Gregori Lohmatski was not smiling. "At least two men on the estate are dead—eaten by a bear. Neither of them was anyone I knew. One was a priest, the other was simply a peasant."

Sherwood's own smile had quickly faded, to be replaced by a look of concern and puzzlement. "Did I just hear you say 'eaten by a bear'?"

Gregori nodded. "I know it sounds like the start of a bad joke. But I fear it is no joke at all. My father would like me to come home and help him deal with the problem, because of my skill as a big-game hunter, and because he knows I have been learning from you. And I think, by implication, he asks also for the help of my friend who's a much better hunter than I am. Absolutely you must come now."

Sherwood smiled, raising his glass. "A man-eating bear, eh? Well, killing large animals is about the only thing in the world I'm very good at. How can a fellow turn down a chance to go after something like that?"

"To a successful hunt!" And their glasses clicked together. . . .

DANCING BEARS

FRED SABERHAGEN

TOR
fantasy ®

A Tom Doherty Associates Book
New York

DANCING BEARS

Cover art by Gary Ruddell

A Tor Book
Published by Tom Doherty Associates, Inc.
175 Fifth Avenue
New York, NY 10010

Tor Books on the World Wide Web:
http://www.tor.com

Tor® is a registered trademark of Tom Doherty Associates, Inc.

ISBN: 0-812-55004-8
Library of Congress Card Catalog Number: 95-45124

First edition: January 1996
First mass market edition: March 1997

Printed in the United States of America

0 9 8 7 6 5 4 3 2 1

ONE

1908

"A re you ready for another hunt, Johnny?" The speaker, raising his voice to be heard in the crowded bar of the London hotel, was a tall man in his late twenties, well dressed in a style favored by members of the British upper class when at their formal leisure. His fluent English still bore traces of his native Russian.

John Sherwood, who stood leaning on the polished dark wood of the bar little more than an arm's length away, was not quite so tall, just under six feet. And, as seemed only natural in an American, a bit more casual in his attire. He frowned, knitting dark brows, and gave the question serious consideration. At last he said: "I don't think I want any more trophies. Not just now."

"Maybe just one more?" The speaker was holding a recently delivered cablegram between his thumb and forefinger; he gave the impression of almost offering the yellow paper to his companion, holding it like a playing card about to be put down decisively.

Sherwood, smiling, shook his head. "I don't know, Greg. The walls of my relatives' houses back in Ohio are full of my victims' staring heads—or so my sister tells me. When I wrote Eileen that I planned to send her that last lion skin, she warned me to cease and desist. Don't know now what I'm going to do with the damned thing."

"Well, you may suit yourself about collecting staring heads. This hunt would have a more serious purpose. Of course, it ought to be good for some excitement, too." The Russian made an expansive gesture, and mellow gaslight evoked the glow of wealth from cuff links of heavy gold.

"Oh, in that case, you know me. I might be talked into it. What's the game?" Sherwood stood up straight and sipped his drink. He was a sharp-featured man of thirty, with a soft voice and a narrow body, wiry arms and legs ending in large hands and feet. His square, clean-shaven jaw had not been well shaded by his pith helmet during his recent exposure to the African sun, and as a result was considerably darker than the upper half of his face.

Gregori Lohmatski hesitated, as if he were at a loss as to how best to explain. At last he ventured: "I told you we have some big game from time to time on our estate."

"Yes?"

The Russian's strong hands crinkled the yellow rectangle of paper which had been handed him by an attendant two minutes ago, and whose contents, approximately a hundred words, had absorbed him intensely during that brief interval. He folded and smoothed it nervously. "The cable is from my father in St. Petersburg, where he spent the winter, as usual. But the news which Father is passing along is from the country."

"Not bad news, I hope?"

The other man's eyes narrowed as if in discomfort. "No, not bad in the sense of personal tragedy—which of course is what one always fears and half-expects—or at least I do—when a message comes by wire." Gregori, who had brightened as he spoke, now paused thoughtfully. "But still the tidings are not happy."

"I'll drink to an absence of tragedy." The American raised his glass and did so.

Greg was not smiling. For the moment he had forgotten all about his own drink. He tapped the paper. "At least two men on the estate are dead—eaten by a bear. Neither of them was anyone I knew. One was a priest, who appears to have been also active in a village council; the other was simply a peasant."

Sherwood's own smile had quickly faded, to be replaced by a look of concern and puzzlement. His glass clinked on the bar. "Did I just hear you say 'eaten by a bear'?"

Greg nodded. "I know, it sounds like the start of a bad joke. But I fear it is no joke at all." Smoothing out the cable on the polished wood, he began to read it again, this time muttering certain words and phrases aloud in English, while his friend listened with keen interest.

"'Killed and partially eaten'—yes. Father makes a point of that. And in two separate incidents."

Sherwood shook his head. He was frowning, as if at something hard to see. "Somewhat unusual," he commented at last.

His companion squinted back at him. "Johnny, you have been spending too much time in London, and are developing a British gift for understatement. You know wild animals much better than I do—but in my limited experience, any bear acting like this is downright unheard of." Then Gregori frowned and gestured. "Oh, of course one expects them to be dangerous. From time to time a brown bear, or even a black, may kill a person. But as a rule the animals avoid humans in the wild. In Europe, at least, such fatalities are very rare."

"In America too."

"But *this* describes a bear going out of its way to attack men." He crinkled the yellow paper again, as if he might be able to squeeze out of it an extra fact or two. "Well, the cable of course does not give full details. One thing is clear to me when I read between the lines. My father would like me to come home and help him to deal with the problem." Greg paused. "I think maybe to help him deal with other matters as well."

"Such as what?"

"Well, my brother and my sister, for example."

The two young men were surrounded by the sounds and bustle of the bar of a swank hotel. From outside drifted the noises of the never-ceasing traffic in the Strand. The stuttering roar of an occasional horseless carriage mingled with the clop of hooves, and the jarring of iron-rimmed wagon wheels on the uneven street. Out there was a glare of electric light; inside the bar, the illumination was the mellow gaslight of decades past.

"Maxim and Natalya, right? What's wrong with them?" Greg had never talked a great deal about his family, and Sherwood had never met any of them. "Or shouldn't I ask?"

The Russian shrugged. "Father is worried about them."

"You mean in connection with this murderous bear?"

"No. Other things. Politics and such."

Sherwood's expression altered slightly. "Oh. Not in my line. If there's trouble in the way of family disputes, maybe I should schedule my visit at some other time."

"Nonsense!" Greg looked up sharply, and waved his hands again. "There are always family disputes. Seriously, my father is asking for my practical help as a big-game hunter, because he knows I have been learning from you. And I think, by implication, he asks also for the help of my friend who's a much better hunter than I am. Absolutely you must come now."

"Well. A man-eating bear—how can a fellow turn down a chance to go after something like that?" And Sherwood, finally smiling, thinking what the hell, why not, raised his drink again.

But a moment later, doing his best from a distance to consider this obscure situation in a foreign family, he frowned once more. "Glad to do what I can, of course. But it occurs to me there must be some good hunters in Russia, too. Maybe among your neighbors in the region—?"

"You are perhaps thinking of how it would be in America."

"I guess I am."

"Well, it's not like that." Greg spoke with the assurance of one who had spent more than a year in the United States. "When you speak of neighbors ... except for the peasants in the nearby villages, there aren't many people living within a day's journey of the estate. And I rather doubt that any of those are eager to help the Lohmatskis."

"Well, killing large animals is about the only thing in the world I'm very good at. But in that department I'll do my best to help."

"To a successful hunt!" And their glasses clicked together.

Later that night, Sherwood sat in his hotel room two stories above the bar, composing a letter by gaslight to his sister in Ohio, informing her of a change of plans. He would not be boarding a steamer for New York as soon as he had expected.

... Greg sends his greetings, and says he's looking forward to another visit to America, but doesn't know when.

Speaking of visiting, as you remember, for some time I've had a standing invitation to spend some time with Greg and his people in Russia. Well, an odd and interesting thing has come up ...

... so there seems to be one more chance for excitement of the hunting type, and you know me. (Don't worry, I promise not to send you a stuffed bear's head.) ...

At breakfast the next morning, the two men planned a quick packing and departure for Russia. Gregori had already cabled his father a reply, telling the people in St. Petersburg to expect him and Sherwood within a matter of days, and giving some details of their travel plans.

"Father may already have left for the country. But they can telegraph on to the town nearest the estate that we're coming. He'll get the message in a few days."

"Good."

Gregori, staring off across the dining room, but obviously thinking of other things than white linen and soft voices and decorum, said abruptly: "I've told you about my brother Maxim."

"You've mentioned him once or twice." Sherwood sipped his coffee. "I got the impression you consider him something of the black sheep of the family."

"We differ politically. Maxim probably would describe me in something of the same way." Greg paused. "I told you my father has a problem with Maxim. The problem I think has to do with the fact that my brother has recently taken a post in the Ministry of the Interior."

"So?"

"This is ominous, because he seems to be in what used to be called the Third Section. Having to do with the suppression of political dissent."

"Politics is not exactly my favorite activity."

Greg came back. "I know, Johnny. Nor mine either. But if when you reach our happy household, you see we are not all perfectly happy with each other . . ."

"So, a family doesn't always get along. That's normal. Is there any more you can tell me about the bear? The more I think about it, the odder it seems."

Greg was only looking at him. Sherwood continued: "In India I've heard of a man-eating tiger pretty thoroughly paralyzing an entire district; I think the record kill there by one animal is something like four hundred people, over a period of eight or ten years. And in Africa a few years back there was that famous pair of lions that virtually stopped the construction of a railroad.

"But I've been racking my memory ever since you read me that cable, and I've never before heard of a true man-eating bear."

"No?"

"No. Big cats are total carnivores, of course. But bears just aren't—except for polar bears, who live where there's no vegetation worthy of the name. Of course polar bears will eat humans—they'll eat any flesh and blood that they can get their teeth into—but mostly they go for seals. Even at their meanest, they just don't seek out people as their chosen diet."

Gregori, plainly unconvinced, had forgotten his remaining bacon and eggs and was gazing at his friend in gloomy silence.

Sherwood pressed on: "Oh, I respect the critters, all right. Bears are dangerous. But frankly, Greg, it's a little hard to believe that even if a bear has killed two people it could be terrorizing square miles of territory. Frightening several villages so the people won't even go out of their houses. After all, except in the Arctic most bears live mainly on plant food. And on fish, when available. Plants are easier to catch than people, and they don't carry guns . . ."

Gregori said: "Not for me."

"What?"

"It isn't at all hard for me to believe, that a man-eating bear is reported on our estate, and as a result all the peasants are afraid to go out. Even when we have a short growing season, and their lives depend on farming."

"No?"

"No. Of course, whether or not the killings actually took place just as described . . . you see, Johnny, according to tradition—or perhaps I should say according to legend—it's not the first time our family has had trouble of this kind. Very far from the first time. And in my country, legends are hard to distinguish from history."

Sherwood thought it over, or tried to. "You mean the two men in the cable weren't really killed by a bear? They died in some other way?"

"How they actually died is perhaps not the most important thing. Maybe a bear really did kill them, maybe not. The important point is what our people believe about the killing."

"I don't understand."

"Of course you don't—how could you? Let me explain. At home there's a tradition, going back more than three hundred years, which says that ever since the time of Ivan the Terrible, certain men of the Lohmatski family have had a tendency to—how does one say it in English?—there is a Russian word, *obaraten*, meaning to change shape. At home we have an old book in the library that I can show you. A certain man can be transformed mystically, into a wolf maybe, or, in the case of the Lohmatskis, into a ferocious bear. And the man who changes in this way generally has a nasty habit of killing people and eating them up. Our family name, by the way? Lohmatski. It means shaggy, or hairy. Like a bear."

There was a little pause. Around them in the restaurant the voices and the cheerful clink of cutlery went on. The London sun was shining, for a change, coming in through clear windows to dazzle on white tablecloths. Greg picked up the silver coffeepot and refilled his cup.

At last Sherwood said: "You're serious. I mean that your farm workers still believe this. That men can turn into animals."

"Oh yes." His companion nodded matter-of-factly. "I'm sure that most of them believe it devoutly. Maybe some of the younger ones know better."

Carefully Sherwood set down his knife and fork. "But this is the twentieth century."

"Not in Russia it isn't." Greg was shaking his head decisively. "There it is more like the fifteen-hundreds still. Officially our calendar is still thirteen days behind yours, but in many ways the gap is several centuries.

My friend, you don't know our peasants. The African natives have nothing on them when it comes to superstition. If anything at all out of the ordinary has happened on our estate—anything having even the remotest connection with bears—I can well imagine that our people are afraid to go out into the fields."

Sherwood was about to ask Greg which of his relatives was currently under suspicion of being a werebear. But the expression on Gregori's face decided him against any remark that might be interpreted as flippancy.

Ordinarily the quickest route to Russia from England would have been by railroad, through France and Germany and Poland, to Moscow. But Gregori wanted to travel by way of St. Petersburg, in the hope that he would be able to learn something of his sister. With a little luck, the sea route would be nearly as fast.

Riding in a horse-drawn cab on their way to the offices of Thomas Cook and Son, where they would make a final choice and buy their tickets, John and Gregori talked again.

As might be expected in a young man who had spent much of his adult life in Europe and America, Gregori was strongly in favor of westernization as the only hope for his own country.

"As an educated man, *I* can be perfectly sure, without having to think about it, that the bear now wreaking such havoc on our lands, or at least in the minds of our peasants, is simply a bear and nothing more."

"Sure, why not?"

"Whereas the peasants . . . well, but let me amend that."

"Sure."

"Johnny, this misbehaving animal is indeed something more than a bear. He stands as a symptom of the attitudes holding back my backward nation."

"You mean he stands as a symbol?"

"Yes, all right. Probably he is both. My friend, this bear could be not only a symbol but a real opportunity.

I mean, to show the stupid peasants and other superstitious wretches, including the priests, that modern
science and engineering are good at solving problems.
In this age of Darwin, electric lights, and repeating
rifles . . ."

His listener shrugged. "Sure. Oh, well. I was nursing
hopes of getting a shot at one damned interesting animal, and here it's turned into a symbol of superstition, about to be overwhelmed by science."

Sherwood's own religious background was Middle
Western Protestant, his inclination toward the here-
and-now, the practical. As a rule, he didn't give the
subject of superstition a great deal of thought.

The latest London newspaper featured a story about
the latest in a seemingly interminable series of terrorist
bomb-throwings in Russia, followed by the latest pro-
nouncement by the tsar. The imperial family and the
government seemed to think that everything would
soon be under control.

When John mentioned these items, Gregori asked
suddenly: "Have I told you much about my sister?"

"Afraid not. You said her name's Natalya. I look forward to meeting her."

"I hope you have the chance."

Sherwood braced himself for more revelations of
family conflict. But Gregori, seemingly on the verge of
something of the kind, evidently changed his mind. He
said only: "In recent years Natalya is not often home."

TWO

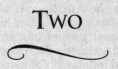

Within a few hours of his arrival in St. Petersburg, John Sherwood was lodged comfortably in the Lohmatskis' luxurious town house, where he filled in some time by writing another letter to his sister in Ohio.

Considerately he added a few words, meant to be reassuring, about his personal safety, knowing that even in Ohio the newspapers must be carrying stories of the violent political unrest in Russia.

May (15, American style; 2, Russian style)
Dear Eileen,
I hope the date above is right. This changing of calendars can be confusing. Here I am. I can report that the voyage just concluded has been of the best kind—that is, uneventful. Ten days, by sea, from London to St. Petersburg, is pretty good time.

He paused, his eyes fixed unseeingly on the open window of his room, through which came an attenuated smell of the sea, along with sounds of distant street traffic. What interesting detail could be put in that would best convey the alien feeling, even for an experienced traveler, of his new surroundings? One of the first sights that had caught Sherwood's eye, as he stood on a quayside street in the Russian capital, overlooking the broad, cold, swift-flowing Neva, had been a small troupe of brightly costumed gypsies and their dancing bear. Sherwood immediately felt sorry for the bear, which looked mangy and indefinably abused.

I don't remember seeing anything of the kind in the States myself, except maybe in a circus. The animal here is muzzled, as they are in England, and led about the streets on a leash, with an iron ring set in its nose, like a bull. It looks docile enough as it walks steadily on its hind legs. One of the human members of the troupe played a mouth organ, another cranked a hurdy-gurdy, and the bear bobbed and swayed and turned almost gracefully. For the climax of the performance, the bear danced with a human partner; one of the gypsies, of course. The show quickly attracted a small crowd, who contributed a few coins when the hat was passed around by one of the gypsy children.

Of course, finding my way around in a new city, or even on a new continent, is nothing out of the ordinary for me. But this time, thanks to Greg, naturally, I have an absolute superfluity of leisure to look at and listen to my new surroundings. All routine matters, as you may imagine, are being made vastly easier for me by the fact that I have a Russian companion, and one experienced in the necessities of travel here. Greg argues with the minor functionaries while I play sightseer.

All in all, St. Petersburg is an impressive city. Large, of course, as you would expect of the capital of a big country, and very different from any other city I have ever seen, despite the fact that much about it reminds me of western Europe.

Things familiar are intermixed with the strange and unique.

I can observe a number of things about the people that are very different, too. The man in charge of all this bureaucratic paperwork regarding passports and residential permits was wearing a sword—and, of course, a uniform. Half the men in Russia seem to be wearing uniforms, in a staggering variety of colors and designs, and I of course have not the least idea which outfits indicate real importance, and which style is worn by those whose job it is to open doors.

This motley army seems splendidly outfitted, but more than a little disorganized, to judge from the difficulty one encounters trying to get anything done. The great majority of it is engaged, I gather, in what we in the West would consider civilian jobs.

From the riverfront, where the English Quay still nursed a number of tall sailing ships among the steamers, Sherwood and his escort had ridden in a horse-drawn cab, on a long bridge over the clean-looking, swift-flowing Neva, to the Lohmatski town house. The St. Petersburg cabdrivers wore their own distinctive uniforms, making them odd figures to Western eyes.

Sherwood, no stranger to the homes of the upper class in England and elsewhere, found the furnishings and general elegance of the Lohmatski house imposing, as were the other mansions making up the neighborhood. The Lohmatski dwelling was three stories high, set back from the street in its own grounds, and surrounded by its own high wall. Attached to the house was an enclosed greenhouse or orangery that would have done credit to the manor of a British duke.

There were an impressive number of servants in attendance, thought Sherwood. Of course he and Gregori had been expected. The staff greeted the young heir to the family fortunes and welcomed his guest with every appearance of genuine enthusiasm.

The servants reported that Maxim Ivanovich, Greg's younger brother, had spent most of the winter and early spring in town, but several days ago had returned with their father to Padarok Lessa, the family estate.

As far as Sherwood could tell, no one was saying anything about Natalya.

On the afternoon of their arrival, Sherwood had come downstairs to see about getting his letter posted, when, on entering the den, he found himself distracted by an impressive array of hunting trophies, mounted on all four walls.

Most prominent were a pair of snarling bears' heads—a great brown and an equally impressive white—whose tongues and teeth of painted plaster showed need of a good dusting. Presently Gregori joined him, murmuring orders to a servant. Soon Sherwood stood sipping strong Russian tea and looking up at this trophy.

He gestured with his tea glass, held in a metal frame to protect the user's fingers from the heat. "Someone's been hunting polar bears."

Gregori gave the head a glance, but at first did not seem interested in this object which must have been so familiar to him. "Ah, yes. Well, Father in his youth was something of a hunter. As was Grandfather before him, I understand."

"They went out together?"

Greg paused, then said: "They couldn't have, very often. Actually I suppose they never did. Father was only about ten years old, I understand, when Grandfather in effect abandoned the family."

"Too bad. So, I suppose the polar bear was shot at your Siberian estate? I remember your telling me once that the family had other lands, way out in Siberia somewhere."

"I doubt this bear was shot there." Suddenly Greg looked vaguely melancholy and very Russian. "That estate is called Padarok Sivera. It means 'The Gift of the North.'"

"Interesting name. Have you been there?"

"Not I. None of my generation have. You can ask Father about it, when we catch up with him. He made the journey once, as a young man." Greg smiled. "I used to wonder a lot about Padarok Sivera, but I doubt I could even find my way there without doing some research. Grandfather supposedly went by sea, taking a ship at Archangelsk and working his way along the northern coast, which is sometimes possible in summer. And I don't know what the inhabitants, if there currently are any, would say if a Lohmatski showed up and proclaimed himself the landowner."

"I guess you weren't kidding when you said those lands are in a very remote area. Must be a long way from here."

"A very long way, indeed. I expect the journey could easily take half a year."

The American thought about it. "You mean round trip?"

"No, not at all. One way. You see, in the north there are few railroads; the Trans-Siberian crosses the continent far to the south, close to the Chinese border. And such roads as we have for horse-drawn vehicles must be seen to be believed—even the main highways. And the rivers, with some exceptions, run south to north; not very convenient for the traveler going west to east."

Sherwood was duly impressed. "Six months. I've really got to get hold of a map. Whatever continent I'm on, I always like to have some idea of the geography around me."

Then he turned, struck by a sudden recollection, and began to inspect the shelves nearby. The library contained several thousand volumes, and he soon discovered almost a full shelf of English titles. "You were going to show me a certain old book."

Greg, nudged out of some memory which had evidently been called up by the thought of unseen Siberia, looked his puzzlement.

Sherwood prompted: "Back in London, you told me there was an old book in your family library, having to do with the local legends about bears . . ."

"Ah, of course!" The shilling dropped, as the English put it. Greg took a couple of frowning turns around the bookcases. He went up a ladder briefly, inspecting the higher shelves, and came back down, dusting his hands. At last he rejoined Sherwood, looking dissatisfied. "It may be at our country house. At Padarok Lessa, I mean, of course. The estate where we are going."

Then suddenly he turned, struck by a thought. "That's the old gentleman up there. My Grandfather, I mean." Gregori pointed to an area of wall, free of shelves, where several photographs were mounted.

Sherwood strolled over for a close look at the indicated picture. Taken evidently around the middle of the nineteenth century, the portrait was of a youngish man with heavy eyebrows, positioned stiffly in a high-backed chair, a long-barreled rifle in his lap. A real antique weapon—Sherwood could see the percussion lock. The man's intensity came through despite the formal pose—or perhaps because of it.

"A hunter," said Greg. "And a real explorer, if all the stories are true. Or even half of them."

Sherwood tried hastily to compute years and ages. "Still living?"

"Oh, I shouldn't think so. Father always speaks of him in the past tense." Then Gregori frowned, as he, too, began calculating decades in his mind. "Let's see. I was born in eighteen-eighty. Father in . . . eighteen-fifty, I believe. That would put Grandfather well into the class of octogenarian, if he were still alive. Probably not likely, for one who chose the edge of the Arctic Circle as his place of retirement—*shto*?"

The concluding word had been addressed to a servant, who now came forward murmuring something, also in Russian, and pressed a folded paper into his master's hand. Gregori after frowning briefly over the note looked up.

"It is from my sister. Someone—one of our servants, I suppose—has informed her of our arrival."

Sherwood didn't understand.

Greg observed his puzzlement. "You see, she is here in town, but reluctant to come to the house. She fears that the police may be watching, and that they might want to arrest her."

"Good Lord."

"She's not sure, but doesn't want to take the chance. She wants me to come and meet her, if I can do so without being followed."

"Followed by the police?"

"Yes, my friend. This is not America."

Sherwood came quickly to a decision. "If you're meeting her, I'm coming with you. What more natural than that you would take your visitor out and show him the town?"

Greg hesitated.

"Come on, man! I want to see some of the city anyway."

"Very well. If I see that we are followed, we will simply go somewhere else, and not meet Natalya."

"I leave that up to you."

Within the hour, the two young men had left the house and hired a cab, eschewing the family carriages as too conspicuous. Greg calmly took precautions against being followed, changing cabs twice, and leading his guest in and out of public buildings on a busy street.

On summer evenings, St. Petersburg evidently tended to live outdoors. The places of entertainment, on some of the city's many islands, were filled with music, dancing, crowds, and merriment.

In May, the capital was entering the period of white nights, entrancing and relatively warm. For a little while the whole population seemed caught up in the delight of warmth and light, under a pearl-gray sky, sunless now for a few hours but mostly starless, also, because it was not really dark.

Here, in the middle of one of the island parks, Sherwood and Gregori took a table in the shadowy section of an outdoor café. Moments after they were seated, a tall, slender, dark-haired woman, simply dressed, approached and slid unceremoniously into a chair, before Sherwood could do more than start to rise politely.

Greg pushed him down into his seat again and quickly muttered an introduction. Then he assured his sister: "I am quite sure the house was not being watched. Nor were we followed."

"You looked?"

"Of course!"

Sliding their chairs closer, Gregori and Natalya embraced warmly; they were apparently on better terms with each other than any other two people in the family.

Then, holding his sister at arm's length, he shook his head as if worried by a change in her appearance. "You are so thin," he murmured.

She responded with a few words in Russian, and paused, considering the stranger.

Sherwood took this degree of attention as a compliment and did not hesitate to return it immediately.

"You didn't tell me how good-looking she is, Greg." The words were perfectly sincere, though Natalya was scarcely pretty in the ordinary sense. Sherwood thought her face was striking, and she was blessed with an attractive combination of dark hair, worn in braids, gray eyes, and a slender, attractive figure.

"You are very kind." Natalya's English was at least as good as her brother's.

Keeping an alert eye out for anyone who passed nearby, Natalya, speaking first Russian, then English, told him that she feared she was in trouble.

Greg glanced at the few people at nearby tables, and evidently decided that speaking English was safer. "You're in with some revolutionary group?"

Natalya made a motion of her head, as if to toss back flowing hair; her braids only bounced a little. "I have been. There would be something wrong with anyone who didn't want to see a drastic change." Her eyes challenged Sherwood to make a comment. He kept silent.

Greg sounded worried. "You have been. That means you've dropped out?"

"Yes. It turned out that there were certain things—like making bombs, or hiding the people who made them—I didn't want to do. Perhaps because the bombs kept blowing up the wrong people."

Natalya fixed Sherwood with her gray eyes. "I suppose my brother has warned you that you may bring trouble on yourself by associating with me? Even sitting with me at a table?"

"I'll take that chance."

"Come home," Greg advised her simply. "Father has influence, as you know. He'll want to help you."

The idea seemed to have considerable appeal. "If only I could . . . I haven't even seen him for a long time. *You* haven't seen him for a year, have you?"

"Ah, but I know him. And I know you. Come home, Natashinka!"

"All right. If you think it wise."

"I do!"

"Maxim will be there." She seemed to offer this as a tentative objection.

"Yes, but we know who is in charge—Father, as always. Anyway, I doubt our brother will bury himself in the country for any length of time." Then Greg suggested gently that Natalya should no longer wear her hair in braids.

Seeing that Sherwood was puzzled by this remark, Natalya explained that braids were a common hairstyle among revolutionary women. "But that's one thing I can easily change. Do either of you have a cigarette? I suppose I'll have to give up smoking when Father is around."

After the waiter visited the table again, she proved that she could knock back a glass of vodka like an experienced drinker. Sherwood knew that she and her brothers were all close to each other in age, all three of them born within a period of four years. Their mother had died several years ago.

"You speak English very well."

"I ought to. I suppose Greg has told you that when the three of us children were small, we had an English nursemaid? And for some years after that, a tutor?"

Natalya said that Greg had frequently mentioned his American friend to her. The two young men had known each other since their university days, when Gregori had spent almost two years in America. In the past they had talked repeatedly about John's coming to Russia sometime and getting in some hunting. Of course they had originally thought primarily of stags.

In consideration of Sherwood's presence, brother and sister continued to converse in English. "Our father and Maxim are not getting on well, it seems; but then, they haven't got on for a long time. They both have the Russian habit of telling people what to do."

Natalya had a momentary hesitation. "Grisha, I don't know what to do."

"But what will you do if you don't come home?"

Natalya shrugged and remarked that she had already made tentative plans to get out of the country, by sea or by rail, into western Europe. "Maybe that would be better, after all," she concluded.

"Are the police actually after you?"

"As far as I know, they are not. But of course one can never be sure."

"To get out of the country, you'd need forged papers. Not easy to obtain, I think."

"Not impossible, either. There are ways. Of course such things tend to be costly, and right now I seem to be out of money."

"Well, you're not going to need any, not right away. You're going to come home with me, and Johnny here, and talk over your difficulties with Father."

The discussion went on. Sherwood got the impression that Natalya loved her childhood home and loved her family. He didn't know what to think of her hanging out with revolutionaries, but he found himself attracted to her with unexpected force.

Eventually Natalya allowed herself to be persuaded that to return home would be best.

"But there must be a revolution of some kind in our country. We cannot go on as we are!"

Seeking to change the subject, Sherwood asked Natalya: "Any fresh news of the terrible bear?"

Natalya seemed grateful for the change. She reminded him that there were no telephones between the capital and isolated estates in the countryside. Nor did the telegraph lines as yet run everywhere, by any means.

Natalya could give her brother and his friend no news concerning the bear; she had heard of the deadly animal only through the family servants who were now in town. Like her brother, she decried superstition. And why any bear should suddenly develop a taste for killing people was more than she could understand.

When Gregori and Sherwood brought her up to date on the cabled reports from home, she too tended to blame at least part of the problem on the peasants' credulity. She too was familiar with the legend about certain male members of her family, shape-changers down through the generations, who tended to become bears.

"Of course if people are actually being killed, someone or something must be doing it. Maybe it's the government!"

Greg did not disagree; Sherwood had often heard him say that, like his American friend, he considered himself apolitical. But now Natalya's brother winced and looked around automatically to see who might have overheard that remark.

THREE

Conversation broke off when Natalya, with a swift but unobtrusive movement, suddenly seized each of her companions by the hand.

"See those two men?" she demanded in a strained whisper. "I've met the short one—they call him Koba."

Sherwood turned his head. Some thirty yards away, a pair of figures had come into view, leaning on the wooden railing of a footbridge slightly elevated above the level of the intervening hedge. At the moment their faces were visible only in profile, in the light of some decorative lanterns.

Natalya was staring at the pair in tense fascination. "I know them, and to hell with them. Gentlemen, I think . . . I think we may shortly be in for a little bombing."

"Did you say bombing?" Sherwood started up out of his chair. "We'd better try to stop—"

"No! We stay out of this!" Hissing the words in a low voice, Greg, with unwonted ferocity, gripped John's arm.

Sherwood, aware that he was wandering in an unfamiliar wilderness, and willing to be guided by the natives, let himself be stopped.

Subsiding into his chair, he looked back at the two men. The bridge afforded them a good position from which to observe—something. Whatever it was they expected was apparently going to happen in the café next to the one where Sherwood was sitting. The intervening hedge kept him from getting a good look at what was there, but music and laughter drifted over.

The watchers on the footbridge gave Sherwood the impression of interested, professional observers who had a clear idea of what they expected to see.

Then abruptly, as if in response to some signal Sherwood had not observed, the man called Koba and his silent companion suddenly turned away and retreated over the bridge, walking unhurriedly but still covering ground. As the shorter man cast a last look back over his shoulder, the illumination of a nearby street lamp fell on his countenance. In the gaslight Sherwood caught a glimpse of a darkly mustached, somewhat pockmarked face, with a suggestion of the Orient around the eyes.

"Are those police?" he whispered, gesturing minimally at the sudden appearance of a squad of black overcoats next door, just beyond the hedge.

"Not your ordinary gendarmes," Greg responded just as quietly. "*Okhrannye otdeliniya*, which means 'protective sections.' The Okhrana, for short."

Sherwood was thinking: *That's the outfit brother Maxim has joined.* But he refrained from commenting.

Natalya chimed in with quiet loathing. "Special units for the investigation of political crime. To hell with them, too."

Greg was just starting to add something more when his sister's earlier prediction was fulfilled not more than thirty yards away, quite close enough to leave a ringing deafness in the ears. Some kind of high explosive, certainly, for it delivered a tooth-jarring blast, centered somewhere among the tables of the adjacent café.

A long moment of stunned silence was followed by

an outbreak of screaming, in both men's and women's voices. Some of the fine debris took a long time to come down. It fell as far as the table where Sherwood and his friends were sitting. This was a variety of violence quite new to Sherwood, and to Greg also, it appeared. But even before the fragments fell, Natalya was trying to drag her two companions to cover under their café table. Then she had them on their feet and moving, away from the site of the explosion.

Sherwood was swearing under his breath. It appeared that no one near them had been harmed, but beyond the hedge there still sounded screams and running feet. Now the whole place was being evacuated rapidly. If the trio stayed put any longer, they would start to become conspicuous.

Within a minute, a rumor had sprung up among the people crowding their way along the paths toward the park exits. Passed along in breathless fragments, it spoke of an attempt to assassinate some eminent policeman or other official, who had been paying a quiet visit to his favorite café. Moments later, the target of the bombing had a name: General Gerasimov himself, head of the Petersburg Okhrana. Somehow the terrorists had known he was going to be there. But the attempt had failed; only a couple of bystanders had been killed.

And now, of course, the police would be taking their revenge, on anyone in sight. Within a minute after the explosion, a squad seemingly composed of the intended victim's bodyguards had deployed rapidly along the nearby streets and paths. Within two minutes, it seemed that they had captured and started beating a suspected revolutionary. Now they were arresting others and throwing them into a carriage.

Greg had now assumed leadership of his small group, and was conducting a masterly retreat. Turning away from a brightly lighted section of path, he pulled his companions to a halt. "If we go that way, we may be stopped and searched."

"What if we are stopped? We haven't done—" The

American, of course, was not in the least awed by police. And the behavior of the terrorists left him angry, rather than afraid. Sherwood was willing to assert himself, and refused to be pushed around—and tried to keep others from being pushed around, if he could do anything about it.

But his two Russian companions were less sanguine and talked him into retreating as soon as possible.

It was plain that both Greg and Natalya knew their way around these islands and their network of paths, roads, and connecting bridges. Tugging Sherwood behind them, they soon emerged from the excitement unscathed, save for a few minor scratches. At one point, Greg had considered it best for them to force their way through a hedge, to avoid police.

With the scene of the bombing now a quarter of a mile behind them, the streets around them peaceful once more, they hailed a cab. The city, once away from the Parisian shopping thoroughfares and the blocks of mansions, offered plenty of evidence of the miserable— by Sherwood's standards—state of the people under the tsarist government. As many poor wretches as you cared to count could be seen cowering in the night shelters, and begging on the streets.

Soon the two men were back at the Lohmatski town house. Natalya was being taken on to some other destination, which she refused to divulge. Before separating from her brother, she promised to meet him at the railway station in the morning.

Late that night, as Sherwood wrote in his final letter to his sister from St. Petersburg, the whole city was buzzing with news of the bomb-throwing attempt at assassination.

In his letter, he assured Eileen that he remained safely remote from all such events. Not even a hint that he had practically been a witness; Gregori had warned him that any mail he sent or received in Russia might be opened.

After spending what was left of the night in the family town house, Sherwood and Greg went to the railroad station, where, amid the crowds, they were joined at the last minute by Natalya.

Natalya volunteered no information about where she had spent the night, and the men did not ask. She had changed her dress, Sherwood observed, and was no longer wearing her hair in braids, but in a glossy chignon at the nape of her neck. It looked lovely, Sherwood thought.

Greg had the tickets ready, and the three boarded a train.

The first-class carriages were easily distinguished; they were painted blue. The second-class were yellow, and the third-class, being swarmed by wretchedly poor people who seemed to have outfitted themselves for a ragpickers' costume ball, were green.

In their first-class car, the three had to themselves a sizable compartment with two wide seats. Gregori demonstrated how the seat backs could be removed, converting the seats into four small beds. Naturally, when bedtime arrived, Natalya had to move into the special ladies' carriage. Still something of an innovation, sleeping cars were lacking on this train.

The train began to move, but Sherwood's sense of the exotic persisted. He had the impression, though he realized it might easily be false, that the political tensions of the capital were dropping away with increasing distance from the city. Out here in the country, the appearance was that nothing might ever change—or at least that nothing *had* changed for decades—maybe for a century or so.

"I just saw a wooden plow." The American commented in wonder as the train pulled out of a village station. He shook his head. "They're still using *wooden plows*?"

Greg shrugged, as if to say: What would you expect? "Nine out of ten farms still use them, I'm afraid."

The ride to Tver took about twelve hours. At the small country stations, women crossing guards were armed with horns and staffs. On the platforms, men in a bewildering variety of uniforms drew Sherwood's attention.

Gregori informed his guest with some pride that there were now more than thirty thousand miles of railroad in Russia—about the same as in Britain's vastly smaller territory.

Sherwood said he supposed that meant there were thirty thousand miles of telegraph line as well.

Greg agreed. He remarked how some things had changed in the comparatively short time since his last visit home, approximately a year ago. There were more telegraph poles now than he remembered.

"On the other hand, I can see also that some things have not changed at all." Whether or not the political situation had grown worse was hard to say.

While aboard the train coming southeast out of St. Petersburg, Sherwood wondered at the almost-straight-as-a-string route of the railroad between the capital and Moscow. One of his companions explained to him that this was the result of an order of Tsar Nicholas I. That monarch, impatient with delays and arguments among his route planners, had seized a pencil and, using the straight edge of a ruler (some said a sword), had drawn a line on a map to connect the two cities. The four hundred and four miles, straight as a string (or almost) of line had been completed in 1851 under the direction of an American engineer. The difficulty with the impetuous decision made by a ruler was that a number of intermediate towns and cities had effectively been bypassed.

The train was proceeding on to Moscow. But Sherwood and his companions disembarked hours earlier and a couple of hundred miles farther north, at Tver, a bustling smallish city.

The next leg of their journey east saw the traveling companions being carried downstream by riverboat on the upper Volga. A steam-powered stern-wheeler, burning wood like an American riverboat, though perhaps not quite as big as the steamboats Sherwood was used to seeing on the Ohio.

First-class cabins were on the upper deck, and supposedly "comfortable." Natalya, of course, was required to retreat to the women's cabin.

Sherwood wrote home:

> The bedbugs and other wildlife were a bit thick in the cabin, which I was privileged to share with six or eight other first-class passengers. As my shooting irons were all packed away, I let the wildlife have the indoors, and spread my blanket roll on deck. I can report that the stars are pretty much the same in Russia as elsewhere.

After proceeding down the winding upper Volga for a day and a half, in which time it covered more than a hundred miles, the boat turned up one of the eastern tributaries.

Sherwood meanwhile had his chance to observe the life of the storied Volga boatmen. In fact it was quite horrible: they were gaunt, ragged figures who labored like beasts towing small boats up some of the tributaries as well as on the giant river. At the end of the day, they wolfed down whatever food was put before them, then lay down to sleep like beasts on the muddy riverbank.

Shortly after marveling at the condition of the boatmen, the American encountered, on the dock, a strange-looking man, wild-eyed, hatless and poorly dressed, who with his traveler's staff in hand approached the foreigner to favor him with a lengthy harangue. Meanwhile passersby came and went, for the most part paying the speaker no attention.

Naturally Sherwood could not understand a word, but he thought the tone and gestures were those of a man delivering a serious warning, as well as the sign of the cross in benediction. He turned to his guide. "What was that all about?"

Greg was vaguely embarrassed. "This fellow is what we call a *starets*, a holy fool. One runs into them everywhere in Russia, I'm afraid—some are truly religious and some are not. In many cases, it is hard to tell. This man means well and gives you his blessing."

"I figured out that much. But he must have said something more?"

"Two other things, actually. He says that you are to be called upon to travel a greater distance than you imagine. And . . ."

"What?"

"Well, that he sees, everywhere on your body, the marks of the fangs and claws of the dancing bear." Greg hastily raised a hand. "Don't ask me; I'm not even going to try to interpret it."

The words had called up a vivid image—in fact, Sherwood had once been mauled by a leopard he was trying to kill—and he experienced a faint involuntary shudder, which he did his best to repress.

"Oh? Not very pleasant, but I suppose I should thank him for the warning." The traveler in far places had encountered soothsayers before, of numerous tribes on several continents, and this was by no means the most unsettling forecast he had been given. He enjoyed a good story, and he had no wish to be rude. "Where does he say I'm going on the extended journey? By the way, I suppose a small donation would be in order?"

Greg exchanged words with the ragged, barefoot man again, then turned back with a faint smile. "The donation would be very welcome. He lives on such kindness and blesses you again for it."

Sherwood dug into a pocket, silently calculating Russian coinage before he deposited a modest portion in the trembling, extended hand. "Here. Tell him I thank him for his blessing. And my destination?"

"You are going to the end of the world, and you will find your destiny in the ice that is filled with fire," Gregori reported a moment later. He shook his head and once more raised a hand, forestalling questions.

"Don't bother asking for an explanation, I'm quite sure you won't get one." Meanwhile the holy fool was bowing extravagantly, sidling away.

Sherwood shrugged. "Well, as prophecies go, I've survived worse."

There was also a shabby group of gypsies to be seen on the road that paralleled the river, a band passing a tin cup for coins, having with them the second dancing bear Sherwood had seen in the past few days. This bear was much like the one in Petersburg, only somewhat smaller and less attractive: a pitiful, tormented, flea-bitten creature wearing a leather muzzle. Naturally, he was reminded momentarily of the prophecy given him by the Holy Fool; but when the gypsy group drew close to Sherwood, he noticed with a sympathetic pang that this bear's claws had been extracted, and this one, too, was wearing a steel ring set into its pierced nose.

After spending three more days on the water, sailing upstream slowly on the unnamed tributary of the Volga, Sherwood and his companions came ashore at a small town where they began the last leg of their journey, which would involve several days on wretched roads. This last stage was on horseback, the mounts being available for hire locally. Natalya put on trousers and straddled her mount like a man. Some of the people who saw her do this were visibly shocked, but she appeared to take no notice. Sherwood needed no translation to understand her muttered words: *To hell with them.*

Traveling overland—it was not an easy journey, but he had undertaken many worse—Sherwood got a close look at several villages.

By now more than two weeks had passed since the long cable dispatched from St. Petersburg had carried to London news of the bear's depredations. Since then the hunters had had no solid information about the bear, though the story had spread in garbled form to the inhabitants of the villages they were now passing through.

As part of this ongoing language study, Sherwood learned the name of the Lohmatskis' European estate: Padarok Lessa.

Meanwhile, he worked intermittently on his next letter to Eileen:

> My companions have graciously explained to me (when I finally thought to ask them) that the name means "gift of the forest"; they are vast land-holdings, though Greg tells me not as vast as they once were, before the serfs were freed. Some of the lands have been sold off.
>
> But the amount the family still owns must still be measured in square miles. Undoubtedly hundreds of them. Greg says he doesn't know exactly how many square miles—or square versts, I suppose there must be such a thing—and hesitates to guess. The impression is inescapable that in this part of Russia, at least, surveying is a distinctly informal art. Still, the Lohmatski domain is big enough to include three or four villages, whose inhabitants work the land. Some of them, if I understand the situation properly, are employed in manufacturing enterprises owned by the family.

Sherwood had heard of small rural factories which built wooden furniture, and looked forward to seeing one. He wondered if they used water-powered lathes. He tried to picture a mill and a dam in a small stream. He'd heard something about machinery for extracting sugar from sugar beets. By all reports, many of the peasants in their villages were small capitalists in their way, making by hand such items as shoes and wooden dishes.

> I suppose it gives them some way to pass the time, and to earn a little money, during the long fierce winters.

Greg and his sister seem to be both growing increasingly impatient to learn what is happening at home. And, as usual, I am looking forward to another hunt.

As ever,
John

FOUR

After two days on horseback, and two corresponding nightly intervals of lodging in poor peasant homes—in the huts were about what Sherwood had been led to expect: the hosts exceedingly cheerful and hospitable, the quarters ill-smelling and flea-infested—the three travelers had, at some indeterminate point, crossed an unmarked boundary and were now on the lands belonging to the Lohmatski estate.

With an air of keen anticipation, the two Russians began to point out to each other, and to their visitor, houses, bridges, and other landmarks, whose recognition took them back to their shared childhood. Sherwood, watching his companions, thought that time must have held considerable happiness. As the versts went by, Greg seemed ever more eager to return to the family home, but soon Natalya began to look doubtful, as if she were uncertain of her welcome when she arrived.

When her brother asked what worried her, she told him, in Russian, that there were things he didn't know. He didn't want to hear any details of what she had been doing since they had last seen each other. And no, she wasn't going to provide him with the story.

Greg evidently felt that good manners required him to translate at least the general sense of this for Sherwood's benefit. He took the opportunity of doing this when Natalya was momentarily absent.

"So she is worried about what Father will say and do when he sees her. Obviously, she has led a—a difficult life since leaving home. And he is a—a conservative man."

It was too late now for Sherwood to wish himself elsewhere.

Around mid-afternoon on the third day of their ride, ten days after leaving St. Petersburg, the three travelers arrived at one of the villages in which nearly all of the estate's workers lived. Sherwood was told that it had always been the usual practice in Russia for farmers to dwell together in small villages rather than in isolated houses.

Sherwood's hosts informed him that the village before him was typical: there was one small church with a little steeple in the form, rapidly becoming familiar to him, of an onion dome. Not far away across a tiny square was the communal well, surrounded by a dozen small log houses and guarded by geese and chickens. A few trees and some tall sunflowers reared themselves out of the dust.

The three companions had hardly ridden into the village before some of the inhabitants recognized Gregori. Several of these folk, men and women obviously distraught, came running to surround the young man and grab his stirrup. When he and his sister had dismounted, they seized him by his sleeve, and began to impart a tale of horror.

Sherwood could see a staggering shock come into the faces of Gregori and Natalya.

"What is it, Greg?" he asked, sliding down from his saddle to stand beside them.

Natalya, white-lipped, her hands clenched, was staring off into the distance. Greg's cheeks and forehead had suddenly gone pale under his sportsman's tan. "It is our father. They say the monster bear has killed him."

"Good Lord!"

Four or five Russian voices were talking together, all obviously consumed by great emotion. The translation came to Sherwood's ears in disjointed fragments from Gregori and Natalya, who were both obviously half-numbed with shock.

The American put his hand on his friend's arm. "Is there any chance of a mistake? Is this only a rumor?"

Gregori shook his head. "One can hope. But . . ." Suddenly he looked smaller.

Details emerged gradually. It seemed that some four days ago, when the travelers had been on the riverboat and out of reach of telegrams, old Ivan Gregorevich had been found dead in the forest. At the same time, and in the same place, Gregori's brother Maxim had disappeared, after joining his father in the hunt for the dangerous bear.

"It sounds to me like Maxim may be dead as well."

Sherwood, feeling helpless, murmured a few words meant to be comforting.

Additional facts came out slowly. Both men's horses had come home lathered, and in a pitiable state of fright. Everyone on the estate had been thrown into great alarm.

A hastily organized search had soon led to the discovery of the father's mangled body. The funeral had already been held—it would have been impossible, particularly in summer, to wait for the expected travelers, because no one on the estate had been at all sure of when they might arrive.

Grimly the young Lohmatskis and their American friend rode on. Fast as they moved, the news of their coming seemed to fly ahead of them. The fields, still unplanted, many of them beginning to spring up in luxurious weeds, were all but completely empty of

workers. The few peasants who were visible seemed to
have come out of nowhere to stand at the roadside, the
men with odd, individualistic hats in hand. The death
of old Ivan Gregorevich was confirmed on every
weatherbeaten face. The people must have thought a
lot of the old man, despite his reputation for harshness,
Sherwood thought. Once or twice, the Lohmatskis
asked for the latest news concerning their brother, and
were told that Maxim was still missing.

The shock of the tragic news blurred all Sherwood's
impressions of his arrival at the great house of Padarok
Lessa, riding up an avenue of lime trees to the front
entrance, and meeting the stricken household staff.

Sherwood realized that of the older generation of
peasants who worked the fields of the estate, quite a
few must have been born on the land as serfs forty
years ago or longer; and that the same must be true of
the stewards and overseers. Many of the peasants and
house servants bowed like serfs and kissed the hem of
Gregori's coat when they welcomed him home. Still,
they were much more informal and familiar than
English servants would have been. They obviously now
regarded him as their proper master.

No, there was still no word of the missing Maxim.
Sherwood gathered that the search for him had been
given up, at least temporarily.

A melancholy, distracted servant who spoke no
English—and responded only weakly to the visitor's
attempts at poorly remembered French—carried Sherwood's saddlebags ahead of him up to a comfortable,
neatly furnished bedroom on the second floor.

There were lace curtains on the single window,
whose glass was double-paned against what must be
ferocious winters, but open now to the spring breeze,
and tapped by a growing tree branch just outside. His
room like all the other bedrooms in the house, as well
as the dining room, had an icon in it. This was a saint's
image, a small, dark painting marked with symbols

unknown and obscure to Sherwood, hanging in one corner of the room. The peasant houses he had already stayed in had been equipped similarly.

The servant reacted with silent shock on observing that the tiny candle on the small shelf before the icon had been allowed to go out. Muttering to himself, the gloomy servant hastened to relight it, before favoring Sherwood with a reproachful look and taking himself away.

In Sherwood's first hours and days at Padarok Lessa, he looked forward to being able to inspect the family library, in search of the old book Greg had mentioned which discussed the family legend. But the first night and day of his visit did not seem a good time to remind Greg or Natalya of the matter.

When Sherwood took notice of the fact, he realized that the entire household was wearing mourning for their deceased master. The steward had arranged with a local priest for a proper funeral service and burial.

With Natalya as his guide, Sherwood, having put on a black armband, went respectfully, hat in hand, to see the site of the fresh burial, in the family plot a few hundred yards from the house.

Sherwood was surprised, when they reached the graveside, to see Natalya kneel there beside her brother (whose behavior in this matter the American found equally surprising).

She said simply: "Father would have been pleased to see me do that."

"I see."

They had begun walking back toward the house. While he was trying to think of some solemn and appropriate remarks, she changed the subject. "And so you and Gregori are going to enjoy your bear hunt."

Striding thoughtfully, hands clasped behind his back, Sherwood answered in a low voice, "That was the way it looked to us from London. Enjoyable. We were approaching the hunt as a kind of entertainment. Now of course it'll be a pretty grim business. I'd like to get on with it tomorrow. And of course get on with the search for your brother, too," he added hastily.

Calmly, she shook her head. "You're not going to find Maxim alive. Not after so many days."

Sherwood didn't say anything, but in his own mind he had to agree with that assessment. If Maxim was indeed dead, his body might possibly have been dragged into a bear's den—bears in general were brainy and curious animals, given to unpredictable behavior. Or, what seemed to the experienced hunter more likely, the corpse had been devoured by scavengers and the remnants scattered. In that case at least some clothing ought to be findable; but of course, if people were too timid to work the open fields, it would doubtless be impossible to get them to search the woods.

Back in the house, Natalya calmly borrowed the dining-room icon candle to light her cigarette. Sherwood supposed it was probably fortunate that none of the servants were on hand to see that; but Natalya seemed to be making at least a minimal effort to avoid scandalizing them.

She said: "My younger brother and my father were both hard men. But of course you are right about the hunt. Kill the bear, so the peasants can get back to work. There should be no loss of agricultural production and profit."

She sounded more embittered than grieving. Sherwood said: "The peasants must have difficult lives. Why not kill the bear, so they'll have one less thing to be afraid of?"

"Oh, you have noticed their hard lives. They are not the only ones who suffer, of course, but it's good you notice something."

On the morning after his arrival at Padarok Lessa, the American had his first real chance to look around.

The more Sherwood moved about the house, indoors and out, the more he was impressed by its deceptive size and by certain aspects of magnificence which it possessed. Though his friend had often enough spoken of his family home, Sherwood thought he had not really done the place justice. The house was basically two stories high, and of pleasingly irregular shape so that it was actually three stories at one point; it would have fitted in nicely as a mansion in the American South.

The house, which Gregori said was approximately a hundred years old, stood on the side of a gentle hill, surrounded by shade trees. Huge white columns rearing from the veranda supported a sizable balcony on the upper floor. The main approach passed through an extensive orchard of fruit trees; pear, apple, and cherry were now in bloom.

Toward the rear spread a flower garden, now looking somewhat neglected, and all the outbuildings to be expected near a big farmhouse.

From a large hall just inside the front entry, doors led off to a big dining room on one side, a drawing room on the other. Beyond the dining room lay a large kitchen, occupied today by subdued servants. The sink was equipped with a long-handled indoor pump.

Elsewhere on the ground floor were several stairways, giving access to both higher and lower levels, a number of store-rooms, and other chambers whose purpose was less obvious. The furniture in general ran to old-fashioned mahogany, and the wall decorations included a number of what must be family portraits.

Among the latter the visitor discovered a lithograph of the current tsar, Nicholas II, wearing an ornate uniform and what appeared to be a yachtsman's cap, who looked enough like his cousin the Prince of Wales to be mistaken for him. Nicholas II had been on the throne now for fourteen years. In the picture he wore an expression of serene pride, as if he had never heard of bombings.

The most immediately interesting place in the house, for Sherwood, was the combination gun room and

billiard room, just down the hall from the entrance.
Two green baize tables waited under decorative
kerosene lamps suspended from the high ceiling.
Natalya did not wait to be asked, but challenged Sherwood to a game. She played skillfully, hitting the ball
forcefully like a man. In a few minutes, she had
defeated him with ease. He tried to comfort himself
with the thought that he had not really played for
years.

"Another?" his opponent demanded. "Keeping busy
this way helps one avoid thinking."

"All right." This time some technique came back to
his fingers. He did a little better, but still lost.

After dinner, a subdued affair, Gregori excused himself to go to one of the peasants' dwellings nearby,
where he meant to talk about getting hounds for
tomorrow's attempt to track the bear. Meanwhile
Natalya walked with Sherwood, showed him around.

"And this you will probably find interesting."

Before them, in a large building that had been converted from a barn, was the theater where decades ago,
Sherwood's guide informed him, the serf orchestra
used to play, and the serf drama troupe had put on
their shows.

Entering the building, he saw that the stage was of a
size for professional productions, and had evidently
been put together by skilled carpenters. Like other the-
aters built in the mid-nineteenth century, this one was
provided with footlights in the form of old-fashioned
oil lamps, now long since dry and dark. What struck
Sherwood as odd was that the space for the audience
was hardly bigger than the stage, with only room
enough to accommodate about twenty chairs.

"What in the—?"

Looming out of the shadows in the wings at one side
of the stage there towered a stuffed bear, mounted
standing on its hind legs. The fur had been nibbled
away in patches, by moths and by God knew what. The
crude dead eyes stared glassily.

"There were several such companies on the estates of the great landowners," Natalya informed him.

She went on to explain that in those years the land-lord of Padarok Lessa, who had been Greg's and Natalya's grandfather, had, like his father before him, owned more than a thousand souls, as serfs were often called.

"In Russia, you see, among the wealthy in those days, one spoke of how many souls could be inherited, or bartered back and forth. Even dead souls had their uses. On paper they might continue to exist, as a kind of bureaucratic ghosts, sometimes helping the man who was supposed to own them in his efforts to claim more land. Have you read Gogol? *Dead Souls*. There must be an English translation."

"No doubt there is, but I'm afraid I haven't read it."

Sherwood and Natalya climbed to the stage and stood there for a little while, observing the dusty chairs and cobwebbed scenery, the eroded carpets. On the walls were several faded, amateurish playbills. These gave every evidence of having been tacked up decades ago and forgotten ever since. Doubtless their printing, like everything else in sight, had been done on the estate.

Studying the announcements, Sherwood tried to sound out some of the unfamiliar names. Natalya was mildly encouraging; he had at least made a start at learning how to pronounce the letters in the Russian alphabet.

He had to admit to himself that so far he had made very little progress, beyond memorizing the alien alphabet, in his effort to learn the language. Basic words for things and actions he found easy enough, but the changing endings and the devious grammar loomed in Sherwood's mind as near impossibilities. Everyone said that Russian was difficult to learn for anyone with English as a native language. Gregori had been tutoring him in some of the essentials, but now, of course, that had been temporarily set aside.

Struck by an idea, Sherwood asked: "Any of the

actors or singers ever become famous? Go to Moscow or Petersburg and perform in the big time?"

His guide looked at him strangely. "They were *serfs*. When the owner, Grandfather, tired of having them perform, he sent them back to the fields."

"Oh." After a moment's silence, Sherwood added: "He was the same gentleman who lost his temper when the government freed his serfs, and abandoned everything here, and went off to Siberia? I've seen his picture in your library back in Petersburg."

"That is our grandfather. Oh, of course the government compensated the landowners for their loss. And the newly liberated serfs suddenly found themselves in debt. Now they were required to pay for the land they had all along thought was theirs. It was one of those government arrangements that leaves no one satisfied."

"Did the peasants have money to pay with?"

"Of course not—but the requirement was officially dropped only a couple of years ago, in 1906. 'The waiving of peasant indebtedness to the state,' as they called it, along with removal of all legal restrictions on peasants as a class."

A little summer sunlight was coming in through a high window somewhere, lighting a high space full of drifting dust motes. Somewhere higher still, pigeons were cooing faintly in an invisible loft.

To Sherwood's surprise, he had to repress a sudden urge to take Natalya in his arms and kiss her. He told himself sternly that now was certainly not the time.

Their strolling tour carried them out of the theater again. The minor outbuildings were all built of logs, calked with mud, like old rural sheds and shacks in America, or with oakum. But the main house was of much fancier construction.

"I suppose all the villages on the estate are very much like the ones we passed through."

She agreed.

Sherwood asked about the other estate, the one far

to the east and north. "Greg mentioned it. It sounded curious."

The legend said, and, according to the Lohmatskis, the old book in the library seemed to confirm, that whatever lands the family possessed east of the Ural Mountains had been awarded to them by a grateful tsar. According to the book, this monarch had been no less than Ivan the Fourth, better known as the Terrible. The land grant, which Sherwood gathered was almost unique in Russian history, had taken place around four hundred years ago, a sign of the tsar's gratitude to anyone who had contributed to the royal treasury such an enormous wealth of furs.

"Apparently we had an ancestor who was a very successful trapper."

Natalya promised to find the old book and read it for Sherwood. But that could wait until tomorrow.

That night, as he lay drifting off to sleep in his comfortable room, Sherwood could hear wolves howling in the forest at no enormous distance from the house. He wondered drowsily if the peasants were as afraid of wolves as they seemed to be of bears. Well, if wolves didn't scare them now, he wasn't going to be the one to suggest the possibility.

On the edge of sleep, he roused momentarily at the sound of a woman, unidentifiable in her grief, weeping somewhere, rooms away in the great house.

Could it possibly be Natalya? But he had no way of knowing what her weeping sounded like. If ever she did weep.

FIVE

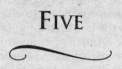

Counting up the number of days elapsed since the death of Ivan Gregorevich, Sherwood was sure that even the best hunting dogs would have trouble picking up a trail at the site of the tragedy. And he was by no means sure that the dogs available were going to be the best.

Explaining to Natalya some of the problems encountered by big-game hunters, and the means commonly employed to solve them, he added that despite the difficulties, he still wanted to be taken as soon as possible to the place of her father's death.

"I would like to make some kind of a start. There hasn't been much rain, in the last few days. With any luck, one or two of the bear's paw prints might be still intact."

Gregori, though not yet legally installed as the new heir, was inundated by duties regarding the estate, with the steward and others pressing him for decisions on a dozen matters. Still he was emphatically in agreement with Sherwood on the matter of the bear, keen on finding out what had happened to his missing brother. He set aside the morning to take part in the expedition.

Sherwood borrowed a sheepskin hunting vest, which turned out to have a few rounds of old Ivan's Mauser ammo still in the cartridge loops, to wear in the chill of early morning. He hadn't brought along a lot of spare clothing, having been assured that at Padarok Lessa every kind of field gear was in good supply.

Greg invited his guest to borrow some kind of rifle or, if he chose, a shotgun. Heavy loads and rifled slugs, effective against bear at close range, were available for the shotgun. Sherwood was basically content with his own Winchester, which he had taken pains to bring along, but looked over the choices anyway. The rack in the gunroom held a small arsenal of rifles, shotguns, and combination weapons, suitable for everything from grouse to bear.

Natalya went with him, and pointed out her father's hunting rifle. Old Ivan's Mauser had been returned to the house, and replaced in its usual spot in the gun rack.

Sherwood picked it out and looked it over casually. It was a sporting rifle, chambered for 7.92 mm ammunition. "Model *1884*, if I'm guessing right. Eight-round tubular magazine, bolt action."

But after a moment he replaced the Mauser, preferring to stick with his own roughly equivalent all-purpose Winchester. He checked the loading with the same religious care he always devoted to the process.

Three horses were saddled at dawn on the morning after Sherwood's arrival at Padarok Lessa, and he rode out with Gregori and Agafon, the old peasant gamekeeper and hunting guide.

Sherwood had invited Natalya to accompany them. There were many young women he would not have asked, but Natalya had not impressed him as the type to disqualify herself—or allow herself to be forbidden—from hunting because of her sex. But she declined,

saying she thought it useless to look for Maxim, and
she had no interest in hunting.

Agafon was mounted on an old horse. Though the
stables held several younger mounts, he disquali-
fied them all, for various reasons. Several times he
remarked upon the advanced age of his steed, giving it
as the reason why they could not go faster. The old
man was also unarmed, and when Sherwood's question
on this point was translated, Agafon declared that he
was only a poor shot, and also his eyesight wasn't what
it used to be.

He led the two armed riders, his master and the foreign visitor, unhurriedly through the farmyard and
into the woods, in almost the opposite direction from
the road by which they had arrived. The morning mists
were beginning to dissipate. The rutted road they had
begun on quickly degenerated into a mere trail, and
Sherwood soon realized that despite the vast reaches of
plowed fields and pastures, much of the land within
a few miles of the house was still forest, a great deal
of it too marshy to cultivate. Innumerable flies were
swarming, along with biting gnats or midges. The fields
Sherwood happened to get a good look at were empty,
going strongly to weeds while they waited for their
workers.

The morning had started cool, but soon the sheepskin was uncomfortably warm, and Sherwood took it
off. Gregori had spoken the truth about his homeland;
the place was beautiful. The dogs, responding to
Agafon's whistles, kept pace uncertainly, as if they had
caught some of the hunting guide's obvious lack of
enthusiasm.

After a couple of false turnings and hesitations on the
part of their guide, they reached the small forest
clearing where the attack had taken place. This was
only about a verst from the house, or a little more than
half a mile. On both sides of the small stream running
through the glade, grass and small bushes had been
trampled heavily by horses and a diverse collection of
booted human feet. The various plants were springing

back, recovering from the assault of several days ago. Whatever blood might have been deposited on the ground or on plants had been scoured away by rain and tiny scavengers, and, as Sherwood had foreseen, any trail the bear might have left was far too old to interest the dogs.

Dismounting, he ordered the others to stay back, and to keep the hounds leashed and well out of his way. Then he spent ten minutes in a methodical search, crouching and crawling over the trampled area, sometimes with his nose almost on the ground. At the end of that time, he was rewarded by one undeniable bear track, of a truly impressive size; its orientation strongly suggested that the beast might have followed the streambed in its retreat. This would render tracking easy, provided the quarry kept to the muddy shore. That was not to be expected, and of course the trail would disappear in the water.

Moments later, in the mud at the edge of the stream, Sherwood discovered another partial paw print, its claws pointing in the same direction as the first. Both specimens were impressively long and broad and deep, and clearly had been made by the same animal. Obviously the tracks were at least several days old, having been pressed by fourteen or fifteen hundred pounds of walking bear into wet mud that later had dried as the level of the stream went down.

Sherwood squatted in the grass to get the best view possible of his discovery. The last of the mists were gone now, the warm sun asserting domination, and the light was good. Each claw still stood out distinctly, but the fine ridges of dried mud between the marks of the claws were crumbling now. Only luck, and the fact that there had been no more than light rain for several days, had allowed him to see the tracks at all.

Without getting to his feet, Sherwood announced: "Well, no doubt there was a bear here, a few days ago. Brown bear."

And I bet it weighs as much as the two biggest lions in

Africa put together. He wasn't going to make that point aloud.

Gregori translated Sherwood's audible comment for Agafon, who was standing by holding the horses and looking mournful. Agafon managed to look impressed. Meanwhile the dogs, out of restlessness, perhaps, had become intrigued by a small fish, days dead and stinking richly, which lay a few paces upstream on the muddy bank. A few yards upstream from the fish, the little rivulet came gurgling out of dense woods.

The old peasant murmured something, in a tone that to Sherwood sounded philosophical.

"What's he saying?"

"Only that there are black bears in these woods as well as brown."

"Comes as no surprise." Sherwood straightened up. He stood sniffing the breeze, trying to absorb the sounds, the feel of this country, these particular woods.

He said: "I believe there are two or three species of black bears in Asia—I know, this part of Russia's still in Europe. But look at the size of this track, Greg!" He pointed at the whole example. "And you can see the toes are in a straight line across, not an arc the way they show in a black bear track. This is your regular brown bear, the same species that used to be seen everywhere in Europe. It's a huge beast, closely related to our American grizzly." Sherwood was trying to remember everything he had read about the Eastern Hemisphere version; he had never encountered that particular subspecies in the wild.

"And you've hunted grizzly."

"Yep."

Judging by the tracks, it was a very big bear indeed. But Sherwood did not want to emphasize that point. Knowing that the old peasant was watching him, paying careful heed to his manner and his expression, he had done his best to look calm and unsurprised while he studied the tracks, trying to dispel the notion that there could be anything supernatural about the animal. Even though he had to admit in his own mind that any brown bear's track had something disturbingly human about it, in the rear portion of the track especially—the slightly raised arch and comparatively narrow heel.

On the chance that their quarry might still be lingering somewhere in the vicinity, the three men took the dogs a quarter of a mile upstream, casting about on both banks for fresh bear signs, but without result. Sherwood was not pleased with the dogs, though of course they had not yet been really tested; he thought they still exhibited something of old Agafon's uneasiness.

There seemed nothing to do now but search the woods at random, or go home. Sherwood opted for the latter course. The bear might easily be ten miles away by now.

Around midday, the party returned to the house.

That evening, when Sherwood had finished another letter home, he handed it to a servant, to be posted the next time someone made a trip back to the town where in summer the riverboats put in. Doubtless there would be a pile of outgoing mail, with all the business accompanying the turnover of the estate.

"Greg, got a minute?"

Watching old Agafon while they were together out in the field, and listening to his translated comments and objections—there were quite a few objections— Sherwood had begun to develop doubts as to whether the elderly guide really wanted to hunt this bear, and even a suspicion that he might make an active effort to keep the hunters from catching up with it.

That evening the American mentioned his worries to his hosts. Natalya and Greg were well aware of the situation; they both assured Sherwood that the peasants, or the great majority of them at least, were still of the opinion that the bear was a supernatural creature, responsible for the death of Ivan Gregorevich, and for the disappearance of his son Maxim. Few of the peasants would be willing to hunt such a creature.

The three were seated in the parlor, before a summer fireplace stuffed with fresh flowers. Gregori was trying to get his pipe to stay lighted. Sherwood seldom smoked, but usually he found the aroma not unpleasant.

"And Agafon is with the reluctant majority."

"I expect he is."

Sherwood started to say something more, and then decided that it was necessary to push on. Now was a good time, when no servants were about.

He said: "There's an aspect of the situation which we haven't really touched on yet. But I think we've got to do so."

Natalya looked at him. "Yes?"

"Fairy tales have to be taken seriously, if people believe them."

Greg was regarding him steadily. "All right. Shoot."

"Greg, the way you describe the legend, the way the old book you've mentioned has it, it's not just about bears as supernatural creatures. The story involves men of your family *turning into* bears."

"Yes."

"Applying that to our present situation, isn't it possible that some of your people here suspect that your missing brother has . . . actually . . . ?"

Greg was nodding before Sherwood had finished speaking. "It is more than possible. You may take it as given that very many of our people believe that Maxim is still alive. That he has turned, at least temporarily, into a great brown bear, and that he has killed our father."

"And the other people before your father."

"Yes." Greg remarked that he had heard they were both men who had fallen foul of Maxim in one way or another. "One on the peasants' council, the other a relative of a girl in whom my brother had, shall we say, taken an interest. So there seems to be some truth in that, which of course makes matters worse."

Sherwood, nodding that he understood, fell silent for a moment, trying to imagine what kind of people would really believe in a thing like shape-changing. How their minds must work, how such folk would be likely to behave. But it was a little more than he could fathom.

At last he said: "So, according to that theory, if we hunt the bear, we're really hunting your brother. Which would be serious business indeed—if you could believe it. So I think we have to decide about Agafon. Is he one of those who might really be convinced . . . ?"

Greg frowned. "I wouldn't be surprised. The problem is that, as far as I know, Agafon's the only one available who's worth anything as a hunting guide. He always handles the dogs, you see. He understands firearms fairly well. And I believe he knows the woods, the lay of the land around here, better than anyone else."

Sherwood nodded. He glanced at Natalya, who was content to listen to the talk in somber silence. Then he came up with a suggestion. "You said you've been away from home for—how long?—a year?"

"Yes. But it's much longer than that since I've done any hunting in these parts."

"So quite possibly you're out of touch. There might now be someone else available who could handle the dogs as well as Agafon, and knows the ground, and is less superstitious. Maybe someone considerably younger?"

Gregori brightened a bit. "That's a thought. Let me see what I can find out."

"Meanwhile—could we look up that old book? If I'm going to deal with a legend, I'd like to know as much about it as I can."

Natalya, seeming glad of the diversion, immediately volunteered to act as guide and translator for Sherwood in the extensive library. She said she knew exactly the old book that he was looking for.

And she needed only half a minute to locate it, in a glass-front cabinet with half a dozen other rare volumes. It was moldering, crumbling paper, bound with a stiff cover, once golden yellow, complete with a metal clasp (long since broken) by which to lock it shut.

Sherwood had never seen anything quite like it. "I'm no expert on old books, but this looks remarkable."

"It is. The bulk of it is supposedly reprinted from what purports to be a sixteenth-century family testament, or affidavit; certainly it is very old, though in any century it would have been highly unusual for a Russian to keep a personal journal or record."

And a personal record it seemed to be, as if someone intimately concerned might have written down the events for his family. There was a suggestion in the wording, Natalya said, as she began her translation, that the story had been written by the very man who had been first to Change—that he had wanted to leave a record, probably for one of his sons.

The archaic Russian was difficult for Natalya, and she hesitated at several words, once or twice calling on her brother for help which he proved unable to provide.

But the sense of the tale came through unmistakably.

"There is, you see, a man, who has fallen foul of the authorities, who were then perhaps not all that much different from what they are today.

"In the time of Ivan the Terrible, in some year past the middle of the sixteenth century, some six or eight members of the tsar's *Oprichnina*, called *Oprichniks* (outsiders), in the course of their reign of terror against the Russian populace—they were, in fact, very much like our *Okhrana* of today—came up with what they considered a new and ingenious punishment—for the sin of rebelling against the tsar.

"At the time that was the only sin, it seems, that could not be forgiven."

Greg raised a hand, signaling that he wished to interrupt. Then he asked Sherwood: "How are you on history, my friend?"

"Not very good, I suppose. Why?"

"Well, if you know a little about the history of Ivan

and his times, it tends to make it more understandable, how such a horrible legend as ours could come to be.

"You see, the tsar had recently been making a special effort to capture bears alive, or buy them—or steal them. He intended to send a special gift to his contemporary, Elizabeth of England. What more appropriate than a bear, or several bears, in some way specially, outstandingly, qualified for bearbaiting?

"At one point in his career, finding himself temporarily wifeless, Tsar Ivan had made overtures sounding out the advisers of the Virgin Queen as to whether she might entertain a royal proposal of marriage."

The overtures had been diplomatically rebuffed. Her Majesty had no intention of marrying anyone, least of all the Tsar of Muscovy, that frozen domain so far away from everything; but Elizabeth, like many of her contemporaries all across Europe, intensely enjoyed the spectacle of bearbaiting. On one occasion in 1575, thirteen bears were provided in one day for the queen's amusement. Maybe Ivan knew this. In any case, he wanted to send her a dozen of the beasts.

At this point, Sherwood's face had taken on a look of disgust; he had the true hunter's loathing and contempt for what he considered unsportsmanlike conduct, cruelty for the sake of cruelty, practiced against animals.

And Natalya commented; "I suppose old Ivan thought that Elizabeth was one of the few women who understood these things."

Then she resumed the translation.

The old book admitted that the victim chosen by the *Oprichniki* had probably done nothing offensive to the common standards of human decency, and perhaps his crime was purely imaginary.

Or perhaps not. In any case, he was condemned to be sewn naked into a fresh bearskin, or the forward half of one, and hunted to death.

"The book says that the man in the bearskin was then hunted by hounds. We don't know exactly what kind, but we can assume that there were at that time dogs specially bred and trained to hunt and attack bears. The Karelian hound might not yet have become a separate breed. The borzoi, or Russian wolfhound, might be used. Norwegian elkhounds? Mastiffs?"

"It doesn't matter," said Greg impatiently.

Natalya silently acknowledged this, and proceeded: "Those who sewed up the condemned man into his furry shroud, using sailors' and tentmakers' cord and needles, allowed his legs to remain free, so that he might be enticed or goaded into running. And they were careful to leave his face at least partially exposed, for two reasons: first, so he could see where he was running, and prolong the game enough to make it interesting; and second so that his executioners, riding close behind their hounds, might be able to watch his face as he died."

Sherwood's imagination, armed as it was with a good store of facts, could paint the scene all too convincingly. . . .

The sheer weight of the raw skin was staggering in itself—if the head had been left intact, possibly almost two hundred pounds. The man, normally strong, was already dazed and weakened by the preliminary torments he had suffered at his captors' hands. He swayed on his feet when they set him upright.

The raw hide stank abominably, even if the weather was cold, and if the weather was warm enough, flies swarmed around it. If the weather was cold enough, the remaining wetness of the hide would cause it to freeze, to crunch and crackle and be difficult to pierce even with a sailmaker's needle.

Maybe those in charge of preparing the elaborate costume had to cut off the trailing part of the pelt, half of the whole thing or even more, so that the man's strength might be sufficient to let him stand and run.

When they were finished with their binding and sewing, their victim's ghastly eyes stared out through the now-toothless gap which once had been the bear's mouth. The man's own hair poked out in tufts through the twin holes through which the animal's living eyes had keenly observed the world. But the man's hands were sewn securely into pockets which had been the bear's forelegs, and the raw hide sewn around his body, with tentmaker's needle and cord, so that with his hands confined, he had no chance of getting out of it.

The victim of course ought to have realized the utter hopelessness of trying to run away—and yet, and yet! His executioners, who were of a sporting disposition, told him what they would do to him if he did not run. And they saw to it that he was allowed a sufficiently long start to make the matter at least a little interesting. A hundred strides, two hundred, finally such a distance that he could no longer prevent his body from beginning to react to hope. His weary lungs gasped harder at the air, his strides lengthened.

The man could not keep himself from hoping that if only he could keep his legs moving under the burden of hide and skin, long enough to carry him to the river—unless the river was frozen solid—if only he could somehow throw the dogs off the track, gain time to work his hands free, a chance to peel himself out of the bloody pelt—

But of course all that, the lure of hope, was part of his tormentors' plan.

The hollow skin of the bear's limbs hung down like long-haired flaps, two on each side of the imprisoned man. Unless they had cut the rear legs off to reduce the weight, dead claws swung and scratched on each side of the two pale, running human legs.

Before they set the human victim running, he had a few last words to say. He might have been uttering a final curse. Or what he spoke might possibly have been a prayer.

Despite the theoretical chance of escape, the ray of hope that would not die, in practical terms it was impossible that the chase should last very long. And it did not. The pursuit wound through bushes and fields and perhaps along the edge of a swamp, before reaching its inevitable end. Although perhaps to the victim it seemed endless. On horseback the victim's

persecutors followed the sound of the hounds, and
sooner or later the savage dogs closed in on their prey,
who perhaps had been making a hopeless effort to conceal himself in a swamp.

One pursuer frowned. He was certain that the bear's
head had been cut off at the last moment, to lessen the
crushing weight—but now he saw the black muzzle,
and the standing ears, and teeth . . . and eyes . . . as if
they were looking straight at him . . .

But to the amazement of the men on horseback who
first caught up with them, the hounds were soon seen
to be worrying only an empty skin. And it was not the
brown-furred hide of the great bear.

An observer saw with shock, like a man beholding an
important part of the world turned inside out, that the
dogs, apparently deprived of their intended prey, were
biting and tearing to shreds something that certainly
looked like a human skin, vastly smaller than a bearskin, pale and almost hairless. So bloodless was this odd
relic that the first man to see it in the hounds' jaws
thought the hide must have been long separated from
the body and soul it once had covered. But the beard
could still be distinguished. And it was very like the
beard of the intended victim.

Some of the *Oprichniki* dismounted from their horses,
the better to investigate.

As they did so, a raging monster broke from a nearby
thicket, with a crashing noise. A brown-furred shape
bigger than a horse, at first running like a horse on
four legs, but then, as it prepared to close with its first
antagonist, rearing up on its hind legs, revealing itself
as a giant bear of supernatural strength and ferocity.

The horse reared on its hind legs, too, but in doing
so rose no taller than the bear.

The amazement of the human watchers was soon
transformed into terror, as they beheld their new
antagonist break a hound's neck with one deft slap,
and in its jaws crush to pulp the skull of another dog
before it could even yelp. The remainder of the pack
went scattering, yelping in cowardly disorder.

This giant bear charged the chief villain and knocked him off his mount, ignored his effort to stab at it with his sword. The blade pierced heavy fur, but drew no blood.

"Though several of the riders fired their flintlock muskets or pistols at the huge bear, the bullets, being not of silver, had no effect."

"Silver, hey?"

"Oh, in all the stories, Johnny, silver bullets are effective."

The bear knocked the leader of its tormentors right out of his saddle, and soon, pummeling them with both forepaws, killed the screaming horse and man alike.

One of the other mounted men also tried to fight. He prodded at the monster with—with a kind of lance, and was quickly mangled.

Another man screamed something about the devil.

A moment later, the human pack, caught up in superstitious terror, was scattering in full flight.

Soon they came together again; no matter how much they feared this devil-spawned Bear, they dreaded the wrath of Tsar Ivan even more. Their report, heard or read by the tsar later in the day, detailed quite a different version of the day's events. Heroic fighting by the survivors had quashed a dastardly plot by more than one man.

An hour or so after tasting the flesh of several of his tormentors, the intended victim, to all appearances, had recovered such humanity as he had possessed before his ordeal.

The physical injuries he had sustained were actually trifling. But some part of his soul had been violently altered, and scar tissue already grown in its place. He had survived his ordeal, but was never the same man afterward.

He returned to his home and talked matters over with his wife, if he had one, or perhaps with his parents—or he tried to talk things over.

In the days and months and years of life that followed, his close relatives were hesitant to accept him as the same man, even though, as they repeatedly assured each other, he *looked* the same.

In time the man, who now knew how to be a bear whenever he considered such a transformation advantageous, had found employment with the family of the famous Anika Stroganov, whose clan was intensely engaged in building blockhouses and settlements on the eastern frontier, near the Urals and even a little bit beyond. The were-bear's immediate employer, who fully understood what kind of creature he was hiring, was old Anika's son Gregori.

In the course of providing this loyal service for their beloved tsar, all the Stroganovs enriched themselves prodigiously. With the riches of an entire continent opening up before them, there was plenty of wealth to be shared with their chief lieutenants.

Years later—some time after Tsar Ivan had gone to be confronted in the next world by his innumerable victims—the bear-man wrote his story down for his sons and their descendants, or when the observing foreigner wrote them down as a warning to the world—or simply for his own satisfaction—the original survivor's family, too, were well established as powerful landlords in their own right. The name "Lohmatski," implying shagginess, seemed to date from this time.

And after Ivan the Terrible, as any knowledgeable student of the era can tell you—*after* Ivan the Terrible came what the Russian people soon began to call the Time of Troubles.

Greg added: "There's a kind of footnote—I heard it from some relatives in another branch of the family— to the effect that the curse which descended upon the family who later took the name of Lohmatski was considered by some members of the clan—notably by some of those directly affected—to be no curse at all. Rather, these men thought the power of Changing an almost-

```
HASTINGS BOOKS, MUSIC & VIDEO #9823
            654 N. 3RD ST.
        LARAMIE, WYOMING 82070
           (307)745-0312
03/03/97 21:10 DONNA   D. TRANS# 9545-01


 1  050 DANCING BEARS            6.29
 1  050 TALES FROM JABBAS        5.39
       CASH               $    15.00



    SUBTOTAL              $    11.68


    TAX                   $     0.70

 TOTAL               $12.38


    CHANGE DUE            $     2.62
With a video membership today, you can
watch all the great summer rentals now!
         www.hastings-ent.com
```

unique reward, bestowed on them by Providence, or Fate, because of their general superiority to the less-fortunate legions of humanity. The first man to formally adopt the new family name did so with considerable pride."

Natalya raised her eyes to Sherwood. "The author's last comment is: 'Very upsetting for the mother involved, of course, but perhaps women do not really understand these things.'"

Later, over a brandy nightcap, Gregori told his friend that it had been a common belief among the local people that the last wild bears in the district had been hunted to death many years ago. But rationally it was quite possible that more of the animals could have migrated in from the vast forests which, according to Gregori, began only a little beyond the estate's eastern boundary.

Sherwood agreed. "Bears in general like to move around a good bit; or at least they don't have any objection to expanding their territory, or even changing it altogether, if such behavior puts more food in their mouths."

The two discussed possible methods of hunting deadly predators, means Sherwood and others had used successfully against big cats in India and Africa. You could sit up in a tree, over a kill, if you thought the beast with big teeth was coming back to the carcass to feed some more, which was what they often did. Or you could tie out a goat or a cow as bait—but neither of those methods seemed applicable here. This bear, which had now killed at least three men, and quite possibly four, had given no sign of being interested in cattle.

The two hunters agreed that it would be worth trying to obtain some better dogs, and Gregori mentioned a nearby village or two where some good hounds might be obtainable.

With some reluctance, Sherwood observed: "You know, we really ought to consider trapping the beast, as well as shooting it. Not very sporting, but under the circumstances, I suppose the idea ought to be simply to get the job done. . . ."

Again Greg looked a little brighter. "I hadn't thought of that. Agafon has never run traps, as far as I know, but some of the people in the villages used to take some nice furs—rabbits, martens, foxes, that kind of thing. Never bears, as far as I know. What kind of traps would you need?"

"If you're serious about using a spring-steel trap on any beast the size of a grizzly—which this one is—you need the biggest made. Number six, I believe. Weighs about forty pounds. Just setting one is a major operation. I've seen 'em, but never tried to use 'em myself."

Gregori shook his head slowly. "I doubt there's anything of the kind on the estate. We could order some, but that might take a long time."

"Of course there are other types of traps and snares, deadfalls and such. Made out of ropes and logs and ingenuity. That can be one line of attack. Meanwhile, let's see what we can do about getting some better dogs."

SIX

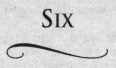

As the new heir to vast properties, Gregori suddenly found himself compelled to grapple with a hundred business matters in which he had previously taken not the slightest interest. Day by day—even, it seemed, hour by hour—the load increased. Fortunately some decisions could be put off, but others could not. Distinguishing the trivial from the important was sometimes difficult, especially for a man who until now had concerned himself as little as possible with the family enterprises.

Lawyers from two nearby towns arrived at the house to talk to him. There were account books to be gone over, as well as other records. Not only were the complicated affairs of the European estate to be dealt with, but also such musty records as could be found regarding the distant Siberian gift of Ivan the Terrible. And there were various other family enterprises and holdings.

With these matters pressing him, Greg was left with almost no time for anything else. Sherwood, despite the language barrier, had to take over the planning and preparations for the hunt as best he could. Natalya volunteered to act as his interpreter.

Pursuing alternate means of getting rid of bears, Sherwood wanted to talk to the villagers who were said to be skilled in running trap lines, in the hope that one of them might possess the necessary knowledge and equipment.

Sitting with Natalya at a small table in the combination gun-and-billiard room, he was explaining his ideas. "I've never tried trapping bear—or anything else, for that matter—but I've talked to men who've done it in the Rockies."

His companion's expression indicated interest. "I've seen some traps, in some of the villagers' houses—what would a bear trap look like?"

"For an animal the size of an average grizzly—and this bear we're after's even bigger—you need a number-six spring trap." Paper and pencil were at hand, and quickly he sketched a diagram, showing closed loops of steel with wicked teeth.

"This thing is about a yard long—a little more than an *arsheen*"—Sherwood doggedly tried to work a few Russian words into his conversation when possible— "and it really needs two men to compress the springs and set it. It has a chain on it, like this—and you secure the other end of the chain to a loose log. Not to a rock or a tree. If the bear can't move at all, he's likely to chew his own paw off to get loose, whereas if he's dragging a sizable log, he'll move around some, but you can find him."

Natalya was studying the sketch intently. "Yes, I recognize the shape. But I doubt anyone around here has a trap that size. I've never seen one." She raised serious, disturbing eyes. "I can imagine an animal wanting to be free, desperate enough to chew off its own leg. But can it survive afterward?"

"Sometimes. It has three more legs, and three are enough for an animal that doesn't have to run. Quite a few beavers have avoided becoming fur coats by sacrificing a foot. And a bear doesn't really have to run to get something to eat. On three legs he can still catch up with plants, or fish, or squirrels' nests, or beehives. And there's nothing in the world he has to run away from—except maybe a bigger bear, now and then."

"Not even people?"

Sherwood shook his head, smiling faintly. "Can't outrun a bullet, even on four good legs."

An hour later, Natalya embarked with Sherwood on a tour of nearby villages, in search of peasants who were known to have been gamekeepers, or thought to have run traps. Sherwood was still determined to obtain better dogs if possible, and continued to nurse hopes of enlisting a competent guide, someone who knew the local land and wildlife but was not disabled by superstition.

Natalya rode with him in a light carriage. Sherwood carried his Winchester, just in case. For a time he gave Natalya the rifle to hold, while he took a turn at driving the odd vehicle, just for the experience. He made a start at learning the proper commands to call out to Russian horses.

The couple failed to locate the former gamekeeper. But in the course of the next few days, Sherwood and Natalya, working as a team, negotiated to buy, borrow, or hire three supposedly superior bear-hunting dogs. Success in this effort did not come until they visited a village a couple of hours' drive away, beyond Lohmatski land, where the people remained relatively unconcerned by the were-bear legend. But even here, the bear was one of the chief topics of conversation. When the dogs had been selected, Natalya arranged for their transportation in a wagon, back to the kennels at Padarok Lessa.

Between long sessions in which he attempted the uncongenial task of managing the business of the estate, Gregori tried to think of some plan to get the peasants back into the fields. A few brave souls were working now, but a majority still refused. The new landowner hoped to make the peasants feel secure by posting armed guards. This required establishing a system whereby some of the local men who owned firearms would take turns on watch. Even Gregori took time away from his paperwork to ride from village to village on this job.

In one of the villages Sherwood visited, he and Natalya met the peasants who had found old Ivan dead. These people, with many oaths and prayers, assured their questioners that the old man's body, which had been buried before Sherwood's arrival, bore the plain marks of having been mauled by a large animal. Other witnesses concurred.

All the clothes Maxim had been wearing at the time of the attack were still missing, along with his rifle, and his small backpack and blanket roll. Sherwood thought that if the man's body had been carried off by a bear, his rifle, at least, would have been left behind.

"But there was nothing."

"What kind of rifle was it?"

Everyone remembered old Ivan's Mauser, which had been faithfully brought back to the house after its owner's death, but no one was sure how Maxim had been armed.

Sherwood didn't want to get the people's hopes up. "Possibly no one has yet searched the woods very thoroughly."

On the other hand, not only the old man's rifle had been saved, but his torn and bloody clothes laundered by faithful hands, and the tears sewn up. Ivan Gregorevich had been buried in his best suit.

It seemed to Sherwood that all reasonable preparations for a serious hunt had now been made. Now they would settle in and wait for another reliable-sounding sighting of the killer bear—the alternative, going out to scour a hundred or so square miles of woods at random, in search of one particular bear, struck him as almost certainly an exercise in futility. Though, of course, such tactics could be tried as a last resort.

Agafon protested that there was no need for the uncle to concern himself. The bear was probably far away by now.

"I'm his uncle? I don't know whether to be flattered or not."

"You'll probably be called *dyadyoshka* by a lot of people—servants and workers. No need to feel flattered. It's just a common form, really meant to be respectful."

Through his faithful interpreter, Sherwood questioned the few peasants who claimed to have actually seen the bear, in the woods or at the edge of the fields, on various occasions over the past month. All of them, men and women alike, were totally convinced that the beast was supernatural—but why they were so sure was hard to understand. Some spoke of how the animal had moved, or how it had looked at them, with the appearance of understanding.

They crossed themselves, and vehemently performed other gestures that Sherwood found less comprehensible. Again and again he thought his ears caught the word *chyort*, which he had learned meant devil.

"Tell them the bear has nothing to do with the devil. It is only an animal."

The man, bowing and agitated, said something else. Sherwood heard *obaraten* again, and also *chelovek-volk*. The wolf-man. He remembered his earlier discussion with Greg about shape-changing legends.

"He begs to inquire of you, Your Honor—that's what he calls you now—if you have seen the animal." Natalya was now looking at Sherwood with faint, bitter amusement; as if she had begun to find all this darkly entertaining, though most of her mind was busy elsewhere.

"No more his little father, hey? Tell him I have seen the big bear's track, and that's all I need to see. What has he observed that makes him think otherwise?"

To begin with there was the size of the bear, which

must have made an impression on anyone who saw it. After seeing the tracks, Sherwood had no doubt that it was very big.

Also the animal had engaged in some kind of odd behavior, real or imagined. And old Ivan was not the first human it was known to have killed.

"Of course some of the people who claim to have seen the bear have seen little more than their own imaginations—maybe they caught a glimpse of a black bear, which are common here, you know. Some may have been frightened by a big wolf, or even a dog."

That evening in the parlor, browsing among the contents of a glass-fronted curio cabinet his hosts had invited him to examine, Sherwood came upon some exotic trinkets, simple but impressive carvings of bears, in bone and walrus ivory. In their simplicity, these artifacts reminded Sherwood of the work of certain European artists who were currently considered very modern, even revolutionary. Some of the objects had designs of unknown meaning lightly incised in them.

A hint, a breath it seemed, of the mysteries of Siberia. Sherwood looked up at the walls, but in this house there were no photographs of Grandfather.

Greg did not seem much interested in the ivory trinkets. None of the younger generation had ever visited the Siberian estate.

"Those things must have been brought here several generations back—though Father did go out there once, as a youth, before any of my generation were born. He rarely talked about the trip, except to say that he had wanted to see, to visit, *his* father at the Siberian estate."

"The one who moved there as protest when the serfs were freed."

"Yes."

"And he found the old man still alive?"

"Yes, apparently, though at that time not so old. Grandfather was then maybe in his forties. Evidently they quarreled bitterly, though Father never told us many details. Family history was not his favorite subject of conversation."

Sherwood considered the story. "So your grandfather actually spent the last half of his life—or maybe more than half—out there, in the Arctic, or almost? Doing what?"

Obviously that question had occurred to Natalya and her brother, but they had never come up with a good answer. "Surviving, I suppose," the young woman offered. "That would seem to be about all one could do in such an environment."

"Surviving without his serfs, evidently," her brother added.

Sherwood asked whether he could see a map of Padarok Lessa, and the surrounding region.

Greg shook his head. "You are thinking Western style, my friend. I very much doubt that a map showing the location and boundaries of this estate exists anywhere—except maybe in the brains of Agafon and a couple of other old people. I don't think we have a decent map of Russia in either of our houses. Probably in London you could have bought one—though I fear even the best maps of Siberia are going to be full of huge blank snow-white spaces. Possibly you could have found one in Petersburg; but then St. Petersburg, as we know, is a half-foreign city."

Sherwood found himself drawn increasingly to Natalya. But so far he had refrained, out of respect for her bereavement, from trying to make love to her. He was also wary of her tendency from time to time to play the hard-bitten revolutionary.

The next day, Sherwood accompanied her on a mission of charity to the hut of an unfortunate peasant family, floored by a deadly combination of illness, accident, and childbirth. Inside the log house, old people groaned with chronic disabilities; dirty children ran about half-naked. The younger adults, who ordinarily would have been out in the fields, were home, but seemed incapable of dealing with their problems.

It was plain that the entire family loved Natalya, though they could not have seen much of her in recent years. The women of the peasant family blessed her, and said that all on the estate had missed her while she was away.

Natalya told the American visitor that whenever she was at Padarok Lessa, she served many of the estate's inhabitants as a midwife, nurse or doctor—although she had not had any formal training.

On their way back to her father's house, Natalya in a pensive mood asked Sherwood what it was like to be a hunter.

"How do you mean?"

"I suppose what I really mean is, do you ever show mercy on the animals you hunt?"

"You mean by not shooting them when I've got them in my sights? Yes, I've done that on occasion. Only a couple of months ago, in Africa, there was a certain elephant . . ."

He paused, groping for words. "See, the killing isn't the important part of hunting. Unless you really need the meat, or it's some beast that's too much for the country to stand, like this bear. For a few years, I was keen on taking trophies—and I've got a number at home, just as your house has here. But lately I've begun to lose interest in that."

"I suppose your wife doesn't mind?"

"No wife."

When Natalya had been silent for a time, he put a question of his own: "Have you ever hunted?"

"Animals? No."

"What, then? Vegetables?"

That got a pretty laugh.

"I do believe that's almost the first time I've ever seen you smile."

She tossed her beautiful hair, worn loose today. "If you want a serious answer, no. Father taught me to shoot, and I have been invited more than once in my life to go along on hunting trips—what do you call them? Safaris—?"

"They call them that in Africa."

"—but I have come to the decision that I am not a hunter. Still, I like to eat meat."

Four days after Sherwood's arrival, eight after old Ivan's death, a hard-riding peasant brought in a report that the bear had killed again.

"The lad who brought the news is frightened, and somewhat incoherent, but the gist of it seemed to be that one man at least is dead, as well as an animal or two. No more than a couple of miles away."

The hunters were both eager to get started at once.

At last it seemed that the Bear had obliged them with a fresh trail. Arms and supplies had been made ready—this household of hunters held a small arsenal of weapons—and the two hunters set out eagerly to follow it, Sherwood once more carrying his own Winchester, leaving old Ivan's Mauser at home.

"Not a real shoulder-breaker like your Nitro Express," he remarked to Greg, referring to the elephant gun the latter had carried in Africa. "But it gets the job done."

Greg armed himself with a somewhat heavier weapon from the rack.

Agafon's grandson Gleb, a slender youth of sixteen or so, wearing a mismatched set of old clothes and a newer model of Agafon's large nose, had been recruited as an additional guide, hopefully less superstitious. Agafon himself, dropping all complaints about his advanced age and poor eyesight, was at first opposed to the youngster's coming along. But when Gregori insisted, Gleb's grandfather admitted that the youngster would be a help with the tasks of packing and managing a camp. Sherwood would have been better satisfied leaving the old man at home, but Gregori sighed and decided that it would be unwise to depend entirely on an untested youth.

The hunters brought along a spare mount, saddled and ready to ride, on the theory that Maxim would need one if they found him still alive. But they counted his survival highly unlikely. A more likely use for the spare mount would be to carry back Maxim's remains. Or a bearskin. If they should be successful in acquiring either.

When they arrived at the scene of the latest killing, three or four peasants on the spot were arguing among themselves whether they should move the dead body off their master's land, to try to avoid the legal difficulties which otherwise might engulf them all.

Sherwood, having heard the substance of the argument in translation, still didn't understand it. "What's that all about?"

Gregori explained: "Whenever a dead body is found, the owner of the land is legally required to explain the death, whether or not he had anything to do with it; or at least it used to be so, and these people have it in their heads that it still is."

The man's body had been mangled savagely, and partially eaten. It seemed to Sherwood, looking on with a queasy stomach, that the body would be unrecognizable even to his next of kin.

But Gregori, struggling against his own revulsion, thought he could identify the victim, and told Sherwood as much, after a brief conversation with the peasants.

"There's his hat, you see, rather distinctive." It lay on the ground, dirty and torn, but the high crown was still gay with feathers. "Many of the peasant men seem to enjoy having unique hats."

"I've noticed."

"And he has a silver ring on one finger, which his comrades here say they can identify. Yes, I think there's not much doubt." Greg paused. "He was a local leader in the campaign for peasants' rights."

"What was he doing out here?" Sherwood looked around; there were no houses within several hundred yards. "I thought the people were afraid to go into the fields."

After another exchange in Russian with the peasants, Greg turned back. "Not Afanasi here. He was progressive and kept arguing in the village against superstition. No sign that he was doing field work, though. He might have come out hunting grouse or rabbits, just to prove that it was safe."

Like Greg's father, Sherwood observed, this victim had been armed. Sherwood picked up the old shotgun from the ground and sniffed at it, then broke it open. Both barrels had recently been fired, but the peasant had evidently managed to miss the bear, for away from the local carnage there was no departing blood-spoor to be found. What size of shot had been discharged was impossible to tell by looking at the empty shells. But even birdshot, if fired at desperation range, in self-defense, ought to have torn out handfuls of fur, a chunk of the toughest hide.

Sherwood looked around again. But there was nothing of the kind.

The dead man's eyes—his eye, rather, because only one of them was still intact—gave away no secrets.

Casting around on the ground at this fresh kill, Sherwood thought he could discover signs enough amid the freshly trampled brush to reconstruct the attack. But what he discovered was disconcerting. Had the bear waited in ambush for its victim? Had it, against all animal good sense, moved along this nearby heavy hedgerow, stalking its victim from upwind?

Yes, the man had come walking along this faint path, just before he was attacked. Here were fresh tracks of the bast-fiber slippers all peasants seemed to wear in summer.

The hunter's senses had gone on full alert. Something here, apart from the blunt fact of human death, was wrong, out of place, not as it should be. Sherwood's instincts had become intensely engaged. He sniffed the noticeable breeze and checked his directions.

Then he asked: "Has the wind changed direction since the attack this morning?"

Greg relayed the question tersely. No one thought it had, but of course it was impossible to be sure. Greg came back: "Why do you ask?"

Sherwood explained. "Looks like the bear could

have been stalking him. If this was a tiger or a lion kill, I'd sure say that the animal had been stalking. Except that it looks like the bear was waiting upwind from the man."

"Well?" Only then did Gregori remember one of the lessons of his recent experience in Africa, and apply it here. "Oh."

Sherwood nodded. "Predators don't stalk their prey that way. Not even man-eaters when they ambush people. Because they don't realize that humans have no sense of smell."

SEVEN

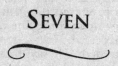

It was late in the day before the hunt actually got under way, and the sun had almost completed its long, slanting descent across the western sky. But at this season hours of white-night twilight still lay ahead. Though Agafon suggested putting off the effort until morning, Gregori brusquely overruled him.

This time there was no difficulty at all about picking up the bear's trail. At the scene of the latest killing, the three new dogs sniffed energetically, and whined in agitation. So far they showed no inclination to bay or bark. But to Sherwood's satisfaction, they seemed—at first—eager to get at their quarry. They strained at their leashes as soon as Gleb had slipped them on.

Agafon pulled his beard and scowled, muttering his doubts that these strange, untested dogs were reliable. Gleb looked at his grandfather but had no comment.

The bear set its pursuers a difficult course, soon leaving open fields behind, going through marshland and forest, uphill and down, among groves of pine and fir and larch and birch. Willows grew thickly along the little streams, which the quarry, this time, did not favor in his retreat—if retreat was the right word for what the bear was doing. The summer forest was beautiful. Several times Sherwood saw deer sign, though the area's wildlife, as Agafon grumbled from time to time, was not as abundant as it had been a few years ago. Still, the old man promised the gentlemen sportsmen that he could show them some fine deer hunting anytime they were interested.

"Or elk," Greg added. "He says there are elk around, though I have serious doubts."

"Looks to me that what he's serious about is distracting us from this bear," Sherwood commented.

"We have to be a little patient with him, John."

"Sure. If our man-eater gives us time."

From the fringes of the settled region, mostly cultivated land, encompassing Padarok Lessa, the wild country extended north to the treeless subarctic grassland of the tundra, and eventually to the pole; east the forest reached for several hundred versts to the Urals, and beyond those mountains almost halfway around the world.

The hunters observed the bear's droppings at least as often as his tracks.

Frowning, Greg wondered aloud: "Has it got diarrhea? I can distinguish several kinds of plants, none very well digested."

"That's normal, for a bear. What it eats tends to move through the gut in a hurry."

They also saw where their quarry had grazed like a bull on small plants, and where the bear's sharp, powerful claws had stripped bark from small trees to get at the tender inner layer, rich in springtime juices. And what was left of some small animal slain and eaten. In one spot at the side of a small stream their quarry had rolled in rotten fish, evidently reveling in the luxurious stench.

Agafon kept looking apprehensively in Gregori's direction, as if the old man feared being given the wrong orders—or perhaps, thought Sherwood, it was the right ones that would worry him. And Gregori, as usual when he was in the field with John Sherwood, looked to his friend who was a vastly more experienced hunter.

Maybe, Sherwood thought, I haven't utterly wasted my whole youth after all. Hunting may be the one thing in the world that I do know something about. To get this animal now, today or tomorrow, to save one human life, would be something of an accomplishment.

Agafon kept wondering aloud whether these inferior dogs were on the right trail. Finally Gregori spoke to him sharply. The tone of rebuke came through without translation.

Sherwood felt somewhat concerned about Agafon's obstructionism, but still pleased that things were actually moving along.

From the start of the hunt the dogs had been held on leashes, only to be unleashed if and when the scent grew very warm and it seemed the quarry could be brought to bay. Agafon and the much younger Gleb took turns holding the leashes and being tugged forward by the beasts.

The day wore on, the sun sliding across the sky but getting only minimally lower. It was hard to tell if they were gaining any ground on the Bear or not, difficult to determine if the tracks and droppings were any fresher. Sometimes now the beast returned to its old tactic of walking in a streambed, and the idea crossed Sherwood's mind that it was making an effort to hide its trail—a very unanimal behavior.

The dogs were gradually becoming reluctant to follow the trail. An hour came when they refused the job altogether, whining and pretending there was no such thing as the scent of a game animal in the vicinity.

Agafon was wearing a faint smile now, as if he felt he had been vindicated.

Sherwood began to get the feeling that their quarry was leading them on a course which, if it was continued, would bring them round in a kind of great circle to a place not far from their starting point.

They had not been tracking for very many hours before they came to a place where the bear's looping trail intersected itself. Sherwood understood almost at once what had happened. The intersection naturally created three possibilities of which way to go, and they had to be sorted out. Which way did the tracks point, which way were twigs broken, which of the trio of possibilities was the freshest? Agafon, ready to claim expertise when it would serve his purpose, twice suggested the wrong trail at these branch points.

Shadows were steadily deepening and lengthening, the sun now down behind trees and almost grazing the horizon. Dogs and men and horses covered several more miles before it seemed that darkness was going to fall at last. The summer twilight had deepened, and was made darker by clouds or mist, to the point where it was necessary to stop and make camp—though Agafon managed to come up with several reasons why it would be better to go home and seemed to assume that that must be his master's choice. The old man was now struck by the revelation that he had forgotten to pack any matches—yes, he admitted he must be getting old!—and therefore it would be impossible to build a fire. Better go home after all. But everyone else in the party had remembered matches.

Greg ignored all these maneuvers as much as possible. "We'll camp here and start again as soon as it's light."

Greg and Sherwood both agreed with the old man's claim that they were now probably no more than a couple of versts from the place where they had started. They did not agree with his conclusion that, since home was so near, they might as well give up.

"The dogs might be able to follow a trail all night, but we can't very well shoot anything in this murk."

The packhorse was unloaded, and all the animals put to grazing. So far the scent of the bear was not strong enough to bother the horses, as it had seemed to perturb the dogs. Agafon and his young helper built a fire, while the old man complained there was not enough dry wood. The smoke was welcome because it thinned out the squadrons of flying insects to some degree. Then the peasants cooked some food. The dogs begged for scraps. The hunters passed a flask of brandy back and forth, inviting their guides to take a nip, and a nearby rivulet provided water.

Sherwood commented to Greg that if they had been after a man-eater of the classic style, tiger or lion or leopard, only a suicidal hunting party would have camped in the open, no matter how well equipped with hounds and weapons. In real life, real bears of course commonly came into camp to rummage through supplies, but they were looking for other food than human flesh. And Sherwood refused to believe that any bear, no matter how cunning or deranged, could approach a camp without provoking a racket among any group of dogs, no matter how derelict.

Tired from the hunt, he soon dozed off like the others, his Winchester within reach.

A few hours later, the men unrolled themselves from their blankets in the dusky dawn, hastily wolfed down what was left of yesterday's biscuits and hard-boiled eggs, then boiled water and drank coffee while the old man and the boy saddled their horses. Then the dogs were put on the trail once more, and the hunt pressed on.

"Where in the hell is he going?" Sherwood asked himself, muttering aloud. There was no question in his hunter's mind about his quarry's sex. This bear had to be a boar; no sow of any species could conceivably have grown to such a size.

But where the big fellow was headed was indeed the question. Having moved on less than half a mile, the dogs brought them to the place where the bear had holed up during the night just passed, a kind of improvised den under the angle made by the fallen trunk and the jagged stump of a broken tree. The small plants there had been pressed down by a great weight. The creature was still eating frequently, as all bears did when given the chance, but it was not simply browsing its way along, or they would have already caught up with it. Rather, Sherwood had a sense of travel at a purposeful speed, as if the animal had some definite goal. But this impression, wherever it came from, was contradicted by the frequent changes of direction.

Ultimately, inexorably, despite many detours, the bear's trail was leading the hunters back to the close vicinity of the place where old Ivan had been killed and Maxim had disappeared.

By midafternoon, having made no real progress at catching up with the bear, Sherwood was ready to make camp again, rest the weary men and dogs, and reassess the situation.

A clouded twilight was again descending when an intense disturbance among the dogs warned the men of an impending arrival—whether of man or beast they could not at first be sure. Sherwood and Greg grabbed up their weapons—only to lower them, a few moments later. The form approaching had now become visible, at a distance of thirty yards or so, and it was definitely two-legged. Slinging his Winchester back on his shoulder, Sherwood experienced a curious mixture of relief and disappointment.

The man who came trudging into the firelight, to the mournful howling of the dogs, was about thirty years of age, muddy, tired-looking and sporting a week's growth of beard, but seemingly unharmed. He had a rifle in hand, a small pack on his back. His clothing did not look particularly dirty for that of a man who had been lost in the woods for more than a week, but it was severely wrinkled. For a long moment he stood there, looking from one hunter to another, having evidently nothing to say.

"Maxim," said Greg, slowly lowering his rifle. The tone of his voice was almost one of disappointment.

Young Gleb, having armed himself for the occasion, looked purely disappointed at having no bear to shoot at. Old Agafon appeared relieved, and at the same time shocked with surprise. And as he greeted his brother, just back from the dead, Gregori seemed hardly less astonished than the old peasant.

EIGHT

As he entered the camp, Maxim stumbled once on a piece of tree limb in the tall grass, and came near losing his balance, muttering what the American supposed were Russian swearwords. For a moment, Sherwood was quite ready to believe that the man was drunk.

But when the new arrival came to a halt, he stood there steadily enough, rifle slung over his shoulder and fists on his hips, a few paces from the fire. From that position he eyed his brother and the two peasants without surprise. But when his gaze fell on Sherwood, a shadow of unease crossed his face. It was as if he found something perturbing in the mere fact of a stranger's presence.

Maxim looked perfectly sober now. At last he spoke. "And who is this?" The meaning of the words was clear enough to Sherwood, even if they were spoken in Russian.

Still looking somewhat numbed, Gregori leaned his own rifle against a tree and performed a quick intro-duction in English, reminding Maxim that this was the

American hunter with whom he, Gregori, had been visiting and adventuring for years. Maxim nodded in
acknowledgment.

"I'm sorry, gentlemen, if you have put yourselves to
a great deal of trouble searching for me." Maxim spoke
English at least as well as his brother. He spread his
arms in an openhanded gesture, demonstrating his
existence. "As you see, it was unnecessary."

Gregori, being very un-Russian at the moment, still
keeping his distance on the other side of the fire, shook
his head. "The truth is, we had pretty much given you
up for dead. We are hunting the bear."

Maxim exhibited no shock on being told that
everyone had thought him dead; it was as if he had
realized that fact some time ago, and it did not bother
him much.

He said: "Well, may you have more success in the
hunt than I have had. No doubt you will, since you
have dogs." Then he added something sharp, in Russian, addressed to the hounds, who were still not happy
with his presence. Ears laid back, they snarled and
growled, and for this were sworn at by Agafon, who
had taken their leashes in his hand. Like the great
majority of dogs everywhere, they totally ignored the
verbal command, whatever it had been.

Taking the measure of Gregori's brother as best he
could, Sherwood saw him from the first as a strong,
energetic personality. Physically Maxim was wiry and
muscular, a little smaller than Sherwood, and bearing a
notable family resemblance to his brother and sister.

Sherwood was observing the brothers' reunion with
an increasing sense that something was seriously
wrong. He had thought that Russians tended to be
demonstrative, and Gregori could certainly be so at
times. He had known that the two brothers were not
the best of friends, but still the demonstration of the
fact was disturbing. Gregori, welcoming his brother
back from the dead, sounded barely cordial.

When the dogs had been subdued, Agafon turned
their leashes over to Gleb for the moment and took his

turn at welcoming Maxim back—an extravagant Russian greeting, of course. Seemingly the old man was determined, by expostulations and by kissing the hands and sleeves of the resurrected one, to make up for Gregori's coolness. Maxim put up with the old man, murmuring perfunctory words of acknowledgment.

Agafon's young relative gave Maxim a much more restrained if no more respectful greeting. The youth seemed naturally curious about this man who had apparently been lost in the woods for several days. But certainly the lad was aware of what the old people thought; and at night in the woods even a normally skeptical youth might feel inclined to credit superstition.

Being urged, at last, to make himself at home in camp, Maxim said at first that he was not particularly hungry, but soon allowed Agafon to convince him otherwise. Nor did Maxim, who now accepted a couple of swallows of brandy from his brother's flask, seem in the least disoriented after his sojourn in the woods. Nor did he even appear very excited at having made contact with the world and his family again.

As conversation developed slowly, the new arrival mentioned how frequently his brother had spoken and written of his friend Sherwood. For the visitor's benefit he continued to speak in English, while Gleb and Agafon looked on blankly.

Then Maxim changed the subject suddenly. "Gentlemen, as you can probably tell from my appearance, I have been—wandering—for several days." He sat down on a small log with a great appearance of weariness. Holding out his hands to the firelight, he appeared to be studying them as if he expected to find them dirty, or otherwise marked in some way.

"For more than a week," his brother corrected.

"Is it really so long? Does anyone have a cigarette, by the way?"

Then Gregori, shifting briefly to Russian, asked something in a hushed voice.

Maxim gave him a look of disdain, and glanced at Sherwood before he replied in English: "Yes, of course I know the old man's dead. I was there when it happened."

"But you could do nothing?"

Maxim gave Gregori another look. "No, there were some bushes between us. I could hear what was happening when the bear got him."

"It must have been a great shock." Gregori now gave the impression that his thoughts were elsewhere, though he was staring directly at his brother as he spoke.

Maxim made no direct reply to that. He gave himself a little shake and clapped his hands together decisively, as if to proclaim that he was ready for another topic. "What day is it, by the way? I suppose I've missed the funeral?"

"Yes, of course you have." Gregori was still peering at him, and now frowning as though having a hard time understanding something.

Maxim had no trouble interpreting the look. "Well, and should I be a hypocrite? I don't suppose you have shed any great number of tears over him."

"No," Gregori admitted. "Not a great number. Nor has Natalya. She's at Padarok Lessa, by the way. But he was our father."

"So he was." Maxim turned a friendly gaze on Sherwood. "You, sir, do you mind telling me what day it is?"

Sherwood told the new arrival the day of the week and date. By now his mind was firmly shifted to the Russian calendar.

Maxim was about to say something else when Gregori broke in: "Did you at least get a good look at the bear? Will you for God's sake tell us what happened!"

The younger brother shrugged. "I really didn't get that good a look. But the old man fired at the beast, and I shot at it through a screen of brush; perhaps one of us hit it, though I didn't find any blood. I didn't have a good shot at all." He eagerly accepted the cigarette his brother had at last got around to handing him.

Sherwood, who seldom smoked, refused the offered

case. He was thinking of old Ivan's rifle in the gun rack back at the house. He hadn't really examined the Mauser, not even to see whether it had been fired or not. Now he thought that maybe he should have done so.

Greg asked his brother, "And then?"

Maxim pulled a burning twig out of the fire and used it to light up. "There's not much more to tell."

To Sherwood, the story as it gradually emerged sounded not entirely convincing. According to Maxim, he and his father had heard a crashing in an alder thicket, and had drawn apart by a few paces, each man trying to find a better angle to see what was making the noise.

"Evidently the bear charged out of the thicket straight at Father; I heard his rifle discharge and I ran back, but I was too late, Father was already on the ground. I got off a shot after the animal as it ran away, but I don't believe I hit it. Then, naturally, I set out to trail the beast. At first I thought it was wounded and would not go far. But it seems that I was wrong."

"You didn't stay with Father?"

Maxim shrugged, and drew hungrily on his cigarette. "What for? One look was enough to show it was all over with him."

"You say that the bear ran away at once. But his body was—partly eaten."

Maxim made a face of disgust. "I suppose some other animal must have come along. Wolves, or a badger—how should I know? I tell you I kept on tracking the bear until eventually I had to give up."

"Without your horse?"

"Naturally one can follow a trail better on foot, having one's eyes closer to the ground—anyway, when the bear came, my stupid mount took fright and ran off. The old man's horse went with it. I suppose they both showed up at home? I didn't want to take the time to chase them. What is this, the Inquisition?"

"Naturally we are curious about what happened.

What have you been living on for the past several days?"

"Not much, I tell you. What does a hunter need? I bagged a couple of rabbits and made a fire. There were some berries, and I found a tree where a squirrel had stored some nuts."

Sherwood, listening, continued to find Maxim's story vaguely unsatisfactory. He found himself speculating that perhaps Maxim hadn't spent the entire time of his absence simply tramping through the woods. But that would mean he had left his father lying dead to hurry off and spend days, maybe as much as a week . . . with whom? Doing what?

Maxim's version of events sounded strange, all right, but it did not seem easy to come up with any more plausible tale.

When a silence fell, Sherwood had a question. "Max—mind if I call you that?"

"Of course." The smiled looked genuine. "To you I shall be Max. And my brother's friend to me shall be John. Was there something you wished to ask?"

"Yeah, if you don't mind, I'm kind of curious. Obviously, you didn't have the old man here"—Sherwood nodded toward Agafon—"or his grandson with you, when you and your father rode out to look for the bear."

"True."

"And no dogs?"

"That is correct."

"Then how did you expect to locate the bear? How did you find it?"

"Sheer luck, I suppose." Maxim's smile was not gone, but maybe a little faded. "Good luck for the bear, bad for Father. Perhaps the truth is that the bear found *us*."

The American nodded slowly. "Where did you finally lose the trail, after you started tracking on foot?"

"Do you know, that's really hard to say." Maxim was studying what was left of his cigarette. Then he pitched it into the fire. "I lost the trail and picked it up again several times. You are an experienced hunter; you know how it is."

Sherwood exchanged a look with Gregori. He had to admit to himself that Maxim's difficulties in tracking were hardly surprising, since the man had been without dogs, and this bear seemed especially given to wandering in vast circles. Still Sherwood was nagged by the feeling that something about the whole situation, as presented, did not ring true.

NINE

Throughout the night and day immediately following the hunters' departure, Natalya Ivanovna struggled to find tolerable thoughts to occupy her mind, tasks to fill her hands until her brother and the American should return. The difficulty persisted during several extended periods of wakefulness in her bed on the second night, and again early next morning. She had no particular interest in the outcome of the hunt, except that a dead bear would probably make the peasants' lives a little easier.

The month-old newspapers in Father's study discussed the latest oppressive measures of the government. Skimming through them in her boredom, she was almost tempted to regret abandoning the revolutionary movement. Almost, but not really. Not when she remembered the shabby apartments, with the bomb builders and their friends, some dirty and disheveled, some painstakingly fashionable, sprawled on chairs and divans making their plans. Or hard at work by sunlight or lamplight, assembling on a kitchen table the mysterious components of fire and death, smiling at any mention of the carnage they were sure to cause among the innocent.

As Natalya waited, alternately thinking over her problems and trying her best to avoid thought, it struck her that the house, in the mornings particularly, was very quiet. And this morning the stillness was more intense than on any of the other days since she had returned to the old house. She couldn't remember all the rooms ever being as still as this, when she was a child.

Again the morning hours slipped away, while she stood listening to the tick of the great standing clock in the front hall, or wandered out to inspect the sundial in the garden. With increasing frequency there came moments when she regretted not having accompanied the men on their hunt. Whatever problems might be looming over her, she always felt more secure when she was with Gregori. And she had to admit to herself that there was a certain fascination about the American.

Feeling very much alone, she drifted into the gun room, which was also the billiard room, and looked once more with vague regret at Father's favorite hunting weapon, resting as usual in its place of honor on the high gun rack. Sherwood hadn't taken it after all, doubtless preferring his own rifle. Once, when she was a little girl, barely strong enough to hold the Mauser steady, he had let her fire it at a deer. She had missed—not entirely by accident.

Odd, but now the pleasant memories in which Father was involved seemed clear and recent. It was her arguments and quarrels with him that seemed unreal.

Turning away from the weapons, Natalya began a solitary game of billiards. The clack of the balls, the feel of the cue and chalk, brought back sharp memories of how Father had looked with his cue in hand, bending over the table. And how he had spoken to her, teaching her the game. They had enjoyed several hours together, doing that—maybe for the last time. Yes, there had been a few good times at home, before her political and social convictions and other things had made it necessary, at the age of eighteen, to take herself away for good.

Perhaps more than a few.

Once the surge of nostalgia had receded, the morning's solitary billiard game quickly became boring. Natalya abandoned her cue on the table, and went down the hall. She caught herself moving almost furtively.

In the library, Grandfather as usual stared down at her from the wall, just as he had in Petersburg, the motionless image conveying his ambition and his pride—and she found herself thinking of John Sherwood. Not that the features of the young man in the old photograph looked much like those of the American.

Moving on, she stood looking into her father's empty study. There was as yet no feeling of abandonment. At least the servants were keeping the place dusted. By now, though the feeling brought with it a certain guilt, she had become aware of a silver lining in the dark cloud of her father's death: with Gregori now the head of the family and heir to its property, she could be sure of influential male support; and to a woman in Russia—to a woman who had decided not to turn her back entirely on civilization—this was still a very important consideration.

She went back down the hall and resumed her billiard game. At the moment, life offered nothing more inviting.

It was still well before noon, when Evdokia, a servant girl whose loyalty Natalya trusted, brought word to her mistress, in the gun room with its billiard table, that mounted rural police had entered the estate and were certain to reach the house at any minute. A young peasant who had dared to venture out, armed and nervous, seeing to the cattle in the far pasture, had hurriedly ridden back to the house, and reported that five uniformed riders were only a few minutes behind him on the road.

Natalya as she absorbed this news was standing with
her back to the gun rack. For a long moment, she
stared at the girl in silence. Of course there was no way
to be absolutely certain that they were coming after
her. Sending five men to arrest one woman seemed to
be overdoing it. Possibly the visit from the mounted
police meant only that Maxim's body had been discovered, and the fact that the deceased had been one of
their number meant that five men were coming. But
after her adventurous life in Petersburg, Natalya
thought she could not afford to take chances.

In a moment, she came to a decision. After a few
hasty words to the faithful Evdokia, meant as grateful
reassurance, Natalya ran out of the house by the back
door. She thought that none of the other servants saw
her go. It was too late to head directly for the woods
because she could easily be seen from the road if she
did that. By instinct, hardly aware of making any conscious plan, the young woman sought shelter in the old
theater.

She was in the doorway of the old building before
she realized that on her way out of the gun room she
had snatched up her Father's Mauser and was still carrying it.

Ducking into the dim, large auditorium, Natalya closed
the outer door loosely behind her. That was how it usually stayed; she could not remember it ever being
locked or barred. The glassy eyes of the stuffed bear
ignored her passage. Holding her skirts out of the way
as best she could, and hauling the heavy rifle with her
by its sling, she climbed swiftly to the dusty and abandoned loft. Once Natalya reached this higher level, she
pulled the ladder up after her. And when she had
attained the highest level of the building, she closed a
trapdoor after her and for good measure dragged an
ancient bundle of roofing shingles onto it.

A few minutes later, peering cautiously down from
one of her favorite childhood observation posts, a high,
dusty window, she witnessed the arrival in the stable

yard of the mounted men in uniform. There were indeed five police, wearing their fur caps even now in summer. One seemed to be a sergeant or higher officer, but otherwise they looked almost indistinguishable from one another in their similar coats, their black leather belts and holsters.

Natalya was not really surprised that the hunters of humanity had come for her, but still felt a little sick—she had allowed herself to begin to hope that perhaps she would be spared arrest.

She was not particularly worried that this gang of intruders would discover her anytime soon. The loft of the old theater was a little higher than the roof of the nearby house and virtually inaccessible once the ladder had been pulled up. No one would find her up here, unless the search should be guided by someone who knew where to look. And apart from one or two servants, Gregori was the only one who might easily guess her hiding place. She could think of no one on the estate at the moment who would be willing to give help to the police.

All below remained quiet, while the passing minutes lengthened into an hour. Natalya had no watch or clock available except the sun, but she could track the summer shadows, making the same familiar patterns across the bare wooden floor as in her childhood. Pigeons, who had their own ways in and out of this place up under the corners of the roof, soon reached an accommodation with her unexpected human presence. Then the fat birds cooed and walked the floor near her, lurching about on their tiny legs that moved at almost-invisible speed. Everything here reminded her with great poignancy of the days of childhood, when she and Gregori had used this aerie as their private game room and sanctuary. Maxim, even in those days, had more often than not demonstrated a crude contempt for such childish things. He had really wanted slaves rather than playmates, and when he could not enforce his authority over the other children, he tended to withdraw from their company.

Once, she seemed to remember, they had pretended that they were lodging on the eastern estate, Grandfather's land, Padarok Sivera—Grandfather of course had been glad to see them—and that they had gone there to hunt polar bears. Grandfather had told them that he was getting a little too old to hunt anymore.

On the previous evening, Maxim, after partaking of a little food and drink and unrevealing conversation with his brother and Sherwood, had fallen, as if exhausted, into an innocent-looking sleep beside the hunters' fire, while Sherwood and Gregori debated breaking off the chase.

Shortly after the sun was fully up, Maxim awoke beside the ashes of the fire, where Gleb had just finished boiling water for tea, and stretched. After a cup of the hot liquid, he took a horse—mounting the suddenly unhappy animal only with some difficulty—and announced that he was riding back to the house.

At first he seemed to assume that the others had only been waiting for him to wake up and announce his intention, and that they would come home with him. But when it became apparent that his brother and Sherwood intended to pursue the hunt, Maxim did not push the matter and rode home alone. He remarked that he, for one, had certainly been out in the woods long enough.

Meanwhile the hounds, avoiding Maxim as much as possible while he was in camp, had reached a state in which they could only slink about, confused and whimpering.

Once Maxim had departed, the hunters saddled up again and pushed on for another hour or so, but the trail had inevitably grown cold, and they failed to discover their quarry.

By midday, Gregori and Sherwood and their two guides had also returned to the house.

With all the patience of an experienced political criminal, Natalya was still looking down from her high window a couple of hours after the arrival of the police. She experienced a shock of surprise, not exactly joyful, on catching sight of the brother she had supposed dead, arriving matter-of-factly on one of the horses the hunting party had taken. Obviously, her brothers had encountered each other in the woods. She experienced relief, but the feeling was mixed with something darker. The result was hardly joy; a cold welcome home on her part, for this political policeman.

Watching with intense interest and considerable surprise from among the cobwebs in her dusty observation post, she realized that she was not entirely happy to see that Maxim was still alive.

Within a minute or two she also observed, with an unpleasant feeling, Maxim's reaction when he was confronted by the police. Maxim did not seem in the least surprised.

Looking down from her high place, Natalya saw her younger brother standing in the yard, handing over first his rifle, and then the reins of his horse, to one of the stable boys, and talking in an animated fashion with the police, who had emerged from wherever they had been waiting, and were now all gathering around him. Maxim was doing most of the talking, and his attitude and gestures were not those of a suspect being questioned. And the attitude of the police was respectful— or it soon turned that way. Natalya was even able to overhear a few words of their conversation when one or another of the men raised his voice.

Maxim showed them a certain document he took from an inner pocket. After the officer in charge had examined the paper, his behavior and that of his men became almost obsequious. Before turning away, the officer in charge actually saluted Maxim.

As soon as Natalya got over her first surprise at seeing Maxim still alive, a suspicion began to grow in her that this untrustworthy brother had somehow managed their father's death. And now, clenching her small fists and muttering swearwords in three languages under her breath, she had good evidence, if she had not earlier, that Maxim was in league with the police.

After a minute or two of further conversation, Maxim dismissed the uniformed men—at least that was how his sister interpreted the behavior of the figures in the yard below—and went on into the house. Distantly, she could hear the raised voice of her mysterious brother, calling calmly to the servants for a bath, his razor, and some food.

Though Maxim had given the impression of dismissing them, the police did not leave the estate. Nor did they change their waiting tactics, as far as Natalya could see; still, they made no effort to search the house or grounds, but were content to remain on watch inside the house or near it. They hung about as if they were waiting patiently for something to happen—or perhaps for someone else to arrive.

The moving sun had marked off another half-hour before she saw the young maid, Evdokia, moving with all the furtiveness of an inexperienced conspirator, come quickly out of the house by the back door and run straight to the lower level of the old theater, at a moment when none of the policemen were around.

First slipping off her shoes, moving as quietly as she could in stocking feet, Natalya ran down to a level just above the ground. From here she conducted a whispered conversation with the servant who had come looking for her, while Evdokia remained at ground level.

Evdokia had heard one of the police say that they were waiting for Gregori Ivanovich to come back, so they could take him in for questioning. They had asked about Gregori's whereabouts, and all the servants had told them that he was out hunting. The visitors had not even mentioned Natalya.

Of course, thought Natalya, that could be an attempt at cunning misdirection.

"What did Maxim Ivanovich say to them?" she asked the girl.

"I don't know, mistress. But he was laughing after he talked to them, and he has ordered the cook to feed them well."

Despite what Natalya had seen for herself, this was a shock for her. She thought of ordering the servant to try to warn her brother Gregori. But she could come up with no reasonable way.

Dismissing Evdokia with a few words of thanks and reassurance, Natalya climbed back to her high observation post, reerecting the barriers behind her methodically. She could see some of the policemen's horses being led to a watering trough. It sounded, too, as if the uniformed men were being fed in the kitchen; she could hear the high nervous laugh of another of the servant girls.

So, it seemed they had really come for Gregori. The natural thing to suppose was that someone had denounced Natalya's harmless brother—though of course that was not necessarily the case. The police could arrest anyone they liked, for any reason or for none at all. As far as Evdokia could tell, they hadn't even asked about Natalya—but having remained out of sight until now, she was certainly going to continue to do so, to be on the safe side.

Urgently the young woman in the loft wished that there was some way for her to get word to Gregori, warning him to stay away. But there seemed to be no way to do that.

Gregori and Sherwood on giving up the hunt rode back to the house, around the middle of the day, talking together. They were greeted by the police, in their official capacity, as soon as they arrived at the house. A conversation in Russian ensued, which even a foreigner could tell was notably lacking in cordiality on both sides.

Sherwood was naturally asked to present his papers, which he did.

But the visitors were really interested in Gregori, who was at once firmly invited to the office of the local magistrate for questioning. For Gregori this was totally unexpected.

Instinctively he asked them: Questioning about what?

But he ought to have known the question was a waste of breath. The men in fur caps weren't going to tell him that.

The temper of the dogs did not improve when they returned to the vicinity of the house. For whatever reason, the hounds continued unhappy, snapping and snarling at each other. When they saw Maxim again and smelled him, they continued to demonstrate an open dislike, baring their teeth at this man who, as his brother marveled, had usually had a way with dogs.

Maxim at first distanced himself from the police, in the presence of his siblings and the American. Then he reappeared on the veranda, napkin in hand, disturbed at his first good meal in a week, and stood by looking concerned, a picture of the sympathetic brother.

Naturally Sherwood, who had come back to the house with Gregori, was questioned too—with Maxim, when Gregori was being kept busy by other questions, now volunteering as a translator.

Then while the police were being distracted by their perceived need to bully the servants, Sherwood exchanged a few words with his friend. "What can I do, Greg?"

"Nothing—no there is something. Get on with tracking the bear and kill the damned thing, if you can. That way we'll have one problem solved at least."

"You sound like you don't expect to be back very soon."

"I hope to be, of course. There would seem to be no reason why I should not. But one never knows, in these matters." The young Russian seemed completely fatalistic. Then, gripping Sherwood by the arm, he charged him in a near-whisper: *"Look out for Natalya."* Then added: *"Don't trust Maxim."*

Sherwood lowered his voice, too. "Gladly. Whatever I can do. But where the hell is she?"

But there was no time for Greg to answer that question; perhaps it had been a mistake to ask it. Sherwood wondered if the police were after her too, if maybe she was hiding out somewhere.

Already the police had come bustling back into the room, upset that their suspect, Gregori, and the suspicious foreigner had somehow been allowed a moment alone to converse—in secret, as they put it.

After reexamining Sherwood's papers yet again, they remained obviously unsure of what to do about him. The man in charge kept saying that he would have to consult his superiors.

Natalya, who was able to see Gregori's arrest and departure from her childhood hiding place in the old theater, was worried and frightened at the sight of her brother led away by uniformed police. They first manacled his hands behind him, then had a hard time deciding whether they could or should make him ride horseback in that condition. Eventually they boosted him into the saddle. Sherwood stood by, looking ready to argue; but at the moment no one was going to interpret for him.

The police and their prisoner were hardly out of sight before she came out of the old theater empty-handed. Not wanting to look like an assassin or terrorist when she emerged, she had left Father's rifle behind.

As she told Sherwood later, Maxim assured her that he would do his best, using whatever influence he might have, to see to it that no harm came to their brother.

To both his sister and their guest, Maxim pretended to think it likely that Gregori would be home again in a few hours, or in a day at the most.

Maxim seemed less concerned and angered over Gregori's difficulties with the police than he was by the fact that the peasants were still on strike—or, as he put it, shirking their duties, glad of an excuse to be lazy. It was something he hadn't calculated on.

Then Maxim left the estate, and started for town alone, on horseback, saying he would catch up with the police, and that Natalya and Sherwood could depend on him to do everything he could for his brother.

Night came, and morning after it, and there was still no word on what had happened to Gregori.

The next morning Sherwood, keeping busy while he and Natalya waited for news of Gregori, rode into the woods once more, looking for the bear. This time the American had the dogs with him, and Agafon, and Agafon's grandson, Gleb.

And this time Natalya, who was torn between wanting to flee, and hoping to be able to do something for Gregori, had jumped at the chance to come along. Now the only interpreter Sherwood had available, she soon appeared dressed in a pair of trousers, which caused old Agafon to look scandalized, and climbed astride a horse, where she looked perfectly at home. Agafon's grandson was less affected by the sight of a lady wearing pants.

The dogs soon picked up a good trail—bear droppings, but Sherwood couldn't find a clear track—and after a chase of an hour or so the hunters tracked down and brought to bay a fairly large, but quite ordinary, brown bear.

Sherwood raised his Winchester and prepared to shoot the bear when the hounds brought it to bay. Natalya wondered aloud if the beast was going to climb a tree; but of course, being a brown bear, it had no wish or capability for such a tactic.

Amid hell's own uproar of growls and snarls, the bear was trying to protect its flanks and rear by backing into a thicket, meanwhile sparring and slugging with the dogs. In this endeavor it continued to have good success, as long as it could keep the smaller animals in front of it. The three hounds in a frenzy darted in and out, dancing and leaping, biting when they could, and howling. Suddenly the biggest dog was on the receiving end of a left hook that sent it flying, then rolling, for twenty feet, only to spring up bloody but undaunted and bound back into the fight.

Sighting down his rifle barrel, aiming as well as he could at a mass of brown fur that churned in furious motion, Sherwood had serious doubts that he was looking at the man killer. But at that point it was too late for doubts. For the sake of the brave dogs, if nothing else, there was nothing to do but shoot the bear. If he failed to kill the beast, the dogs would keep attacking it until good luck gave out for at least one of them. Shouting over the animals' noise, he did his best in a couple of staccato sentences to explain this to Natalya.

Then, with the stock of the weapon tight against his shoulder, he estimated the location of the heart behind the fur and squeezed off one shot. The bullet—it crossed his mind that this one was only lead—did its work. The bear was dead before it hit the ground.

The dogs rushed forward in a frenzy. Sherwood levered another round into the chamber and gave the quarry another bullet for good measure.

As soon as he felt satisfied that the bear was dead, and his helpers had regained control over the dogs, Sherwood recruited old Agafon, who now seemed entirely satisfied with the success of the hunt, to help skin the animal. The quicker you could take the skin off, the easier the process was.

As soon as the job was under way, the dogs were rewarded with some fresh bear meat.

Gleb and Agafon tended the wounds of the dog most seriously hurt.

Agafon kept saying that he would be proud and delighted to carry the hide around to all the villages as a trophy, to demonstrate to the frightened peasants that the devil-bear was truly dead.

For a time the two men struggled with the huge dead weight of the carcass. They had no hope of being able to lift that mass and did not try. Merely rolling it over when necessary was difficult enough. Natalya, not a bit squeamish, volunteered to help. Tugging her sleeves above her elbows, she grabbed one of the dead furry legs and, at Sherwood's direction, pulled like a man.

The men were cutting and pulling, the hide.coming loose with a sound like tearing cloth.

Already the flies were gathering.

TEN

Even working with the benefit of long experience, skinning any large animal while keeping the hide in one piece, or even almost in one piece, was a tedious and bloody business. Fortunately, Agafon proved to know what he was about, and was able to help out with a minimum of direction. With two knives cutting, the work went faster; try to use more than two, and people would simply be getting in each other's way.

Sherwood, working diligently with his shirt off and his prized bone-handled hunting knife in hand, kept at it for a while in silence. But after a quarter of an hour, hoisting one of the dead beast's feet at the end of a massive, raw-fleshed, white-tendoned leg, he commented flatly: "This's no good at all. It isn't the right bear."

Natalya had been sitting on a log nearby, watching the gory operation with an air of detachment, while she waited for her next assignment of tugging and heaving. Now she looked up with surprise. "How can you be sure?"

"Too small. The feet just aren't big enough." Sherwood brushed flies from the lifeless paw and, with something of an effort, measured it against his hand. The dead bear's appendage impressively dwarfed that of the live human, but still the paw was too small. "Look. This animal never made the big tracks we found at the place where your father was killed."

Natalya did not bother to translate for Agafon; the old man observing the maneuvers with the bear's paw needed no great shrewdness to understand what the American was saying.

Agafon burst forth with a comment, which Natalya translated: "For the love of God, Little Father, let the peasants believe that we have slain the monster! The fields must be worked."

When he heard the English translation, Sherwood shook his head. "That's why I hesitated just now about speaking out. If everybody thinks the killer bear is dead, the field workers can get back to work, and the crops the people need will get planted. But then I figured, no. Everyone who's at risk has the right to know the truth."

Natalya seemed to be of two minds. "It's quite true. For their own sakes, the peasants had better get some planting done. Even now it may be too late. But how dangerous is it, really, Sherwood, for the people to go back to field work?"

He hesitated, frowned at his fingers all scummed with drying gore, then instead of using them to scratch his head picked up a little twig with which to do the job. "I want to say 'not very.' But if I say that, sure as shootin', someone else will get chewed up. That bear is one weird animal, and I don't pretend to know what it's going to do next."

"So far," Natalya remarked, "only one of the victims has been a peasant."

She still looked uncertain, and Sherwood tried to explain. "You'd like me to describe the habits of the man-eating bear, and I can't. Because by all the rules there just ain't any such critter." He sighed. "So hell yes, I guess the farm workers ought to go back to work. I don't know much about what crops you put in here, but from the way everybody talks, it sounds like the farmers are in real trouble if they don't get some seed in the ground soon."

She translated some of this for the old man, and came back to Sherwood with his eager answer.

"Agafon agrees. He says the devil-bear is certainly dead now, we should not worry our heads for a moment about that. The danger is over. He also says he is quite ready to go on with the skinning, even if you think it's useless. There is no reason why a gentleman should have to soil his hands with such a job."

"Let him go on with it, then." Sherwood puffed out breath in a sigh, gave his knife a few preliminary wipes on the leaves of a handy shrub, then drove the blade repeatedly into a spot of sandy ground. "Maybe he wants to teach his grandson how to skin a bear. Maybe he wants a bearskin rug. That's fine. But otherwise I just don't see the point." And Sherwood, his arms and shirtless torso a bloody mess from the skinning, went a little distance to crouch beside a stream where he could wash.

Natalya followed slowly and sat on a fallen log where she could talk to him.

Old Agafon and Gleb finally finished the job of skinning. It took both of them just to lift the raw bearskin, with most of the head and the four paws still attached. Bundling the hide onto the back of a mule, to whom all cargoes were the same, they started for the nearest village. There Agafon eagerly began his self-appointed task of displaying the trophy to convince everyone that the terror was dead.

Riding back to the house with Natalya, Sherwood told her: "When Greg and I went out with Agafon the first time, I got the impression that the old fellow didn't really want us to kill the dangerous bear. And now he wants to convince everyone that the dangerous bear is dead—even though he knows it isn't. He's actually trying to protect the beast."

"No doubt Agafon thinks the people will be better off if they get the planting done."

"They'll also be better off if nothing's eating 'em," Sherwood persisted. "When we were out on the trail, he kept finding reasons why we shouldn't go on. He'd forgotten things; first the matches, then the spare ammunition. He kept telling us we could have more fun hunting deer. Kept coming up with crazy arguments, like a child trying to get out of doing something."

Natalya listened carefully, then shook her head, marveling. "I have to admit, it all fits together if he really believes that Maxim is—that he became—the bear."

"That's disturbing."

"Of course."

Sherwood looked at her. "I don't mean just the superstition."

"What then?"

"Did Agafon get along with your father at all?"

Natalya thought about it. "I really don't know. Now that you mention it, I have the impression that most of the time he kept out of Father's way. Why?"

"Well, if you think it through, old Agafon here wants to ally himself with the animal that killed your father."

Sherwood and Natalya reached the house to find Maxim going over some papers in what had been his father's study. Evidently he had found it necessary, for this purpose, to break open a locked desk drawer. The poker he had apparently used was still lying on the desk among a new scattering of papers.

As the pair entered, Maxim immediately pushed aside this litter and greeted them heartily. He appeared keenly interested in the results of their hunt. He broke into a smile and offered hearty congratulations when told that Sherwood had shot a bear.

When Natalya pressed him for news of their arrested brother, Maxim looked sad, but said he had no fresh information.

Natalya could remember a time when she and Maxim were both small, when she and her younger brother had been on good terms, apart from the ordinary childhood squabbles. But then she remembered his chronic need to be in command and wondered how much of the happy memory was only a golden haze. With the passage of the years younger brother and sister had increasingly come to distrust and dislike each other. Natalya's distrust had been much magnified by knowing that Maxim was now working with the *Okhrana*—which he was now ready to admit openly.

Speaking in Russian when Sherwood was absent, she asked Maxim: "How canst thou do that? Cast in thy lot with such people? They are torturers and murderers."

"My dear Natashinka, thou knowest how it is. I might ask thee the same thing: how dost thou make common cause with the bomb throwers?"

"The truth is that I found I couldn't. I left them because I could not throw bombs that blew up innocent women and children. Maybe I was wrong to leave them."

"That question thou must decide for thyself."

"Gregori did not throw bombs. He supported the government loyally, but now he has been arrested."

"Dost thou believe that he was loyal?" And Maxim shook his head in solemn reproof.

"Well, and what if he was not?"

"Thou shouldst be careful what thou sayest, beloved sister. Other ears than mine might be listening."

Natalya walked out in a quiet rage.

Agafon, when he returned that evening from touring nearby villages with the trophy bearskin, soon made a point of getting to talk to Maxim privately.

When the two men were alone, old Agafon said he wanted to assure his new master that most of the peasants were now convinced, or soon would be, that the bear killed was truly the deadly one.

"Are they going back to the fields?"

"Some have, Your Honor. Tomorrow I think the rest will join them. The seasons will not wait. Besides . . . "

"Yes?"

"Why should a bear not want fields planted? Why should a great bear be angry at mere peasants?"

Maxim toyed with a letter opener on the desk. The way Agafon was talking now removed all his doubts about how much the old man might know.

"Dost thou know a great deal about bears, then, old man?"

"Not nearly as much as Your Honor knows about them, I am sure!"

"Why dost thou think I know so much about them? Hey?"

"Because Your Honor is a wise man. Wiser even than Your Honor's father, of blessed memory." And Agafon's old cheeks glowed like apples when he smiled. Perhaps without even realizing it, he slipped briefly into the familiar form of address: "As wise as thy grandfather, whom I remember well!"

Maxim stared at the old man. He said slowly: "My grandfather left here more than forty years ago. Nay, almost fifty years! More than once my father has told me that story."

"But I remember, sir! Oh, I remember, the wonders I have seen with my own eyes, and heard with my own ears!" And Agafon laughed. "In that very year, when the Tsar Alexander of blessed memory chose to set free the serfs. That was the last time that a bear wrought such havoc in our fields. That bear did not like those who had displeased Your Nobility's grandfather! No, it did not like them one little bit!"

The small boy Agafon, then still an enslaved serf, had been awed and enthralled. Freedom was an abstraction, other matters of far greater practical concern. Oh, if only he could have gone to Siberia, too!

Maxim, feeling the grip of fascination, said: "I wish that I could have known Grandfather."

"Oh, indeed sir, indeed! The two of you would have gotten along famously, I'm sure!"

Eventually Maxim dismissed the old man, with mixed feelings about him. It was tempting to try to find a use for anyone who understood, even a little, the challenges of being a bear as well as a man. But in Agafon's case, how much danger was there that he would talk too much, and how great were the chances that anyone outside the villages would believe him?

All their lives, Gregori and Natalya had been close to each other, and now her feelings for her older brother had intensified. The tie seemed to be strengthened by the fact that Gregori had now been arrested. Whether he wished to be or not, he was now his sister's comrade-in-arms, against the oppressive government.

Sherwood made what seemed to him an obvious suggestion: that the family retain the best lawyer they could find to determine what had happened to Gregori and work for his release. The Lohmatskis, sister and brother, looked at the naïve American with an initial lack of comprehension that in Maxim's case quickly turned into something like amused contempt. Brother and sister both assured their guest that there was nothing for a lawyer to do in the present situation. It was common for the Russian system of administrators, courts, and prisons to swallow people without a trace.

An hour or so after Sherwood and Natalya returned to the house, Maxim mounted his horse and rode away, saying he was going into town, where he intended to resume his efforts to help Gregori. "Don't look for me anytime soon. I'll be back when I get here."

Sherwood and Natalya both volunteered to come along, but Maxim assured them that they had better stay at Padarok Lessa. "Take it from me; to have a foreigner pleading dear Gregori's case would not be helpful." He stared at his sister. "Nor do you wish to bring yourself to the attention of the police. Besides, our friend Johnny would be left without a translator."

Maxim had not been gone much more than an hour before the rural police, this time only three of them, returned to the estate.

This time they had come looking for Natalya.

Sherwood was in his room, half-immersed in a small tub. Servants had carried buckets of water to provide him with a hot bath, which he badly needed after his hours of killing and skinning.

Meanwhile, Natalya had received a timely warning, from Evdokia again. She had just time to scurry back into the old theater and up again into the loft.

The first thing that struck her eye, on reaching her snug hideaway up under the eaves, was her father's rifle. The Mauser still stood leaning against the wall in a corner of the small, high room, where she had left it.

Sherwood was unaware that the police were back until one of them came pushing into his room while he was bathing, looking into wardrobes and under the bed without attempting any explanation. Sherwood, out of the little tub and grabbing for a towel, trying to establish some kind of dignity, asked questions in French and English without result. Fearful that the men might have come after Natalya, he threw on some clothes and went looking for her, to warn her if necessary, and to get her to tell him what was going on.

Policemen seemed to be everywhere in the house at once. Sherwood, hastily dressed, walked outdoors. Moments later, he entered the old theater, after seeing that the door to that building was ajar and hearing an angry voice. Just inside he discovered one of the fur-capped police involved in a furious altercation with a young servant girl. Sherwood recognized her as Evdokia, who was especially close to Natalya.

The uniformed man was gripping the small girl by her wrist, twisting her arm in a way that must be causing considerable pain, meanwhile menacing her with some kind of short whip, which he held raised in his other hand.

A raw new mark on the girl's face was swelling and

discoloring even as Sherwood watched. Now the uniformed man shouted at her in a loud voice, and the girl cried out and tried to pull away and run. But the young policeman was too fast and much too strong for her. Now he again used his knout, raising a bloody welt on the servant girl, trying to force her to tell where her mistress had hidden.

The policeman looked up sharply at Sherwood's entrance, and replied to Sherwood's shout of outrage by saying something—obviously nasty—to him in Russian.

Sherwood could not understand anything said by either the policeman or his victim, but the brutality on one side and terror on the other spoke in a language that needed no translation. And no words could have excused what he was seeing.

The front of the girl's dress had been torn, and the knotted leather whip had left her skin bloody.

Sherwood too had only one language to work with; he also had to trust to tone and bearing to make his meaning clear. "I think you better let her go. There's no call to beat a girl like that."

Pushing the girl violently aside into a corner, so that she staggered and fell, the policeman raised his whip, threatening Sherwood. Then he threatened a back-handed swing against the fallen girl, who gave a soft, hopeless, despairing cry, to Sherwood's American ears more chilling than any scream.

It was too much. Sherwood took a long step forward, and knocked the policeman down with his fist.

The uniformed man on the floor, his face suddenly a mask of shock, outrage, and his own bright blood, fumbled his revolver out of its holster and took aim at the man who had floored him.

The sound of a powerful rifle exploded in the confined space. The policeman's body convulsed instantly, and a bullet's impact rolled it against the wall. In the succeeding silence, with the smell of burned cordite hanging thickly in the air, Sherwood looked up to see Natalya, her father's Mauser in her hands, standing braced on the upper part of the narrow stair. Obviously, she had just emerged from a hiding place somewhere above.

The servant girl, crouched on the floor and cowering away from violence, let out another little cry.

For a long moment, no one moved. Then Sherwood, pulse hammering, mind racing, said: "Someone must have heard the shot."

The woman on the stair stood straight and still. "Sherwood, get out of here. Don't get involved in this." Her English was as precise as ever, but her voice had a hard tone that the visitor had never heard in it before.

He said: "It's a little late for me to try that."

He started looking for some way to bar the door leading out into the yard. But in fact, people outside, somewhere in the distance, were now laughing. There was no indication that anyone had heard the shot or any other alarming noise. Perhaps the acoustics of the cavernous place had tended to keep the sound indoors.

In a moment, Sherwood was bending over the policeman, opening the man's coat to reveal the spreading stain inside. The man's eyes were open but sightless, and all experience testified that he was dead.

Sherwood grunted. Firearms and blood were his home territory. He said assertively: "Anyway, I'm the one who killed him. You'd better give me that rifle and hide again." And he stretched out an open hand.

"*You* killed him? Are you crazy?" And Natalya, keeping a tight grip on the Mauser, descended swiftly to ground level, where she could inspect the corpse at close range. Sherwood could see now that she was in her stocking feet under her long skirt.

"The man is dead," he cautioned her.

"*I* am the one who shot him!" She glared at Sherwood as if he were attempting to deprive her of some long-desired reward. "At last I have done something I can be proud of. If you must get mixed up in this, help me hide him."

Sherwood, looking around, noted that the servant girl had disappeared. After a last useless attempt to find a pulse or heartbeat, he caught the policeman's body under the arms and dragged the lifeless form over to the stage, then stuffed it into a storage space beneath that Natalya opened a low door to reveal. He noted with cool relief that so far no blood seemed to have dripped onto the floor. After a moment's hesitation, he picked up the pistol and weighed it hesitatingly in his hand, noting dazedly that it was of American make, a Smith & Wesson .44, then threw it in after its owner.

A moment later, Natalya had closed up the cabinet again, as well as the door to the outside, and was standing with her back against the latter. She said, with pride rather than guilt: "I must get out of here. The responsibility for this is mine."

"All right, but I'm coming with you. There'll be plenty of blame to go around."

There was no sign as yet that the other policemen on the grounds suspected what had happened to their comrade. Evidently, thought Sherwood, they had not heard the shot, contained as it had been within the walls of the old theater. Or else they attributed the noise to some other cause.

Natalya led him to the theater's back door, on the side away from the house. From there it was only a few strides to the back door of the stable.

Horses were right at hand, all being held in readiness for expeditions. Gleb happened to be in the stable, a pitchfork in his hands, and his face turned white under its tan as Natalya told him in a few words what had happened. The youth quickly helped the couple to saddle a pair of horses, and saw them off.

Young Gleb goggled momentarily at his mistress's legs below the hiked-up skirt, bare to the knees and higher. As Natalya swung herself up into the saddle, skirts and all, she had time to tell the trustworthy Gleb where he could meet the fugitives later, with information and supplies, when the police were gone.

A couple of minutes later, Natalya and Sherwood were riding at a good clip into the forest, for the first minute or so keeping a barn and other outbuildings between themselves and the house.

They were bringing with them only a single weapon. Sherwood, whose saddle happened to be equipped with a rifle sheath, had now been allowed to take charge of the Mauser.

Minutes later, Sherwood and Natalya were cantering briskly along a shallow streambed, trusting to running water to hide their trail. As they rode, they discussed their situation.

"Can we trust that kid? I could see that you were telling him a lot."

"I think we can trust him if anyone. He's going to meet us later, if he can, and bring some things. I told him the essentials."

"What about the girl?"

"She will say nothing."

Natalya was determined to flee, but evidently she still questioned whether Sherwood ought to do so.

"Certainly I have no other choice," Natalya said angrily. "I was a fool ever to have thought otherwise. But for you things may well be different."

"Well, I don't feel like hanging around to be arrested."

She thought the situation over for a few moments before admitting: "In that you are probably wise. If you return to the house later, you can claim you were simply out riding, and you know nothing about what happened to the policeman."

"Right now I'm not thinking along those lines. Where are we going?"

"When we have put some distance between ourselves and the house, I'll have time to think about that."

"Fair enough." He rode on for a few more moments in silence, then asked: "Why was that cop beating up that girl, anyway? To get her to tell where you were hiding?"

"That might have been the reason. Or it's quite likely

that the police simply had discovered that the girl was Jewish."

Sherwood had the feeling that he had missed something. "She was? Why the hell should that earn her a beating?"

"Well, you see there are special laws for Jews. As there are for blacks in your country. And they are always much more likely to be beaten."

"What a system!" Shaking his head, he gave voice to his general disgust at the turn events had taken.

Natalya rode in silence for a time, but seemed to be gradually becoming more upset. She slapped at a stinging insect which had its own way of expressing its appreciation of her exposed legs.

"You fool!" she whispered fiercely, suddenly rounding on Sherwood once again. Her attitude toward him seemed to be swinging violently back and forth, as the various implications of what had happened sank in. "What were you thinking of? Why couldn't you stay out of this?"

"Well, sorry. Sure, I could have stayed out if it . . . if only I'd known you were hoping to get yourself arrested . . . or maybe you wanted to see the hide ripped off your girl back there."

They rode on in silence for half a minute.

"It is I who must apologize. Sherwood," Natalya said at last. "You are risking your life trying to help me. It is not your fault if such help is impossible."

Natalya reassured her companion that she thought there would be no quick pursuit. She felt reasonably confident that the servants and any other workers around the house would try, on principle, to give the police as little help as possible.

What Maxim might do was, of course, another matter.

"It seems our brother now has an even more important connection with the police than we suspected. So important that he would like to keep it a secret." And she told Sherwood of the conference she had seen from her hiding place. "He has arranged to have Gregori put away—I feel certain of that now. In my case—well, I was probably due to be arrested anyway."

The day wore on. Sherwood and Natalya rode for several hours, covering a great number of versts through almost-trackless woods, avoiding villages and roads and fields with workers in them. Sherwood, when he knew in which general direction Natalya wanted to go, took charge of making the trail difficult, keeping their horses as much as possible on rocky ground or in streambeds.

Since the start of their flight Natalya had had a goal in mind. After a ride of three hours from Padarok Lessa they reached the place, the abandoned remnants of a burnt-out manor house.

The site was peaceful, but with the tranquillity of a cemetery. In the middle of an extensive clearing stood a ruined house, obviously once the main building of a manor, originally somewhat smaller than the Lohmatskis'. Around it, a number of lesser buildings had been eliminated more thoroughly. Only the remains of chimneys and stone foundations were clearly visible save for one small shed which was more or less intact.

"Looks like someone had a fire not too long ago."

"They certainly did. It was in nineteen-oh-six, when the last rebellion erupted among the peasants in our region. The people on our estate did not take part, they got on fairly well with Father, and I think they feared him too. But the landowner here fled with his family to the city, and so far no one has come back."

She told Sherwood there was no reason to suppose that the police would come looking for them here—she doubted that Maxim, who for several years had been spending so much time away in Petersburg, even knew about the place.

She dismounted, walking gingerly, and he remembered that she wore no shoes.

Enough of the house remained standing to form a crude shelter, that ought to at least keep the rain off their heads during the night. They had other reasons to welcome a good rain, which would tend to wash away their trail.

Gleb, faithfully keeping the appointment to meet with Natalya, arrived at the abandoned estate several hours later, at twilight. He had brought his mistress a pair of her own shoes and some boy's trousers to wear. There were a few more items of clothing and some food. Gleb assured the pair that he was sure no one had followed him—back at the house, all was confusion. No one, the police least of all, seemed to know whether they were coming or going.

The lad also had bad news to report. The policeman's body had been found, hidden in the theater. The fugitives were certain to be charged with murder, and with concealing evidence, or something that came through translation sounding like that. The police were already talking of posting rewards.

Sherwood said: "Ask him again if he made sure he wasn't followed."

"He has already assured me of that, several times. He knows his way around the woods, and I suppose he's right. Not much we can do about it if he isn't."

The youth said he had been afraid to arouse suspicion by trying to bring along any kind of firearms. Sherwood found himself longing wistfully for his Winchester—but it probably mattered very little. He wasn't going to win any serious gun battle with the police, however he was equipped.

Sherwood took note of the way Gleb looked at Natalya and felt sure that the young peasant was fiercely devoted to the beautiful young daughter of the family, only a few years older than he. Well, he certainly couldn't blame the kid.

As far as Gleb had been able to find out, Evdokia, the Jewish girl, had fled—even though no one had as yet connected her with the policeman's death—and was taking her chances on the roads, trying to reach some distant relatives.

He had seen very little of Maxim and Agafon, but he thought they were both now at the estate.

The couple gratefully looked over the additional supplies Gleb had brought them. The bread and other food were especially welcome.

"A pretty mess you've gotten yourself into," Natalya told Sherwood when the boy and his horse had disappeared back into the woods. He said there would be some moonlight, and he expected no difficulty in finding his way home.

"By shooting the policeman? Well, maybe as an American I'll get off lightly, if they catch me. I guess maybe it was a dumb idea, hiding him under the stage. But that might have bought us a little time."

"Don't be absurd! No one gets away with shooting a policeman, though I suppose being an American might help. But don't try to be a hero. I shot the man, and I will acknowledge the fact, with pride, whether I am caught or not."

Sherwood thought about it. He really couldn't see how he was going to help Natalya out of this situation—she was the one they had come to arrest, even before the policeman was shot.

Looking at his own situation as realistically as he could, matters certainly appeared grim. But not so bad as hers: he supposed that if he could somehow reach the American legation in St. Petersburg, some means of avoiding the worst could be worked out. He might claim self-defense. No one could testify to seeing him pull the trigger that killed the policeman. Most important, he had no doubt, was the fact that his family was not without influence.

But even at best it was a hell of a mess. Of course getting himself off would accomplish nothing at all for Natalya. Or for Greg. In his attempt to help an unknown servant girl, Sherwood had only succeeded in getting Natalya into worse trouble, and the shooting certainly wasn't going to make Greg's situation any better. Or the servant girl's, for that matter, he supposed.

Maybe he'd been a fool to challenge the policeman, but it was done now, and so be it. Sherwood looked at Natalya. There was only one factor in the situation about which he felt no doubt: "I'd do it again, you know. I couldn't just stand by and watch."

She snapped back immediately: "Then you are a fool."

"Why can't you ever just simply say something nice? If I'm a fool, what about you?"

This time her answer was a while in coming. "It is well known that I am a fool also."

As usual, Sherwood's mind was perfectly ready to turn from fruitless worry to practical matters. After a little thought, he suggested to Natalya that there was no reason to despair—not that she showed any sign of doing so. Making their way to St. Petersburg offered real chances for them both. For Sherwood there would be the American legation, and at minimum the promise of good legal help. Sometime earlier, when her situation had been considerably less desperate, Natalya had mentioned a plan by which she hoped to be able to get out of the country from there. By good fortune, Sherwood did have some money in his pockets—several hundred dollars, as well as a respectable fund of rubles—but of course riding a train would probably be impossible for a pair of fugitives—rail travelers could expect to be asked for their identity papers at any moment. And with a policeman dead, they had to assume that the regular roads would be watched, and an intense search made for the missing suspects.

Concentrating on what he knew of Russian geography, he tried to develop in his head the map he had been unable to find on paper. Details were hazy or nonexistent, but he thought the essential distances were clear enough. Reaching the capital would mean working their way across country, or along small roads, for a good five or six hundred miles—maybe a thousand versts. It would be a difficult trek, certainly, but when he talked it over with his companion, neither could find any reason why it should be impossible.

Obviously, Natalya also preferred thinking in practical terms, rather than worrying. The two of them seemed well matched in that respect at least. After thinking things over for a minute or two she agreed that they should start for Petersburg, heading northwest.

"I don't see why we can't do it, Sherwood. Of course, we are not going to have much success if you are going to be a fool and insist on knocking down more policemen."

"How far are we going to get if you keep shooting them?"

The look they exchanged had humor in it, and a good bit of mutual respect.

ELEVEN

B efore Sherwood and Natalya reached the abandoned estate where they were to rendezvous with
Gleb, Agafon, who had hastened into town to
find Maxim, discovered his master in a back room of
the small police station, and was first to bring him news
of the policeman's death. The slain man's comrades
were still in a confused state, Agafon said, and hoped to
solve the crime before they reported it.

As soon as he had heard the news, without waiting to
learn any details, or to notify his colleagues at the station, Maxim hastened back to the estate.

On the way, Agafon gave his master more facts. The
police on the scene of the crime had so far failed to
accomplish much of anything. They seemed to be proceeding on the assumption that the missing American
was the murderer, though they had yet to determine
what kind of firearm their colleague had been shot
with. Within minutes after the discovery of the dead
policeman, it had come to the attention of the police
that the foreigner, the American, had disappeared.

Meanwhile Natalya Ivanovna, the woman they had come looking for, was still not to be found.

Agafon's own interpretation of events was that the American Sherwood had fought with the slain policeman, and had indeed killed him. The body had been found stuffed into a storage cupboard under the stage of the old theater. The strange behavior of one of the household dogs, whining in agitation, sniffing at the door to the old theater, had led people to the body.

Riding on side by side, the two men now speculated briefly as to whether Natalya Ivanovna might have done the shooting. They recalled old Ivan teaching his daughter to shoot.

"She is fierce enough and strong enough," her brother mused. He grinned. "Yes, a fierce little bitch. And she certainly has no liking for the police." Maxim muttered to himself. Without really being aware of the fact, he had switched to English, so of course Agafon could not understand: "Natalya was always playing in the old theater as a child—so was Gregori. Yes, she might well have used it as a hiding place when the police came."

When Maxim returned to Padarok Lessa, one of the uniformed men grumbled to him: "None of the servants seems to have any more wit than a turnip when it comes to knowing where their mistress is."

The servant girl Evdokia, the little Jewess befriended by Natalya Ivanovna, seemed to be missing, also. Agafon soon noticed this, though it was doubtful that the police had yet realized the fact. In what seemed an effort to convince themselves that they were in control of the situation, they were grilling several of the servants, none of whom were likely to have had anything to do with the matter. Agafon thought that Evdokia had probably fled by herself, taking her chances on the roads, intending to join some relatives.

Agafon, having conducted a further investigation of his own, whispered to his master that two horses were

unaccounted for. The old man did not believe the
police had yet discovered the fact.

"Do you suppose, Your Excellency, that the American and the servant girl have run off together?"

"Unlikely," Maxim commented dryly. He was still in
no hurry to speed up the official investigation.

Everything Agafon told him tended to confirm his
assumption that Sherwood and Natalya were both vulnerable to being charged with murder. Logically, there
was still a remote possibility that one of the two women
had done the killing and they had then run away
together, and Sherwood the hunter had simply gone
wandering in the woods. But Maxim found that possibility much less attractive and was ready to dismiss it.

Maxim made a dismissive motion with his hand. At
the moment he was not particularly interested in servant girls, Jewish or otherwise.

Agafon, after a quick look around to make sure that
he and his master were quite alone, suddenly burst out:
"Dear master, dear Maxim Ivanovich, I must warn you
that the American still does not believe that he has shot
and skinned the deadly bear, the true man-hunting
animal." Agafon finished this statement with a meaningful sly emphasis.

Maxim looked at his servant thoughtfully. "Couldst
thou not convince him of that fact, old man?"

The peasant became nervous under that steady gaze.
"I tried my best to manage that, Your Excellency, while
we were still together in the woods, hunting and skinning the bear. Later there was no chance to discuss the
matter. Should I tell the police about the Jew-girl, call
their attention to the fact that she is missing? And I
think it might be possible for me to find out where
Your Excellency's sister and the American have gone."

Maxim considered the situation. "I would like to talk
to my sister and the American before the police arrest
them—if indeed, they are going to be arrested. No
doubt they are together somewhere. If thou art able to
find out where they have gone, come at once and tell
me, old man. Tell no one else."

"I will tell only you, Excellency." Agafon allowed himself a little shiver of delight. Again putting a certain sly emphasis in his words, he added: "Perhaps the American will find the bear while he is hunting in the woods. Or it will discover him. At some moment when he is not expecting the bear, perhaps, it will suddenly be there."

"Thou hast told me the bear is dead," Maxim reminded the old man sternly.

"Of course it is dead, Excellency, of course! I myself have taken its skin around to the villages." And the old man, smiling, actually winked.

Maxim gazed thoughtfully at the old fool, who was so insistent on sharing the joke that was going to be the death of him. At last he asked: "And were the people satisfied?"

"Of course, Little Father. Of course they were. I tell thee, they are returning to work."

Maxim regretfully found himself coming around to the conclusion that the old man would soon have to be disposed of. Agafon was too full of self-importance. He would not be able to resist the temptation to brag, to drop sly hints about his secret knowledge. But the matter could wait a little longer; it would have to be managed with some care.

Police were coming and going at Padarok Lessa through the remainder of the day. Maxim soon ceased to play any active role at all in their investigation, and then he ceased to pay any attention to it.

In the middle of the night, with everyone else in the house asleep—the policeman who was supposed to be standing watch was snoring as loud as any—Maxim walked out of his bedroom and prepared to do some tracking.

He had decided that he would either have to kill John Sherwood, or recruit him to his cause—that would be worth a try, though Maxim had little hope of success. If Sherwood had grasped the truth about the Bear, there would seem to be no other way. As a for-

eigner of status, Sherwood could not be simply disposed of through administrative means, as had been
possible to do with Gregori. Nor was he subject to the
peasants' superstitious awe, their habit of obedience.

Determined to discover where the couple had fled,
Maxim walked silently to the stables. He was just in
time to watch, from concealment, as young Gleb came
riding in, obviously returning from some clandestine
journey. Maxim, standing in the shadows at a corner of
the stable, remained a silent observer as Gleb cared for
his horse, then climbed into a hayloft and fell into an
exhausted sleep.

Maxim needed only a few minutes to quietly saddle a
mount for himself, and lead it out.

At the edge of the woods, a couple of hundred paces
from the house, the scent of the trail left by Gleb's
horse, very fresh, awaited the keen nose of the Bear.

Once the bear-man realized the direction in which
the trail was tending, his human intelligence made a
shrewd guess as to the rendezvous place.

Maxim alternately rode his horse and dismounted,
pausing to change forms and sniff out the trail again.
When his horse, senses outraged, tried to express its
objections to carrying a man who was no longer
entirely a man, he whipped it mercilessly about the
ears and eyes.

With his mount too cowed to rebel any further, he
located his quarry just where he had expected to find
them—thirty versts or so from Padarok Lessa, at a
deserted, half-ruined manor house, a remnant of the
peasant uprising of two years ago.

He supposed that Sherwood the hunter had made
sure to have his rifle with him when he fled. It was
amusing to anticipate how vastly surprised the American was going to be when he discovered that his favorite weapon would do him no good.

According to the old book, and the stories told by
Father he could remember from his childhood—and
Maxim had no reason to doubt those sources—silver
bullets were the only kind the *obaraten-medved* had to

fear. And no one—certainly, no American hunter, in this modern, disbelieving age—was going to load a firearm in such a way.

The two fugitives had taken shelter on the upper level of the ruined manor house. The remnant of floor, about eight by ten, on which they rested was approximately twelve feet above the ground. Natalya, unused to sleeping in the woods, had insisted on wanting a floor of some kind beneath her. Sherwood could not see that it made much difference—if the police tracked them this far, they were caught anyway.

The half-house offered them a fragment of a roof over their heads, and shelter against any wild animal, notably a bear, that might represent a danger. On floor and walls was evidence, in the form of rubbish and scrawled chalk markings, that other wanderers had sheltered here recently.

The narrow stairway, mainly intact with some of its supports missing, still clung to one wall of the ruin, giving the only access to what was left of the upper floor.

Meanwhile Sherwood and Natalya, while bringing their modest food supply and their rifle up with them, had left their horses in the shed, the only building that had escaped extensive damage.

By midnight Natalya was sleeping, her head pillowed on a horse blanket over some pieces of wood, and it was Sherwood's turn to stand watch, sitting on the platform with rifle in hand.

The strange, murderous bear crossed his mind as a possible danger, but his ears were really listening for the approach of the police. They would come on horseback, he supposed, to the accompaniment of neighing, jingling, and creaking sounds, with now and then the splash of a hoof in a wet place.

He considered, not for the first time, how striking Natalya's features were, with the moonlight shining on her face. He wondered, not for the first time, if he was ever going to become her lover. He supposed that, since they had run away together, everyone would assume they were sleeping together. In a way, he supposed, it was good that her earlier behavior with the revolutionaries had left her social reputation irretrievably in ruins.

Yes, they were both going to have to get out of Russia. America was the place for people who wanted to start over.

Someone—some other lover years ago—had cautioned him with great seriousness how unlucky it was to let the moonlight fall on a sleeper's face.

Sherwood was first alerted by a noise made by one of the horses—something was bothering the animals.

And now there came a sound from the deep woods, slight but very plain. Obviously the approaching creature, whatever it was, was making no great effort to be quiet. Now Sherwood could readily hear the sound, drawing nearer, of four careless feet, like two men walking.

In a moment he was going to see the new arrival because the moon was full, or nearly full, giving almost light enough, he thought, to read by.

And then he saw the bear quite plainly, moving between trees at the edge of the clearing, moon-magic frosting the rounded, lumpy clown-form with faint color, transforming it into a silvertip grizzly from the distant Rockies. It walked with the lordly indifference of a big bear, and it was coming directly toward him.

Sherwood's instincts told him that the bear now approaching was the genuine article, the deadly beast he had been hunting. There seemed something unnatural, something suggesting human intelligence and purpose, in the slow purposeful way that it moved closer. It was certainly huge enough in the moonlight. But still he was totally unprepared to accept the idea of there being anything supernatural about the beast.

Gripping the Mauser tightly in his right hand, index finger just off the trigger, Sherwood reached over with his left to shake Natalya awake. Meanwhile the bear

was prowling around the ruined house, past the out-
building in which the horses were sheltered, as if intent
on making sure that its victims were entirely alone, cut
off completely from the rest of the world.

Natalya awakened at the first touch and sat up alert
and silent.

And at that moment the horses began kicking and
snorting in sudden terror, hooves thudding on the
shed's ramshackle walls, loosening what attachment it
still had to its foundation.

Maxim, looking up with a bear's keen vision, could see
the moonlight gleaming on the barrel of the rifle in
Sherwood's hand. He knew the American to be an
expert shot. But the man at ground level only smiled.

Maxim began a Change to man-form, meaning to
call Sherwood down—and then, if necessary, revert to
bear-form to destroy him.

The were-bear did a dancing step or two.

From Sherwood's viewpoint, looking down, in what
appeared to be some masterstroke of stage illusion, the
bear was gone. Where it had been, just at the foot of
the stair, a man was standing now, his naked body pale
in moonlight, hands raised as if to demonstrate that he
was concealing nothing.

"Come down, John Sherwood." It was Maxim's easily
recognizable voice. "The bear is here."

But actually, Sherwood observed, the bear *wasn't*
there. At the moment, by means of whatever wizardry
was being worked, by hypnosis or whatever, the huge
animal was nowhere in sight. Only the man stood
below.

Sherwood's next coherent thought was that either he
himself, or the man below, had gone insane. All he
could think of to say was: "Where are your clothes?"

"The bear has hidden them." And Maxim laughed,
as if that were the wittiest joke anyone had ever
thought of. Then he burst out spontaneously: "He
thinks it is marvelous to be a bear!"

"How did you find us here?"

"I smelled horses—and humans."

Sherwood was standing at the top of the stairs, holding his rifle ready. The hunter wasn't in any hurry to come down; the naked man below looked crazy at best. A lifetime of experience was shrieking at Sherwood that trickery was being worked on him—and some attempt at worse than trickery probably impended.

"Your rifle will do you no good, John Sherwood. Your bullets of lead are harmless. The Bear has already been blasted with a shotgun at close range, and it did him no damage at all."

And in the next instant Sherwood saw, with a clarity tending to wipe away all thoughts of stage deception, what appeared to be a ghastly transitional stage: a naked man with a bear's head.

Then the reverse. A voice, monstrously deep, came out of the furry torso through the human mouth. "I see you are a hard man to convince, John Sherwood. But you have no choice. Either you must serve the Bear from now on—or the Bear will kill you. Which will it be?"

Whatever exactly Maxim was proposing to them, he was demanding that a decision be reached now.

His voice, filled with the certitude of madness, came drifting up. "You may be the first man, and the first woman, to see this Bear and live."

Natalya, now fully awake and standing a little behind Sherwood, confronted her brother—who once again appeared entirely human—and demanded of him again what news there was of Gregori.

Whatever she was seeing in the moonlight, whatever tricks she thought her eyes and mind were playing, Natalya was going to insist on explanations. She started instinctively to speak in Russian, then switched to English for Sherwood's benefit. In her mind, what she asked about was more important than any trickery with bears.

"Maxim, will you admit to me it was your doing, having Gregori arrested? Why did you do that?"

"Understand that dear Gregori is not coming back. He is already well on his way to Siberia. To one of the mines near Irkutsk, to be precise." Maxim spoke like a man firmly in control of the situation, and seemed to think, with evident enjoyment, that he was proving it. "The family property is all mine now. But you can share it with me, dear sister, if you like." His tone was contemptuous. "There are much, much greater prizes—there is a whole world to be won—and we can share that too."

"Is that why you did it—got rid of your own brother—simply to get your hands on the property?" Natalya finished with Russian that sounded like an oath.

Evidently, Maxim had decided to ignore his sister. He addressed the man beside her. "You must not dream, John Sherwood, of trying to kill a Bear like this one. You ought to be his friend instead. This Bear has great power to reward his friends—and to punish his enemies."

Sherwood was still struggling to grasp the reality of what was taking place before him. "I don't understand what you're talking about. Show me the bear."

"I said, he can reward his loyal friends. What happened to Gregori is a sad tale; but there is no need for either of you to face exile or imprisonment simply because a stupid policeman died."

Natalya refuse to be ignored. "What did happen to Gregori?"

"They tell me he was found in possession of treasonous documents. It is too bad, as I say. But an administrative order had been issued. Only a short sentence at hard labor in the mine—that was the best I could do for him, in the circumstances—and then I fear a lengthy term of exile, in some dismal village. Maybe you, dear Natashka, would like to join him there? Of course you would do better to join me. You had better take the opportunity while you can."

Maxim, grinning up from the bottom of the broken stairs, added something to his sister in Russian.

"You are mad," she breathed.

"Nyet, nyet," Then Maxim switched to English. "Only those who say they have seen a man change into a bear will be proclaimed mad, by the authorities. But still such mad people could be dangerous, not only to themselves. Unless they are among the Bear's best friends, they have to die."

"You killed your father." Sherwood voiced the words that Natalya had been unable or unwilling to pronounce. He thought perhaps that he was dreaming. *You ate part of the old man's body.* He didn't say those last words.

But perhaps Maxim read them in his face. "Among others," he replied. Then he added obscurely: "Your American bullets are the wrong kind."

And on that last word the bear reared up, fully ten feet high when it stood on its hind legs. Surging forward, it mounted the old stairway's lower steps—and from that position lunged at Sherwood, who was standing with one foot braced at the head of the stair, some twelve feet above the ground.

The lunge—the bear striking at Sherwood with its right foreleg at full extension—came within an inch or two of killing him. When the sharp claws grazed Sherwood's head and left arm the Mauser in his hands went off.

The bullet fired at point-blank range struck home on fur and flesh. At the same moment, two steps of the old stairway splintered and gave way, under the sudden load of more than half a ton of weight. The whole remaining upper portion of the house, only precariously supported, shook and tilted, and Sherwood, with one foot braced at the head of the stair, came near falling. He dropped the rifle and managed to catch himself only at the last moment with his good arm, by grabbing what remained of the upper bannister.

Below him the brown bear, racked with pain, uttering roars of incredible outrage and astonishment, tumbled on the ground. It appeared that the wounded creature had no hope of climbing the stairs again to reach its victims; it thrashed about on three legs, rolled briefly on its back and gave voice to a hideous noise, roaring and snarling, terrifying the horses.

Natalya clutched at the injured Sherwood to keep him from falling off the edge of their platform. A moment later, Sherwood, his left arm and the left side of his scalp and forehead torn by that glancing blow from the bear's claws, had collapsed into Natalya's arms, his wounds pouring blood.

The wounded bear went lumbering, howling, limping on three legs, off into the woods.

"Sherwood. Sherwood!" The words came out in a fierce whisper, though it was all Natalya could do to keep from screaming.

The man in her arms was unconscious. The rifle, their only weapon, had fallen to the ground.

Sherwood was not completely unconscious. In his mind, as in a dream, sprang up now the image of one of the old superstition-mongering peasants, who had earlier mentioned the belief that anyone bitten by the were-bear or wounded by its claws, who survives, eventually suffers the same fate himself.

In the strange realm where Sherwood's mind was drifting, he seemed to be ice-skating with Natalya. And he was asking her, while he held both of her smallish hands in his, just what "ice palace" meant. In his dream he found himself still puzzling, or puzzling again, over the prophecy given him by the holy fool he had encountered before his arrival at Padarok Lessa.

The dream, or vision, persisted, now taking on a brilliant, fevered clarity. In it, Natalya was explaining to him a true story he had heard somewhere once before—maybe years ago, from Greg—and then forgotten. How, at the court of the Empress Anna, almost two hundred years ago, an actual palace of solid ice had been built and decorated. The whole enormous structure had been constructed as part of an entertainment, a building decreed by the courtiers for their own amusement—and when the building was complete, a pair of dwarfish newlyweds, clowns and jesters of the empress, were tucked into a marriage bed of ice, sacrificed by freezing to complete the joke.

. . . the music played on in the palace of ice, and Natalya on her skates went swirling off in a waltz with the ragged and barefoot holy fool . . .

TWELVE

$\sim$

Sherwood was fighting his way up out of the realm of visions, trying to establish a foothold in reality. He remembered, in a vague and disconnected way, that he had been hunting, somewhere, and that a charging animal had knocked him down . . .

. . . and then suddenly he regained enough awareness to understand that for some reason he was lying on the rough wood planking of the upper level of the remnant of a burned-out house, with his head pillowed on Natalya's lap. He realized that he must have been knocked out for several minutes, because his companion had had time to tie crude bandages on the upper part of his left arm and around his head. Obviously Natalya had done all she could do in the circumstances, given the lack of materials, to tend his wounds. His own clothing and Natalya's were alike sticky with someone's blood. Painfully he concluded that it must be his own.

And now the events of the last few hours were coming back to him.

The full moon had descended completely behind the tall trees to the west. In the east, Venus had appeared, sharp and clear and enigmatic this morning. The world had entered the brief interval, in the white summer night of the far north, when darkness seemed to deepen before dawn.

"Sherwood?" Even in his half-conscious state he was keenly aware of the fear and uncertainty in the question.

Am I dying? Damn it all, no, I can't die, I refuse. Abruptly he remembered the bear lunging up the stairway at him, and the rifle in his hands firing.

Aloud he said, in a voice that surprised himself with its clear strength: "I'm all right."

"Good." Natalya let out a deep breath. "I was beginning to be worried. That arm is probably going to need stitches. Maybe your scalp too."

"Great."

"But I think nothing is broken."

Jumbled visions were receding, being rapidly forgotten. He had now found a snug harbor in the real world—though after what the real world had shown him tonight, it could never be the same world as the one in which he had spent the first thirty years of his life.

He demanded: "Did I kill . . . the damned thing? How long have I been out?"

"You certainly wounded it. Only a couple of minutes."

He groaned, struggling to get a sitting position. Natalya helped him with a boost. Obviously stitches were going to have to wait. Right now what he really wanted was a drink of water, but even such a simple matter as getting a drink was not going to be that easy . . .

. . . moments later, coming out of his second fainting spell, he once more raised his head, with an effort, out of Natalya's lap. This time he asked: "Is the bear gone?"

The fear was still evident in her voice. "Gone for now. It ran off. To me it looked like it was running on three legs only, as if it were badly hurt, and the noise it made was horrible."

Ursus horribilis popped into Sherwood's mind. No, that was the American grizzly's fancy title. And *Thalarctos maritimus* was the polar bear. They all had nice impressive scientific names, though right now he couldn't think of the brown bear's.

Realizing that he was still light-headed, he took a few deep breaths. "And Maxim?"

Natalya needed a little time to find a good response and made two false starts. "Sherwood? I want you to tell me if you saw the same thing I did. Just before you shot the bear. If so, God help us. Maybe the devil is real. Maybe he rules the world."

"Then God help us. Because I think we *did* see the same thing. I know I saw what was there, but I don't believe it." He closed his eyes again, ran a dry tongue over dry lips. "Yes I do—I have to believe it. God, I need some water."

"Of course. For water, and other reasons, it is necessary that we get down to ground level as soon as we can. I can help you down the stairs. You can walk, can't you." It was more a statement than a question.

"Sure."

With Natalya helping him, he inched over into a sitting position at the top of the stairs. The remnant of the building swayed beneath him. Again Sherwood noticed her wiry strength, though she wasn't big. Then, before they started down, she was silent for a moment, crouching on the edge of the platform beside the stair, looking off into the moonlit woods. He grunted, groping with his right hand for the top end of the banister. Every time he moved, pain surged through his upper left arm and his head. At least he could still move the arm. When he got down to the ground, he would have to walk—there would be no choice about that. Walk, and then get on a horse. But still his mind was elsewhere, not really thinking at all about these details, important as they were.

He said: "I can climb down, I can walk." Then he demanded urgently: "But tell me what you saw."

Natalya drew a deep breath. "I saw Maxim—I saw my brother. I have not the least doubt about that. The moonlight was good and bright. He was standing right down there on the ground, at the foot of the stairs, and you and I both talked to him."

"Right."

"He told us—he even bragged about it—how he sent Gregori away into exile. He even told us where he sent him."

Natalya paused, then added: "Also, Maxim admitted that he had killed our father—and other people."

"All right, yes, I heard him say those things—and then I saw a bear. Maxim was gone, vanished just like that, and a bear was standing there, right where he had been—"

"You saw the transformation, too!"

"That's exactly what I saw. The bear must have been ten feet tall on its hind legs. Its head almost reached up to the floor here. Standing exactly where Maxim had been a moment earlier."

"Yes. Yes." Natalya had closed her eyes. "That is what happened."

"The bear roared like hell, and it started to charge up the stairs at me—and once the bear was in view your brother was nowhere to be seen. What happened?"

"Maybe we were hypnotized."

"Do you believe that?"

"I don't know—Sherwood, wait a minute, hold still. You're still bleeding. Damn, these aren't very good bandages." He realized now that she must have torn pieces from her skirt or petticoat to bind his injuries.

After a pause she said: "You certainly hit the bear when you fired at him."

"Yes, I think so too. But only by sheer luck. The rifle went off when he clawed my arm."

"Your shot hit the bear, and it ran away. It was making an awful noise. I'm sure it was wounded."

"Maybe it's lying there dead somewhere. Maybe we

can see some blood." And imagination, unbidden, showed him a picture of Maxim lying dead and naked.

Grimacing, Sherwood got himself into position and started tentatively down the stairs, placing his feet carefully, nursing his hurt arm. He could see now that the two or three lowest steps of the stair were all caved in.

Sherwood suddenly began looking round him. There was something like panic in his voice. "Where's the rifle now?"

"It fell to the ground."

"We've got to get it." He started moving.

Natalya, following him down, went on: "You're still bleeding. When we get down on the ground I can fix the bandage again."

Shakily he descended, grunting, cautiously shifting the grip of his good arm as he progressed. He said: "I don't want to drip blood down here and confuse the trail. I think I hit him when I fired. I think I hit it—the bear."

"I know you hit him. I tell you, the bear was wounded."

The Mauser still lay on the ground where it had fallen. Sherwood picked it up in his right hand and tried to make sure that the muzzle wasn't clogged with mud; but doing anything was very difficult, as his left arm was practically useless. Natalya took the weapon from him.

"Can you shoot?" For a moment, he had actually forgotten the policeman.

"Need you ask?"

The light was failing further, the world receding into the shadowy darkness before dawn, with the moon now well down behind the nearby trees.

He wondered whether the bear, running away wounded, afraid of another shot, had been aware that the rifle had fallen to the ground. But if the bear was hurt badly, maybe that would have made no difference—whatever kind of bear it was.

The fact that the lowest stairs—the ones the bear must have trod on in launching its attack, were completely smashed—now made it difficult for a dizzy man with only one arm to finish his descent. But once Sherwood had his feet solidly on the ground he could see, dimly in the poor predawn light, how the wood had been broken cleanly, as if by some great weight. If those thin boards had held, he supposed he would be dead by this time. Eaten by—

Suddenly feeling worn out, Sherwood sat down in the soft grass to rest, at a little distance from the house. Sitting down beside him, Natalya demanded: "How about this for an explanation? Maxim has somehow trained a bear. It roams the woods with him, and—"

He broke in harshly: "Gypsies train bears. Maybe other people do too. But anyone who trains bears just wants to put on shows and make a little money. They teach the bears to dance and beg, not to kill. Anyway, I don't think Maxim is the type to spend his time training animals."

"True," Natalya admitted. "He would rather spend his time training people, forcing them to do what he wants."

"And everyone says he's spent most of the last years or so in Petersburg. Working his way into some kind of political or police job. Right?"

"All too true."

"Another thing," Sherwood continued. "Your brother was stark naked when we saw him. Right?"

A hesitancy. "Yes, he was. But—"

"But what?"

When she didn't answer, Sherwood pressed on. "I don't know why a bear trainer would take off all his clothes on the job. Whatever the explanation is, *I* didn't see a bear with a man, or a man with a bear. And you tell me it looked the same to you. What we saw was first one and then the other. Standing in the exact same place."

Natalya could find no words.

Presently they got to their feet and moved around again. They found some water, at the edge of what had been a barnyard, in an old rain-replenished watering

trough carved from a mossy log, and had a drink.
Sherwood could walk, slowly and shakily. He decided
that he would be able to ride—provided that the horses
hadn't run off, or crippled each other with their frightened kicks.

When Natalya got back from visiting the horses, and
reported that they were all right, he said: "Whatever
else happened just now—with the bear—Maxim was
really here. True?"

"Yes."

"And he knows we're here."

"True."

"And we know he's in with the police. That means, I
think, that now he will send the police after us." Even
as he spoke, Sherwood's imagination presented him
with an image of the wounded bear, talking on a tele-
phone, holding the receiver in its paw.

"Maybe it does."

Both fugitives felt an urgency to get moving, get
away from this place, where things could be seen that
were so crazy and unexplainable, that the structure of
the world seemed to have something wrong with it. But
the urge to relocate was only a part of an even greater
need: to find out, once and for all, whether they were
both crazy, or whether the world was a very different
place than either of them had ever thought.

They saddled the horses, but then delayed. With the
sky brightening slowly, the tracks of huge bear-paws
were becoming visible in the patches of muddy ground
around the house.

Still mesmerized by the events of the preceding
hour, Sherwood and Natalya followed the trail back to
the west. He was well bandaged now, no longer dripping blood to confuse a possible trail.

No special skill in tracking was necessary to see that
along the way the prints of three paws somehow
evolved into those of two naked, man-sized human
feet. Two of the footprints gave evidence of what
looked absolutely like a transition stage, the slender

human heel blurring into the marks of bear-sized pugs and claws.

Was it possible for anyone to fake a thing like that? Maybe someone could, given the time and inclination and the tools to play around with. Of course, the trickster would have to leave his own tracks nearby—but there were none.

Staring at the monstrous prints in mud, Sherwood felt his scalp crawl. The unbelievable tracks were just as real as tree stumps, solid and plain in daylight just like every other detail of the everyday world. They were not unverifiable dreamlike events having their existence only in the darkness before dawn.

As the intensity of morning light increased, the sun now really pushing up at the horizon, he and Natalya could also see the blood trail left by the bear. There were big, dull, dark splotches, the venous blood dripped by all flesh wounds. No sign of the pink frothy stuff, beloved of big-game hunters, that would indicate he'd hit a lung. Sherwood, in the grip of awe and bewilderment, wasn't even sure this bear had lungs, or needed them.

Soon the tracker began to feel fairly confident that the bear had been wounded in his left hind leg, because, as he studied the tracks, it appeared that that limb hardly ever touched the ground.

The spatterings of gore led from the foot of the broken stairs back into the woods for seventy or eighty yards. There was a spot where the man whose trail had begun as a set of paw prints had tied up his horse.

"Sherwood, look at this."

Behind a bush were indications that the creature, now possessed of human feet once more, had managed to pull on one boot, on his one good human leg, and had got on at least some of his clothes, before he'd managed to drag himself into the saddle and had ridden away.

Two abandoned items of clothing nearly looked as if they might be Maxim's. The least convincing was a glove for the left hand. But what could not be ignored was the left boot of a pair. Naturally a man would not try to pull a boot onto a seriously wounded leg.

When Natalya handed him the boot he held it up and turned it over in his hands. "Your brother's?"

"Yes." Natalya's eyes were closed. "Those are the boots Maxim was wearing the last time I saw him, at home."

Fearful that the police might very soon be on their way, the pair of fugitives hastily drank again from the watering trough, then led out their horses. Natalya had to delay long enough to retie one of Sherwood's bandages yet again before she helped him climb into the saddle. He doubted whether he could have made it without help.

The horse, as if newly disturbed by the man's presence in the saddle, moved restively under him.

"All right?" Natalya asked.

"A little dizzy. I'll manage. Where are we going? We need some kind of plan."

"We'll just go north, for the time being. The woods will be thicker in that direction, I think. Fewer people. We'll go slowly. Later, when we see how well you can travel, we will make a plan."

Waves of dizziness assailed Sherwood, and he was forced to hold his mount to a walking pace. Dabbing gingerly with one finger at the edge of the bandage on his forehead, where finally the ooze of blood had stopped, he felt compelled to talk the thing all over again—the matter that had to take precedence over everything else.

"Natalya, I never saw any bear *with* him. I saw your brother Maxim, and then I saw a bear. One turned into the other, right before my eyes, like a caterpillar turning into a butterfly—only a hell of a lot faster. It wasn't the darkness; there was plenty of light to see by. It just happened while I watched. Am I right? Is that what you saw?"

"Sherwood. What are you trying to tell me? That . . ." She couldn't finish.

"Am I right?"

"You are right. But—"

"I'm trying to tell you the same thing you've been trying to tell me. That we both saw the same thing: Your brother changing into a bear. Maybe I've been hit in the head, but you haven't. We can't both be crazy, or hypnotized."

Sherwood gritted his teeth and managed to stay on his horse's back, though with some difficulty, and in occasional danger of falling out of the saddle. They stopped to rest at frequent intervals, and in general kept a slow pace, with Natalya riding beside him when the way allowed enough room. From time to time, his wounds oozed more blood.

As the morning advanced, Sherwood's horse continued to display an increasing strange reluctance to carry the injured man. Swapping horses with Natalya seemed to help a little.

For Sherwood, the question had become a feverish repetition, beginning to shade into delirium: "What did you see? Never mind, I know what I saw."

THIRTEEN

A s the day wore on, Natalya and Sherwood made what progress they could, putting distance between themselves and the burned-out house. Around noon, with a thunderstorm breaking, they took shelter in a small, isolated building, made of logs in a fairly crude construction. Natalya identified this as a bathhouse belonging to a tiny village, a hundred yards distant through the woods.

Natalya thought it highly unlikely that anyone would come to the bathhouse except on the eve of one of the frequent holidays—which today fortunately was not. Even if they were discovered, she thought the peasants more likely to shelter them than turn them in.

The sound of more rain on the leaky room was welcome, because it meant whatever trail they had left was being steadily washed away. But Sherwood could not shake the certainty that the Bear could find them again, somehow. . . .

Reflexively, as he would have done even with his own familiar Winchester, Sherwood started to check out the rifle with which he had shot the bear. He worked with difficulty, because of his wounded arm, but he had plenty of time and was in no hurry.

It was, as he had noted in the gun-room days ago, a sporting rifle, bored for 7.92 mm bullets.

The chamber held only an empty casing because he hadn't worked the bolt to reload following the half-accidental discharge of the one round that hurt the bear.

The box-type magazine, fastened under the breech, with a capacity of five cartridges, held only three.

The weapon looked to be in excellent working order, but something else caught the hunter's attention.

Sherwood extracted a round from the Mauser's magazine. At first glance, something about the ammunition had struck him as odd, and he wanted a better look at it. The cartridge looked perfectly ready to fire. But the look and feel was odd, and for a moment he held his breath. He balanced the compact weight in his hand, rubbed the pointy nose of the protruding bullet with his thumb, and stood silently contemplating it.

He turned to Natalya, and without speaking held it out to her on his palm.

"What is it?" Natalya stared at the loaded metal casing, almost as long as a man's finger, lying on Sherwood's palm.

"Unless I'm much mistaken, your father had his rifle loaded with silver bullets. That's what these three are."

"What are you saying?"

"Silver bullets," he repeated. "I don't know that I've ever seen one before, but I've heard that they're supposed to be effective against werewolves. I suppose they're equally deadly to supernatural bears."

Natalya was more taken aback than Sherwood had yet seen her. She lifted the cartridge from his hand, as if just touching the object would tell her something, and then put it back. At last she managed: "But that's impossible. Father wasn't in the least superstitious."

"Look for yourself. This isn't lead." With the small blade of his pocketknife, he scratched the tarnish and the faint film of gun oil from the tip of the bullet, revealing brightness underneath.

"Silver bullets," she breathed in wonder. "To kill the *obaraten* . . ."

"If I had a standard round or two here, I could show you the difference."

Suddenly remembering that he had put on old Ivan's hunting vest, he hastily patted the loops and special pockets and came up with three more cartridges. All were of the same caliber, and all were tipped with ordinary lead.

Natalya had been frowning intently, but now her face began to clear. "Of course, there is an explanation. One of the old peasants loaded the weapon for him . . . that must be it! Maybe Father didn't realize what they were doing, or maybe he let them do it, just catering to their nonsense." Natalya raised startled gray eyes as a new idea struck her. "Oh, damn it all, Sherwood, did they kill him somehow with their foolishness? Trying to provide him with magic bullets? Oh, it would be utterly ironic of he died like that!"

Sherwood said that he could see no evidence that the unusual ammunition was to blame in any way for old Ivan's death.

"Maybe one of the old peasants put these cartridges in the rifle, as you say. But someone with fairly sophisticated equipment must have made them—I suppose the estate has its own gunsmith?"

"Yes, there used to be a man who worked on guns, years ago . . . I don't know how it is now."

He sniffed at the opened breech, then tried the familiar expedient of inserting his thumb, the pink nail serving as a dim mirror to illuminate the rifled barrel as he peered down it from the muzzle. One round—presumably of the silver ammunition—had wounded the bear last night. Old Ivan, in the course of his last tragic hunting trip with his younger son, might have fired one round, or maybe two, if he'd been carrying a sixth round ready in the chamber.

Sherwood felt a chill. Maybe old Ivan had known exactly what he was doing, when he went bear-hunting that day. Maybe—

As evening approached, he could feel a slight fever coming on. The fever was accompanied by the first indications of an extraordinary mental state.

That night, with Natalya dozing wearily nearby, he felt sure that he was sliding into deep delirium.

But his fever never became more than slight, and soon he had to admit that what was happening to him was something much harder to describe than the onset of an ordinary illness.

Later, Sherwood retained only a dim memory of Natalya bundling him, wounded and only semi-conscious, into a crude cart stolen or borrowed from a farmer. One of their horses pulled the cart, while the other was tethered behind. He was shivering, though she had covered him with straw. Then she cracked her whip and began to drive the injured man to relative safety. Old Ivan's rifle was hidden in the bottom of the cart.

Caught in a fever dream, he tried to devise fantastic stratagems for escape. Natalya ought to paint his face and arms with red or black spots to suggests the signs of some deadly disease. Certainly a change of clothing was in order. And his beard! He would try to force it to grow faster, and his hair, and in no time at all, with a little luck, he could hope to pass for a peasant or gypsy or even a wild-eyed holy fool.

Sherwood's fever dreams passed into ordinary sleep. Jolting along in the peasant cart, he had a comparatively ordinary nightmare. This concerned one of his hunting adventures of several years ago, involving a leopard which had charged him and got close enough to maul him, before his bearer shot it dead. In his nightmare now it appeared as a great cat with Maxim's face—a countenance that changed, as he watched, into the face of the holy fool who had accosted him on his way to Padarok Lessa.

Suddenly Sherwood awoke with a hoarse outcry. It was night, the road jolting under the wooden wheels as if it were no road at all.

"What is it now?" Natalya, still driving, sounded impatient.

"Nothing. Bad dream. I'm all right."

The wound on Sherwood's arm—he couldn't see the wound on his head—alarmed him by displaying the usual signs of infection: redness and a slight swelling in the area.

Clear-minded again, though still lying in the cart, he was listening to Natalya telling him, with triumph in her voice, that his fever had gone down.

In reply he said: "The big cats usually have little traces of rotting meat clinging in the grooves along their claws, and that tends to make for nasty wounds."

"Gone down, poor Sherwood, but you still have it." She stroked his forehead. Sitting back, she added: "Then you're lucky it wasn't a big cat that clawed you. Only a nice, clean bear." She made a sound that tried to be a laugh. "Maxim was always quite—what is your word?—quite fastidious. Clean fingernails."

Sherwood wasn't listening very carefully. "I don't know about bears. They don't eat that much meat, usually. Of course they'll eat some if they can get it. They even kill cattle sometimes, or sheep. They especially like fish. Fish is very good, I wish I had some now."

"Maybe you *are* delirious."

For the next day or two he had to struggle for recovery while hiding out with Natalya in the woods not far from Padarok Lessa, in a series of small camps and abandoned huts, getting ever farther away.

Even with the fever fading, Sherwood knew that he was in the grip of something truly extraordinary. He had undergone a strange alteration in his mental state—he was beset by thoughts and sensations he had never known before. For one thing, there was the memory of

a certain dead fish he'd seen and smelled, beside the
first of the great bear's tracks that he'd ever seen. He
remembered those tracks very clearly—those deep
impressions in dried mud, on the bank of the tiny
stream. Now Sherwood was troubled by the thought of
how good that rotting fish would taste if only he could
crunch it in his jaws. In his imagination, the morsel
tasted like nothing other than a dead and rotting fish,
and yet if he were to try to explain this to someone else
he knew he would give his hearer the wrong idea
entirely.

By God, the odor was delicious, and the taste would
simply have to be!

Meanwhile, off in some relatively lucid corner of his
mind, Sherwood was speculating that, besides fever
and delirium, there were two more possibilities which
had to be seriously considered: one was that he was
dreaming; the second, that he was going mad.

But what followed this onslaught of bizarre appetites
and sensory vagaries was, at first, worse than any
dream—if this was madness, he thought he might
prefer death. He realized in horror that his wounded
arm had swelled alarmingly, threatening to split his
shirt-sleeve, making him hastily pull the sleeve back;
the bandages came loose. At the same time, the arm
grew long, and the articulation of all its joints was
altered. While this was happening, the limb also
became immensely furry; meanwhile the bones of his
affected hand changed—a lesser transformation was
required than he would have thought—and the hand
became a massive paw, furred on the back, black-
skinned on the palm side, all but completely finger-
less—yet it seemed to Sherwood that he could identify
the precise locations of his finger bones. They were still
there, though now they were pretty much bound
together, inside the strong, firm flesh—his left hand,
his left paw, had no fingers any longer, but was armed
with long, sharp claws. He stared at his claws, and

the thought crossed his mind that they must be non-retractable, unlike a cat's.

He became aware also of the immense strength of his arm—which had now become a leg—even if it was still wounded.

The Change, having started at the site of the first wound inflicted by the Bear, bloomed out in less than a minute into a whole-body transformation. The process reminded Sherwood of a segmented balloon being inflated, one section after another changing, swelling up.

In a panic, he pulled off all his clothes, imagining that his swelling body would somehow be pinched and strangled if he did not.

Natalya, turning round from her high seat on the cart, watched in horror—and screamed as the Change reached its climax.

Sherwood, despite his injuries, scrambled out of the cart, walking four-legged beside the shabby little vehicle. Panic was threatening to overcome the old horse harnessed at the front; Natalya had to fight, using the whip, to control it.

Meanwhile Sherwood was stricken by sudden cramps in his two forelegs, which had been his arms, and in the two limbs that were still legs. Cramps that staggered him, then sent him rolling on the ground. Delirium took over again, and it seemed to Sherwood that he was sitting on the darkened veranda of the great house at Padarok Lessa, smoking a cigar to keep at bay any nocturnal biting insects that might show up, listening to dogs barking somewhere in the background. For once, it was actually a warm night. He could see clearly now that his left arm was a bear's leg, but he felt quite reconciled to the fact. There were advantages to being a bear, or partly a bear; his physical senses had grown vastly sharper, so that the world around him had become quite different. Sherwood's nostrils inhaled a symphony of odors from the woods nearby, and his ears distinguished a whole directory of little sounds.

When he looked into a mirror—or dreamed he did—how could there be one on the veranda or, for that matter, in a farmer's cart?—the emotion that swept over him was almost relief, because now he could see the proof that he was dreaming.

His eyes had changed, though less than the rest of his body, and so had the angle of vision encompassed by each eye. Still he could see, overall, just about as well as he had when looking out of a human face. No more human face now. Instead, a furry, muzzled mask looked back at him. The pinkish tongue, the predatory teeth. You'd have to call them fangs. He made his thin, blackish lips curl back. Good God, but what a dream this was! And he could think of no way to jar himself back into wakefulness. He stared in horror at his arm. . . .

He was awake, and they were in the dark woods, on the road at night. There were no mirrors, except maybe in his own mind. The cart was waiting nearby, while Natalya crouched back, away from him, her eyes enormous. Her voice had suddenly gone tiny, become the squeak of a little girl.

"Sherwood?"

He tried to speak, to tell her that she need not be afraid. Only a hideous rumbling growl issued from this throat. When Natalya seemed on the verge of running away, he lay down, making a piteous noise. Only if he lay still would she be reassured that he was not going to attack her.

In a way, the most terrible aspect of the whole experience was that through all he retained a human awareness of what was happening. There were only a few brief intervals when consciousness was completely gone, like being under ether.

Perhaps an even more horrible aspect was the ease with which his mind and body accepted the hideous, tremendous transformation. *At bottom, this kind of thing—this folding and re-forming of the stuff of life—was as*

natural as birth or death. Instinct told him that anyone
ought to be able to do it, if only they knew the secret.

The Change brought with it a taste of seductive,
intoxicating power, strong as the imagined salty tang of
blood.

When full awareness returned, Sherwood found himself already standing on his hind legs, growling low in
the new chambers of his speechless throat. His physical
form had lost every track of humanity. The Bear,
coming from somewhere inside himself, had devoured
him from the inside out.

He had been fully clothed when Natalya put him
into the cart, but he had somehow freed himself from
these constraining bits of cloth before they were torn
apart by his expanding flesh and bone, before the fingers of his right hand, too, had disappeared.

His acceptance at last gave way to panic. Sherwood
was desperate to change back before someone saw him
in this condition.

Dogs somewhere nearby were howling, strangely,
mournfully. But it seemed to Sherwood, listening with
new and keener ears, that they groaned and mourned
if at a loss, not as in the presence of an enemy.

. . . and suddenly the aroma of the dead fish on the
muddy bank was excruciatingly delicious. Fully as glorious as that other fish, smelled on the day he had
started tracking the were-bear, Maxim the *Obaraten,*
now seemed in memory.

It was Sherwood the *Obaraten* now. Yes, of course.
Yet, throughout the Change, he had remained himself.
Or almost. At least, the lumbering bear-man assured
itself, he could remember very well what it had been
like to be the man who answered to the name of Sherwood. What it had been like to be confined in a small,
weak body, balancing uncertainly on two puny, almost-
hairless legs, sensitive to every chill wind, to every
thorn or pebble in the path. And all but blind to the
world's odors and half-deaf to most of its sounds . . .

Sherwood the bear was perfectly aware that he had spent his life, until just a few minutes ago, as a human; but it was somewhat difficult to remember what it had been like to think at full human capacity. He had a poignant awareness that something had been lost, but no way to recall the details of what the rare and precious treasure had been like. Thinking it over later, Sherwood decided that while in bear-form, he had retained a great deal of his human intelligence—much more than any natural bear could ever muster. Without actually making the attempt, he felt sure that a man in bear-form could read, and that he could write, given some way to form his letters.

Unfortunately, the nerves and muscles of the ursine throat were insufficient to allow him to talk

On changing back to man-form, Sherwood found himself stumbling at first when he tried to move about on only two legs. Suddenly he recalled how Maxim had stumbled earlier, walking into the camp of the men who had been hunting him.

When his first full experience of Change was over, Sherwood found himself once more beset by serious doubts that it had been real. In what was left of his mind, he did everything he could to nurture and encourage his doubts.

Only the fact that Sherwood had earlier seen Maxim changing kept him from convincing himself that it had been only a dream, or a hallucination.

His wounded arm had remained only slightly sore when it became a furry foreleg. But it was fully, humanly painful again when he Changed back. And his wounds, once the body supporting them was once again human, began to bleed and hurt afresh.

Natalya had to bandage them once more. She said: "It's really happening, isn't it?"

He nodded.

For a moment, he thought she was going to cry. Then she said: "I thought maybe it was . . ."

"What?"

"When I was—with the rebels in St. Petersburg—there were people who took drugs. Sometimes they saw strange impossible things. I tried the dirty business once . . . but this is different. This is real."

Sherwood couldn't argue with that.

FOURTEEN

On emerging from the turmoil of his own first Change, regaining a brain and body that were once more entirely human—in outward form at least—Sherwood had to struggle monumentally to reorient himself. Simply coming to terms with the fundamentals of what had happened to him required an all-out effort.

The consequences, the implications, however immense, would have to wait till later.

He sought to reestablish himself—who and what he was—by deliberately taking note of time and place. Of the apparent state of the universe around him, and of the company he was in. The human presence of the woman beside him served as an anchor for his own humanity. It seemed to him that he needed strong medicine to keep himself from flying to pieces like a shattered bullet.

He and Natalya sat for what seemed a long time on the worn benches of the otherwise unoccupied bathhouse. They sat there scarcely moving, staring at each other, and he could see the horror and compassion and fear all mingled in her gaze. For a full minute she kept repeating his name, over and over, as if it might have the magic power to keep that massive inhumanity at bay.

This, he told himself, is a village bathhouse, its hand-hewn timbers mossy and damp. I think it's the second one we've stayed in. Over there's a fireplace, and in that stained and ancient kettle they heat the water. The structure seemed as insect-infested as any of the peasant houses, and that homely detail made it real.

Somewhere in the distance, village dogs were barking.

"It's all right. It's all right now, I'm back." And with the feeling that he ought to at least try to resume normal social functioning, to stop being a patient in care of a nurse, he reached for some clothing to cover his nakedness.

When it came to sleep, neither of the fugitives could find relief in slumber. Now Natalya and Sherwood were both numbed, stunned, by the realization that the fact of the Change was true: not only Maxim, but Sherwood himself was subject to this tremendous transformation.

But even as the couple struggled to come to grips with this truth, other matters of life-and-death importance continued to demand their attention and could not be put aside.

The paralyzing shock of Sherwood's transformation had left them capable of little more then sheer mechanical flight. He was well enough now that they could leave the cart behind and ride in the saddle again. But gradually, with continuous physical movement, the shock started to wear off.

"Which way do we go tomorrow?"

They took turns asking the question of each other, while neither could frame a satisfactory reply. It seemed that after what had happened, all their plans, everything about their lives, would have to be rethought.

Once they had established a purpose, Natalya was able to recall hearing of someone who could be helpful in achieving that purpose.

"One revolutionary ought to help another, right? But very often it does not work that way at all."

Natalya shared with Sherwood such shaky knowledge as she had picked up, here and there, of supposed revolutionary contacts in different cities. Many of these people were more than a thousand miles away. One was in Vladivostok (she smiled at the mere idea of trying to make their way there), a quarter of the way around the world.

Natalya told him that according to all the information she had available, their best hope would probably be in Nizhni Novgorod, a city at a moderate distance, and a center of illegal as well as legal commerce. This, she explained, was because of the fair.

"What fair?"

She made an impatient gesture. "It's the greatest one in Russia, and held every summer. Thousands—tens of thousands!—of people come, and everything in the world is bought and sold. I've heard there's a source in Nizhni Novgorod from which it's possible to obtain the very best in forged documents. They look even better—more convincing—than the genuine papers the government hands out."

"How far is that from here? Who do we have to see when we get there?"

"It's not even a thousand miles; if we are lucky, we'll be able to travel most of the way by boat. As to whom we must talk to when we get there, naturally I don't know—that information isn't passed around loosely. I only know the means by which it is possible to get in touch with him—or her."

Sherwood tried to give all this the serious consideration it deserved. He had no idea whether or not Natalya knew what she was talking about. He had the feeling that ever since the encounter with the bear he had been living and operating in a dream. "Well. I don't know what else to do. We have to go somewhere, and I suppose it's worth a try. Whatever help we are offered will have a price, of course."

"I am told that one qualifies for these superb documents not by having money, but by demonstrating true revolutionary fervor."

"Can you be sure about this?"

"Of course not—one is never entirely sure. One hears things sometimes, and remembers them. And the person one wants to find may be arrested or killed any day."

"You said you had dropped out of their movement. And I'm not a revolutionary."

"Pardon me, but if you will claim credit for killing a policeman, you certainly are."

"All right, maybe I am. The way this government goes about its business would turn anyone into a rebel."

"If you have a better idea, Sherwood—?"

"No." At the moment, he seemed to have no ideas at all. But life had to go on. If you lost an arm, or you went blind, or you started turning into a bear—still, life had to go on.

Proceeding very slowly and tentatively on the day after Sherwood's first Change, more freely and boldly during the next few days, Sherwood and Natalya made their way east. At first, they traveled across country during the hours of daylight, and rested at night in what shelter they could find, sleeping in the open, if necessary. Even while remaining unequivocally in man-form, Sherwood adapted to these conditions with the ease of an experienced woodsman. Natalya was by no means used to sleeping out of doors in the wild. Still, sheer weariness soon overcame her unease.

During this interval of shocked retreat, Sherwood more than once awakened to find the arm of his sleeping companion thrown across his chest. He had been worried that the monstrous wonder that had overtaken him would drive her away, and he was enormously grateful that it had not.

"You look a mess."

"Thanks. You don't look so great yourself."

Apart from the dried brown stains of blood from Sherwood's wounds, their clothing looked as if they had been living in it for several days, which they had. He was unshaven, and his head and arm were still bound in bandages that needed changing.

In general, the mornings were sunny, but the warm afternoon and evenings frequently brought rain, which they welcomed as making it more difficult for anyone— or any Bear—to follow their trail.

Such supplies as Gleb had brought them were exhausted now, and in general food was difficult to come by. Natalya discovered some delicious mushrooms in the woods, and a few berries were ripe enough to eat. Sherwood considered shooting a rabbit or a squirrel, with their only weapon, the old man's comparatively heavy Mauser—although the sound might alert others to their presence. But including the finds in old Ivan's vest, they had only half a dozen rounds of ammunition, three of them silver.

After some thought, he had put the silver-tips back in the loops of the hunting vest, and reloaded the Mauser with regular cartridges.

Even after a couple of days of slow, difficult travel, Natalya estimated that they were still no more than twenty-five or thirty versts—maybe fifteen or twenty miles—distant from the boundaries of the Lohmatski estate.

At intervals the fugitive pair saw a few peasants, mostly at work in the fields. These the couple avoided, staying as much as possible in the deep woods.

Once or twice Natalya hesitated. "I expect that if we absolutely needed help, then we would be likely to get it in any peasant house we stopped at—I mean, if it was the kind of help that they could give." In general, as she told Sherwood, peasants could be counted on, more often than not, to be helpful to any fugitives. A traditionally generous hospitality was more the rule than the exception among the peasants. Unlucky refugees were not at all uncommon in the Russian forests.

While the couple kept on the move mechanically, their thoughts were dominated by the undeniable reality of Sherwood's shape-changing power—or curse. But for some time they avoided any attempt at a serious discussion of the matter between themselves.

On the fourth day after Sherwood's first experience with Changing, they were forced to take shelter from the chill rain in a peasant's house when it seemed that Sherwood's fever might be coming back, and one of the wounds in his arm was bleeding lightly again. Also, the lack of food was becoming a serious problem.

The couple had earlier lodged with peasants, when traveling with Gregori, in an infinitely happier time. So Sherwood knew more or less what to expect now.

Stopping at an isolated farm, Natalya introduced herself and Sherwood as a woman and her brain-damaged brother, hoping to become colonists in Siberia. She called Sherwood by the name of Dmitri.

The peasants seemed ready to accept such visitors, or whatever else God sent them, without dispute and almost without question.

Sherwood's clothes, their foreign materials and cut, attracted some attention. But no one commented openly. The two fugitives were obviously people who needed help.

So it was that half-witted Dmitri, letting his jaw sag and his eye go vacant, and his watchful sister spent a night inside a typical peasant hut—perhaps not so typical because it stood at some distance from the nearest village. Everyone slept on the floor, like random campers who had happened on a shelter, except grandfather, *dedushka*, who had the place of honor, on the broad, flat shelf of bricks atop the stove.

Natalya listened with interest as a peasant relayed a third- or fourth-hand account of recent events at Padarok Lessa, brought to this village by a passing peddler.

She heard (and later translated for Sherwood) that several days ago the man who seemed destined to be the new master of the estate, Maxim Ivanovich, had been carried home by peasants who had found him in the forest with gunshot wounds in his leg and arm, the leg wound reportedly the more dangerous. The witnesses had reported that Maxim seemed likely to survive, though they disagreed about how badly his left leg was shattered. At the very least, he had sustained a deep flesh wound, and for the time being he was unable to walk. The bullet had passed completely through the limb, which in general was considered a good sign. But reportedly the doctors were still considering amputation, which they often deemed necessary when a limb was seriously injured.

The victim publicly attributed his injuries to a hunting accident.

At a moment when the pair of fugitives thought no one was paying attention to them, they exchanged meaningful looks. They had no need to remind each other that the bear had been wounded in its left hind leg.

Their conversation with the peasants also confirmed that Gregori Ivanovich had never returned to his home following his interrogation by the police. Now it was considered certain that he had been sent, exiled by administrative action, to Siberia.

Of course, Maxim claimed that his brother's troubles had nothing to do with him; they were Gregori's own fault, for engaging in some kind of subversive activity.

Other news relating to the Lohmatski family concerned the intensive search now under way for Natalya Ivanovna and the American, John Sherwood.

The peasant hosts did not seem to connect the people who were their guests with the stories of a vanished lady and a foreigner.

Several of the old servants at Padarok Lessa had recently been arrested. Nothing was known of their fate beyond that.

Meanwhile, some nurses and a doctor in the employ

of the police had come to Padarok Lessa to care for the wounded master of the house.

Sleeping in some peasants' hut, or as they sometimes did, in their little barn, Sherwood could only hope that he would not turn into a bear overnight.

Change had never yet overtaken him in sleep and it didn't now. But he knew beyond doubt that it wasn't gone. More than once he woke in fright from a dream in which his hands and arms had gone to thick brown fur. At these times he was never sure whether or not he had undergone an actual, partial Change, whether he had been able to reverse by the act of waking.

In the morning, moving on, after receiving a simple blessing from the elders of the house, Natalya and Sherwood talked. He felt greatly relieved at hearing English once again, after listening, in the guise of a deaf-mute, to incomprehensible Russian all through the night.

Both of them could feel their attitudes altering, even though their basic purposes remained the same. The couple were now compelled to think and act in an entirely new world—a world where men could change to animals, and savage animals once more resume the guise of human beings.

This revelation had thrown new light on—and also raised new questions regarding—the death of old Ivan.

Trying to reconstruct the course of events, Sherwood decided that old Ivan must have realized that his son Maxim was a shape-changer only after he had sent the cable to Gregori in London.

"Your father wouldn't have wanted help on the particular kind of special hunt that he had planned."

"Father knew . . . about Maxim."

"Yes, he must have known. Found out, somehow. So then he got the silver bullets out of storage, or had them made for him by a local gunsmith. It seems to me that casting a silver bullet wouldn't be very easy.

Melting point is much higher than that of lead, if I remember right."

"Perhaps Father had known for a long time," said Natalya, "that what it says in the old book is true."

"I'm beginning to think he did. About the truth of the book, I mean. I don't know when he learned about his son."

If old Ivan had been long aware that the family curse was a reality, then he would have been ready to believe the truth, when presented with any kind of evidence, that his son Maxim, long a troublemaker, had fallen victim to the family curse.

Natalya said: "Therefore, the truth is that our father rode out, on that last day, deliberately intending to kill his son. I suppose it would have been easy to make the death look like a hunting accident."

Sherwood agreed, almost inaudibly. "Looks like that's what happened."

But when the time had come for action, Maxim had been too fast, too cunning, and too strong for the old man. He had separated from his father, hidden his clothing, Changed, and come back, stalking quietly on four huge paws, to where the old man waited, and had taken him by surprise. It seemed that none of Ivan Gregorevich's silver bullets had struck the were-bear on that day; perhaps none had even been fired.

Travelers traditionally traded news items when the opportunity arose. Here and there Sherwood and Natalya gleaned other bits of news from gossiping peasants, carters, peddlers, or holy fools. Some of the latter were as ready to gossip as to prophesy. From one such person they had one more confirmation of Maxim's statement that Gregori had already been dispatched into exile, by administrative action.

Natalya mused that administrative action seemed to be coming more and more in favor, being quicker and more certain than a trial.

"Can they really do that? Just lock people up and ship them away?"

"Oh, Sherwood! Our government has been doing

that for generations. For centuries. Many exiles—I suppose a great majority of them—go by that route, mixed in with common criminals sentenced to hard labor. They are all jumbled together—the so-called political offenders, many of whom are as innocent as Gregori, along with common thieves, rapists, and murderers. When will you get over your naïve idea that people who live in this country have rights?

FIFTEEN

⌒

The next morning they started off early, scratching themselves in tribute to the vermin they had picked up sleeping in the latest peasant's barn.

The couple had ridden less than a verst before Sherwood called a halt.

"Nellie, we've just been wandering. That has its good points, because if anyone's after us it's unpredictable, and so far it's kept us from being caught. But eventually we've got to have a plan."

"I know. We keep saying that, but we never actually make one."

Looking at her, his heart turned to see how haggard she had grown. Thinking he really had to take charge, for her sake, he said: "This time we do. We don't move from this spot until we have a goal."

"That might be a mistake." Natalya sighed. "Plan or no plan, we must keep on moving, getting farther from Padarok Lessa, even if we don't know where to go. Where we are now, there is still a chance of my being recognized by someone who would turn me in."

"All right. I agree. The farther we get away, the better. But I insist we choose a direction. Pick a goal."

"Very well. I suppose we must. The choice is still open to try to work our way west, to Petersburg, as we planned originally. You can get help there at your legation, even if Maxim has accused you in the shooting. If he hasn't, I don't doubt you can get permission to leave the country."

"I guess I might be able to do that. But what about you?"

Natalya started to run her fingers through her hair, then withdrew them when they encountered a hopeless tangle. "I can take to the woods, live as an outlaw. In Russia thousands of people do that every summer. But going to Petersburg won't help me now."

"Why not?"

"Because, whatever else may happen, I could not bring myself to leave the country, knowing that Gregori is even now on his way to exile in Siberia. Even if I were absolutely sure that there is nothing I can do to help him."

"You sound like you're not absolutely sure. You think there is something we can do for him."

"I don't know yet. But . . ." She stared at Sherwood as if she were trying to read the depths of his soul. Suddenly the horse under him shivered as it walked.

"Damn it, Nellie, tell me. The fact is, I feel the same way you do. I don't want to go to Petersburg. Because the way things have developed, my getting out of the country isn't going to do anyone any good, not even me. And I want to help Greg." He looked at her intently. "Another reason for my staying is that if you're going to remain in Russia, I don't want to leave."

Natalya appeared to be making an effort to pretend she hadn't heard that.

He let it pass, and added: "And if you're seriously planning to take to the woods, you're going to need help. From the little I've seen, you're not all that good at living out in the open, off the land."

Her eyes flashed. "Other Russian women do! I can also."

"I bet you can. But maybe there's a couple of things you ought to learn, like building fires, and not leaving a big trail, and not getting lost. You said we should go north, and then you weren't sure which way that was. I'm pretty good at all those things. I want to stay with you—or for you to stay with me."

"On what terms?" She still sounded ready to strike.

"I haven't got that far in my thinking. Remember, I'm the man who just . . . became . . . well, you saw that happened to me. Damn it all, I turned into a bear!" At last he snapped out the plain blunt words defiantly, as if daring Natalya to dispute them.

"I saw," she breathed. For the moment her voice and her eyes held a mixture of fear and something like reverence.

There was a brief silence while Sherwood groped in vain for useful words on that subject. But there was nothing he could do about it, and life had to go on somehow. He would have to cope with bearishness as he went along. Other problems needed attention, too. At last he said: "Let's get back to Greg. What is it exactly you think we can do for him?"

Natalya too was ready to put aside the overwhelming fact, the crack in the universe, which they had tried repeatedly to talk about—so far without really getting anywhere.

She spent a minute in renewed concentration on Gregori's problem, which, by comparison, seemed more manageable. Then she said: "First of all, are you ready to agree that simply getting a lawyer, as you might do in America, is utterly hopeless? Useless!"

"Okay, no lawyers for Greg. Not now anyway. Then what?"

"There are other ways of setting people free."

"Yeah? Bribery?"

"Yeah!" She imitated the word with a mocking intonation. "Bribery is a way of life here. Even in remotest Siberia, money can be very useful for other things than starting a fire. That is probably our best chance, but not the only one. Yes, really, Sherwood. If Gregori is exiled after only a short term of imprisonment, as it seems may be the case, then he would be sent to live in some Siberian village, comparatively without restrictions. Probably. Once he is in exile, he will only need to report to the local police every day or so. And even while he is still a hard-labor convict, I am told that for a young and active man, simply getting away from a prisoner convoy, or even from a prison, is far from impossible. The hardest problems come after one has escaped, trying to survive, on the tundra or in the *taiga*—the forests—and avoid recapture. There are natives, Siberian tribesmen, who hunt the prisoners—how do you say it?—for bounty."

He thought for a couple of minutes. This young girl might not know as much about the prison system as she thought she did—but she sure as hell knew more than he did.

At last he said: "You're saying that wherever Greg has been sent, prison or the mines or exile, we ought to have a good chance of arranging an escape, or buying him out. If we can only find out where he is, and get there."

"Yes, I think so." Natalya nodded. "I can tell you stories. But it won't be easy. Understand, Sherwood, most of the prison mines and camps are as far east from where we are now, as your New York is from your San Francisco. And some are very much farther than that. Siberia goes on a long, long way."

"In my time I've made a couple of journeys even longer."

In America, heading west had been the traditional route of those who for one reason or another no longer fit into the settled part of the country. In Russia, the seekers of greater freedom or a new start went east.

And Natalya still insisted that the best forger of identity documents known to the revolution was to be found in Nizhni Novgorod.

Sherwood had money, but it was hard to find a way to use it. Natalya decided that their best chance of being able to ride a train to Siberia lay in adopting the guise of volunteer settlers. The government had been trying for a long time to encourage population movement to the east, and peasant volunteers were allowed to travel at one-quarter of the regular railroad fair. They also stood a good chance of being allotted government land, provided they were willing to settle in some of the more remote regions. Hundreds of thousands of such people were now thronging east every year, many by railroad, and thousands more in wagon trains. Some established themselves in the east. Others failed. Listening to Natalya's account of such treks, Sherwood was reminded irresistibly of what he had heard of the settlement of the American West.

Here the geography was reversed, but otherwise the similarities were considerable. The farther east one got, apparently, the more open the society and the greater personal freedom—if one were not in prison or exile.

Even without special orders, the trains and stations would be watched for fugitives—and the *Okhrana* could be very efficient when they put their minds to it. Still, it sounded worth considering. While Sherwood struggled to learn the language, he could continue to pose as a slightly brain-damaged man, and Natalya as his wife or sister who spoke to him in simple, soothing Russian, whispering English only when no one else was listening.

"All right, east it is, then. It ought to speed things up if we could knock off a thousand versts or so by rail."

Natalya hesitated. "Yes, possibly. But of course, there is something else we ought to talk about before we undertake any course of action. Your condition."

"The fever's gone. I'm healing. I feel strong." Tenderly he touched the claw marks on his forehead.

"That's not what I meant."

He paused, looking down at his hands. "Yeah, I know," he said at last.

"What I meant was, naturally I would like to know, if you think you are going to, once more . . . ?"

So of course they were going to have to talk about it. He would have to do his best to find the necessary words. He drew a deep breath. "If I'm going to change into a bear again. Yeah, I expect I am. It's too bad that wasn't all a dream a couple of nights ago."

"Certainly it was not."

Natalya's answer was quite calm. Both of them had been preparing themselves inwardly for this discussion, and now it seemed they were as ready as they could be.

"I—I think the question is not *if* I will change again, but when." Sherwood realized that such an answer was inadequate, and tried again. "I've been thinking it over, and I'm pretty sure it's inevitable. When the bear . . . when Maxim . . . when he drew my blood . . . it brought on some kind of permanent transformation. But it seems to me that I do have at least a certain amount of control." He looked at Natalya to see how she was taking this, and sighed.

But still he persisted. They had to reach an understanding. "This changing—the *obaraten* business—is still with me. I think it will be, from now on."

Observing his companion's expression again, he shook his head. "Really, it's not at all like being ill, or crippled. I'm over that part now. The truth is, it feels like I've grown up, grown into a new power. It's kind of an inward feeling. I've had the feeling, that a change is coming on, several times since the other night, and I've been able to prevent it from happening . . . maybe this sounds silly, but the best way I can describe it is to say it's something like trying to control a sneeze. I guess that sounds ridiculous, but . . . so far I've been successful."

Natalya was still looking at him hopefully, but not with understanding.

"I've got a better comparison," he suggested. "Think of puberty."

She stared blankly for a moment, then said: "Oh."

"Of course, it's not quite the same thing either." Despite enormous difficulties, he had to make the effort to explain. "Obviously Maxim was exercising some control over his own Changing, that night when he attacked us. And in my own case my changing back—back to my right form again—was at least partially voluntary."

The man and woman paused to smile at each other with mutual relief. It seemed that they were going to be able to discuss the business matter-of-factly.

Natalya asked, "What about changing in the other direction? From man to bear?"

"I've been trying to tell you that I *do* have some control over that." He lay back, closed his eyes, and thought about it. It seemed to Sherwood that he could feel the potential there, permeating his whole body. Just like the potential of being able to move his arms and legs, even though at the moment they were quite still.

"Yes," he said at last. "I will Change again—sooner or later. I don't think I'm really going to have much choice about whether I do or not. Some choice about the circumstances of where and when, yes. But I think it could possibly even happen in my sleep."

Suddenly looking directly at Natalya, he caught her watching him with quiet fright. "You'll be safe!" he interjected, and reached impulsively to take her hand. "I mean, the bear that I became was still me. Maybe for the moment, I somehow had a different brain, but I still had the same thoughts, as far as I could tell. I wouldn't have hurt you for the world. I think I might have gone crazy with the shock of it—except I knew I had to hang on, to behave. Because you were there. At all costs I had to keep from scaring you into running away. Whatever else happens, I'm never going to hurt you."

Natalya did not withdraw her hand. For what seemed a long time, she was quiet, watching him. Then she asked: "How are we going to deal with this—this power you have? Make sure about your control over it?

And about the—the risks. There must be some risks involved? To you and . . ."

"To anyone who's with me. You'd think so, but I swear I'll never hurt you, whatever I turn into. I know that's true, I can feel it."

She didn't answer.

"I suppose there's only one way to be convincing," he said at last. "If you agree. I'll see if I can do a controlled Change. Maybe just a partial one at first."

When they reached a deeply isolated spot in the thick woods, as secure from interruption as they could hope to be, they stopped and tethered their horses in such a way that the animals could graze. He handed over the rifle to her.

She took it wordlessly, then deliberately set it down, leaning the muzzle against a trunk. "What now?" she asked.

Sherwood made an uncertain gesture. "It seems to me I ought to prepare by taking off my clothes. They had to go, right away, when I changed involuntarily. If I don't—I'm not sure what would happen, but they might get torn to pieces, when I—get bigger."

"Well, go ahead, then. What, are you shy? Don't be a fool. I'm not exactly a novice in a nunnery." And then, surprising and confusing herself as well as Sherwood, she blushed.

Facing away from his companion, somewhat embarrassed despite the certainty that there were vastly greater things to fret about, Sherwood removed his garments quickly in the warm summer afternoon. He gave each piece of clothing a shake automatically, trying to get rid of last night's bugs. As he turned back to his companion, he held his shirt wrapped loosely around him.

Then he let the Change happen. It was amazingly easy, and a little frightening. How he did it would have been impossible to explain. But this time there was nothing in the least dreamlike about it. For the moment, at least, he felt that he had almost full voluntary control over the process.

In a moment he was considerably shorter than he had been. Now he was standing on four legs, his senses assailed by sounds, and especially by odors, quite imperceptible to human senses. His vision had not been greatly affected.

Natalya, the expression on her face beyond description, had withdrawn a step. She whispered: "Is it—painful?"

It seemed to Sherwood that his command of language was as good as ever, and he tried to say: "No. No, not in the least. A little scary, but—"

But all that issued from his ursine throat was a slightly modulated growling.

He was worried that Natalya was going to scream and run away from him. Quickly he lay down, that being the best way he could think of to reassure his companion; he tried to imitate a cat that wanted its ears scratched.

For the moment his companion was still paralyzed. "Sherwood, this is . . . this is—" Words failed. "Sherwood? You can understand me? It is still you?"

The bear nodded.

When he had submitted to having his head scratched behind the ears, and his tummy rubbed, he let out a *whuff* of sound and sat upright.

"Well, Sherwood, what now?"

With Natalya looking on, no longer truly frightened, he capered, roared, and tore down branches. In a few moments Sherwood discovered, to his delight, that he was now surrounded by tempting food, just what he needed to assuage his newly ravenous hunger.

After doing his best to growl some reassurance to Natalya, who once more looked somewhat apprehensive, Sherwood gobbled berries off nearby bushes, and then, struck by inspiration, broke open a dead log; the pale little creatures inside looked tasty, and smelled absolutely delicious. After only a brief hesitation out of respect for his companion's sensibilities, he spent a couple of delightful minutes eating them.

His appetite dulled for the moment—though far from sated—he sat down, rolled over, and once more invited Natalya to pet him.

From being terrified at the seeming miracle, Natalya now looked almost enraptured.

Grabbing handfuls of fur, she tugged the new bear to his feet, then up on his hind legs; her imitation of his movements led the two of them into a kind of capering dance.

The dance, the celebration, grew wilder and more abandoned. Now her clothes, too, were coming off. At the sight, Sherwood's humanity and manhood came roaring back. The dance ended moments later, with woman and man locked in each other's arms. Yes, he noted with great relief, they were four human arms.

A minute later, in the midst of a feverish embrace, she whispered into his blood-red human ear: "What if you Changed again, *now*?"

Vaguely but deeply shocked, he considered the possibilities. "No," he said. As a bear, he could not—would not—want to lie with any woman, any more than as a man he would have wanted to embrace a bear.

After a while, after the world had settled down again, and they were lying quietly, he said, "I hadn't expected anything like this." He was trying to say that what had sprung up between them was as great a miracle as shape-changing. "I mean . . . I guess I had hopes about you and me, days ago. Before I turned into a bear."

They were lying quietly in the warm grass.

Natalya put out a hand and stroked his human hair. "I had hopes too, Sherwood. My crazy American. From that first day when I saw you in Petersburg."

He put out a human hand and stroked her hair, then her bare shoulder. "This is crazy. I'm afraid I'm mucking up your life entirely. And that's the last thing—the very last thing—in all the world, I want to do."

A little later again, as they were pulling on their clothes, she said, "Sherwood, Sherwood! Have you realized what this means? I mean, it seems horrible, in a way, especially at first, but . . ."

"That we are lovers?"

"That you are a bear, you fool!" He had to dodge an awkward blow from a small fist. "That you can *become* a bear. It suddenly occurs to me that there's definitely a positive side to it. If the condition recurs, if you can control it. What power it will give you! All the things that you might do, quite beyond the capability of all other men."

"Not quite *all* other men. We better never forget that Maxim has that same power. And that he must still want to kill us."

At that same hour, Maxim, still recovering at Padarok Lessa, lacked firm evidence that the wounded Sherwood was still alive, but suspected that he was. And the possibility was dawning on him that he, Maxim, through his own claws had passed on to Sherwood the power (or the curse) of taking on bear-form. He wondered how much of an hereditary predisposition was required.

If Sherwood was still alive, he knew. And that meant of course that Natalya also knew the truth.

At their next meeting, Maxim thought, assuming there was going to be one, he would approach the matter more carefully. Once more he would propose, this time calmly and thoughtfully (though with treachery in mind, of course) that they form an alliance.

What caused Maxim the greatest wonder was the realization that he must have been wounded by a silver bullet.

Not that the bullet had been recovered—it had grazed his left foreleg, gone straight through the hind leg on that side, and must have buried itself in the dirt. But there was no other reasonable explanation. Only silver, the old book said. The frightening question was: How had Sherwood come to be carrying a rifle loaded with silver bullets?

Sherwood too was pondering an effort to obtain more of those effective cartridges.

If it became necessary to fabricate more, a blacksmith's forge would probably be needed, to provide a fire hot enough to melt silver. The melting point of that metal, he seemed to remember, was much higher than that of lead, for which a campfire was sufficient.

But soon he decided against trying to enlist a blacksmith or gunsmith. "I've still got three rounds left. If I can't kill him with three, I might as well cash in."

"All right. That should simplify matters to us, at least a little."

"Do you think your brother was telling the truth about Greg? About where he was going to be sent?"

"I don't know. I can't see that Maxim would have had any reason to lie."

The latest rumors, spreading third-hand and fourthhand from Padarok Lessa, indicated that Maxim had been spared the loss of his leg. But he was said to be recovering very slowly from his bullet wound and might never get over it completely. He might spend months getting about on crutches, and walk with a permanent limp thereafter.

Maxim, returned to man-form, had reported to the authorities, and to anyone else who expressed an interest, that he had managed to track his sister and the man she'd run off with into the woods. Sherwood, after admitting he'd killed the policeman at Padarok Lessa, had also shot him—though Maxim did not mention his suspicion, hardened by now to virtual certainty, that he had been the victim of a silver bullet.

That had to be the only explanation. Thinking it all over, Maxim had come to a private conclusion, which he'd been able to verify to his own satisfaction when he confirmed that his father's favorite hunting rifle was now missing.

So that had been the weapon Sherwood was holding when Maxim charged him. One implication was that

Father had loaded with silver before starting out on that last hunting trip with his younger son. Another was that Sherwood, after all, might not have known the truth about the *obaraten* business.

Well, if the American was still alive, he must now understand the truth.

Somehow Father had discovered that the family gift of power, having evidently skipped a generation, had descended on Maxim; and, in consequence, Father had been prepared to shoot his son down in cold blood.

Well, what had happened to the old fool when he tried had certainly served him right.

In all of these reports, Maxim Ivanovich Lohmatski also omitted to say that at the time he was shot, he had been trying his best with his own fangs and claws to rend John Sherwood into little pieces.

Nor did he mention to a single living soul his most serious personal problem: ever since the silver bullet had hit him, his Changing capabilities had been distinctly crippled. And there was every indication that they were going to remain so.

Now, when Maxim in the privacy of his own home or inner office, tried to stand up in Bear-form, his left hind leg remained stubbornly, whitely, almost hairlessly human, with all the weakness that implied. Of course the limb was now completely useless when it came to supporting anything like a full leg's share of a large bear's weight.

Maybe, he told himself, when the wounds were healed completely . . . but each day that passed reinforced his terrified doubts.

Never mind being able to stand on his hind legs. The truth was that he could scarcely walk at all!

His head, unwounded, became all Bear.

A large part of the problem was due to the fact that his left foreleg, grazed by the silver bullet, was also frozen in the shape of a man's arm, emerging pale and bald and practically useless from a massive chest and shoulder covered thickly in brown fur. A bear could get about on three legs, but not on two. And there was no way he could use crutches. Obviously some of the muscles and bones in this newly hybrid shape were human, others evidently ursine—and some perhaps in a transitional shape. When he looked at this monstrous mosaic in his bedroom mirror, he could only wonder that he was able to move the arm and hand at all.

A servant, coming into the room a minute or two after Maxim had resumed man-shape, sniffed at the bear's lingering smell, and without comment opened a window farther, and quietly sprayed some lavender water about.

Thinking about the situation, Maxim suddenly realized that his grandfather might be still alive. The one man—and also the one bear—in the whole world who could really understand his, Maxim's, situation.

There was only one place in the world, as far as Maxim knew, where he might be able to go for help. Perhaps, in all the world, he had only one potential ally: Grandfather.

If Grandfather existed anywhere in the world, the only place Maxim knew to look for him was on the family's Siberian estate. But he did not even know exactly where that was.

SIXTEEN

~

For a few days immediately after his first voluntary experience of shape-changing—and the tremendous sequel with Natalya, which to Sherwood had been almost as momentous an event—he remained in man-form.

During that time he and his new lover pressed on, working their way generally to the southeast. When hunger became serious, he hunted, expending a couple of mundane lead bullets to collect a rabbit and a squirrel. He decided he could get to like the Mauser, though not as much as his own favorite rifle. They gathered nuts and berries and mushrooms. Sherwood wished he had a pole, or even just a hook and line, for fishing.

At night they sheltered in abandoned huts, or sometimes only fallen trees. At intervals during the day they stopped to make love, talk, or nap. Just now they were resting drowsily, while their horses grazed nearby with the afternoon forest seemingly so peaceful around them.

The spot they had happened on appealed to them as invitingly secure, sheltered under overhanging willows

on the back of a stream some twenty paces wide.
Natalya was sure that this little river emptied into the
Volga. If they could find a suitable boat, the way to
Nizhni Novgorod by water would be open.

On this secluded bit of shoreline, shielded from view
of the occasional river traffic, and a hundred yards or
so from the nearest road, a bout of lovemaking was followed by a practical session of bathing and washing
clothes.

Sherwood was just in the act of pulling on his
drawers when a faint sound of low voices reached
them, followed almost immediately by the gentle splash
of an oar. And the rest of his clothes were spread out
on a bush to dry. Natalya, ignoring the worn remnants
of her undergarments, pulled her dress on quickly
over her head, and was immediately farther along than
he was on the way to respectability.

Neither of them had time to do any more before the
nearby branches parted, and they were confronted by
two bearded, ragged men aiming rifles at them.

In another moment it was apparent that the pair of
men with rifles were only the advance guard of a much
larger band. The five well-armed outlaws, the greater
part of their number walking along the shore, had
approached as silently as any Indians Sherwood had
ever met.

Now the leader of this group came upon the couple,
amused himself and his followers with a few obviously
bawdy comments, and then with threatening commands and gestures began to relieve them of their
horses, and of Sherwood's rifle.

There was no chance for either victim to leap into
the saddle and gallop off. In the first place, the horses
had been unsaddled; in the second, they were grazing
well out of leaping distance. Sherwood began to reach
for his own rifle, which he had stood leaning against a
tree, but saw that he was too late. He was seriously out-
numbered and outgunned.

In a few moments the unhappy couple were also
completely surrounded.

Now three or four more bandits came into view. They had been rowing quietly upstream in a small boat, which, at a wave from the leader of the band, pulled into shore, stopping just under the overhang of willows.

The bearded man who seemed to be the leader was speaking to Sherwood, seemingly making some kind of demand. Natalya speaking Russian warned the newcomers that Sherwood spoke no Russian. A sharp exchange volleyed back and forth between them.

Breaking off this confrontation, she turned to Sherwood. "I've told him you speak no Russian—I don't know if he believes me. He says we will both be allowed to join the band, once we've turned over to him all the good things, as he puts it, that we are carrying."

"Doesn't look like we have a whole lot of choice at the moment," Sherwood muttered. He started to reach for the rest of his clothes, drying on the bush, and then abruptly aborted the movement as a better idea came to him. As if his reaching had called the clothing to their attention, two or three of the men with rifles, grinning, stepped forward to look over the display for themselves, like shoppers about to make selections in a market.

Two or three people, who evidently formed a kind of rear guard, came out of the woods, and began to examine the horses appreciatively. These later arrivals were no longer making any effort to be quiet. Evidently there were about a dozen people in the band. Eventually what seemed to be the total was gathered in the little clearing: eight or nine men, three or four women. The great majority did not look like Sherwood's idea of bandits, but rather resembled lost souls who might have drifted into playing bandit. Most of them looked at Sherwood and Natalya without any particular curiosity.

Sherwood noted that the leader posted a pair of informal sentries, one a little upstream and one down.

Most of the laundry that had been drying on the bushes was now in the hands of its new owners.

Two or three of the men were obviously beginning to take a personal interest in Natalya.

For some time Natalya had been wanting to tell someone, proudly, that she and the man with her had killed a policeman. Now she had a chance to brag to these outlaws.

"I'm going to tell them, Sherwood."

He thought about it and shrugged. "Don't know if that's wise. But maybe it is. You decide—you're the one who has to do the talking."

Then Natalya translated one woman's scornful comment for Sherwood: The report in revolutionary circles was that Natalya Ivanovna Lohmatskaia was a quitter, someone who had turned her back on the struggle in Petersburg, just when the going was getting particularly tough.

But at least one of the bandits had been a quitter too. "She says she and her comrades here have all given up on the revolution, and that we will do the same, if we have any brains at all. The only way to live is to try to survive from day to day."

"That's fine. Any of them speak English?"

"I doubt it very much, but keep it short."

"Looks to me like we're really in trouble here. I'm going to take some strong action to get us out. I'm really going to bear down. You know what I mean."

She nodded. Her expression, though she was doing her best to control it, expressed sudden hope, tinged with something less happy.

He nodded back. "That's right. When you see me duck into the brush, just look out for yourself for half a minute. Smile and do whatever they want. I'll be right back."

She understood that even with their lives in peril, he felt an instinctive need to avoid revealing the great and fantastic secret, as long as there was any chance at all of doing so.

After taking control of the horses, they made sure Sherwood was otherwise unarmed—the old Mauser was treated as no great prize, and was left leaning against a tree.

Sherwood picked up his vest from the bush, opened the inner pockets so the money inside began to fall out, and tossed the garment to the nearest of the enemy, distracting them for just long enough for him to make his move.

Suddenly Natalya, in the grip of two men holding her arms, was being forced down on the ground. She swore and kicked and struggled. "Sherwood!" It was a desperate cry for help.

But Sherwood was no longer anywhere to be seen. He had turned away when the eyes of the dangerous men were busy with the woman and the money; and when the outlaws looked for him, they saw only his abandoned underdrawers, and the quivering of a thick-leaved bush to mark the spot where the naked man had disappeared.

One of the women called out with a laugh that the coward must have been overcome by a sudden need to relieve his bowels.

Well, how much did it really matter if the fellow ran away in that condition, anyway? He'd left behind everything he owned. . . .

And he'd left his woman. The men who had Natalya in their grasp were getting down to serious business, grunting, beginning to breathe more heavily than was required by the effort of holding one small woman still. Their leader was unbuttoning his trousers.

In her rage, Natalya bit the hand of one of the men. The man cursed her and lifted a thick arm to strike.

Before the blow could fall, a vicious crashing sounded in the thicket, coming from the same direction in which the peculiar foreigner had just vanished.

"*Medved!*"

Medved—the bear—coming into view would have checked out at three-quarters of a ton if anyone had measured, ten feet tall as he reared on his hind legs, and to the handful of people standing directly in his way, he looked half again as high and wide, his brown fur erect with the fury of his movement, little wicked eyes, red mouth gaping like a basket of ivory knives. Brush crackled, saplings snapped before the charging bulk.

The great mass of brown fur darted against the bandits much faster than a man could move. Gigantic forelegs were spread like arms, as if *medved* wanted to embrace them all.

The men struggling with Natalya let her go and grabbed for weapons, but not nearly in time. Their screams rose up. Still, not all the outlaws were panicked enough to drop their firearms and run. Fortunately for the Bear, their weapons were not loaded with silver bullets.

The man who had raised his fist to hit Natalya turned at the sound of rumbling, crackling onrush just in time to catch a clawed slap squarely in his face. Natalya, suddenly released and sitting on the ground, heard the sound of a dropped pumpkin. She saw the front of the man's head go fleshless in a spray of red pulp, his hat fly toward the treetops, his spare frame lifted clear of the long grass by the blow, his body turning once in midair, brushing willow boughs with seeming grace and slowness, before crashing back into the grass to move no more.

Even before the faceless body hit the ground, the knives in the great bear's jaws had closed upon the shoulder of a second victim. The man screamed, being lifted, arms and legs vibrating like leaves on a shaken twig, before his broken body was cast aside. Somebody's gun went off, seemingly almost in Natalya's ear, and a moment later another weapon fired. Then one more, all without visible effect upon the bear. Natalya hurled herself back flat on the ground, seeking cover with her face buried in her arms; and for a little while she saw no more.

The roaring and the screaming, the thuds and grisly crunches and crackling of trampled bushes, kept her facedown while she held her breath. Another gunshot was fired, and then yet one more; but that was all.

In much less than a minute, the skirmish was completely over.

Natalya raised her head and looked around. A small mountain of brown fur was swinging, swaying back and forth across the clearing on four tree-trunk legs. Turning in short circles, pacing, intently on patrol. Three men were down—no, four. One of their bodies lay very close to Natalya, the others, some with weapons nearby, scattered around the edge of the clearing. The survivors of the outlaw band, both men and women, were all gone. Vanished. She could still hear people rampaging through the woods, screaming, scattering in a desperate attempt to get away and save their useless lives. The sounds were fading rapidly.

The boat the band had brought with them, oars neatly shipped aboard, was just starting to drift away, when the bear caught the nearest gunwale gently with one paw. An effortless tug brought the small craft sliding hard aground, up far enough on muddy shore to be secure from the light pull of the current.

The bear, still on all fours, continued patrolling the edge of the small open space. Now and then he stood up again on his hind legs, looking and sniffing and listening, alert against the possibility that some of the enemy might be coming back.

Natalya closed her eyes and began counting. When she had reached fifty, and still could hear no sound except the growls and lumbering prowling of the bear, she opened her eyes, jumped up, and started trying to pull her torn clothing together.

One of the men who had been knocked down still moved, and the bear coming to his fallen body sniffed at it, as if uncertain what to do about these signs of life. Then *medved* evidently decided that no action was required, and moved on, shaking his great furred head, growling and mumbling, through the short fur around his mouth that was all clotted red, making inhuman sounds that were almost words.

He prowled the clearing in circles, most of the time on all fours now, employing the keenness of nose and ears as well to make sure that all the surviving members of the gang were well on their way to somewhere else.

Every few steps, the great beast stopped and turned its shaggy, massive head toward Natalya, and looked at her to make sure that she was still all right.

In Sherwood's altered perception, the sounds of panicked flight, the trampling feet of horses and of men, were fading in the distance. The smell of terror was drifting slowly from the clearing, leaving the interesting tang of blood to dominate.

He sniffed at his own vest with some of the money still in it. He had never noticed before the symphony of smells with which the garment was invested. The rest of the money, paper and gold coin together, was scattered on the ground. Only when he moved to pick it up did Sherwood realize that he was going to need fingers.

When Natalya looked back at the bear again, she saw a much-diminished figure. Only a naked human, only Sherwood, gathering his clothing from where the bandits had dropped it.

Before Sherwood finished dressing, he looked his pale body over carefully. "No harm done, anyway." The enemy's bullets, presumably of mere lead, had left no trace.

He looked at the dead bodies, and muttered: "They had it coming."

Hungrily, the two fugitives inspected the boat and roamed among the dead, eager to pick up whatever they could find in the way of food or other assets abandoned by the fleeing gang of outlaws, or left in the pockets or in the hands of the dead, or stowed aboard their newly captured boat. They had their choice of weapons, a little spare clothing, a bundle of paper money, rubles, from the leader's inside pocket. Old Ivan's Mauser still stood against the tree, where one of their attackers had propped it.

There was a good supply of food, a veritable banquet

for two hungry people, including black bread, some mushrooms wrapped in muslin that looked freshly picked, even two live chickens with their legs tied together. A compass, matches. In the bottom of the boat, even a folded small tarpaulin that could make a tent for two, pots and pans, and a bottle of vodka and one of wine. A fishing line and hooks.

"Looks like we take to the river for a while."

SEVENTEEN

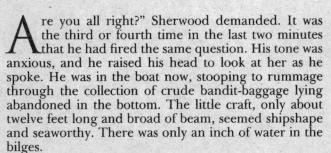

A re you all right?" Sherwood demanded. It was the third or fourth time in the last two minutes that he had fired the same question. His tone was anxious, and he raised his head to look at her as he spoke. He was in the boat now, stooping to rummage through the collection of crude bandit-baggage lying abandoned in the bottom. The little craft, only about twelve feet long and broad of beam, seemed shipshape and seaworthy. There was only an inch of water in the bilges.

"As well as can be expected." Natalya, who was examining what the fleeing enemy had dropped on shore, patiently repeated her earlier reply. Her nerves were slowly coming back to something like normal. "You came out of the bushes just in time. Very neatly done. And how are you? It sounded like a lot of shooting."

Sherwood straightened to his full human height (making himself momentarily aware of just how small he was), giving the question serious consideration. Standing up carefully in the boat, he pushed with his hands at the small of his back, like a man with a slight backache. Then he said, as if surprised: "I feel—very good. A little strange, but good." He paused. "The shooting meant nothing to me, you know. They were using only ordinary bullets." He shook his head, still somewhat awed.

When he smiled tentatively, Natalya noted that there was no blood around Sherwood's mouth. The fur around the bear's mouth had been stained with human blood. Maybe he'd wiped it away, or else he'd . . . She forced herself to think of something else.

In their hurry to run away, the outlaws had dropped several backpacks, along with a miscellany of other items. Natalya now opened a good-sized blanket roll, and let out a little cry of satisfaction. Immediately she began digging through the contents, mostly women's clothing, for some garments to replace her own torn dress. Her first choice was a sweater. After giving it a fierce shake to dislodge at least a majority of lice or bedbugs, she pulled it on over her ruined dress.

Having examined the rest of the package, she moved unhurriedly on about the clearing, picking up one discarded bundle after another, going through them ruthlessly. It was necessary to unstrap one pack from the dead body of a would-be rapist, a task she accomplished as emotionlessly as an expert surgeon conducting an autopsy. The fallen man who a minute ago had still been moving, now breathed no longer.

Sherwood, watching his companion, had it once more borne home to him that this woman had not led a sheltered life during her revolutionary period in St. Petersburg.

His own emotions since the start of the fight were complex and puzzling. From one moment to the next he still kept expecting some kind of substantial impact to hit him, because he had never killed a human being before—only a great many animals.

"You could help," Natalya called briskly, seeing him standing idle. She indicated the remaining bodies.

Sherwood nodded, and balanced his way on two

human legs (legs that for the next few minutes seemed to him abnormally thin) out of the boat again onto the shore, where he crouched beside the man who had been dead the longest, the one who no longer had a face.

I did this, he thought, as he reached out (noticing as he did how beautifully human fingers were designed for such an action—but how weak were all his muscles!) and with a firm unhesitating touch started to rifle the corpse's pockets. He experienced no more emotion in this than in handling a dead animal. In his human shoulder he could feel the remembered motion of the blow struck by the bear: *I think, just before I did it, I had the idea that it would be like striking a man with my right hand. . . .*

But it hadn't been like that at all. He looked down at his right hand, which was only a hand, unmarked, as human as it had ever been and no more deadly. It was all very curious. But he felt no overwhelming shock. The killing seemed to have taken place in another world. He remembered the event only as he might have remembered a story. A story about a bear.

No human hand had dealt that blow.

How easy and how simple it had been to call upon the power of the Bear.

A few minutes later, when it seemed that every item likely to be useful had been removed from the dead men's clothing, Natalya asked: "What do we do with them? Put stones in their pockets and dump them in the river?"

"I don't know." Sherwood considered. "No, that would be a waste of time. I say just leave them where they are."

"What about our horses?" She gestured toward where the animals were still tethered in the brush.

"Can't very well take them in the boat. We might as well let them go free."

"And the saddles?"

"Leave them here too. All that stuff. Can't burden ourselves with things we're not going to need. We've got more money now than we had before." The bandits seemed to have had some earlier success along that line. "When we come to a place where we need horses again, we'll get them somehow."

Natalya and Sherwood loaded the boat with all the food they could find, tucked in a few weapons—making sure they had the Mauser aboard, and its silver bullets—some spare clothing, and a couple of other items that seemed to prove useful. After seeing to it that the horses were free to make their own way in the world, Sherwood shoved off, Natalya paddled, and they went gliding out from under the willows.

Fifty yards downstream, only a minute of drifting down the small river and with Sherwood just settling into a rhythm at the oars, and the little glade was out of sight. It occurred to him, not for the first time, that the biggest forest on earth would likely be good at keeping secrets. If and when the dead men were discovered by anyone who took an interest in their fate, it might well be assumed that they had died fighting among themselves.

Before the couple had been boating for half a day, their modest stream had been vastly swollen by a couple of substantial tributaries, raising it in Sherwood's estimation respectably into the category of real rivers. Staying in the middle of the river now put them far enough from both banks to be out of easy conversational range.

In silence the two people in the boat looked at each other. It was time—and past time—for a constructive conversation. But that was easier said than done.

"Nellie, I want to talk about it—about what it's like when I become a Bear. I want to talk to you about it, and I've started several times. But the funny thing is, every time I try, it seems to me that there really isn't much to say. What happens is just—beyond words."

She had stretched out in the bottom of the boat, eyes closed, her head pillowed on captured packs. "Maybe later, Sherwood. What has happened has happened. Let's enjoy a little peace and quiet while we can."

"I'm all for that."

After they had enjoyed near-silence and green tranquillity for a couple of hours, rowing when they felt like it, drifting between times, Sherwood tried again. "So, we have this fair at Nizhni Novgorod as our immediate goal."

Natalya stirred, opened her eyes, and sat up. "Yes. Being there should put us closer to Gregori—assuming that Maxim was telling us the truth about Gregori's fate. Also, in Nizhni Novgorod, we have our best chance of getting some important help."

"You mean from that expert forger, the one you mentioned earlier."

"That's right."

Somehow the skirmish with the bandits had the unexpected effect of alleviating anxiety. Sherwood and Natalya now showed themselves in public more openly and confidently, felt less and less impelled to turn away and hide when someone saw them.

Learning that Natalya was unacquainted with *Huckleberry Finn*, Sherwood tried to tell her the story. He decided to emulate Huck and Jim in their successful fugitives' strategy, traveling downstream by night and lying low by day, tied up in a thicket or on an island. Several days passed in this fashion.

During this period, Natalya and Sherwood were encouraged to note that the people they saw, on shore or on the water, fisherfolk and peasants and small traders, appeared to pay them little or no attention. There were plenty of other small craft on the river, going upstream or down by oar or under sail.

Going ashore repeatedly, they felt more and more at ease with every casual encounter, increasingly confident that they were unlikely to be recognized.

So far their plan was unfolding satisfactorily. They

would make their way downstream to the Volga, this time approaching the river from the east.

The closer Natalya and Sherwood came to the Volga, the greater the number of people, of all classes, they encountered traveling by water and land in the same direction—toward the fair.

Sherwood said thoughtfully: "You know, there's a good chance that this boat we're in is stolen; we might possibly run into the rightful owner."

"Not a very good chance that he could recognize it, though." The boat was comfortably nondescript, the color of its paint indistinguishable with age and weathering, and it bore no name. A number of other very similar craft were plying up and down the river.

"Nellie, how soon do you suppose we'll reach the Volga?"

Natalya refused even to guess. Sherwood squinted at the passing bank, visualizing a walking figure just keeping pace with the boat. It was his way of estimating speed. Three miles an hour, he thought, without rowing. So just drifting would make about seventy-five miles a day, which would mean about three days or four for this leg of the trip.

When their tributary river bore them at last into the mighty Volga, Sherwood was no longer sure of the exact date, on either the American or Russian calendar. Natalya estimated that they still had a hundred miles or more to go to Nizhni Novgorod.

The numbers of people who were traveling in the same direction by land and water continued to increase steadily. There were many moments during those days on the great river when Sherwood could half-close his eyes and almost convince himself, by sound and smell and feel, that he was home again, on the Ohio or the Mississippi.

Between intervals of rowing, he got out the hooks and lines which had been among the equipment in the captured boat. Then Sherwood, recalling boyhood skills, pulled in some large fish. A few of these turned out to be tasty, when he cooked them with the bandits' flour and bacon, in a captured pan over a small fire on the shore.

He managed to teach Natalya something about fishing, and also, with wood plentifully available and captured pots and pans, the craft of cooking in the open air.

Under cover of darkness, they swam to cool off, then climbed back into the drifting boat and made love. Steam-powered craft of any kind, running at night, were reassuringly less common here than on big American rivers.

Under Natalya's constant tutelage, Sherwood's Russian had made some progress. He could understand a number of words and express a few simple wants.

Sherwood, trying to retain a grasp on the world around him, was nagged by a pointless worry over the correct date. He remembered that he had arrived in Russia in late May. It had been sometime in early June when he and his companion had taken to the woods. She was now as uncertain about the date as he was.

At several of their stopping places, Natalya took up a little stick and in the mud drew crude maps of shores and islands. Thus Sherwood tried to fix the geography of Russia in his mind, but the imagined shapes and distances kept stretching and changing, like those of some fairy-tale kingdom in a book. Really, he had to get a decent map, or several of them if necessary; he was going to try his best to do so at the fair, where everything in the world was said to be on sale.

As they drew near their goal, traffic on the water, the majority of it headed downstream, steadily increased. There were places where the surface of the river, broad as it was, seemed almost covered by paddle wheelers, rafts, sailboats, barges, and dinghies.

Sherwood figured that it had to be sometime in early July when they reached the fair, having enjoyed a slow-drifting, anonymous progress down the Volga. Frequently they rowed to speed the journey.

Speaking of the contact which she hoped to establish in Nizhni Novgorod, Natalya lowered her voice to a whisper. She confided to Sherwood that the place where they had to look was not at the fair itself.

At last the city of Nizhni Novgorod appeared, an unlikely collection of brightly painted church spires and onion-shaped domes, a wayward fragment of the Arabian Nights looming atop a lofty tree-clad bluff, a couple of thousand miles from Araby.

He asked Natalya: "You've been here before?"

"Once, when I was a little girl, my parents took us to the fair. I don't suppose it's changed that much."

The city on the bluff was gliding closer. Domes of gold and silver, and white walls, of cathedrals and monasteries, stood out most plainly. Part of the upper town was surrounded by stone walls, and from a distance looked like a city of the Middle Ages. But the fair itself, deployed between two rivers on a narrow plain under the bluffs and below the town, on rocky land that appeared to have been raised artificially above flood stage, was most impressive. Here there were hundreds of buildings, permanent and semipermanent, hundreds of tents and makeshift shelters. As many shops and dwellings as in the upper town were thronged with people, of all classes and sizes and ages. Oriental faces and straight black hair were common. Where did all these people come from? Where did they all sleep and eat? Sherwood had never seen a marketplace like this one on any continent. Marble buildings with plate-glass windows stood on some of the highest ground in the immediate area, next to crude lean-tos and small ornate churches.

He found it surprising that no real docks or piers had been built along the shore. But then he decided that the water level probably varied too much. Obviously trade was brisk, and business was good. Loading and unloading were carried out in a constant turmoil of small craft and workers sometimes wading

armpit-deep, singing as they carried things, coming
and going to the floating platforms of landing stages.
The shipping was dense as far as one could see, for
miles upstream and down.

The couple tied up their small captured boat, at a
place where it seemed unlikely to be noticed among a
hundred other boats. There they quietly abandoned it,
after removing the few things they were most likely to
want. With money in their pockets and the fair with its
hundred food vendors just ahead, there was no need to
carry anything to eat.

As the couple started on foot for the upper town, gradually separating themselves from the crowd, Sherwood
was reminded of the possibilities of rapid communication when he saw the line of fresh new telegraph poles
carrying wires into the town. Whatever authorities ruled
here must be in at least occasional contact with St.
Petersburg.

Having trudged up the long, curving road leading to
the upper town, and having enjoyed briefly a view
from above of the river and its thriving commerce, the
fugitive couple found themselves almost alone in what
appeared to be an abandoned city. Followed at intervals by curious dogs, they searched cautiously among
almost-deserted streets and buildings, for street names
and secret landmarks, seeking Natalya's contact with
the revolutionary underground.

"Where is everyone?" Sherwood marveled.

"They'll all be at the fair."

At last Natalya stopped in the middle of an eerily quiet
street, gazing at a crude sign on a nearby building,
white chalk lettering on a black-painted board.

"'Bolkov's Blacksmith Shop,'" she read in translation. "This is the one I want."

EIGHTEEN

⌒

Asmithy, equipped with forge and anvils for heavy metalworking, obviously couldn't readily be relocated to the lower fairgrounds in the summer. But naturally business would be slow in these days when almost everyone had left the upper town. The enterprising thing to do, thought the American visitor, would be to set up a new branch shop down there.

He said quietly to Natalya: "Well go ahead then. Remember our signals."

The smithy was not deserted, as all the nearby buildings appeared to be; men's voices and the clang of metal drifted out of the dim opening. Smoke drifted from a chimney, and some kind of work was evidently going on. Sherwood, with a Krag-Jorgensen carbine captured from the bandits slung casually over his shoulder, kept watch just outside. (Old Ivan's Mauser had been wrapped in oilcloth and hidden away, inside a hollow log near the edge of the woods.) Meanwhile, Natalya entered the half-open shed and confronted a grimy, muscular worker. This, Sherwood thought, was probably the master smith's helper or apprentice, because he stood, bare torso gleaming with sweat above his leather apron, with a bellows in hand, rather than a hammer or other metalworking tool. A couple of other men, hovering in the dim interior background, seemed to be listening in.

Sherwood could barely hear her voice, calm and musical. Since he knew in general what she was going to say, he could pick out a few Russian words. She was introducing herself as Madam Sarban, and asking the question she had been taught to ask; about what special types of horseshoes were available.

Trying to appear casual, Sherwood stayed where he was, now and then shifting his weight casually from one foot to the other. With an effort he kept himself from fingering the Krag. News of the murdered policeman at Padarok Lessa could easily have spread this far by this time, though it might pass almost unnoticed in the welter of reports of similar revolutionary violence around the country.

He watched vigilantly for any of the hand signals he had prearranged with Natalya. One motion would summon him to approach in a casual, friendly way, another would bring him quickly with carbine aimed. A third would invoke the Bear. But moment after moment passed, and Nelly's hands, in fashionable gloves captured from the bandits, stayed clasped in front of her in ladylike fashion.

Now the voice of the blacksmith, heavy but gentle-sounding, was rumbling in a hesitant reply. Picking out words, Sherwood could hear him saying that he didn't know the answer about those special horses and their shoes. But he would do his best to find out. Where can we find you, madam? or words to that effect. And now Natalya was telling him: We'll be at the fair.

Unhurriedly, Natalya turned away from the men inside the smithy, and came walking steadily back to Sherwood.

"What do we do now?" he asked in a low voice, as soon as they had turned their backs on the shed and were casually moving away together, along the empty street.

"Wait."

"For what?"

"For them to make contact with us."

"Where do we wait? And how are they going to know where we are?"

"We will be at the fair most of the time, like everyone else. I told him that. The people we want to talk to will have no trouble finding us."

Certain practical questions needed answering, such as whether they ought to seek indoor lodging, or instead find somewhere to camp out, avoiding the crowd. The mobs visible at every kind of hostelry near the fair suggested that the second plan might be the only real choice.

The couple started into the woods, and presently were about a quarter of a mile from the great fair, walking a narrow path which clung to the flank of a steep, wooded hill. Below them the slope fell down sharply to the busy river's edge, a long stone's-throw below.

In this way they covered another quarter of a mile, but still they were not alone. The woods continued to be uncomfortably full of other people who had already set up their own camps, or were looking for places to do so.

"Seems we might have to hike a long way to get any elbow room. I'd like at least a minimum of privacy, where we can't hear our neighbors in the next camp snoring."

"So would I. But what choice have we? The more I think about it, the less I want to rent indoor space, even supposing that we could find it."

The couple hiked on, and gradually the population of the woods thinned out. They had settled on what seemed a feasible spot to spend the night, almost a mile from the fair, and had just started to relax when a faint crackle of brush, repeated immediately and slightly louder, signaled that some group of people must be approaching through the woods.

"Hush! What's that—?"

"Look out!"

Sherwood, with the recent memory of bandits and deadly peril all too vivid in his mind, and with the thought of the police never far from his awareness, was on his feet and had already begun stripping off his clothes . . .

Moments later, the ominously noisy party came in view, and at the same moment childish voices gave away the unintended joke. The small group with which Sherwood and Natalya were suddenly confronted was the perfect picture of harmlessness. It consisted of a pair of young women, teachers or nurses, in charge of a group of half a dozen small children, five or six years of age, all well dressed, no doubt the offspring of prosperous merchants.

These folk, bursting in upon the couple unexpectedly, were astonished to see a young woman with a kind of rifle slung over her shoulder, alone with an enormous brown bear, but not in the least frightened of the beast. She was talking to it, in the manner of a woman speaking with a close relative, with one arm wrapped around its neck, the thickness of a human waist; and with her free hand scratching and petting the animal's head.

Meanwhile the bear sat on his haunches. In that position he was still as tall as a man. But with forearms half-folded before his chest, he looked droll and no more dangerous than an alderman.

The children, after a moment of silence, wide-eyed and openmouthed, were encouraged by Natalya's smile to raise a chorus of delight. The two young women who had them in charge hesitated only momentarily before joining in.

"A man's clothes!" she heard one child whisper to another, pointing at a small heap of garments behind a bush. "But where's the man?"

"The bear has eaten him!" the second shrilled, in a mixture of horror and delight.

"No no, little one! Napoleon here does not eat people!" Natalya laughed an icy crystal laugh, inviting the world to hear what a strange idea the little girl had voiced. "The clothes are only part of a new trick that we were practicing."

Seizing a moment of opportunity when all eyes were on the bear, Natalya gathered up Sherwood's discarded clothing hastily and stowed it in her pack.

One of the two young women marveled aloud that the bear had no iron ring in its nose. "Not even a collar or a leash!"

Natalya, as though she were in the habit of talking to herself, translated this into French. The bear appeared to be listening with interest, while the two women looked blank. Then Natalya added in Russian: "But my dear Napoleon doesn't need such things. We are practicing, you see, for our performance at the fair. Let me show you how tame he is!"

And she called out some commands, in French, to Sherwood, who obligingly shuffled into an awkward dance on his hind legs, while Natalya kept time clapping her hands. Then he was commanded to bow, and entreated to nod his head.

"And now, dear Napoleon, listen to me! How much is two and two?"

The shaggy head responded with four nods. What a remarkable bear, indeed!

One of the young teachers, or governesses, had decided on glum disapproval, while the other was quickly becoming enchanted.

She asked eagerly: "But the beast understands only French?"

From somewhere Natalya produced a hat—Sherwood's own—placed it on the bear's head, and the animal contrived for some time to keep it on.

Then, holding the same hat delicately between his massive forepaws, he passed it in front of the tiny crowd, as trained bears generally did, in search of donations. One child put in a kopeck, another a button, and the nursemaid, looking flustered, picked and threw in a wildflower. Napoleon bowed and nodded, showing each the same amount of gratitude.

The little band of watchers clapped their hands and cried out in applause. The other young woman dropped money in the hat. Other children contributed candy. Even the woman who at first had not approved now began to thaw a little.

Even when she spoke to the bear in French, Natalya was cautious about what she said, thinking that the young woman might well understand.

Over her shoulder she said, brightly, to the small audience: "Napoleon, you see, does not yet understand Russian. But he is a bright pupil, and he will learn."

Drawn by the sounds of laughter, a man on horseback happened by. And then a few more people. Even at a mile's distance from the fair, these woods were more thickly inhabited than had at first appeared. Some looked poor, while others were well dressed.

The crowd had grown to more than a dozen when a minor local official, dressed in a uniform even more garish than most, came nosing his way through the woods to investigate. He took the position that the woman needed some kind of license to keep the bear. Others, taking Madam Sarban's part, disputed with him. Inside his human brain, the bear was thinking that there seemed to be some law of nature, to the effect that the farther east you got in Russia, the less seriously most people took the subject of paperwork.

Meanwhile, Sherwood kept looking for a chance to turn unnoticed back into a man. Then he could hope to slip away with Natalya, while the minor officials continued wrangling with each other. But for the moment at least they were being watched so steadily that Sherwood could find no opportunity for an unnoticed Change.

Natalya kept petting him reassuringly. Then a couple of small bribes, delivered to each of the officials in turn, did the trick, allowing the bear and his trainer to depart unmolested. The woman casually put on the pack containing the man's clothing before she walked away.

And the bear, its mistress said, was now scheduled to perform at the fair.

The comparatively few people who watched the first full performance, held a couple of hours later at the edge of the fairgrounds, were willing to testify that the bear called Napoleon was much different from the usual animal found in that role. This bear, which understood French, seemed to be somehow of a higher social class than other bears; he was very large, also, and his fur was glossy and healthy. And such clever tricks! At times he looked fierce and proud, unlike the broken-spirited animals one usually saw. Yet he allowed himself to be petted by children; his mistress even encouraged such intimacies, as though she was perfectly confident of the monster's good temper.

He accepted several gifts of candy and fruit, sniffing and nibbling them with such delicacy that the watching crowd gave voice once more to its amazement.

Maxim, in the course of his efforts to alert everyone he could think of to watch out for the couple, had already telegraphed at least one *Okhrana* agent at the fair. But, as had been the case for several years, the official wires were busy with reports of arrests and conspiracies, of bombings, shootings, robberies, and other violence, from one end of the tsar's empire to the other. Only messages given the highest priority were likely to spur any energetic action.

The fair, as Sherwood saw it successively through both human and ursine eyes, continued to impress him, accustomed as he was to the sophisticated ways of Europe and America, as an overwhelming spectacle.

Here, their numbers seemingly increasing day by day, were thousands of people, from all corners of the empire, milling around, conducting trade. Hundreds of diverse buildings, many serving as informal hotels. Bearded monks soliciting alms. Prostitutes. Peddlers, screaming the virtues of everything from mushrooms to anvils to lace scarves.

Think of something, and you could find it: tea, dried fish, pig iron in rusting stacks. Fine fabrics from everywhere in Asia and many places beyond; furs from Siberia, the cold land-ocean stretching from here east to Japan.

The smell of the river, a compound of tar and fish and mud, permeated everything. A babble of languages rose to the summer sky, bargaining for jewels and gold, machines and fine woodwork and pottery. Poles and Persians, Jews and Chinese, bought and sold. Sherwood wandered, mouth agape, his own problems forgotten for the moment.

Here were furs, everything from squirrel to sable, the startling white of polar bear. Here were the carriages, furniture, firearms of every description.

Here were houses, huts, and tents, offering food and every kind of entertainment. And it was here, walking meekly along a kind of midway with Natalya's gently guiding hand on his furry neck, that Sherwood in bearform had his first chance to see himself in a large mirror.

After a moment of shock, he realized that he was looking into a distorting mirror, in front of a large tent, evidently some kind of carnival fun house. The moment had produced a kind of vertigo, a fear of returning too suddenly to humanity.

Over the next two days, the couple put on three more performances, with considerable success. Napoleon's reputation was spreading quickly.

At the fair Natalya had no difficulty in obtaining a man's belt that made a suitable collar for Napoleon, and a leash, intended for a large dog. When attached to the collar, the leash looked as if meant to go with it.

Sherwood had occasional moments of near panic, wondering how he was ever going to get a moment of privacy in which to change back to human form. After giving three performances he was more than ready to enjoy the powers conferred by fingers and clear thought.

In fact, his first good chance to resume his human form without discovery did not come until dusk, when they reached the river. A bear went plunging into the muddy stream, and when no one else had a good view of the necessary transformation, a man emerged, shaking off a spray of droplets like any human bather. Here among the heterogeneous masses, men and women alike went into the water naked. Sherwood had already observed that in Russia there was much less concern over casual nudity than there would have been anywhere in the Western world.

No one really noted the fact that the bathing bear had suddenly disappeared—everyone assumed that it had come ashore somewhere else—and there was now one extra man in the water.

Of course, at such an immense gathering as this fair, there were other performing bears, as many as ten or a dozen of them, along with a hundred other entertainers. The real bears had gypsy owners, who tended to be jealous of the new arrival, so superbly talented. These animals and their masters stayed in their own encampments, a little apart from the fair itself.

"That was a good idea, taking up a collection. We don't need money, and I wouldn't have thought of it."

"It's what the people with bears always do. Would have seemed strange if I didn't. And anyway, we may need money tomorrow."

Throughout her first full day with Sherwood in Nizhni Novgorod, Natalya kept waiting and hoping to confirm the contact with the important revolutionaries.

Sherwood realized that he and Natalya could easily have searched the town and the fair for days, and never have got a hint of the presence of these canny intriguers, had not those they wanted been trying to locate them as well.

Late in the day, a message was brought to the couple by someone they had never seen before, a dark-haired gypsy-looking girl of ten or so, barefoot and in a ragged dress.

"Yes, child. What message have you for Madam Sarban?"

In a singsong voice the girl recited Russian words obviously memorized: "Madam, I am to tell you that your horse can now be shod at Bolkov's Smithy. The special shoes that were needed have come in."

"Thank you."

After Natalya had translated this exchange for Sherwood, and he had nodded, the couple followed their now-voiceless guide on foot along the long, climbing path.

Ten minutes later, in the almost-deserted upper town, the girl brought her silent followers to another building, two stories high and nondescript, several blocks from Bolkov's Smithy. There with a small fist the child rapped on a street door badly in need of paint.

Immediately the knob turned, and an invisible hand inside the house pulled the door open into dimness.

NINETEEN

At about the same time that the fugitive couple were abandoning their boat on the bank of the Volga thousands of versts away, Maxim Ivanovich Lohmatski, gnashing his teeth over his unhappy fate, stalked about his ministry office in St. Petersburg with a cane—the crutches he had been using until last week, and for which he soon hoped to celebrate a suitable ceremony of destruction, still stood in a corner of the large room. His human body was healing, and gave every sign of eventually being as good as new.

But the damage to his nonhuman self—the ursine nature he now considered the most important component of his being—was quite another story.

During the past few weeks, Maxim had spent considerable time planning one scenario after another of elaborate vengeance on his sister, and above all on the damned American. Burning alive the man who had done this to him would be much more enjoyable than burning crutches.

One reason, perhaps the most important, for Maxim's

journey to the capital, had been to consult the best doctors in the country.

The doctors—he sometimes thought that the more famous and high-priced the scoundrels were, the more dull-witted—had been telling Maxim for weeks that under their expert treatment he would soon be completely recovered from his wounds. At each consultation they looked approvingly at the newly healed scars (not knowing they had been engraved in his flesh by precious silver), and tested with satisfaction the strength and range of motion of his human limbs.

But of course the would-be healers never dreamed that he was anything more than a man—they didn't know the half of it!—and he was not about to enlighten them.

It had been a surprise to realize that none of these medical men knew enough, or were going to discover enough, even in the course of close examination, to bring his real problem into their view. In this, as in so much else, they simply did not know what they were doing.

In his imagination he could hear himself explaining: "You see, doctor, my real trouble is that, whenever I turn into a bear, my left arm and leg remain discouragingly human. This, as you may imagine, interferes terribly with my activity in that other shape."

In his imagination he could see the graybeards nodding, polishing their pince-nez thoughtfully. Oh, that explains it, sir. Now we understand your situation. Yes. Of course.

Bah!

The more he contemplated his own situation, the more his thoughts turned to his grandfather, whom he had never seen, but who had evidently enjoyed the same powers that were now his own. Agafon had testified to as much, and so, toward the end of his life, had Maxim's own father.

And the more Maxim thought about Grandfather, the more the question obsessed him: was it possible that the old man could be still alive, out there at the frozen northern edge of the world? As far as Maxim knew, no one in the family in his lifetime had even communicated with the Siberian estate. Father had been out there once, but he had undertaken his only expedition before any of his children were born, and had never been willing to say much about it afterward.

But now he, Maxim Ivanovich, was going to do it.

Padarok Sivera. Gift of the North, and what an ambiguous gift! Land no one could use—or could one? One of the little jokes of which old Ivan the Terrible had evidently been so fond.

Yes, he, Maxim, was going to have to locate that strange domain in the vast northern fringe of Siberia, and go there. No matter that such a journey meant putting off, or abandoning, his struggle for power within the bureaucracy, in which he had so far enjoyed meteoric success. He had already seen Minister Stolypin himself, volunteering to go on a long tour of inspection that would require at least a year of traveling, and take him to remote camps and exile villages in the far north. Stolypin had been pleased with such enthusiasm in one of his high-ranking subordinates. The arrangements had already been set in motion. Only out there, among the tribesmen in the region, might he hope to find the answers that he needed.

Meanwhile, of course, one had to get on with the business of the Ministry.

Despite continuing efforts on the telegraph, Maxim had yet to receive any convincing reports concerning the whereabouts of his sister and the man she'd run away with, the American who'd been struck down by his Bear claws, but who had probably survived. Last week some half-credible story had come in, that the couple had been seen in Moscow. But attempts to follow up on it had accomplished nothing.

Now one of his relatively well-trusted lieutenants, his chief clerk, brought him some garbled news of the bandit massacre, a story told by one of the foiled rapists who had been attacking Natalya when the Bear came to strike them down.

Maxim grabbed the dossier and examined it. The man had long been wanted for several major crimes, including robbery and rape, and had been brought to Petersburg to stand trial for them. He was about to be locked up in the common jail.

"Sir, you said you were interested in any news concerning unusual bears, anywhere in the country—and we've a fellow here with a strange story to tell about a bear."

"Bring him in."

In another minute Maxim was interrogating the bandit.

One of the first things Maxim wanted to know about this man was whether the mysterious Bear had wounded him at all. The fellow wasn't bandaged, and did not appear to be hurt or limping. No, Maxim was assured, the bear had not so much as scratched him. He'd been very lucky indeed.

The improbable tale of how, in the *taiga* thousands of versts to the south and east of Petersburg, a woman and her trained bear had launched a completely unprovoked onslaught, caught Maxim's attention. He took it for granted that the story had grown somewhat and changed its shape in the retelling: but still . . .

Training a gaze of controlled professional ferocity upon the wretched prisoner, he observed: "This group that you were with in the woods—you and a few friends, as you say—you make it sound like an innocent band of picnickers."

The felon's face brightened. "That's the idea, Your Honor. Yes, something like that."

"Don't lie to me, scum!" Maxim half-rose behind his desk, and then subsided as the prisoner shrank away. "Fortunately for you, I don't give a damn what you were doing there. Understand that? I don't want to know about you and your scum companions. For now you can get away with murder. It is the woman and the bear who interest me. Tell me the absolute truth about them, and I'll see what I can do for you."

"Oh, yes sir! The truth, of course!"

"Is there any way you can identify this woman? Would you know her if you saw her again?"

Surprisingly enough, the man explained that Natalya had given the bandits her right name, and Sherwood's. "She said that her companion was an American."

It was all rather suspiciously neat. But—who knew?—it might be possible.

Maxim listened for a while as the story went on, then interrupted sharply: "You claim you shot this bear, but didn't kill it?"

"Yes, Your Honor."

"What really happened was that you shot and missed."

Slowly, stubbornly, the prisoner shook his head.

"Oh? I suppose you hit the beast, but the bullets didn't hurt it?"

"I swear it on my mother's soul, Your Honor."

"Your mother was a pig. A lying pig, no doubt, like you."

"Quite so, Your Excellency."

"How can you know you actually hit the bear?"

"Sir, the range was very close. I could hardly have missed with my eyes shut." The man took thought. "Besides, the fur—at the moment one shoots, one sees a little . . . a little *puff*, stirring the fur where something moving very fast strikes home."

Maxim stared hard at the man. The detail struck him as convincing. "And so, since the bear wasn't hurt, not even slowed down, I suppose it took a bite out of you, despite all your heroic efforts?"

"Out of me, sir? Not a bit. No, when I saw there was something wrong with my cartridges, I ran like a maniac. I managed to keep well clear of its claws and teeth."

"Lucky for you. Now tell me again about the woman you say was talking to the bear."

"She must have been a gypsy, Your Honor. Or a Jew."

"Why do you say that?"

"The—The way she acted, sir . . ."

"Never mind that. What did she look like? How old? How tall?" Maxim played with the riding crop he liked to keep lying on his desk. The prisoner's eyes nervously followed the slight movement.

"And you say that when you first saw the woman, there was a man in company with her—and her bear?"

The prisoner blinked. "Yes, actually, sir, there was a man."

"A young man or old?"

"Youngish, sir. A-Actually about the same age as Your Honor."

"Possibly this man was the bear's trainer?"

The prisoner shook his head vehemently. "No, Your Honor, that could not have been. Because just when we—just before we were attacked so unfairly, the man ran off into the bushes. It was obviously the woman who was giving orders to the animal."

"He ran off, did he? And what else did he do? Did he by chance do anything—very much out of the ordinary?"

"Your Honor has great insight. Actually the man pulled off his clothes, just before he ran away. No doubt he was quite mad."

Maxim stared at the prisoner for some ten seconds before he spoke again. "Pulled off his clothes, did he? And then what?"

"Then he ran away, Your Honor. I lost sight of him at that point."

"You heard him speak?"

"Once. But not in Russian. It was German, I think."

"Possibly English?"

"That could have been it, Your Honor. I don't know a word of German or English, either one."

"And you never heard the man give the bear any commands, in any language?"

"No, Your Honor. Not one."

"How can you be sure?"

"Because the man was gone before the bear appeared."

"Gone where?"

"Again, I don't know, sir. The man went into the bushes, and the bear came running out at us, and I was busy shooting and running away. I never saw the man after that."

Maxim gave up toying with the whip, and looked down meditatively at his own uninjured right hand. He was remembering the blow he had struck Sherwood— evidently not a fatal blow, as matters had turned out. At least, not fatal for Sherwood.

Just bad luck, with the collapsing stairs in the burned house, and there was nothing to be done about it now. But it could easily be fatal to strike a dangerous enemy, and not kill him.

The description of the strange man, especially his lack of Russian, certainly tallied with Sherwood, while that of the woman sounded like she might very well have been Natalya. And supposedly she had given the hooligans their right names.

What motive could this criminal have to fabricate such an improbable story? None was apparent to Maxim. After another half-hour of questioning, which gained him no new information, he ordered the man put in a cell nearby. The business of his common crimes could wait; he might be wanted again for private questioning.

Then Maxim hastened back to the telegraph office, where he dispatched new orders and warnings.

Maxim particularly sent word to agents who were loyal to him personally, in several cities, including Nizhni Novgorod, to watch out for John Sherwood, American, and Natalya Ivanovna Lohmatskaia, thought to be traveling together. It was of the utmost importance that they should be intercepted.

If Maxim was right in his suspicions, it would doubtless be beyond the power of any ordinary police to make a captive of this bear. But if they failed to do so, failed in some spectacular fashion, that would at least provide proof that his fears regarding Sherwood were justified. And he would have to go looking for his enemy himself—damn it! If only he could regain his full Bearhood!

Maxim, enjoying his private plans, asked himself silently whether he would prefer to be in bear-form or man-form when he paid Sherwood back for the pain and disability brought on by that silver bullet. There were advantages to each mode of operation. Man-form allowed one to carry on a conversation—and to think up all kinds of refinements. As for Bear-form, well, he didn't want his enemy to be able to gloat over his crippled two-and-a-half-legged self. For a time, he lost himself in almost-blissful reverie. . . .

And yes, of course, his dear sister—what to do about that? Now he could be certain that Natalya knew his secret. Not that anyone who mattered would be likely to believe her if she told, but that was too much of a chance to take. It was necessary that she be silenced permanently—unless she and Sherwood could still be recruited, which now seemed impossible.

What would Natalya Ivanovna and her lover, that lucky survivor, be doing now? It seemed they hadn't been in Moscow after all. Most likely, thought Maxim, they would be heading for St. Petersburg, hoping to get abroad from there, by way of Finland. Natalya was experienced in revolutionary tricks.

Maxim's urge to visit the family's Siberian estate was swiftly becoming an overwhelming compulsion. There, if anywhere, Maxim could find the shaman's skill, the magic, whatever was needed to make his Bear-self whole again. Besides that, there were actually moments when he had the feeling that Grandfather was actually summoning him to the estate, by some extraordinary means.

Maxim was beginning to wish intensely that he had at some time taken an interest in his own grandfather. By this time, maybe, he'd know . . . but all he had to

remember was the dim portrait at Padarok Lessa, and
another in the Petersburg town house.

Even though presently living in the family's St.
Petersburg town house, spending many hours of each
day in some secret *Okhrana* telegraph office, Maxim
Ivanovich was already thoroughly enjoying his new
role as the new owner and master, the sole proprietor,
of at least Padarok Lessa—not to mention all, or most
of, the Lohmatski family's other properties. Already
most of the legalities were in place to allow him to take
over officially as sole owner, but he would have to visit
the Siberian property in person before he had everything in order to his own satisfaction.

In recent years, as the forces trying to overturn the
government demonstrated surprising strength in most
regions of the country, Maxim had seriously begun to
consider whether someday there might really be an
effective revolution in Russia. Slowly, reluctantly, he
had been brought around to the conclusion that such an
event, long considered the mere stuff of nightmares,
was, in fact, quite possible.

The real trick, of course, would be to make sure that
when the real revolution did arrive, one was on the
winning side at last—whichever side that turned out
to be.

Outside the open, softly curtained windows, deep
summer still held sway. Maxim, who in general preferred winter to summer, was looking forward to the
journey—which would have to wait, it seemed, until he
had finished off his sister and the American. There was
a lot to be said for Siberia—out there, if all reports were
true, a man, or a Bear, could make his own way, with a
great deal less interference.

There, where there were in practice no other authorities to interfere, he could dispose of his enemies in
proper fashion.

He was getting regular reports from Agafon regarding
events at Padarok Lessa. Peasant or not, the old man
was quite capable of riding into town every few days,

finding the telegraph office, and printing out a few essential words of message. No elaborate evaluations were required. Let the local peasants continue to hope that the bear was dead—though, since Maxim was still alive, some of the peasants ought to know better.

From time to time Maxim also made tentative plans to dispose of Agafon—he would have to be taken care of sooner or later. No matter how useful he was on occasion, the man could not be trusted—and that was that.

Natalya talked with Sherwood about the dangers of a police trap. They could not assume that the *Okhrana* would be always stupid and disorganized. Sometimes, as had been amply demonstrated in the past, they could be truly cunning, and employ a deadly patience. There had been cases where someone who was really a police agent pretended to be a revolutionary, and the police set up what they called a mousetrap apartment in a town, lying in wait for weeks or months, arresting everyone who came to the door.

She related to him stories she had heard about the Forest Brethren, a revolutionary group of partisans, who had been active in the countryside near Nizhni Novgorod two or three years ago.

When the little girl had led Sherwood and Natalya to the silent building in the midst of the silent upper town of Nizhni Novgorod, almost abandoned now at the season of the fair, a new guide appeared to take charge of the couple. This was a tall man who seemed to have the knack of keeping his face in shadow. He conducted the pair through the darkened ground floor, almost devoid of furniture, into a small room, where they were ordered in a few words and gestures to stand still and be searched.

Sherwood at this point was still carrying the Krag carbine slung over his shoulder. He had been expecting to be relieved of all weapons, and surrendered the carbine without an argument, then submitted to being searched. But he did this with a feeling of relief. Surely, if this were some police trap, it would already have been sprung. And years of hunting in strange places had taught him that once you decided to trust someone to help you, you had better trust them all the way.

Natalya, searched by a woman, had to surrender her pistol, one of the items captured from the bandit gang, which she had been carrying concealed under a shawl.

In a moment another door had opened, a staircase appeared in the light, and their tall guide motioned them up. The man warned them, in excellent French, to watch their steps.

On the second floor another door opened, admitting them abruptly into bright daylight. They entered a large room whose wallpaper strongly suggested that once it had been a nursery. There an elderly, ascetic-looking woman, in a plain gray dress that almost matched the color of her hair, was waiting for them.

While the tall man who had brought the visitors upstairs stood behind them, the elderly woman, who introduced herself as Comrade Svoboda, received them seated behind a workman's bench that served her as an ordinary desk would serve a bureaucrat, and was well lighted by the lowering sun in the windows behind the lady's chair. Her thin hands, almost transparent with age and aristocratic breeding, rested on its surface. Heavy curtains had been pulled completely back. The smooth, broad top of the bench was almost covered with neat stacks of paper, most of them blank sheets, with little pots of ink in a rich variety of colors, with other containers of glue and paste, two racks of pens and pencils, blotters and envelopes of various sizes, and an assortment of rubber stamps.

Speaking in French after Natalya had warned her Sherwood spoke no Russian, she courteously asked her visitors to sit down. Her assistants, shadowy and nameless, seemed to have disappeared.

Comrade Svoboda was tall for one of her sex, and somewhat stooped when at last she stood up from behind her bench.

She began by telling Natalya and Sherwood that she

knew who they were—the couple who had shot a policeman and fled for their lives—and who had now appeared in charge of a trained bear.

She congratulated them in the name of the people! They had earned the praise and gratitude of the workers, the common people, of the whole world. By the single act of killing a policeman, "punishing him directly with the blood of his crimes still red on his hands," they had earned all the help that a true revolutionary could give them.

Having said that much standing behind her worktable, the Gray Comrade now came around in front of it to press her visitors' heroic hands, one at a time, in a grip surprising for its strength, and look closely into their eyes.

Sherwood and Natalya meanwhile had exchanged glances, conveying a silent communication: *If we can't trust this woman, whom can we ever trust?*

Speaking in turn, Natalya translating English when Sherwood's halting French proved inadequate, they told the lady of their hopes to rescue Gregori, as an explanation of their expected need for at least one extra set of false documents beyond what they were going to require for themselves.

Natalya asked: "You knew, Comrade, that we were coming here?"

"I thought that you might appear in Nizhni Novgorod; almost everyone does, sooner or later. You have become a famous couple in important circles. You may be sure that I soon learn of every police dog who is killed."

She had many other skills, but did not speak English. Or simply did not admit to doing so?

The elderly forger began to ask them about the Bear. Her agents had correctly informed her that Natalya was the popular bear trainer called Madam Sarban.

Sherwood in trying to respond, wondered whether Comrade Svoboda was ruthlessly realistic enough to accept the fantastic truth of the Bear? Probably not, though she obviously prided herself on her realism.

Considering Comrade Svoboda's calm rationality, Sherwood choked on his first words when he thought of telling her about the bear Napoleon.

Exchanging looks again with Natalya, he decided they had better not even try, at least not at first. Maybe after they got to know Svoboda better.

In turn, Natalya hinted at the truth and repeated what some people believed about the bear.

"In my family," Natalya said to her, "the old tales of *obaraten* men are taken seriously."

Comrade Svoboda nodded briskly, accepting the point and dismissing it immediately as of no importance. The minds of many peasants were still crammed with these absurd beliefs; more cobwebs that the revolution was going to sweep away. Many in her own family still clung to various superstitions; the upper classes, who encouraged such fantasies among the poor, were not entirely immune.

To both Sherwood and Natalya it seemed obvious that this woman was likely to think them mad if they tried to tell the truth, or would be enraged by their impudence. Every word of her fanatical materialism strongly indicated that she would be totally unable to admit the possibility of were-animals. All were nonsense, along with the whole of religion, and the theory of the imperial right to rule—all must be consigned to the realm of superstition.

She only doubtfully approved of the tactic of spreading superstitious fear among the revolution's enemies.

Already having firmly identified Natalya with the supposed Frenchwoman from the circus, Svoboda asked where the bear was now.

"In a safe place, Comrade."

"It's not dead?" That seemed an accusation.

"Yes, dead!" Natalya put something like defiance in the answer. "We had to dispose of it." She shot a glance at Sherwood that seemed to say it was time to come out with the truth.

The old woman looked at the young one sharply for a moment, then nodded. If *her* agents had been unable to find the animal, it must be in a safe place, indeed.

"I can understand that. Just leaving such an animal tethered or caged somewhere would have created great difficulties."

As soon as they were out of doors again, and free, with the promise that the papers they needed would be created, Natalya explained to Sherwood that the word *svoboda* meant "freedom."

TWENTY

The gray-haired comrade, she who in the struggle for the people had taken the name of *Svoboda*, sat thinking over the story the two young folk had told her. She was willing to believe at least its main points, though she was equally certain that the pair were holding back something of importance. Well, so be it. But from the beginning she had serious doubts that the young woman and the foreigner were being at all practical in their plans to rescue the young woman's brother. Besides, to one steeped in revolutionary theory, it seemed a quixotic and useless goal: the man they had pledged themselves to save from prison and exile sounded like a mere social parasite, an aristocrat beyond salvaging, who would better be left to share the doom his system had inflicted on so many others.

But then Comrade Svoboda reminded herself that she herself had come from a family even more prominent and aristocratic than these Lohmatskis. There was always hope.

Seated again behind her workbench, looking at the couple when they came to her again, she asked gently: "How do you plan to get your brother away from the escort who will certainly be guarding him?"

"That aspect of the matter is already taken care of." Natalya, fearful that she had already said too much, and instinctively rebelling against this mother-figure seeming to try to take over her life, did not translate this exchange for Sherwood.

"So?" The thin shoulders shrugged. "Then you are perfectly right not to discuss it with anyone unnecessarily. Not even with me." Still, there was a touch of coolness in the reply. Every instinct told Svoboda that the couple before her were not double agents. Their shaky knowledge of political theory tended to confirm that. But in their arrogance, brought on, one supposed, by their good fortune in avoiding the police thus far, they were holding back too many things.

Again Natalya translated.

The old woman would have preferred the couple to accept her offer of a secure hiding place until their new papers were ready. But no revolutionary authority had placed this couple under her discipline. She accepted Natalya's protests that they must be able to come and go quite freely.

She also warned the couple that whatever they did, they could not expect any direct help from her in freeing Gregori.

When Sherwood and Natalya elected to leave, she ordered that their firearms be given back to them.

The fair—and indeed the whole vicinity of Nizhni Novgorod—was swarming with agents of the *Okhrana*. And these, as well as the regular police, had received their respective telegraphic orders in code, from headquarters in the capital.

In the local headquarters, at one end of the fairgrounds, one agent grumbled: "Surely they can't hide very well, even among thousands of people. Does this

make any sense to you? An American man and a bear?
It's described as a very big bear."

"One doesn't always expect orders to make sense,"
one of his colleagues reminded him. "Maybe it's
become confused in the decoding. That happens all too
often." Pause. "Are you sure there wasn't a woman
involved?"

"I think that was another case altogether. Do we
have a file on that?"

"Of course we have a file. Altogether too many files."
In every corner of the office, the dusty cabinets were
overflowing.

They received a fresh impetus to action when a
report came in, from one of their many part-time
agents roaming the fairgrounds, that one of the couples
who were being sought had just been spotted.

Dourly, and with no great enthusiasm (being assigned
an important job meant incurring a risk of very noticeable failure) a chosen squad of ten men, led by the most
senior officer who could be ordered to accept the risky
job, went out from their headquarters to make the
arrest.

While planning how to go about this job, the officer
locally in command and his lieutenant discussed their
orders and puzzled over the situation.

"Can you tell me, Vladimir Ignatovich, is it one
couple or two couples that headquarters wants us to
find?"

"I don't know."

"Well, is it one American or two? And how many
bears are involved?"

The commander scowled. "I tell you I don't know.
And they don't like it at headquarters if we complain
that their coded messages are garbled. Probably they'll
be satisfied, as usual, if we at least arrest someone." He
brightened momentarily. "I think we can safely assume
that there is only the one bear."

Trying to follow the dictates of headquarters as best
they could, the commander and his lieutenant made

their plans. Their secret orders were to capture or kill Natalya and Sherwood, while their orders regarding the woman and her bear were even stranger.

After a serious discussion with his lieutenant, the local police commander had decided to arrest the man and woman at dusk. What was the use of waiting around? If the bear ever showed up, they meant to cage it, in accordance with instructions, as soon as they could do so without provoking a great disturbance among the crowd. Meanwhile, one officer had already been dispatched to seek among the fairground merchants for a suitable cage, and requisition it. At any other time and place, that might well have seemed like an impossible assignment; but at the fair at Nizhni Novgorod, everything imaginable was routinely offered for sale, along with a number of things that seemed beyond imagination. It never occurred to anyone familiar with the fair that a bear cage might be unobtainable.

"Why not simply shoot the beast?" one junior policeman whispered to his colleague.

"Orders." The other shrugged. "They say it's wanted alive, as some kind of evidence."

At a signal from their officer, a dozen police closed in on the unlucky couple from all sides. The arrest would have been easier with fewer bystanders swarming around and getting in the way, but at fair time there was really no way around that problem.

Once the commanding officer had his men deployed, he himself stepped forward, raising his arm in a gesture of command, and with a voice of authority called on Natalya Ivanovna, under her true name, to give herself up.

The bogus Frenchwoman made no attempt to resist. Instead she peaceably, and without any great appearance of surprise, raised her hands in apparent surrender.

Meanwhile her male companion promptly vanished, among stacks of exotic merchandise. It looked as if she had seen the police coming, after all.

But hardly had the man disappeared when the bear came into sight, stalking out from between two piles of

Persian carpets. And when it first appeared, it seemed quite docile.

But this time the totally unexpected cleverness displayed by the bear—an initial appearance of docility, followed by a treacherous outbreak of roaring rage—coupled with its overwhelming physical power, foiled their enemies.

As long as the police remained poised, hands on gun butts, to quell resistance, the bear looked meek as a kitten. As if in testimony to its mild temper, Napoleon was unencumbered by any physical means of control—the beast wasn't even wearing a muzzle or a collar. But this deceptive behavior lasted just long enough to put the officer and his men off their guard, as if the beast were capable of reading the subtle signs of human intentions as easily as it smelled food.

Then, with a bloodcurdling roar, dropping instantaneously its pose of meek innocence, it attacked the men in uniform so fiercely that Natalya was able to get away.

The woman also played her part superbly and managed to avoid arrest by darting into the crowd just as the bear's attack exploded. By the time any of the police were free to look for her again, she had completely vanished among the thousands of fairgoers.

As some dozens of those onlookers who happened to be nearest the violence went scattering away in terror, even greater numbers from a little distance away came running, crowding in to see what all the disturbance was about.

Sober witnesses were later found quite prepared to swear that the supposed Frenchwoman had tucked up her skirts and leapt astride the animal, and had ridden bear-back into the water, clinging to the heavy fur of her galloping mount with both hands, by this means escaping at twice the speed at which any policeman on foot could chase her. Such a tactic might well have put the woman in increased danger because the police would be shooting at the bear. Of course, in general they were poor shots, and by that time at least the great majority of them were no longer firing their guns at anything, either having been knocked down and chewed up or having chosen to run away themselves.

Natalya and Sherwood rejoiced that they had earlier made plans to follow should the police attempt to arrest them. Of course, a variety of plans were actually required, depending on when and where the attempt to arrest them was made.

Having been carried into the water on the bear's back, Natalya had to put up with wet clothing for a while on her emergence. Clinging to Sherwood's fur, she rested while he helped her swim all the way to the far bank of an untenanted small island.

Not until after dark, almost an hour after the attempted arrest, when most of the excitement had died down, did she return on bear-back to the river-bank on the same side as the fair. There her first act was to steal a dry peasant dress which had been left on the bank by some other woman swimmer. Then she went to pick up clothing they had had the forethought to hide away for Sherwood.

After carrying Natalya away, the bear returned to the near shore, where he kept the police occupied for a time. Once more being surrounded, and despite having been riddled with bullets (witnesses aplenty were available to testify to this) the beast broke easily through the lines of those trying to head him off, and plunged again into the river.

In the water this time the bear went out of his way to upset a small boat or two, so the river locally became a thrashing whirlpool of desperate swimmers. Under cover of this turmoil, the bear changed back into a man underwater, and then the man bobbed to the surface to join other bystanders in their excited effort to avoid the deadly animal.

Of course, the police had boats in the vicinity, but darkness had fallen before they could be mobilized, and it was hopeless to attempt to search the river at night.

A couple of bystanders had been wounded by stray police bullets. None of the officials involved paid much attention to the fact, except to blame those shootings on the woman who had got away.

The officer corrected his lieutenant. Neither woman nor animal had escaped; both had succumbed to a hail of well-aimed bullets. "If we can't recover their bodies, well, we can't—that's all."

"Sir, the actual orders were to take the bear alive."

"I can't help that." A shrug. "Sometimes what an order says, and what the people who wrote it really want, are two different things. Tell you what; take out the bit about 'well-aimed.' Emphasize that it must have been really the woman's own pistol shot that must have killed the bear."

A couple of hours later, when Natalya and Sherwood were both finally out of the water, clothed in dry garments, and they felt confident that no one was following them, they made their way, by a roundabout route, to the upper town. From there they once more managed to get in touch with Comrade Svoboda.

Already news of the Bear's latest victory had spread. Like most stories, this one was traveling in several versions, some of them closer to the truth than others. But all variations agreed that one or more police had been severely injured, perhaps killed, in the struggle with the bear—and by one or more pistol shots fired by the woman.

When the young couple stood once more before Comrade Svoboda, she at first accused them of having lied to her about the bear. But she finally accepted their explanation: they had left the animal with someone who solemnly promised to shoot it and dispose of the body, but then had not kept the promise.

Obviously one thing concerning the Bear that Comrade Svoboda was resolutely refusing even to consider,

was the truth—and she persisted in this attitude even
after a couple of her own subordinates later proved
superstitious enough, and foolhardy enough, to suggest it to her.

Meanwhile she openly admired the skill with which
the animal had evidently been trained, and she
hoped—to those near her it almost seemed that she
prayed—that its masters, whoever they might be,
would succeed in once more escaping the police.

When Maxim got the report of the fiasco at the fair
later that night, (he had been waiting for the news in
the police telegraph station in Petersburg) he put out
an alarm to all his remaining agents, especially those in
southwestern Siberia, to be on the lookout for any performing bears that demonstrated any tricks or abilities
out of the ordinary.

Of course the official report of the police, which he
did not believe for a moment, said that both bear and
woman had been shot dead, their bodies unfortunately washed away in the swift-flowing Volga. That
way, of course, the fools on the scene would claim
success.

In Maxim's mind, no doubt now remained that Sherwood had now become an *obaraten* like himself. That
confirmation was not unexpected. The question that
nagged at Maxim was: what in hell were his sister,
along with the American-turned-Bear, doing in Nizhni
Novgorod? Maxim had more or less assumed they
would be heading for Petersburg, in hopes of getting
out of the country.

Back in his office, paying a last visit before departing
on the tour of inspection he had agreed to undertake
for Stolypin, he went at once to look at his maps. From
the place where the outlaws had been massacred,
Nizhni Novgorod was, of course, practically in the
opposite direction from the capital. But the city with
the famous fair lay directly on the route most often

traveled by prisoners, including Gregori, who were being sent to Siberia.

It occurred to Maxim that the fugitives, relying on the power of the were-bear, might well be trying to rescue Gregori—he himself had told them, in a general way, where his brother was going to be—and it occurred to him that with such an advantage, they might succeed. He would certainly have to take steps to prevent that.

Some who saw the decoded form of Maxim's latest orders, dealing with a dangerous bear and a wandering Frenchwoman, assumed that they were doubly coded, with "bear" and "Frenchwoman" mere symbols for people somehow too important to be named directly.

And now Maxim, walking on his two thin human legs, without even his cane, was actually boarding a train on the first leg of the journey secretly planned to take him to Padarok Sivera, in northern Siberia.

In man-form he still limped slightly, but what the hell! Excitement helped deaden the persistent soreness. He was quite ready to travel now, and his real crippling, like the special strength that it negated, was still hidden from the world.

Maxim had done his best to arrange, indirectly, to have his brother's term of exile served somewhere near the Siberian estate of which he—Gregori—was really the rightful owner. That appealed irresistibly to Maxim's sense of humor.

He had to assume that Colonel Zagarin, whom Maxim had never met face to face, but who was rapidly emerging as his chief rival for advancement in the Ministry, knew that Gregori Lohmatski was now a captive in the prison system. The colonel was going to try to get his hands on his rival's brother.

Well, Maxim knew what to do about that.

What he ought to do about Colonel Zagarin himself was quite another question. But it was indeed beginning to seem that action was going to be necessary.

As report after report came in to Comrade Svoboda from her own local people, corroborating the story brought by the two fugitives, she waxed ecstatic at the casualties inflicted by the trained bear on the police, who had been trying to arrest its trainer.

She was almost equally elated by the escape of the people she had sworn to help. Her doubts about their capabilities were much diminished, swept away almost completely.

The loss of the bear, of course, was to be regretted, like that of any effective fighter for the cause. Another crime for which the enemy must someday be made to pay. But whether the loss was of a human or an animal, it was necessary to close ranks and press forward. Ultimately the individual counted for nothing; it was only the cause, the fulfillment of historic destiny, which mattered.

Behind her workbench, the Gray Comrade redoubled her efforts to help Sherwood and Natalya.

She ran through her list of possible contacts, people who might be able to aid them in one way or another. Comrade Svoboda was ready and able to provide a pair of swift horses for the heroic couple's escape; but, after discussion among the three of them, that idea was rejected in favor of disguise, superb documents, and railroad travel.

Completely reoutfitting oneself in new clothing was certainly easier at the great fair than it would have been anywhere else, even in Moscow or Petersburg. Especially now that the revolutionary contact sought out by Natalya had proven to be fanatically devoted to the cause, and miraculously helpful.

Yes, one could buy at this amazing fair just about anything one was willing to pay for. It was a carnival, a giant marketplace, an ongoing marvel which even foreigners—at least those who knew what they were talking about—rightly praised as one of the great wonders of the world. Good evidence for that lay in the fact that the police now found themselves in possession of a bear's cage they didn't need, and the price of which would be a difficult item to explain on their budget.

In fact, at Nizhni Novgorod, one could find almost anything one could imagine. And, year after year, a few things even beyond that.

TWENTY-ONE

~

Three days passed while the fugitives remained in hiding. Well fed and well sheltered, Sherwood and Natalya under the guidance of Comrade Svoboda and her aides occupied a succession of otherwise-untenanted small houses in the nearly deserted upper town, spending no more than half a day in each. Once, in the middle of the night, in response to a warning from some unknown source, the couple were awakened and transferred hastily to a different dwelling. Whatever had triggered the midnight relocation must have been a false alarm; for as far as they could tell, no search came through the neighborhood.

Their only real problem during this interval was an earnest discourse on the necessity of revolutionary Free Love, presented to the two new comrades by three unwashed revolutionaries, two male and one female, who obviously lusted after Natalya. Sherwood reacted with quiet—if reactionary—ferocity, and Natalya with icy disdain. The subject was quickly dropped.

During this three-day interval, while Sherwood and Natalya did little but kill time, the Gray Comrade and her shadowy assistants, working steadily and secretly in their attics and cellars, completed the preparation of new clothing and forged papers. The passage of three days also guaranteed that the police would have begun to lose whatever edge of alertness they might have acquired in their pursuit of the dangerous Frenchwoman and her bear.

Sherwood without really thinking about it had expected this small illegal shop to have serious problems in providing so many elaborate documents on short notice—but in fact this well-equipped establishment kept on hand a comprehensive stock of stolen or illegally printed credentials, even a small printing press, turning out forms which required only the bearer's name and description to be filled in. The necessary official signatures were already forged and seals affixed.

Sherwood and Natalya also had taken advantage of the master forger's skill and generosity to obtain from her a third internal passport, eventually to be used by Gregori, under the assumption that they would somehow be able to set him free. The spaces for the bearer's name had been left blank, to be filled in as needed when the time came. So had those for personal description, because, as Comrade Svoboda briskly reminded them, their Gregori Ivanovich might well have changed during the long weeks he'd already spent in custody. People did change when they spent time in prison, particularly when their guards and cellmates alike were likely to be murderers.

A fourth internal passport was readied as a spare, insurance against unforeseen contingencies.

The old forger, Comrade Svoboda, sat frowning and glaring at her visitors (though she was extremely proud of them) while she kept working—at night in front of heavily-blacked-out windows, and under the latest in electric light. Most of Nizhni Novgorod was yet to be electrified, but the Freedom Comrade enjoyed a connection to a steam-engine generator half a mile away (when that was unavailable, the steam-engine's place was taken by dedicated, hardworking fanatics pedaling fixed bicycles, connected to a much smaller generator in the next room)—worked, and muttered fanatical revolutionary litanies.

And as she worked, brushing back again and again a strand of gray hair that kept swinging before her eyes, she never tired of hearing the story of how the police had been defeated at the fairgrounds, and at least one of their number killed. She was especially eager for any evidence suggesting there might have been more.

Still it bothered her somewhat that the untidy bear was back, after having been reported dead. Success had depended upon this creature, whose very existence seemed irrational, tainted by superstition.

The only part of the official story to which the Comrade Forger was ready to grant unqualified belief concerned the bear: that the beast had been riddled with bullets by the police, and it had drowned and been swept away in the river.

Natalya and Sherwood were quietly agreed that the Bear had better stay completely out of sight for the foreseeable future. An exception would be contemplated only in an extreme emergency.

Whether or not the massacre of an obscure outlaw band thousands of versts from Nizhni Novgorod had ever been taken seriously by the police—indeed, whether they had ever noticed it at all—was very doubtful; but certainly the outcome of this latest fight, in which the police themselves had been mangled, would get the attention of every constable and militiaman between the Polish border and Vladivostok. All must now be alerted and watching for the Bear.

And that afternoon Sherwood went boldly out into the sunlight again, carrying his suitcase across the platform and through the waiting room of the railroad station in Nizhni Novgorod. Here he experienced his first chance in what seemed like years to see himself in a mirror. His most recent opportunity, at the fair, had

come when he had been a bear—and bears looked
much more alike than people did.

This time he beheld a scarred and bearded face,
whose nationality he thought would be hard to determine. He could discover no reason to think that it
belonged to an American. It was the visage of a man
well over thirty, a man in whom vast inward transformation had left its signature in modest permanent outward change.

After a moment's shock, he decided with relief, and a
tinge of wonder, that a casual observer would have pronounced his countenance entirely human.

In a bad light, the scars on the left side of his forehead
might escape observation altogether. But in healing
they had contracted slightly, subtly changing the ten-
sion of the skin and flesh around his eyes, the left eye
more than the right, turning him asymmetrical and
giving him something of an oriental look. He was now
more evenly sunburnt than before, although he was
wearing a Russian gentleman's broad-brimmed white
summer hat. In anticipation of the Siberian weather,
he had also been provided with a fur hat. But it was
packed away.

Having done for the moment with studying his own
face—in fact, he was beginning to be afraid to study it
any longer—Sherwood looked down, as he now caught
himself doing quite often, at the backs of his hands.
The dark hair there grew no more thickly than it had
before he came to Russia. His hands, like the rest of his
body (as far as he could tell) were no less human.

He found it necessary to keep assuring himself, with
disconcerting frequency, that he had suffered no permanent change. Having resumed at will the form of
humanity, he was still as human as he had ever been.
The nagging question, of course, was whether he would
even realize the fact if there actually was a difference. . . .

No, he certainly didn't *feel* any less human than
before, however the Change was effected. . . .

Looking at the people around him out on the railroad
platform, the usual self-preoccupied faces to be observed

anywhere, Sherwood wondered which of them if any might know the Secret, as he knew it. He was ready now to believe the stories of werewolves. Look at that prosperous matron now, traveling with her small pet parrot in a cage. . . .

Trying out his rudimentary Russian, he offered to help a woman with her luggage, and was disconcerted when she swung her handbag at him.

Natalya, who had been standing at a little distance as if they were not together, hurried to his rescue. An incident drawing the attention of everyone else on the platform was averted only narrowly.

As soon as they could talk without being overheard, she hissed at him under her breath: "Do you know what you said to that woman? I had a terrible time convincing her you meant no harm."

"I was *trying* to say I was a porter. You know, just meaning to convey, with my limited vocabulary, that I wanted to be helpful—"

"Oh, very helpful! What you *said* was: 'I am a rapist.'"

He strolled the platform away from Natalya. But at the moment they were once more pretending not to know each other, avoiding immediate identification as a couple. No wonder the rebels had wanted to assign her one job after another. She was good at this kind of thing; once their eyes met, and it was as if they were perfect strangers to each other.

It was a hot day in what he estimated must be early July, and he was elegantly dressed in a pale summer suit as some kind of foreign businessman, very likely Swiss, waiting for the train to Tomsk, smoking a cigar and inspecting the summer haze over a distant curve of river. The piercing blasts of steamboat whistles, somewhat more distant, vied with the similar shrilling of a train. What were people doing in America now that the Fourth of July had come around? No doubt, what they

always did. But no, he was forgetting the official calendar difference of thirteen days.

Police came on to the platform now, half a dozen of
them at least in their dress uniforms, and began
moving up and down, in and out of the station,
checking papers in desultory fashion and examining
some baggage. These, Sherwood noted with some
relief, seemed to be only the ordinary police—he had
come a long way in being able to interpret uniforms—
and were therefore probably not very sharp.

When they stopped in front of him, he handed over
his forged papers and waited in silence, casually
smoking his small cigar. When one of them made some
routine comment, he responded in French, and fortunately one of them understood that language. If he
had to Change here . . . he couldn't let himself think
about it, for fear of bringing on the very transformation he now dreaded.

Think about something else.

The first-class carriages of the train they were about
to board, now waiting on the eastbound line, were
blue, the second-class yellow, and the third-class green.

With a strange mixture of feelings he remembered
his first Russian train trip, with Gregori. And Natalya.
It seemed impossible that that journey had taken place
only two months ago.

Today his papers were accepted with boredom, and
returned to him the same way.

Sherwood and Natalya could afford to travel first-
class to Tomsk, or all the way to Irkutsk. But they had
to stop en route, perhaps at a number of places, to look
for Gregori.

Of course it might have been more secure in third
class, where no one would be looking for the Frenchwoman Madame Sarban, or even for Natalya Ivanovna
Lohmatskaia, and certainly not for a wealthy American
big-game hunter.

Fortunately, at the time of their flight from Padarok
Lessa, Sherwood had been carrying a fairly large sum

of money in his pockets, primarily in an inner pocket of the hunting vest where he had packed away a good supply of American dollars as well as rubles. He had had with him almost a thousand rubles, each worth about half a dollar. In the long run, of course, they would need some way to support themselves while they traveled. Both of them had a repugnance for begging. Of course a bear act as good as theirs, at the great fair of Nizhni Novgorod, had not failed to bring in quite a lot of coin—although they did not manage to hang on to it through their mad escape from the police. Most of that money had been lost.

By this time both fugitives, but Natalya in particular, had gone through several changes of clothing. The man was no longer wearing a single garment that had come to Russia with John Sherwood of Ohio. Sherwood's baggage and that of his companion now represented quite an interesting variety of clothing, and if it should ever be searched by an enemy of any intelligence they were probably both done for. For example, should Natalya choose at some point to play the part of an emigrating peasant, she could wear a skirt and then wrap her legs in leggings under it, as the peasant women sometimes did.

But they were dealing with the problem of suspicious incongruity by stowing away the peasant garments in a carpetbag strongly suggesting poverty. If the police should take an interest in it, easy enough to say: "Why no, that one's not ours. How did it get in here?"

Even after buying two first-class railroad tickets, Sherwood was still carrying a substantial sum of money.

Traveling separately from Natalya would deprive him of his translator—in emergency, if she were nearby, she might come forward and volunteer, as a helpful stranger.

Natalya had for a time considered putting on the guise of an Englishwoman headed for her new employment as a governess. No one in the vicinity was likely to have the ear for English necessary to discover that she did not really sound like the person she pretended to be. But of course some native English speaker might be encountered.

Anyone in Russia going anywhere by rail could expect to have his or her papers inspected at least once. Several times, if the journey was of any considerable distance. Even in the line of people waiting to buy tickets. They might persuade and pay some peasants to buy third-class tickets for them.

Soon, without incident, Sherwood and Natalya boarded the eastbound train. Some minutes later, after the usual unexplained delay, the engine snorted steam, belched smoke and sparks, and jerked like a weight lifter at the burden of its cars. After a minute of repeated jerks and stumblings they were under way.

Eventually, after four days and as many nights of lurching progress and maddening delay (getting on toward the middle of July) including scores of intervening stops and pauses, where passengers bought food from private vendors at the stations, their train dragged them to their intermediate destination, which lay some two thousand miles east of Nizhni Novgorod: this, coming into view as the sun appeared over the ever-retreating eastern horizon, was the city of Tomsk.

Clearly this was one railroad line the tsar had not drawn on a map with a straightedge; but even as the crow might fly, it had covered an impressive distance.

All the more impressive when Sherwood considered that they had not yet come halfway across Siberia.

At times during their exhausting journey, especially when they were tired and tempted by despair, Natalya and Sherwood indulged in dreams of a glorious future, which was coming to seem increasingly improbable: Once they had done whatever they could for Gregori, ideally having set him at liberty, then separately or together all three might find some way out of the country to safety.

Natalya was aware that according to the law of the

United States, she would become an American citizen by marrying Sherwood.

"There's no doubt about that, is there?"

"Absolutely none."

No doubt it would be difficult to find an Orthodox clergyman to perform a ceremony for a couple of refugees, one of them a Protestant and a foreigner. Natalya reminded her companion that the established church in Russia was very much a part of the system of government.

"There must be other kinds of marriages. When we got to America, I'd want to have a document of some kind, so there wouldn't be any trouble proving you were my wife."

Of course, to be useful, the marriage certificate would have to carry the couple's real names.

"I think I shall like it in America."

"You will. You certainly will."

"What shall we do there?"

"Walk the streets of the cities and look into the display windows of the stores. And I will buy you anything you want." And he contributed, whatever his imagination could come up with, to a pleasing fantasy. They were strolling under shady summer trees, and eating ice cream.

"And will you be going off on another one of your trips, to hunt animals in some distant land?"

"Huh?" For a moment he really didn't understand what she was talking about.

In whispered conversation, he and Natalya tried to draw encouragement from the thought that some time in the last month Gregori had almost certainly traveled this same line. They did not dwell on the fact that his journey would certainly have taken place under vastly different circumstances—on a convict train, under conditions which would make even the third-class carriages look like luxury.

TWENTY-TWO

Tomsk was a sizable city, a bustling place which offered upper-class travelers a choice of good hotels. But in Russia, as Sherwood had discovered weeks ago, the outward signs of quality gave no guarantee against vermin.

He and Natalya obtained a suite of rooms in one of the better hotels, confidently surrendering their forged proofs of identity to the desk clerk for the duration of their stay, as was required of all guests. Since they had arrived in Tomsk in the guise of prosperous travelers, and had no private lodging awaiting them, they thought any other course would be likely to attract attention.

Eavesdropping on other travelers in the lobby and dining room, Sherwood received the impression that a considerable number of relatives of the condemned were putting up briefly in Tomsk, while making an effort to achieve some kind of contact with their unfortunate loved ones.

Natalya, in her year-long immersion in the political underworld, had heard that this town was full of tricky agents and would-be go-betweens, men and women who promised, in exchange for sometimes extravagant fees, to obtain, for worried relatives and lovers, the information they desperately wanted about prisoners. Many of these helpful people were government informers.

Newspapers, in this city connected by telegraph and railway to the great world, offered some news of world events. It seemed that two American bicycle mechanics, brothers named Wright, had been demonstrating their heavier-than-air flying machine in Europe this summer.

The obvious place to begin their search for Gregori was the huge Forwarding Prison, near the edge of town. Natalya's secondhand knowledge of the penal system had convinced her that each and every convict and exile destined to central or eastern Siberia passed through these gates.

She had heard also that it was possible in most cases to learn, simply by asking one of the clerks in the prison office, whether a particular prisoner was inside, or had already been processed through. Tentative questioning of a few citizens in the vicinity of the prison indicated that this was indeed so, at least in the case of ordinary prisoners, given the usual payment of a small bribe to some underpaid member of the bureaucracy.

"All that you really learn that way, or course, is whether there is a prisoner answering to a particular name." On thinking it over, she decided that the risk of entering the office was too great.

After standing uncertainly with Sherwood for a while outside the high gray prison walls, Natalya drew him away from the stream of passersby, to a vantage point from which it was possible to see for more than a mile or more down the straight, busy street. There, with a cautious nod in the direction of the unpaved road that stretched ahead of them, she informed him in a low voice that this was the very highway along which the prisoner convoys always marched away. The dusty lines of ruts failed to impress Sherwood as much of a highway, but then he had yet to see the Russian road that did. About a verst from where he stood with Natalya, this road left the town behind, running on between green fields of summer crops, dwindling and dwindling until it nudged at the horizon—that ever-present flat Siberian horizon, which was beginning to give Sherwood the sense of being on an ocean voyage.

During her time on the lower levels of St. Petersburg society, Natalya had heard several of the older revolutionaries describe the ordeal of transportation at considerable length. She could describe the procedures and the difficulties.

"There are *étapes*, rest houses—though that is hardly an accurate name for them—spaced about twenty-five versts apart, all along the way to Irkutsk, a thousand miles. Ordinarily the prisoners march for two days, and then rest in one of the *étapes*, for one. The shoes they are issued generally wear through before they have walked a hundred miles, while the manufacturers and the corrupt officials enrich themselves. The unfortunate ones in their leg irons spend three months, trudging from here to Irkutsk. Those who are too old or too ill to walk are hauled along in little open carts. A great many die along the way, as you might imagine."

"What happens in the winter?"

"What would you expect? The system keeps going the year around, chewing up people. No doubt a higher percentage die in winter."

Sherwood murmured something inadequate. The Russian prison system sounded to him like a monument to utter foolishness. But at least monumental stupidity in your enemies was more heartening than efficiency.

Natalya had turned away from him, and was now approaching an old man who came herding his little flock of geese along the dusty street. The fellow seemed about the least likely candidate for government agent Sherwood had ever seen. Following Natalya, he managed to understand several words of the questions she put to the old man in Russian. She was asking when the next prisoner convoy was scheduled to leave.

"Convoy? Convoy?" The ancient laughed at them, his face dissolving into a mass of wrinkles. "Ten years and more have gone by since the unfortunates had to wear themselves out walking. Now they are privileged to go by train. Someone's been telling you tall tales, young lady."

Natalya blushed, reluctantly translating the man's remarks for Sherwood as the couple walked away. For just a moment, for the first time in Sherwood's memory, she seemed to be near tears.

Trying to keep up her spirits, he squeezed her arm. "Come on, Nellie. So, some of your information is too old to be useful. Well, that's only to be expected; it can't be helped. What do we do now?"

With an effort Natalya pulled herself together. "We wait, as we waited in Nizhni Novgorod. Try somehow to gather the information we must have."

Fortunately, they were still carrying the equivalent of several hundred dollars, divided about equally between dollars and rubles. Sherwood hesitated about spending the dollars, not wanting to reveal himself as an American. Spending little time in their hotel, they loitered around town, listening and learning. On the first afternoon in Tomsk, they heard that there was a glut of prisoners, the harvest of drastic government measures which so far had kept simmering revolution from boiling over.

After one night in the high-class hotel, Natalya and Sherwood moved to less-expensive lodgings. They spent money grudgingly, determined to hold a sizable fund in reserve, against the day when it would be necessary to bribe someone—or several people, if necessary, to find out if a particular prisoner was indeed now in the Forwarding Prison. Also they wanted to know where and when Gregori was going next, whether he was scheduled for convoy or train transportation.

The only safe assumption was that by now the police had received orders to arrest anyone making inquiries about Gregori Ivanovich Lohmatski.

Natalya was bitter. "We must assume that Maxim continues to take a personal interest in Gregori's welfare."

Back at the fair in Nizhni Novgorod, the police had called Natalya by her real name when they were trying to arrest her. Obviously, they had known whom they were after.

In Tomsk, afraid to say or do anything that would even hint at their own identities, the couple considered bribing someone to show them the list of all men currently being held.

Better still would be the list of the men's names going out on the next train. And the next train after that, and so on.

The bribery was successful; it seemed almost routine. Gregori's name was on the list of those scheduled to be shipped out in the next batch.

Maxim, having departed St. Petersburg by rail, on the first leg of his northern tour of inspection, was traveling with a single military orderly, and a servant to see to his personal wants. He and his modest entourage were to stop at almost all the police stations along the way. He had already visited several, and in each had gone dutifully through the motions of inspection. It was pleasant to see the local officials petrified in his presence, and trying to think up newer and more subtle ways to offer him bribes; but his thoughts were elsewhere, and he could not really enjoy the situation to the full.

The railroad took him east for a thousand versts or so; the next two or three stages of his journey were accomplished by riverboat.

At his latest stop, reading between the telegraphed reports on the recent fiasco at the fair, he had alerted a

loyal *Okhrana* agent at Tomsk, where there were so
many loyal agents that he had a choice, to be on the
lookout for Natalya and Sherwood, either as a human
couple or as a woman with a bear.

He was too experienced in the ways of the corrupt
bureaucracy to put any faith in the official reports that
both woman and bear had been shot dead, their bodies
lost in the Volga's great moving tide. That was what the
local police would naturally say, in an effort to protect
themselves. But Maxim knew with certainty that this
particular bear was never going to be killed with ordinary bullets.

Over the last few months, the name of a certain
Colonel Zagarin, his colleague in the Ministry, and a
man of approximately equal rank, although stationed
in Irkutsk, had become more and more familiar to
Maxim as that of a potential rival.

Maxim could only suppose that Zagarin was seeing
the same reports, concerning the fact that Maxim's two
siblings were in trouble with the law—and also concerning the wonderful bear.

So far the colonel and Maxim had avoided even a
direct exchange of telegrams. They continued sparring
at a distance.

Bursting into the small rented room she shared with
Sherwood, Natalya awoke him from a doze. Leaning
over the couch where he was lying, she spoke in a
fierce whisper: "Sherwood! I was right about the convoys after all!"

Eagerness restored, she hastened to supply details.
The authorities, struggling to cope with record numbers of prisoners, the threatened breakdown of a railroad burdened with terrorist acts of sabotage as well
as bureaucracy and corruption, had reverted temporarily to the nineteenth-century methods of prisoner
transport.

"Do you know what Lenin is supposed to have said?

He had to go into exile—I mean, out of the country—a year ago."

"Who's Lenin?"

"Never mind. He's a revolutionary."

"I figured that."

"He said that so many people are being arrested, and will be in the next few years, that the government will literally have no place to put them all. Not enough trains or carts or wagons to transport them all to Siberia. I'm beginning to think he's right."

"Of course," Natalya added, "the mere fact that an exile has been ordered to a particular destination does not mean that he will actually arrive there; identities are confused, sometimes by accident, sometimes deliberately by the prisoners themselves. The penal system, like everything else in Russia, works slowly and poorly when it works at all."

"Would Gregori try to change identities with someone else?"

"Ordinarily that would be a mistake for a political prisoner. But in his case it might be very wise."

At a busy pawnshop in the middle of the city, Natalya bought a good pair of field glasses in a leather case. While they were there, Sherwood picked up a few other items, including the map he'd wanted for so long, weapons, and a compass that seemed likely to prove useful. His three silver-tipped cartridges were still packed away securely in the ammunition loops of his hunting vest.

Then the two of them improvised an observation post near the prison, climbing to an upper-story window of an empty building, from which they would be able to observe the next convoy of prisoners as it made ready to set out on foot. "We can't be sure whether they are marching all the way, or only to the railroad station."

Obviously a violent attack on the convoy, culminating in a rescue, would require some advance planning, even when one possessed the strength and near-invulnerability of a *medved*, wedded to human intelligence.

One of the larger problems was how the three of them might get away when Gregori had been set free. Besides the new papers, new clothes for Greg would be required, and an extra horse.

Now that Gregori had been more than a month in one prison or another, living on wretched food, lacking exercise and exposed to maltreatment, it was not possible simply to assume that he would still be in good health. Therefore they investigated the possibility of boats as an alternate means of transportation.

"Unfortunately, boats become useful only when there is adequate water on hand. For example, if we were going north down the Ob—it goes all the way from here to the Arctic Ocean. . . ."

They studied the map. Before coming to Russia, Sherwood had never dreamed that its rivers were so many, and that so many of them could be so huge.

"By the way where's Padarok Sivera?"

"Somewhere far to the north." But Natalya wasn't sure just where; her small fingers, moving tentatively, brushed at the white spaces on the map, where land and ocean seemed to blur into an Arctic nothingness. The white spaces were enormous.

Nezvedani. Unexplored.

It was also necessary to choose a destination—to have a goal in mind—before Greg was set free.

Petersburg was one possibility. Returning to the capital from here would mean a long difficult journey, but certainly not an impossible one. Once near St. Petersburg, it should be comparatively easy to slip over the border, or else out to sea, and reach Finland by either means.

Weeks ago, on that night at the abandoned estate near Padarok Lessa, the coming of the Bear had forever removed them from the ordinary world. In the expanded universe where Sherwood and Natalya now dwelt, the mere freeing of a prisoner from among dozens of armed guards seemed nothing to be marveled at.

"There's no use making an attempt here, so near the prison. The whole area is swarming with police and soldiers."

If necessary, the Bear, impervious to ordinary gunfire, could methodically destroy the entire escort. But how to pick out the man they were trying to save from the mass of doubly terrorized prisoners? Gregori would have not the faintest idea that a giant bear was coming to rescue him.

Natalya and Sherwood considered smuggling a note to Gregori beforehand. It might well be possible to bribe some peasant woman or child to pass it to him, under the guise of selling eggs or whatever, when the prisoners had been brought out to be marched away.

But after agonizing thought, they rejected the idea as too dangerous.

To watch the prisoners' departure, Natalya and Sherwood concealed themselves about a block away from the Forwarding Prison high up in their observation post. With their new binoculars, they examined the prisoners in this convoy, when it started out on the long march.

"My God, I think some of them are branded."

And indeed, a few of the older convicts still bore on their faces the small branded "K" for *katorga*, meaning hard labor, indicating that they had been sentenced at some time before the turn of the century. The practice of branding had officially been discontinued generations earlier, in the 1840s; but like other cruelties had persisted for a long time in out-of-the-way corners of the vast penal system.

Natalya was too excited at first to hold the glasses steady, and Sherwood took a turn. His eyes were somewhat keener than hers anyway, and he was more accustomed to using field glasses.

Scarcely had he begun to look when he exclaimed:

"There he is!" The familiar figure was unmistakable, though his head was shaved on one side like all the others, and he was wearing the prison uniform. This included a dull gray jacket with a yellow diamond sewn into the back, and a gray Scottish-looking cap without a visor. The cap was removed when an underofficer came by to make sure one side of each man's head—whether the left or right side did not seem to matter—was newly shaved.

"Are you sure?"

"No doubt about it." And Sherwood handed over the glasses.

Natalya found her brother, and feasted her eyes on him. "But he is pale and thin—Sherwood, this is our lucky chance. The best chance to break him loose that we're likely to get anywhere. We've got to take advantage of it."

Taking another turn, Sherwood stared through the glasses, with wonder, at an unfortunate who was cradling a small pet mongrel dog in one arm. Evidently that man intended to march, carrying the animal with him, for at least a thousand miles.

The prison blacksmith arrived, burly assistants behind him wheeling into position a small portable forge and anvil, a hammer or two, and a whole armload of spare chains and fetters. These technicians made sure that every prisoner's legs were chained securely together at the ankle. One or two had their present leg irons methodically replaced.

In bustling and accommodating Tomsk, there was no problem hiring a carriage and driver for a planned trip of several days; evidently, there was a regular demand for such among the well-to-do businessmen who traveled between east and west in considerable numbers.

Renting a carriage without a driver would have been more difficult, and might have drawn the notice of the police.

It was relatively easy for Sherwood to play the part of a businessman from Switzerland; he had taken advantage of the time in Tomsk to have some cards printed, proclaiming himself the representative of a mining company, albeit one who spoke only a few words of Russian. Natalya of course fell easily into the role of the businessman's secretary/mistress/interpreter, accompanying him east. The ride, almost certainly in an unsprung vehicle, over the eternally unpaved roads, would certainly be at least as grueling as third class on the train. But of course a mining executive is interested in minerals and land and timber, and no satisfactory survey of these matters can be taken from a train.

Two or three months from now, when the snow and cold appeared in earnest, it would of course be necessary to switch to a sled.

Getting rid of their driver, when they were a dozen versts out of town, posed no serious problem. It was simply a matter of making vodka available. As soon as the man was good and drunk the couple simply abandoned him and drove away—then, riding swiftly over back roads and lanes, sometimes across fields and pastures, easily outdistanced the convoy of prisoners in which Gregori was included.

It seemed a practical impossibility that they should have to worry about ambushing the wrong convoy. The shipments of human refuse traveled a day or two apart on the long road between Tomsk and Irkutsk.

When Sherwood and Natalya had regained the main road, and reached what they thought was an ideal place to set their ambush, they ditched their carriage too, and waited to intercept the convoy on a relatively deserted stretch of dusty road, where it passed through a sizable patch of forest.

They were sure the convoy would come to this spot, next to an *étape*—Natalya said this was one of the smaller ones, a "half–rest house," or *polu-étape*. This was a collection of red-roofed buildings surrounded by a wooden palisade, whose wooden gates were now standing open. Obviously the place had not been used as a prison for years. Sparrows and mice had taken possession. There were fields of summer crops nearby, empty of workers at this day and hour, but no other buildings were within sight.

The buildings inside the palisade were low and dim, unfurnished except for broad, low platforms that Natalya said were where the prisoners slept. In America these buildings would have been shelter for livestock; they might have accommodated several hundred pigs, Sherwood thought. The interior walls were still almost covered with Cyrillic graffiti. After a decade or so of standing unoccupied in Russian weather, the stench was gone.

Natalya, armed, waited on horseback just inside the palisade.

Moving methodically, aware of a pleasurable excitement underlying his concern, Sherwood stripped off every stitch of his clothing and packed the garments neatly into a saddlebag, except for his new boots which he tied hanging to the saddle. Everything ready to go. Then, naked, swatting absentmindedly at the insects who viewed him as a banquet, he stood at a little distance from the uneasy horses. There was no great hurry about accomplishing the Change, and no uncertainty— he could sense the power waiting, at his command.

His bear's blood was up now. They were going to make this thing work, he and Natalya, they were going to get away with this right in the middle of the tsar's Russia. Damn Nicholas and all his thugs! Another skirmish here, and then away with Greg, and the three of them would somehow, if it took them a year, work their way back west, all the way to the vicinity of Petersburg. And from there, over the border.

Even as slowly as the marchers moved, they stirred up sufficient dust for the couple waiting in ambush to see the approaching cloud a mile away. The marching chain gang of two hundred men or more would be choking on their own dust as they moved, just beginning to get the feel of the three months' march they had been sentenced to accomplish in heavy fetters, and worthless shoes issued to them by a corrupt government.

Closer they came along the rutted, unpaved road, and closer. There seemed to be no more than a dozen guards in all, about half of them mounted. Now it was possible to hear the prisoners' chained feet moving, like the jingling of a million key rings all together, a dreadful burlesque of cheerful bells. And the prisoners' mournful chanting. Like a parody, thought Sherwood, of a body of soldiers singing on the march.

Nearer still. And now, looking out of the stockade, around the corner of the crude wooden gate, Sherwood could discern some of their faces.

"Can you see him?" Natalya whispered feverishly, meanwhile using the field glasses to continue her own eager search.

"Not yet." The gray cloud was too thick, there were too many men in identical prison jackets, marching too close together. "But he's got to be there."

When the faceless mass of humanity had drawn within fifty yards, Sherwood smoothly and easily changed to bear-form, dropping to all four legs as he did, losing sight of the marchers momentarily.

Natalya dropped her arm in signal.

And with a coughing snarl he charged.

TWENTY-THREE

Tactically the attack was an immediate success. The nearest members of the armed escort, as Sherwood had expected, initially recoiled from the bear's charge—the mounted men had no choice, when their horses panicked—then rallied, and came back shooting. But they had all they could do to manage their terrified mounts, and their aim was wild as they tried to gun down the attacking predator.

A trooper's horse reared up immediately before the bear, the rider shouting Russian curses and trying to aim his Mosin-Nagant. Just as the rifle went off, the bear grabbed the man's booted leg in his broad jaws, crunching leather and bone together, tearing the screaming man out of his saddle, trampling him, and charging on.

Meanwhile Natalya, mounted, was holding herself and the other two horses in reserve at a little distance from the fight, doing her best to keep everything in readiness for a getaway. She remained poised, watching past the edge of the opened gate in the palisade, rifle in hand, ready to defend herself and the saddled animals.

Under the attack, the prisoners' crude formation dissolved like a pile of leaves in a high wind. The gray mob was thrown into turmoil by the ambush, becoming a mass of men milling about, at its fringes beginning to scatter at such speed as they could manage with fettered legs. Not all of the unfortunates had yet caught sight of the charging bear, but several of those who had were screaming, in terror of their lives.

In less than a minute the shackled men were widely dispersed, their leg irons clanking and jangling as they moved, sending up a storm of dust, scattering along both sides of the road. Now Sherwood thought that a substantial minority of the prisoners were cheering the bear on. Meanwhile, Mosin-Nagants barked in the hands of those guards who had not yet been subdued, and bullets flew wildly. Sherwood, rampaging savagely in Bear-form, chasing down one soldier after another, was conscious of only two or three harmless penetrations of his body. Dull lead carried only transitory pains that vanished as quickly as they came.

Meanwhile Natalya had begun to return fire, shooting at any man who shot at Sherwood. She thought she might be firing blanks for all the damage she was doing, and she bemoaned her recent lack of practice.

At every moment Sherwood kept expecting to discover Gregori among the prisoners. But they remained only a throng of half-shaven heads and yellow-diamonded jackets, scrambling away in terror whenever the huge bear came near them. Once or twice the hunter thought he had discovered his man, only to realize he had been mistaken. The one face Sherwood was looking for stubbornly refused to appear.

Another bullet tickled harmlessly at his vitals and passed on. Here was persistent opposition. He roared and turned, but could not identify the marksman. These soldiers were more powerfully armed and better disciplined than any of the bear's previous opponents.

And there were more of them than Sherwood had first
estimated. Even if only half were ready to fight . . . now
first one rifleman and then another tried to bayonet
the Bear. But the attempt was futile, and in at least one
case fatal for the man who made it. Sharp steel was no
more effective against the Bear than speeding lead.
Sherwood found the sensation produced by a bayonet
passing through his shoulder or his flank only slightly
more unpleasant than that left by an ordinary bullet.

In the confusion of battle, time took on a different
meaning. Still, he had the feeling that this fight was
lasting longer than either of his previous brawls in
Bear-form, because he was forced to wage it against
more serious opposition. Long before it was over, the
Bear, his species not built for endurance, had begun to
feel winded and heavy-limbed.

Minute after minute the struggle dragged on, until
Sherwood began to suspect that some at least of the
escort must have been hunters before entering the
military life. These men, rejoicing in this unexpected
boon of a regular bear hunt, persisted in trying to fight
back. Fiercely Sherwood taught them that they were
not—could not be—the hunters here. Though gasping
for air and forced to move more slowly, he continued
to press his attack, pulling down one mounted man
after another, overturning their steeds. Heavy losses
had been inflicted on both horses and men before the
last of the troopers lost confidence altogether and
abandoned the idea of armed resistance.

Sherwood's strategy in this attack was based on the
idea of getting rid of the officers and noncoms, generally distinguishable by being mounted, would be the
surest way to disorganize and rout the guards. At the
same time he felt an impulse to avoid maiming and
killing horses. But once his Bear-self started fighting,
their bulky four-legged opposition was too challenging
not to be accepted. None of the horses were more than
about half his weight. Not even the biggest could withstand the wrestling grip of his mighty forelegs.

But then pain shot through him as one horse came

near crippling him with a lucky kick. The impact of an
iron-shod hoof struck home powerfully against the
great bear's belly, thickly padded with fur and fat and
muscle.

The Bear, full fury mobilized for the first time in Sherwood's experience, reacted with instinctive violence.

Ten seconds later, Sherwood, gasping hoarsely
through huge ursine lungs, looked down through his
beastly eyes at the red ruin which had been a horse. *I
didn't mean to do that*, flashed through the human component of his mind. But at the same time, rising from a
lower level of his being came deep satisfaction in
having done it, all the same.

Two or three horses were down before the fighting
came to a sudden end, their injuries serious enough to
keep them on the ground. After that Natalya, or Sherwood—when he had regained man-form—shot the
crippled animals in passing, to put them out of their
misery.

Four or five of the human escort, including the
officer in command, were down as well. In a scene that
had begun to acquire all the familiarity of a repeated
dream, the others broke at last and fled, whether on
horseback or afoot.

When, at long last, he could feel confident that effective resistance had been crushed, the enormous bear
turned, rearing on two legs in a good imitation of a
giant man dressed in a furry costume, and beckoned to
Natalya with one massive forearm, a very human gesture. Immediately she left two of the horses where they
were still securely tethered just inside the palisade, and
spurred her own mount out to join the search among
the prisoners for her brother.

By this maneuver, Sherwood was given a few
moments' opportunity to transform privately into man-
shape, and then pull on some clothes. Now he had a
painful bruise across his belly, in the spot corresponding to that where his Bear-self had been kicked
by a hoof. He could only thank whatever powers were

in charge that it hadn't been a little lower. The iron horseshoe might not have hurt him—none of the incursions of steel or lead into his body had left the slightest residue of pain or injury—but the impact of the hoof had been impressive.

In another moment he had mounted his horse, armed himself, and, leading the spare horse, joined Natalya as she rode about. But neither of the searchers, for all their efforts, had any success in finding Gregori.

The pair of would-be rescuers swung their mounts this way and that, crossing and recrossing the barren ground just in front of the *étape*, calling until their throats were sore the name of the man they were determined to find, doing their best to avoid trampling confused unfortunates beneath their hooves.

They had of course foreseen that their attack might have the effect of scattering the prisoners, making it impossible to get a close look at every one. But they had been unable to devise any way around this difficulty. Only now was it becoming fully apparent to Sherwood and his companion how easily they might have lost one man in the confusion. By the time Sherwood regained man-form, some of the prisoners had already run off into the woods. It was impossible to say that Gregori could not have been among them.

But if Gregori was here, he could not have failed to see his rescuers by now; he must have heard them hailing him.

The seekers, still shouting his name, went chasing into the woods on horseback.

"If he's run into the woods already, he can't have got very far!" No prisoner could run very far or very fast until he had rid himself of his chains.

Almost half the original number of prisoners were still huddled in small groups in the road or close beside it, near where they had been when the fight started. The only goal in life of these men seemed to be to avoid being shot. As far as Sherwood could tell, none of these particular unfortunates was hurt, but many were groaning, screaming, and praying, covering their half-shaven heads with their arms, as if convinced that their last hour had come.

Others were already scattered over an amazingly large area, sitting down, some behind trees or bushes and others in the open, pounding their leg irons industriously with rocks. Sherwood thought it a foolish hope to try to break the steel that way; but then, to his surprise he saw first one prisoner, then another, freed of his chains and running into the woods.

As with every large group of prisoners, no matter what their means of transport, there had been a couple of dozen ill, elderly, and otherwise disabled prisoners, judged unable to walk any considerable distance. In the convoy, these followed the marchers, riding in half a dozen uncomfortable little springless carts—*telegas*, Natalya called them. But Gregori could not be found here among the helpless, either. And if he had been riding in a *telega*, he would scarcely have been in any shape to run away.

Sherwood and Natalya exchanged a despairing look, and then, after a few more moments of renewed exertions, another. Had they after all, attacked the wrong convoy, despite the seeming impossibility of such an error? But no, there was the small mongrel dog which one of the prisoners had been carrying in Tomsk. It was now running in circles, as if looking for its master.

Still unable to find the man they sought, Natalya and Sherwood grew almost desperate. While she held the horses, Sherwood dismounted, and at gunpoint recklessly interrogated one injured guard after another. Finally one of men, demoralized by injuries and threats, told him through Natalya's translation that the man called Gregori Lohmatski had been taken out of the convoy only a few hours ago, this very morning, freed of his leg irons and put on a horse, then hurried on to Irkutsk in the midst of a special escort formed by a squad of cavalry.

Sherwood jabbed the man with his rifle barrel. "You saw them do this, with your own eyes?"

"*Da, da!*"

"Why was it done?"

The guard had no idea—or so he claimed.

"How do you know they took him to Irkutsk?"

The man said he had heard the officer in charge of the cavalry tell that to the commander of the prison convoy—a man who now unfortunately was dead, and could not be called upon for confirmation.

At this point a voluble prisoner, a baby-faced youth who looked about twenty years old, came forward, gave the dying guard a casual kick in passing, presented himself before the successful raiders with a kind of military salute, and announced that he had become a friend of Gregori Ivanovich in prison, and what the dying guard had just told them about that fine man was quite true.

Sherwood growled and aimed a weapon at the youth. Natalya demanded: "Who are you?"

"Anton Fedorovich Miushkin, at your service." For just a moment Sherwood had the impression that the young man (who had somehow freed himself of his leg irons with the speed of a magician) was about to click his ill-shod heels and bow.

"And what can you tell us about my brother, Comrade Miushkin?" Under stress, Natalya fell into an old revolutionary mode of address—then, in a hasty aside, relayed to Sherwood what the man had just said. In the background, prisoners moving singly and in pairs, many with unfettered feet, continued to vanish in a steady trickle into the woods.

The prisoner complimented his interrogators on the planning and execution of their bold rescue attempt and assured them he had much information to convey. Once again he went over the circumstances of Gregori's departure.

At that point, Miushkin paused to observe that a little food would be good to have, as well as a change of clothing. Casually he helped himself to a dead officer's pistol, belt, holster and all. He announced that he might as well ride on with Natalya and Sherwood, for a little way at least, as long as they seemed to have an extra horse available. He wanted to join their band—he kept shooting glances around the horizon, evidently assuming that a sizable group had made the attack and more of them would appear at any moment.

They searched a little longer, calling Gregori's name a few more times.

For a minute or two longer, Miushkin ran alongside them, calling Gregori's name. Then he broke off to assure Natalya once more: "I tell you, Mistress, your unfortunate brother is gone."

There was nothing to do but ride off, a trio debating in two languages, leaving the confused mass of freed prisoners and injured guards to shift for themselves as best they might.

Somehow or other, it seemed easier to allow Miushkin to come along than to take the stern measures which would obviously be required to get rid of him. Anton Fedorovich now quickly climbed aboard the spare horse.

Even while he made every effort to attach himself to his liberators, Miushkin savagely discouraged other prisoners from trying to join the little group. There were no more horses available anyway; the soldiers' mounts whose saddles had been emptied had all run off, or had already been commandeered by convicts who had managed to get free of their leg irons, and who were putting into practice their individual ideas as to what to do with their new freedom.

Pressed for more information, Miushkin described in convincing detail how, during the long days while they were both confined in the Tomsk Forwarding Prison, he had seen Gregori Ivanovich writing letters.

"Would Greg try to change identities with someone else?"

"He might let himself be talked into it. He's such an innocent about some things . . . ordinarily, that would be a mistake for a political prisoner. In fact it's a trick that's been worked time and again by the realistic criminals on the naïve politicals. The guards at the mines and prisons don't give a damn what a man's right name is, or whether he belongs there or not, as long as the number of prisoners comes out right and they can't be blamed for allowing an escape.

"The truth is that a mistake in a prisoner's identity, once made, is almost never rectified. Admitting a mistake, redoing all the paperwork—that would cause too much trouble and bother for the guards and the clerks who keep the system functioning—if that's the right word to describe what it does. The convicts in the mines are worked much harder, under even worse conditions than the political exiles.

"But of course, in Gregori's case, a switch might have been the wisest thing that he could do."

TWENTY-FOUR

L ooking back over her shoulder, Natalya hesitated. A hundred or so wretched prisoners, through fear, or weakness, or hunger, or sheer inertia, had not yet melted away into the woods and fields. She appeared to be on the verge of wheeling her horse around and plunging back in among them to continue the search for Gregori.

But Sherwood pulled his mount beside hers, yelled at her and grabbed her arm. "Natalya, come to your senses! Come on! If he had been there, we'd have found him!"

"You are right." There was nothing to do now but ride on, leaving the confused mass of freed convicts, and the terrorized remnant of their guards, to resolve the situation somehow for themselves.

Not until they had ridden half a verst did Sherwood look closely at the talkative prisoner who had begged and pleaded to come with them. Then the American, his temper still set at ursine pitch, began glowering at the man suspiciously. His first impulse was to drive

Miushkin away, employing whatever level of violence proved necessary. He began to order the man, at gun-point, to turn away.

Again Natalya had to plead the convict's cause. "He may be able to tell us something more about Gregori. Besides, he is a victim just as we are."

Because Natalya was so desperate for more news of Gregori, Sherwood tolerated the brash presence. The fellow, keeping his seat rather skillfully on his newly acquired horse, had begun to retreat in the face of Sherwood's wrath, but he did not go far. He continued to follow the couple at a little distance, until presently Sherwood relented and waved him forward.

On rejoining the couple, Miushkin gazed at them uncomprehendingly as they conversed in English. In Russian he swore fervently that he was loyal and dependable.

Sherwood remained unconvinced. "Well, what would you expect a man to say?"

When Natalya had translated Sherwood's demand to know why he had been arrested, Miushkin, calling upon the Holy Virgin of Kazan as his witness, claimed that it had all been a hideous mistake, he had been unjustly accused. His trial had been a farce, and he had been convicted with no real evidence against him.

In the aftermath of failure, Sherwood continued iras-cibly: "Yes, I'm sure. They'll all tell you they're inno-cent. Can't you get him to say what he was convicted of, exactly?"

More questioning ensued in Russian. "All he says is 'all a most hideous mistake, Your Honor.'" Natalya was somewhat cooler now and looking at the man more critically. "I suppose he might very well be some kind of scoundrel. But Sherwood, I think we must keep him. What crime he might have committed hardly matters—not if he can give us some real news of Gregori."

"All right then. Let him ride with us for the time being, anyway."

Sherwood led the way at first. Natalya followed closely, riding beside Anton Fedorovich, whom she kept prodding to tell her something more substantial about Gregori.

The convict seemed always ready to talk, in fact constitutionally unable to stop. He strove manfully to provide Natalya with reassurance about her brother, though very little of what he uttered could be described as news. What few nuggets of information did come through was reassuring.

"Your brother, Natalya Ivanovna, is a man of noble nature, I was sure of that in the first minute I knew him. And quite innocent, of course—that goes without saying—as innocent as I am myself. Might there be among the supplies of this expedition anything for a man to drink?"

"You'll find a full canteen on your saddle."

Eagerly Miushkin uncapped the container and lifted it to his lips; his expressive face seemed to fall a little when he tasted nothing but water.

But a moment later he had resumed his chattering. Sherwood thought the problem might come in trying to shut him up.

Still, he could not help being somewhat reassured by what Miushkin said. The man their new companion was describing sounded recognizably like the Gregori they knew, and indeed like a Gregori who had been coping quite well with his unfamiliar and frightening situation—at least, up until this morning.

Though Miushkin repeated himself at great length on the subject of Gregori, and of the prison conditions they had both endured, he actually conveyed little more of substance. He said he had first encountered Gregori Ivanovich some uncounted number of days ago on the prison train from Moscow, when they found themselves among forty or fifty men jammed into a freight car.

The yellow diamond was sewn integrally into the back of the convict's jacket, not just on it. Miushkin took off that garment and hurled it away the moment Sherwood offered him a spare shirt as replacement.

Miushkin began to impress Sherwood as someone who might be useful. Here was an undoubted Russian speaker of nondescript appearance—except, of course, for his half-shaven head.

Natalya, when the three paused for rest after several hours of riding, dealt with this problem by cutting very short the other side of Miushkin's tow-colored hair, reducing it to a mere stubble. Now both sides could grow back more or less together. Meanwhile, the result could be hidden by the spare cap that was to have been Gregori's; and in a stroke of inspiration, the amateur hairdresser decided to stuff the ends of some of the long, cutoff hair under the cap, so that it protruded as if it were growing, firmly rooted, on both sides of his head.

"Just remember, don't take off your cap," she cautioned her client. "Not for several days at least." Miushkin swore in fervent obedience that he would not.

The man as he emerged in the aftermath of prison and violent rescue was a nondescript Russian youth. No one could mistake him for the American who was being hunted by all the police. At least a hundred other convicts were going to be reported missing at the same time, so there was no reason to think his description would be especially circulated. There seemed a good chance that he could ask questions at prisons and in towns with anonymous impunity.

Having been wrung dry, as it seemed, on the subject of Gregori, Miushkin reverted to asking questions of his own. Displaying a bright and curious mind, Sherwood's and Natalya's new companion kept wondering aloud where the mysterious bear had come from, and why it had attacked the soldiers so fiercely while leaving everyone else alone.

"You trained it to go for the uniforms, Mistress? Is that it?"

Natalya did not bother either to answer or translate the question, but simply ignored it.

Miushkin was not easily discouraged. He wanted to know what had caused the beast to disappear so conveniently into the woods as soon as its usefulness was over; and just what its connection was with the people who were seeking their lost brother and comrade.

When his first series of questions along these lines went unanswered, he tried again in a few minutes, starting over with the patience—if not the tone—of a police interrogator, squinting back along the way they had come, and then inspecting the land on all sides, as if he half-expected to see shaggy Napoleon loping along, coming to join the party. "What happened to the bear?"

Sherwood saw the questioning look and caught the word *medved*.

"Just tell him that the bear is gone."

Natalya did so.

"I can see that, Natalya Ivanovna. Maybe it died of being shot?"

"Maybe."

"I don't suppose it's coming back to join us at some point?"

"I have no idea."

"But it's your bear, all the same?"

She didn't bother to answer.

With Sherwood she discussed the question of whether the man might be old-fashioned enough, peasant enough, to believe something like the truth.

"Is he a peasant, then?"

"I don't know." Natalya shook her head. "His speech is quite different from that of most of the peasants I've met."

"Better educated?"

"Or at least trying to appear so."

"Maybe he's the grandson of one of those peasant actors you were telling me about. . . . I suppose if and when the truth about Napoleon really dawns on him, he might run away from us as fast as possible."

After a while Miushkin seemed to forget about the bear. But he remained curious about other matters. For one thing, he wanted to know what had happened to the rest of the revolutionary band, of which he assumed that Sherwood and Natalya had to be the leaders. That only two people might have ambushed a prison convoy did not seem to occur to him as a possibility. He remarked that the others doubtless had taken the trained bear with them when the band split up. He did not seem discouraged when Natalya continued to be reticent.

Thus the three people headed into the endless Siberian *taiga*, angling east and a little south through the forest in the general direction of Irkutsk, while doing their best to leave a trail that would be difficult to follow. Once more they were blessed with a good fortune of rain. And when the air dried out, they entered marshy ground, where tracking them would be extremely difficult.

As they rode, Natalya and Sherwood discussed their situation. They had ordered their new recruit to ride a little distance ahead of them, for the time being. In that position it was easy to keep an eye on him.

Sherwood said: "We have to start with the fact that Greg just wasn't in that convoy. He absolutely wasn't there, or we would have seen him."

"Yes, all right. It's good you stopped me from going back, wasting more time there. But we did see Greg in the very same group when it started out from Tomsk."

"Right. Therefore Greg did leave the convoy sometime in the last few days. So it's probable that our friend Miushkin is telling the truth when he says Greg was taken away this morning, transported on to Irkutsk. That guard said the same thing. I remember his exact words—well, the way you passed them along in English: 'The convict Lohmatski was taken on toward Irkutsk.' "

"Damn it! If only we could have been a few hours earlier—but no use crying over that. Two people giving us the same story tends to make it more believable."

"Yes. But the implication, I am afraid, is that dear Maxim is once more taking a personal interest in his brother's fate."

"Or someone else is."

"So which way are we going to turn? West or east?"

After several hours, when they thought they had confused their trail sufficiently to foil pursuit, Natalya and Sherwood decided to turn east.

When Natalya informed their new companion of their plan, he strongly advised against it. The young unfortunate suggested, as an alternate scheme, that the three of them conduct some robberies on a modest scale. But he did not seem much put out when his suggestion was turned down.

Sherwood thought he had met the type often enough in other countries: men who made one surprising claim after another. Now and then, one of their amazing affirmations turned out to be true.

Miushkin exuded confidence and trustworthiness. But his new companions remained wary about taking his suggestions on any matter of importance.

Sherwood and Natalya considered trying to overtake the special escort that had kidnapped Greg. But if those troopers were in a hurry and had a start of several hours, that would be hard to do. The soldiers would have fresh mounts at frequent intervals.

Of course it ought to be possible to ride the railroad to Irkutsk much more swiftly; and that was what Gregori's special escort would do, or must have done: board a train at the nearest convenient station. But none of the three knew offhand just where that was.

Miushkin, now carrying in his pocket, just in case, one set of the faked papers made out for Gregori, made inquiries at towns and stations along the way, and with his natural open curiosity and guileless appearance found out a number of useful things.

"Yes, Your Honor, I can read quite well, if only in Russian. Road signs, and 'wanted' notices, and all. I'm ready for a test."

Getting to Irkutsk by road, or cross-country, was not a journey to be undertaken lightly, as it lay near the shores of Lake Baikal, just over a thousand miles east and a little south of Tomsk. A convict convoy, marching two days out of three in every kind of weather, had commonly needed about three months to cover the distance. Two or three people on horseback, making inquiries along the way, to find out in which direction a single prisoner with a special escort had passed by rail or unpaved road, might cover the same ground in about two months. That would put their arrival in Irkutsk in September. By then, Natalya told Sherwood, the weather would have started turning chilly. Autumnal rains might well turn the roads to mush.

Natalya was determined to remain optimistic about her brother's fate. "If they were simply intending to shoot him, they'd have done it out here, away from everyone and everything. No, if Gregori survived to be put aboard the train, they're really taking him somewhere, with a purpose other than putting him to death."

Sherwood allowed himself to be convinced. "Well, they can't be taking him back to Petersburg or Moscow. If they were doing that, they wouldn't have got on an eastbound train."

By the time Miushkin had successfully completed three or four scouting missions, visiting villages and isolated railroad stations while his companions waited for him at a distance, Natalya and Sherwood had gradually begun to trust him a little more. Still they observed certain precautions, taking care that they never waited for him at the exact spot where they had said they would, watching for his approach to make sure that he was not leading police back to them.

Miushkin returned with one eyewitness account of a

lone prisoner taken aboard a train, and at least one other story of a lone prisoner seen passing through. They had what seemed convincing evidence that Gregori was bound, willingly or unwillingly, for the mines or one of the prisons near Lake Baikal. Sherwood and Natalya, accompanied by their new ally, pressed on to Irkutsk.

TWENTY-FIVE

The fugitive couple, wary of the hue and cry raised against them across half a continent, hesitated to approach the city directly. Fearful of being recognized, they sent Miushkin ahead to scout out side roads, looking for police checkpoints and traps. Fortunately Irkutsk was large, a booming town for a hundred thousand people or even more, its stoves and fireplaces making a pall of wood- and coal-smoke on the horizon, an emblem of its presence before any of its buildings came in sight. And this city of central Asia turned out to be cosmopolitan enough that the arrival of three anonymous strangers made no impression on any one.

Taking their time, they made their way around the city by a circuitous route. As they advanced, walking their horses, Natalya said to her companion: "I regret that recent events have forced me to say good-bye to the gypsy woman, sole proprietor of a dancing bear called Napoleon—I must say, Sherwood, I found that bear rather attractive in his way."

"He kind of liked you too, ma'am."

Approaching Irkutsk in the characters of a prosperous and well-traveled foreign businessman and his mistress/secretary/interpreter, with Miushkin as their servant, they heard from local people several stories about a near-miraculous Bear. The beast seemed well on its way to becoming something of a cult and legend among the people.

Just inside the city limits, Natalya on entering a post station heard people discussing the mysterious Frenchwoman who had been a member of some small circus, now disbanded. Reports were being passed along regarding her clothing, and her accent, and her cigarettes. And of the fact that all the police were looking for her.

"They say she has been in this country so long that her French has a Russian accent."

"I've overheard some similar things." Linguistically, Sherwood was no longer totally helpless. He had been struggling, day by day, to reach and then improve a minimal facility in the Russian language. Recently he had been thinking that if he continued hearing Russian every day and trying to speak it, he could look forward to the time—certainly within a year—when he might understand and even speak Russian well enough to consider obtaining the proper uniform, and posing as some properly stupid and dignified high governmental official.

Weeks had now passed since Maxim's departure from St. Petersburg. He was sure that his leaving, with the ostensible purpose of conducting an official tour of inspection, had left his chief rivals in the Ministry, most of them snugly ensconced in their Petersburg offices, alternately rubbing their hands with glee at his stupidity, and worrying that they had missed the point of a cunning maneuver on his part.

Well, they had missed the point, all right. They could hardly have done otherwise. Maxim Ivanovich told himself that he was now well on his way to Padarok

Sivera. Of course, he could not be sure. Whether he was even halfway to his real goal was more than he could tell himself with any certainty.

Spreading a map before him in his latest lodging, he looked at the police outposts scattered along the map in the form of an irregular chain of dots. Far ahead, the chain of dots grew thinner, skirting the white spaces. The numerous police outposts could be found even in regions where there seemed no human activity to police or spy on.

He read additional telegraphed reports concerning the bear's purported exploits. Nine out of ten, he was sure, were totally imaginary.

At the nearby regional police headquarters, he had recently learned that half a dozen additional dancing bears, both east and west of the Urals, had been taken into custody, or shot, and their owners, who were for the most part gypsies, had confessed to an interesting variety of crimes, a great many of them, Maxim was sure, quite imaginary.

From time to time he was ridden by a nightmare involving a silver bullet.

In Irkutsk, Sherwood was also looking at a map. He could see that he was now well over 5,000 versts from Petersburg; that translated to more than 3,000 miles. Also he was now only about 150 miles north of the Chinese border. To the north and east, Siberia stretched on for distances that made the mind ache.

From where he stood, Asia extended for literally thousands of miles in every direction. People rode the streets of this city not only on horses and mules, but astride camels, which were common enough to draw no second look from any of the citizens. In certain neighborhoods, almost half the faces in the streets were Oriental.

Entering the city for the first time, in midafternoon, Sherwood was surprised to see unlit electric streetlights in the center of town. A proud native, enthusiastic about progress, boasted to the newcomers that Irkutsk had had electric street lighting since 1896, years before the main streets were paved—of course many of the side streets still formed a branching sea of mud. But never mind—they'd all be smooth and hard come winter.

And Sherwood realized that something about this city—its feel or spirit—reminded him somehow of San Francisco.

The three new arrivals had gone into a café to eat, when a youngish man in stylish civilian clothes approached their table. Holding his hat in his hand, speaking in nervous, stilted French, he asked Sherwood: "Excuse me, but are you German, monsieur? Don't I know you from Berlin?"

The American paused in the act of unfolding his napkin. "That can't be. I am Swiss. My name is Lavater."

"Ah, then it must have been Zurich, last year or the year before. You must remember me. My name is Golikov."

Sherwood the Swiss could not very well protest that he had never been in Zurich. The man kept hovering beside the table, determined not to be put off. He remained adamant that he had met Sherwood somewhere before. "And it is very fortunate for us both that I have encountered you again. Because I now have a business proposition to put to you; no one else will be so well qualified to take advantage of it. I pray you, let me speak to you alone."

Sherwood exchanged glances with his companions. Obviously, the best chance of remaining inconspicuous lay in humoring Golikov, whose agitation seemed to be quietly increasing. Natalya and Miushkin, after a final exchange of meaningful looks, were soon on their way outside.

Eagerly Golikov slipped into the chair opposite Sherwood. When the waiter came, he ordered tea.

"Let us speak English," he suggested in a low voice,

with a sideways glance that might have been meant to indicate the dangers of being overheard by the waiters or other customers.

"Very well," Sherwood agreed warily.

Natalya, on emerging onto the street, noticed a cluster of distant figures, mounted and in military garb.

Miushkin by her side was staring in the same direction. "Shall I see what's going on down that way, Mistress?"

"Very well. Be cautious."

"No need to worry about that." And the little man was off, walking briskly.

Meanwhile, in the café, Sherwood was clinging tenaciously to his character of Swiss businessman. He found himself launched on what proved to be a difficult discussion, with a young man who soon impetuously confessed his identity as a Russian army officer. "It is Captain Golikov, at your service—Mr. Sherwood."

"I don't understand," Sherwood protested. He was trying to conceal his shock at hearing his own name, fighting down panic as best as he could. Already he was totally convinced that the explanation when it came would be one he did not like.

Meanwhile, he was very much aware of the pistol in the inner pocket of his coat. He loosened another button on the coat, as if he felt the room growing somewhat too warm.

In halting English the man across the table quietly let him know that he had some contact with Colonel Zagarin's staff.

Sherwood stared, with a real lack of comprehension. "Colonel who?"

The officer smiled faintly, not to be put off by any such pretense of ignorance. He proclaimed, softly but with a flourish, with bold fatalism, that it was widely known among the police and military that Sherwood was an American agent. But the time had come for the old corrupt regime to be swept aside. Half-measures were no longer sufficient. He, Golikov, and his comrades were ready to support the scheme.

Solemnly he raised his metal-framed tea glass as if it were a wineglass and he were about to propose a toast. In fact, he was: "To the United States of America!"

Sherwood raised his own glass of tea reflexively and took a sip. He had the feeling that the dirty boards of the café floor might be about to open up and swallow him. "What scheme?"

Miushkin had not been gone for more than a minute when Natalya, cautiously pretending to inspect a shop window, saw in its mirror the little man being picked up by the authorities—grabbed right off the street by uniformed men, who in a moment were putting him in a closed wagon, hauling him roughly away.

It would not be wise at all, she thought, to depend upon Miushkin to resist interrogation. With great urgency she turned, to take the risk of reentering the café. At all costs she must warn Sherwood. She turned up her coat collar against a sudden chill breeze.

But Natalya had taken only two steps back in that direction when the uniforms, seeming to pop up out of nowhere, were at her elbows too.

Colonel Zagarin's office was a large room near the center of a walled compound. Sentries on every exterior wall were alert against bomb throwers, and other terrorist incursions. The chamber boasted marble walls, pierced by only two small, high windows, which would not have looked out of place in some ministerial office in Moscow or St. Petersburg. In the place of honor behind the colonel's desk hung a large hand-colored photographic portrait of the tsar and tsarina. Below, diplomatically smaller, hung a framed photograph of Minister of the Interior Stolypin.

There were many bookshelves, most of them—but not all—filled with dossiers and other official records. At the right side of the desk stood a large terrestrial globe. A map of the district hung on one wall.

The colonel liked his office. He fully enjoyed his
job—most of all, he reveled in the possibilities his job
had opened for him.

At the moment, Miushkin, flanked by two burly
guards, stood more or less at attention just inside
the door.

Settling himself behind his desk in the pose of an
examining magistrate, Zagarin said to the two arresting
officers: "Leave me alone with the prisoner."

One of the guards hesitated. "Are you sure, sir?"

"Don't be absurd, I'll tell you when I want help. I'm
twice the prisoner's size. I take it you've made sure he
isn't armed?"

A moment later, the police who had brought in their
captive saluted and went out. And as soon as the door
had closed behind them, leaving the colonel and
Miushkin quite alone, Zagarin's face ceased to wear a
threatening expression. And Miushkin's countenance
relaxed from its appearance of controlled terror.

Only a few seconds later, the two were seated comfortably, doing a good imitation of a pair of old friends,
on opposite sides of Zagarin's desk. The man who had
just come in to face his doom now had a bottle of vodka
and a glass before him, and was leaning back in his
chair, puffing at a Russian cigarette tipped with a card-
board filter.

In the nearest corner of the room, close behind
Zagarin's desk and handy to his chair, stood a tall
wooden icebox, the upper compartment filled with ice
cut last winter from the purity of Lake Baikal, the
freezing downdraft keeping the colonel's vodka in the
lower compartment deliciously chilled.

Zagarin, amused, sat examining his visitor for a little
while in silence. At last he remarked, in Russian:
"Enough of prison life for the time being, hey? By the
way, what happened to your hair?"

The other tossed down iced vodka, expressed his satisfaction with a sigh of ecstasy, and drew on his cigarette. "Very much so, sir. I look forward to that

vacation you promised me when this job is over. The hair? Oh, they shave your head for you."

The colonel knew little and cared less about the common details of prison life. His duties and interests lay elsewhere. "We'll see about the vacation. I think the job is far from over yet. Now tell me how you've fared since your last telegram. The last arrived three days ago, the one telling me the three of you were about to come into town."

"First let me repeat, sir, that there was absolutely nothing I could do when Lohmatski's men descended on our convoy and snatched away his brother. He sent a whole squad of cavalry."

"You are sure they were acting on the orders of Maxim Ivanovich?"

"Oh, sir! Beyond any doubt."

"Well, of course you—being alone, unarmed, and in chains—could not very well stop them. Nor could you invite yourself to go with him. At least you can provide me with the details of how it happened—but let that go for now. First I want to hear about the two revolutionaries and their marvelous bear."

The agent, who had had plenty of time to mentally prepare a concise report, began speaking, smoothly and unhurriedly. He told of the second attack on the convoy in the space of a day, this one by a man and woman and a bear—"No sir, they had no other help"— their routing of the military escort, and the effective liberation of many prisoners who eventually had hammered themselves free of their fetters, stone-age style, and walked off into the *taiga*.

Zagarin was intrigued enough by this last detail to digress momentarily. "I've heard of similar incidents; they seem to happen whenever prisoners are left unguarded. Then is it really that easy, to get out of leg irons? Are we using cheap metal, or what?"

"Yes sir, we are. But the real point is that one doesn't actually have to break the steel. Just bend it a little, deform the circle into an oval, and nine times out of ten one can slip the foot right out. This seems to be common knowledge among the prisoners."

"I see. Go on." Having satisfied his curiosity, the colonel was ready to put the matter of leg irons out of his mind—keeping prisoners wasn't his job. And no one ever rose in the Ministry by proposing practical improvements in the day-to-day routine.

Miushkin resumed his story precisely where he had left off. The colonel listened with intense concentration, and almost without interruption. Fantastic as Miushkin's talk sounded, it coincided almost exactly with the official version of the raid given him by the surviving soldiers. Of course they were Zagarin's own people and had been under orders to divert the prisoner Lohmatski here, to his headquarters, as soon as his convoy reached Irkutsk.

When at last the young man paused, Zagarin prompted: "What about the American? Where is he now?"

"That's the very devil of it, sir. Your people just now picked me up at a most inconvenient time."

"I told them I wanted to talk to you; I didn't suppose I was ordering your arrest. Well, the devil take it—there's no help for it now. Go on."

Miushkin reported that some mysterious individual, undoubtedly a conspirator of some kind, probably a military officer but one he didn't recognize, had made contact with Sherwood only an hour ago.

"I don't know how their conference went off, sir. But the American will be in the city, somewhere. Certain to get into trouble if he's alone."

The colonel leaned back in his chair. He spoke in a slightly different tone. It now appeared that something was weighing on his mind even more heavily than American conspiracies. "And where, now, is this amazing bear?"

"The bear? I couldn't say, sir."

"Have you been able to find out any more about it?"

Miushkin responded with a knowing smile. Having eavesdropped, unsuspected, on days of English conversations between Sherwood and Natalya, the small man now had some were-bear material to report.

"They spoke in English to each other all the time, never dreaming that I could understand. Sometimes they talked about the Bear, though indirectly. Their favorite topic was their plan for rescuing the woman's brother, Gregori Ivanovich Lohmatski, who is also, of course, the brother of Maxim Ivanovich, Your Excellency's esteemed colleague in the Ministry." The secret agent allowed himself a broader smile.

"Any word of dear Maxim Ivanovich, by the way? My friends in the capital tell me he's off on a tour of inspection that will take him to the far north. Everyone's speculating as to the real reason behind his journey."

Miushkin's manner gave his words a significant emphasis. "You would know best about that, sir. But you might find it interesting that his sister and the American spoke of a certain power that they believe Maxim Ivanovich possesses."

"A power connected with the Bear?" At the moment Zagarin seemed not so much intent on learning about the Bear, as in discovering just what Miushkin thought about it.

"Inseparable from the Bear, it seems, Your Excellency."

"An occult power?"

"Yes. Your Excellency. Everything they said on the subject suggested to me that this couple, though certainly educated people, believed in—in certain events which most people would class as supernatural." The little man's expression was bright and unapologetic.

Zagarin took his time about lighting his own cigarette. Then he leaned back in his chair, and with a practiced motion elevated his booted feet atop his desk. "Did they tell a lot of *obaraten* stories in your village when you were young, Miushkin? Let me continue to call you by that name, for I think it may stay with you for a while yet—you grew up as a peasant, didn't you?"

"I did, sir."

"Then tell me honestly what you think about this

question of people who can at will turn themselves into animals."

The secret agent on the other side of the table made a little seated bow. He replied immediately and with apparent sincerity: "I believe in whatever Your Excellency believes. No more and no less."

"A perfect answer, Miushkin." The colonel squinted his eyes against the smoke of his cigarette. Briefly he slipped into the familiar form of address. "Sometimes I think thou art the perfect agent."

"It is vital to me to have your good opinion, sir . . . so I take it Your Excellency is rather deeply interested in this bear, which was able to rout an escort party of twenty-five soldiers, five of them mounted, most of them armed with military rifles? I had a good look at the beast while it was tearing up the convoy escort. A very good look—I even felt its hot breath once or twice."

"I am indeed interested."

Miushkin described the Bear, including its immense size, its strong white teeth, its apparent immunity to Mosin-Nagant bullets and bayonets. He had as usual been a keen observer, and his description went so far as to give the exact shadings of color in the fur.

At last he added: "And when the three of us were riding on, Your Nobility, my new companions talked in English several times about 'the bear coming back'—it seemed that bringing back the bear was not something they were eager to see happen."

"Nevertheless, I have the feeling that it will be coming back."

"They seemed to think that it had better not, except in the most serious emergency."

"I see. And they don't really have any clear idea of where their precious Gregori Ivanovich is just now?"

"I'll stake a month's pay, sir, that they do not."

"Whereas we know where he must be. Headed north, one way or another. Into the tender custody of his brother, who had him arrested in the first place." Zagarin sat up straight in his chair, reached for his glass, tossed down some vodka of his own. A thoughtful smile was growing on his ugly face.

"Will they still trust you, Miushkin, the American and his lady?"

"I wouldn't bet on it, sir. They're not fools. They've simply had to take a lot of chances, and everything is pretty much against them."

Here word was brought to Zagarin—the confidential aide who entered was not surprised to see Miushkin at his ease and drinking vodka—that the ordinary police had picked up the woman, Natalya Ivanovna.

Sherwood's conference in the café did not last long. Golikov, if that was really his name, having delivered his enigmatic pledge of support, soon took himself unhurriedly away. He moved quietly, with the air of a man who had accomplished a heroic deed.

Sherwood paid the bill mechanically and drifted after him, downstairs and out into the street. Traffic had diminished for the time being. Dusk was gathering, and in the distance some electric lights were coming on. There was no sign of either Natalya or Miushkin, but he assumed that they were not far away.

Irkutsk boasted some beautiful buildings, he thought to himself, but most of the streets were a sea of mud.

A few people passed, paying the idle foreign businessman no particular attention.

A few minutes passed as well. Sherwood decided that he couldn't simply stand waiting for his friends to reappear; a loitering foreigner probably would begin to make people curious. He'd walk around the block, and Natalya would be here when he got back. He now had plenty to think over while he walked.

He wondered if Maxim, too, supposed him to be some kind of American secret agent.

At the local headquarters of the regular police, Colonel Zagarin was saying to Natalya: "You are coming with me now. If you will answer some questions for me, freely and truthfully, it is not at all impossible that you will see your brother again."

Natalya, her face pale with fear but set in an expression of defiance, nodded slowly.

A minute later, as deferential officers were ushering and bowing them out of the station, the colonel added: "You may even see the American. I have a kind of appointment with him too, though he doesn't know it."

Sherwood, having walked twice around the block in the middle of Irkutsk, was wondering what had happened to his dear companion.

Now, in early September, the weather had suddenly turned chill, and he turned up the collar of his summer coat.

The American was distracted from his contemplation of the weather by the sight of a large dog, a wolflike, shaggy and unbarking beast, that came trotting toward him from out of the gathering dusk. It sat on its haunches eight or ten paces away, and looked at him, tongue lolling, almost a hungry expression on the canine face. Sherwood noticed that the street had somehow become almost deserted.

Here came a second dog, which very much resembled the first. And now a third, sitting also, all taking their places in what was now the beginning of a semicircle, which seemed as if it might be intended to hold Sherwood against a doorless wall.

When he started to walk away, the dogs growled and moved to contain him in their formation. They were very large indeed—for dogs.

Four hounds, now. Now five. Now six. Muttering faint snarls and inching closer to him.

He drew the pistol from under his coat, and as if the act had been a signal the dogs leapt to the attack. Sherwood fired, and fired again, using up two silver bullets, and brought down two hounds, before one of the surviving dogs leaped on him from behind.

In self-defense, he Changed. His clothes went

bursting, ripped to shreds. He got his vest off just in time.

Great *Medved* reared up roaring.

Most dogs, except for hunters bred and trained, would have scattered when challenged by a bear. But these large canines only gazed at him with expressions of warm regard. Obviously they felt themselves quite up to the task of dealing with any *medved* however large. Fangs savaged him from behind, his legs and flanks, no matter which way he turned.

No doubt about it—it was Sherwood the Bear that the dogs wanted, and they were coming after him with murderous enthusiasm.

At last he caught one hound in front of him and mangled it. But killing one or two was not going to save his life. The fury of the combat blocked out pain, but he could feel that his blood was running out; the pack was chewing out his life.

A man with a gun appeared, no, in truth at least half a dozen men, all obviously members of a trained team of bear hunters, except that they were coming to his aid and not to kill him. Maybe dog hunters would have been a better description. A commanding voice was barking orders. Whips and truncheons rose and fell, beating off the hounds, who were too steeped in bear's blood now to willingly relinquish their kill. But the men were determined that the bear's life must be saved. Pistols cracked and banged. Dogs that had not heeded the command to retreat were shot dead.

At last the attack dissolved in outraged howls and whimpers. After the surviving bear-hounds had been beaten off, Sherwood, reacting with a wounded animal's instinct to hide, tried desperately to retreat, first tottering on two bear's legs, then lumbering on four. No longer able to outrun mere human beings, he staggered and collapsed. Strength failed with loss of blood, and he fell at his full ten-foot length in the muddy street.

Clinging to his last shreds of consciousness, he fought down an impulse to revert to man-form.

Something told him that were he human, his terrible injuries would kill him on the spot. Animal vitality clung to life where it seemed that the merely human would be hopelessly inadequate.

In a moment of horrible, sinking, drowning sensation, Sherwood was convinced that he had fallen into a trap. Some agent of Maxim's—or of some other power, even more mysterious—had caught up with him successfully.

But he was not yet too far gone to experience surprise. Human hands, skilled but rough, bringing neither death nor healing, were actually putting a metal collar around his neck, closing two segments of a ring, locking them like a giant handcuff. Something fiery in the touch of the cold metal, a contact his Bear-self had never felt before, alerted Sherwood to the fact that it was silver.

One of the armed men picked up what was left of Sherwood's clothes, including the vest with one silver bullet still in a cartridge loop.

At the same time a figure whose beard and robes suggested a Russian priest, holding aloft a beribboned book that might have been a bible, mumbling what sounded like a mixture of Latin and Russian, was showering him with blessings—with invocations, rather, meant to keep him in confinement.

Now once again the more commanding voice was ordering the other men to hold him securely; in the mist of horror and the fear of death, it crossed Sherwood's mind that yes, his persistent Russian lessons were paying off. He was able to understand the last words that he would ever hear.

But still he wasn't dead. One astonishment was piled upon another. Unless he was delirious again, the sides of some portable wooden cage were now being tightened on him, oaken bars thick as a man's arm putting on pressure like the jaws of a slow, enormous vise. Distantly he remembered once talking with Greg and Natalya, about the different varieties of bear traps. But who could have prepared anything like this, for him? Maxim? But how could Maxim have known that the Bear was going to be here in Irkutsk?

What happened next was worse. Inflicting incredible pain in the process, they pierced the septum of his nose with a silver point and began to insert a silver ring.

TWENTY-SIX

~

S herwood, his bear-form body badly torn up and
dripping blood, his hybrid mind drifting in and
out of awareness, lay helpless in the dark street,
surrounded by half a dozen fur-coated men whose
gunfire had killed some of the crossbred canine mon-
strosities attacking him, and had driven the rest away.

He observed, without understanding on either the
human or animal level, that none of their weapons
were pointed at him.

Now a folded cloth—it tasted horrible, like water-
proofed canvas—was stuffed into his mouth, so that the
great ivory knives of his teeth bit down on it in reflex.
Meanwhile another rag filled with entrancing vapors
was clamped over his muzzle. The chemical fumes
surged into his nostrils to soothe his pain and shock,
even as they left him less in control of his own mind
and body. Next a sting in his haunch (human thought
made the reassuring identification of a veterinarian's
needle) added one more wound, almost microscopic, to
the nearly overwhelming total. In a few moments the
bear-man could feel some powerful drug take hold.

Essentially immobilized and barely conscious, his furry form was maneuvered onto a tarpaulin, then dragged away, still faintly snarling his pain and anger. Lifting a fully grown male brown bear would have been a practical impossibility. Someone, because of his phlegmatic nature speaking slowly enough for Sherwood to comprehend, swore in Russian that even ten men would not be enough—each would have to hoist one hundred fifty pounds. Almost six *poods* apiece. Hoists and pulleys would have to be mobilized. Someone had evidently been exercising forethought on the subject of kidnapping bears, for it turned out that his captors did indeed have such machinery ready for the occasion.

Faint with drugs and loss of blood, Sherwood was vaguely aware of the grappling hooks, pulleys, and hoists. With great effort, broad canvas straps were worked underneath his body and their ends attached to machinery. Eventually a force was applied that not even an unwounded bear could have resisted.

The bear-man regained imperfect consciousness to find that it was still dark, and he was riding on a kind of wooden sled pulled by a mule. After half a mile or so of this, he was rolled off the sled and dragged through a narrow doorway into some kind of dim shelter, a converted storeroom, out of the wind. A solid door was closed, walling him indoors.

However, he was not going to be left alone. Presently a man came to tend his wounds with skilled and knowing hands, while other guardians held kerosene lanterns or portable electric lights and sat helpfully on Sherwood's four legs, one or two to each limb, while he lay spread-eagled, belly down on a stone floor. In his weakened and drugged condition his human captors were able to hold him almost still, quiet enough for the veterinary surgeon to get on with his work.

Around him now the air was a little warmer, and the absence of wind indicated that he had been brought indoors. Eventually Sherwood ceased to snarl and struggle, made every effort to lie still. Despite the roughness of the men surrounding him, it was clearly apparent that their purpose was to save his life.

Every instinct warned Sherwood against attempting to Change, in his present mangled condition. Underlying this perceived limitation was the horrible feeling that even if he did risk everything in making the attempt, he would probably not succeed in regaining his humanity.

The huge bear's fur was shaved away in three or four places, with a blade whose tingling passage warned the bear that it was silver-plated. And then the surgeon stitched up the worst of the gashes—by now he could tell, from the special quality of the pain, that the needle, too, was at least a strong alloy of silver. A muzzle was fitted on, holding his jaws almost shut.

Finally, there came a time when Sherwood was left alone. No more than semiconscious now, struggling and thrashing around in this bemused state, he tried repeatedly and without thinking of the consequences to regain his humanity, but the silver collar and the agonizing nose ring effectively prevented the transformation he sought to bring about.

New sounds awakened him. The cellar around him was aglow with kerosene lamps and candles—one of the latter held in a small white hand. To his surprise, he realized that a woman, dressed incongruously in a silvery evening gown, was speaking to him, as if to a hurt child. She crooned soothing words in Russian as she bent over his tied-down form. From time to time she shifted as if unconsciously into French, so that more of the meaning came through to Sherwood.

"Those terrible dogs—I don't know what he can be thinking of, to keep them."

Timidly, cautiously, she reached through the iron bars of a heavy door to touch his shoulder and his neck with her small, jeweled hand—stroked the bear's fur, over and over, as if she could not keep herself from touching him. "And I think he set them on you deliberately. But why should he want his hounds to do this to you?"

Before he passed out again, Sherwood heard one of the men present, whether guard or servant or veterinarian he was not sure, address her respectfully as Eva Pavlovna.

Evidently fascinated by this giant beast who seemed almost on the point of death, Eva Pavlovna—her family name still remained a mystery—was again on hand the next time he regained consciousness. He wondered if she had deliberately scheduled this visit at a time when all the men who had the bear in charge happened to be absent. Or was the timing of her visit merely accidental?

"Poor beast," she murmured impulsively, petting him again. "They have caged you as they have caged me."

Sherwood rumbled something in response.

"Ah, it's almost as if you understood. As if you knew your mama wanted to help you."

And once more she lapsed into French, a language Sherwood understood much better than Russian.

"There are times when I think he would find it amusing to set the dogs on me . . . what are they doing to you, poor *medved*? Are you wild, or did they get you from some gypsies? Ah, that must be it. Look at the ring in your poor nose—so sore, and bleeding. That's a fresh wound. Why would he . . . ? Don't worry, I won't even touch it. Ach, I wish I could kiss your poor sore nose!"

Sherwood whined.

From Eva Pavlovna's tone and gestures, even more than through the mixture of imperfectly understood languages, it was obvious that she sympathized with him—even if she did not actually try to kiss his nose. She tried to give him a drink of water and succeeded partially.

And as the man-bear drifted in his drugged and dreaming state, it occurred to him that now, at last, he was being granted an experience of the redemptive power of prison, of which Dostoyevsky had written so fondly. Now he could describe to Natalya the great honor of being one of the Unfortunates.

Returning to clear consciousness, being brought to full awareness of his condition in his cell, which might have been a converted storeroom, brought the certainty of defeat and imprisonment. But by whom, and on what terms, he had yet to discover.

His body and limbs were very weak, his wounds, mostly on his back and his hind legs, all hurt. His nose, in the ursine scale of sensation, had ceased to be a hellish torture and was merely sore. The silver ring remained firmly in place, and he thought that a tiny padlock held it closed.

Sherwood had not been fully awake for long when some men came. This time the man with the commanding voice was with them, and Sherwood heard other men address him as colonel.

Again the woman, this time dressed more practically, came with them, to give him some better organized help in drinking and eating.

Before long the sympathetic Eva Pavlovna volunteered to hold the bear's head, and was pressed into service. Soon she was cradling Sherwood's massive, furry skull in her lap, and had virtually taken over the operation. In a crisp voice she issued orders to the men, which they obeyed.

Water was poured through a funnel into his muzzled mouth, one bucket after another. Much was spilled, but what was not began to quench his thirst. After the water came some kind of nourishing soup. The hot liquid would have been more to the human than the ursine taste, but the bear was more than usually ready to consume anything.

Then some lard, half-liquefied with warmth, as a delicacy. The bear's stomach loved it.

Meanwhile his muzzle, devised of silver rings and odorous new leather straps, had been removed to let him eat the semisolid food. Eva gave him a sternly playful warning against biting, and having done so, seemed to consider herself perfectly safe in his company.

Next time he awoke, he was again feeling a notch better. He could halfway believe that he had only dreamed the woman's presence. The pain of his wounds remained fierce and almost constant, but his bear-nature was incomparably better equipped to ignore pain than his human self had been.

Daylight had come outside his cell, making itself faintly visible through a few scattered chinks in the windowless outer wall of stone and concrete. A whiff of brisk air, smelling of acorns and early autumn, came in through the cracks as well. Chestnuts were roasting somewhere, perhaps a mile away.

The room was about twelve feet by fifteen, with an iron grating closing a doorway in its inner wall, and in the outer wall a single solid door, of heavy wood reinforced with iron bands and rivets. That must be the way he had been brought in. There were no windows.

The next time he looked, he saw a couple of snowflakes drifting in. The first wave of winter's scouts. Inside the cell, warmed by its connection to the big house around it and above it, the temperature remained comfortable—for a bear.

This time a large basin of clean water was waiting at his side. His limbs were free of straps and restraining weight, the muzzle had been removed—though the damnable nose ring was still in place—and he tasted the water as soon as he could lift his head sufficiently to drink. He retained human sense enough to refrain from biting at the pain in those wounds that he might reach. Instead he only licked them, tasting, smelling stitches, ligatures crafted from sheep intestines, along with the last traces of the burning antiseptic.

The feedings were repeated, during his intervals of wakefulness. Some strength returned. At last there came a time when, with a strong effort, he could stand

on his four feet. But he was glad to be able to lean
against a wall. He was a long way from being able to
fight or run.

He could smell the woman approaching—a blend of
human flesh, and sweat, and exotic cosmetics—before
she was close enough for him to hear her soft footsteps.

"Ach, but you are standing up! Misha, how marvelous! But don't hurt yourself, don't overdo!"

"And your limbs are free." The woman stood just
outside the cell, gripping the bars and watching. "But
you must not bite or claw away the bandages, dear
Misha! Ah, you won't do that, will you? What a beautiful animal you are!"

She was so surprised and delighted at Sherwood's
good behavior that he realized she did not suspect that
he was anything more than an animal.

Presently some of his regular keepers reappeared.
Good solid food was now brought him, in plentiful
amounts. Of course to a bear all food was good, and
almost any organic substance qualified as food. Today
men came in carrying fruit and vegetables, oatmeal
and sour rye bread, and as a special treat, ten pounds
or so of raw horsemeat.

From the start of Sherwood's captivity, the Colonel himself was a frequent visitor to the Bear's den. His first
visits were invariably brief, and sometimes he appeared
only as a silent figure in the background. As the Bear's
recovery progressed, Zagarin came more often, and
soon—after making sure that all other humans were out
of earshot—started asking him questions.

The first time they were alone, the Colonel stood just
outside the bars, holding in one hand, tossing and
catching it casually, the silver-tipped cartridge Sherwood had been carrying in a loop of his vest.

"Greetings, John Sherwood. I am Colonel Zagarin—
you may have heard of me?" The bullet-headed man
with the monocle actually clicked his heels and bowed.

Zagarin spoke quite passable English. But sometimes, in giving orders to his subordinates, he failed to allow for the fact that Sherwood could now understand a fair amount of Russian. Thus he dropped small nuggets of information, possibly to become useful later.

Sherwood wondered if Zagarin's subordinates thought it strange when the colonel regularly told them he wanted to be alone with the bear. But quite possibly they were accustomed to eccentricity.

"Of course you cannot respond in human speech. But that will come in time; you would not want your humanity restored just now."

The Colonel leaned on the door of the cell, gripping one of its bars, and gazed at Sherwood fondly. "Remarkable beasts, my hounds. A hybrid of the Karelian bear-hound and the wolf. Not that I bred them for your benefit; no, my original quarry was merely ordinary bears. You and I must have a chat about hunting—when you are farther along on the road to recovery."

Zagarin bragged carelessly about his dogs, and boasted of the effort and expense he had had to make to get them. The dogs were kenneled somewhere nearby, so that the Bear could hear and smell them. He was not particularly worried that they would be loosed on him again; this colonel certainly wanted him alive.

And Zagarin's ongoing monologue confirmed this: "I wanted them to bring you to bay, not chew you up. They were supposed to drive you into a corner, make you hold still, so that I would have a chance to discuss certain very serious matters with you."

He held up the silver-tipped cartridge between finger and thumb. "This you obviously intended to use on Maxim Ivanovich, when you caught up with him."

Talking more to himself than to the Bear, the Colonel wished aloud that he might have the chance to use the dogs on his rival Maxim Ivanovich Lohmatski—as if he knew quite well that Maxim too was *obaraten-medved*.

"I know you are the American John Sherwood.

There are several questions I should like to ask you, but of course any detailed answers will have to wait. For the time being, at least, you will have to remain a bear—for your own health, if for no other reason. I am sure we can find a way around any mere difficulty in communication. In the meantime—I would like you to just nod your head."

The bear, motionless and enigmatic, looked steadily at the man.

"Oh, and by the way—I suppose you are interested in the fate of Natalya Ivanovna?"

The bear's small eyes glittered, looking at him.

Zagarin offered vague reassurance. "She is well. She is not too far away. If you are interested in her welfare, nod your head. If you are only a bear, or you are not interested, well, there is not much point in my keeping that difficult woman around—a little nod, if you would like to see her? Ah, that is better."

A little later the colonel brought Natalya down to his cell. She was dressed just as Sherwood had last seen her, and appeared to be quite unharmed.

With the three of them quite alone in the locked cellar, she said: "Sherwood? I am all right; they've given me quite a comfortable room upstairs." Natalya was speaking English, slowly and distinctly, as if to a child. "You must allow yourself to heal. . . ." Suddenly, in fear and outrage, she turned on Zagarin. "What in hell have you done with him? What's that in his nose?"

The colonel, his arms folded, was leaning comfortably against the wall. "It is a silver ring. It won't do him any harm. It is just insurance that he remains a bear, until I say otherwise, and plays no tricks like trying to get away."

Zagarin shifted to Russian. Sherwood could pick out most of the meaning. "You see? The one you care about is here, alive and . . . certainly I want him to remain alive . . . we have much to talk about."

Eva Pavlovna was immediately suspicious of the attractive foreign woman and assumed she had a rival for the colonel's affections, but remained all unsuspecting of what was really going on. Eva continued—and even increased—the frequency of her visits to the animal's malodorous cell.

When he realized that his mistress was trying to make a pet of Sherwood, the colonel was rather amused by the fact.

Obviously, Eva Pavlovna really had great sympathy for animals. Once she came down to the cellar carrying a small kitten, cooing to it and petting it.

A day soon arrived when the veterinarian announced, in Sherwood's hearing, that *medved*'s life, barring unforeseen complications, ought no longer to be considered to be in danger. His recovery was well under way, but it looked like it was going to be a long process.

From the way the man spoke, it was obvious that as far as he was concerned, Sherwood was simply a bear. It would not be possible to get a professional opinion from him as to when Sherwood might safely resume human form—the Bear knew, he could feel in his bones, that there was no chance of a full Change as long as the silver ring was in his nose, the silver collar around his neck.

Colonel Zagarin came down to Sherwood's cell at least once a day—except one day when he was kept too busy by some emergency—to observe his prisoner's progress for himself, and to carry on a one-sided conversation that really sounded as if it might be meant to be encouraging. For the most part, the colonel stayed outside the bars.

Sometimes he wore a holstered pistol, which Sherwood was able to identify as one of the standard old Smith & Wessons, much favored in the Russian army. The colonel did not mention—and his prisoner had no way of asking—whether he had silver bullets loaded.

Sherwood's clothing, most of it shredded by his last

Change, along with whatever was in his pockets, and whatever weapon he had been carrying, had been picked up and brought along by Zagarin's men. He wondered what Eva would make of this collection of abandoned male garments and equipment, assuming she saw them.

Zagarin had to admit that there had been nothing in Sherwood's pockets to identify him as a secret agent. But then it was hardly likely that an agent would carry incriminating material about.

Sherwood, as he continued his physical recovery, naturally began to study the possibilities of escape. His body was much stronger now, and his legs, he felt sure, were capable of running. He could make a break for it when the outer door was open, as happened daily when his cell was being cleaned. But even if he got away, the silver ring in his nose would keep him frozen in bear-form.

Also tending to discourage any remote hope of fighting his way to freedom was the fact that he could hear and smell the Karelian bear-hounds, kept no more than a room or two away on the ground level of the house.

Zagarin on his repeated visits delivered various political, social, and religious opinions, sometimes in the form of a stern lecture.

One night the colonel, quite drunk, paid a late visit, with bottle in hand and a drunken prostitute on his arm. He still wanted Sherwood to confess, once more by simply nodding his head, that he was in fact a secret agent of the American government. The prostitute thought the whole thing—the business of talking to a bear—was hilariously funny; she sat down on the floor in the corridor outside the cell, and laughed and laughed. Trying to maintain his dignity, and probably retaining some shreds of caution, the colonel was content, for the time being, not to press the matter.

"I will of course want to hear the details later, when

you are sufficiently healed to take the form of man again."

Sherwood slowly shook his massive head from side to side.

The gashes left by wolfish fangs were healing, perhaps more swiftly than anyone had anticipated. Animals and civilized humans had quite different ways of dealing with pain and disability.

Soon he was allowed out of his dim cell, to be taken for a walk within the security compound on a light chain linked to his silver nose ring.

The colonel seemed to have no serious trouble believing in were-bears, just as he—in his own way—believed in all of the other accoutrements of mystical Mother Russia.

Colonel Zagarin, like his colleagues, the other district chiefs of eastern Siberia, ruled for the most part with a great deal of independence from the authorities in the great cities in the west.

Presently he mentioned to Sherwood a certain impending event of great importance.

The Minister himself, Pyotr Arkadyevich Stolypin, was coming to visit Irkutsk in person, as part of a tour of inspection. Stolypin was generally acknowledged the second most powerful man in the empire, after only the Holy Tsar himself.

The colonel was amused by Maxim's telegraphed orders, demanding repeatedly that the woman with the trained bear called Napoleon should be arrested.

Zagarin considered just what kind of reply he might send to Maxim Ivanovich, telling him that his sister was now living in Zagarin's house and hinting that the great plot had been discovered.

Sherwood overheard enough to make him realize that Zagarin was locked in a vicious struggle with Maxim, among other men on the same level of the bureaucracy, in a perpetual rivalry for position and importance.

Sherwood's worries about Natalya were mounting swiftly once again. He had not seen her for several days, not since that first visit in Zagarin's presence.

TWENTY-SEVEN

Before dawn one morning Sherwood, finding himself alone and unobserved, the darkened lower portion of the house seemingly deserted, tested the strength of one of the iron bars which kept him in his cell. To his great surprise and secret joy, he discovered that if he pushed hard, the metal interpenetrated the were-bear flesh of his foreleg without doing any harm. The temptation to try the experiment with his whole body was irresistible, and a moment later he was standing in the dark corridor outside his cell.

But he was still muzzled and bound with silver. And there were the dogs. And, somewhere nearby, Natalya, without whom he could not leave. Escape was going to have to wait. In another moment, Sherwood was back inside the cell.

He couldn't tell how much time had passed since his capture—he guessed three weeks or a month. Winter had certainly settled in, though in his fur he was almost uncomfortably warm, out of the wind in the unheated cellar. Anyway, his physical healing was virtually complete.

Now he had to get free of his silver nose ring and collar. And let Natalya know how matters stood.

Eva was still visiting the prisoner an average of once a day. She was treating the bear like a pet now, calling him "Misha"—and the fact that Sherwood could think of no explanation for this name worried him unreasonably. He knew he had real things to worry about. He felt sure that as soon as he was sufficiently healed, Zagarin would insist upon his resuming man-form and answering some questions.

Meanwhile, Eva seemed to have no suspicion that he was anything but a pure beast. In Sherwood's presence she sometimes fretted aloud, in a mixture of French and Russian, about what her master might be planning to do with his captive Bear.

"The trouble is, I don't know what my Sasha intends to do with you . . . there are only two reasons, dear Misha, why he might want to keep you. And at least one of them would be terrible. No, I can't allow him to do that!"

And reaching in through the iron bars, she impulsively, fearlessly, hugged the puzzled Bear around the neck.

With the sounds (laughter, song, dancing feet on hollow boards, the occasional crash of glass or crockery) of yet another of the almost nightly parties drifting down from the upper levels of the house, Sherwood began thinking furiously of some means by which he might influence Zagarin's mistress to set him free. There came down also the smells of sweaty bodies, perfume, food, and liquor.

His nose ring was not a solid circle of metal, but a thin clasp, locked shut with a tiny padlock.

He had a feeling that this woman would probably be credulous enough to believe in the *obaraten*, if someone told her the truth.

"Ach, I wish that you could talk!"

Slowly, solemnly, he nodded his great head.

"Ah! You frighten me, almost."

He shook his head from side to side.

A minute later Eva—she had a good eye for precious metal, if the jewelry she usually wore was any indication—noticed that his nose ring was of silver.

Daily, now, Sherwood was led out of the compound on a chain attached to his nose ring, walked around and brought back. These expeditions were conducted late at night, Sherwood supposed, to minimize the number of potential observers on the street—not that there were many idle onlookers anyway, in the vicinity of the security compound.

He moved slowly, with a limp more pronounced than was really called for by the soreness in his stretched wounds. As he passed, surrounded by his walking escort of grim-faced men, among the darkened houses and shops, sniffing the coolness of the suddenly autumnal, almost wintry air, one of his captors kept a firm grip at all times on the chain connected to his nose ring; the other men were all armed, and Sherwood had little doubt that at least one of their guns was loaded with silver bullets. How many knew or suspected that he was *obaraten* he could not guess; perhaps none of them.

One day Eva's personal maid, a little old woman with bulging eyes, happened to accompany her mistress downstairs. Eva happened to mention the silver in the metal objects by which the bear was constrained.

The maid, who was old and superstitious, gasped and recoiled. She pointed out to Eva in rapid Russian that her master and his associates were treating this prize bear as if it were a were-creature: *obaraten*. That was the only possible explanation for the silver bonds.

Her hands suddenly raised, one to her breast, one to her mouth, Eva stared at the bear in fright and astonishment.

Sherwood, maintaining the calm demeanor he had affected lately, stood close to the bars while the women reached in from outside to inspect the silver items more closely. They commented on the fact that both ring and collar were fastened on with small padlocks.

The maid retreated fearfully while Eva tried talking to the bear as if it were a man.

"Who are you?"

Sherwood grunted. He tried to growl with some intelligence.

Eva snapped an order over her shoulder. "Run upstairs and get my planchette!"

In a minute the maid was back. And what Sherwood could recognize as a Ouija board was put in carefully between the bars, on the floor of his cell. Fortunately the device was of French make, and in the Latin alphabet.

Holding the board down with his left forepaw, he ticked off letters with the index claw of his right. He was surprised at how well the ursine nervous system was adapted to small manipulations.

J–O–H–N–S–H–E–R–W–O–O–D soon appeared.

"What kind of name is that?" the cowering maid demanded in a minor shriek.

"Anglais, certainement!"

Further questions spouted from the women. Sherwood answered them all with: H–E–L–P, until at last his questioners, frightened and upset, retreated upstairs.

Next morning Zagarin, having evidently decided that the bear was now healed well enough to risk a Change, came down to see the prisoner, bringing along keys for the silver rings. He was also carrying a bag under his arm, and emptied this inside the cell, restoring to Sherwood what was left of his clothes.

He looked with satisfaction at the bear. "Well, how about it? Ready to try standing on two legs? Come here!" He jingled keys.

Any real improvement in his condition would have to start with getting the nose ring out. Sherwood came to the bars. The rings were unlocked, removed.

Sherwood Changed—and his wounds tingled with the transformation. They were sore, but they remained healed. He felt almost dizzy, standing on only two feet.

Before Sherwood had finished dressing, the questioning began.

Zagarin had lighted a cigar, and after a moment's hesitation offered Sherwood one.

The American declined. He seemed to have lost all taste for smoking. Returning to man-form had so drastically reduced his sense of smell that he felt his head was stuffed.

Zagarin began, "You admit that you were sent to Russia by the American government?"

Sherwood stared. "I admit nothing of the kind." After weeks as a bear, the tones of his own human speech resounded strangely in his head.

"Come, come! Make it easy on yourself. Others involved in the plot have confessed. They've told me the whole story."

"I don't know who's told you what story, but I'm no agent of any government." Sherwood wondered whether to mention the young officer in the café, and decided against it for the time being.

"How deeply is your friend Gregori Ivanovich involved?"

"Greg's never been involved in any kind of plot that I know of—where is he?"

Zagarin shrugged. "If I had had my way, he would be here—but at the moment he is still his brother's prisoner. On his way to exile, in a small village just above the—what do you call it?—*Cercle Polaire Arctique*."

"The Arctic Circle."

"Precisely. His brother is taking no chances, keeping him out of the way."

The questioning went on. Zagarin really did not seem very good at this kind of thing; probably he was more accustomed to interrogations where the prisoner was beaten routinely. But, for whatever reasons, he was not adopting such methods here. Not yet.

At one point Zagarin seemed to be offering Sherwood the possibility of a secret commission in the *Okhrana*, to give him authority to act in the north.

Sherwood, openmouthed, could only shake his head in wonder.

Zagarin shrugged. "I am sure that plenty of people will unquestioningly take orders from a bear—as long as it presents the proper credentials."

Gradually Sherwood understood that this policeman truly believed that he had come to Russia as part of a plot between the American government and dissident Russian officers. The scheme seemed to be to break Siberia—or at least a large part of it—free of tsarist control, first establishing an independent government, and eventually attaching it to America.

At last, turning away without explanation, Colonel Zagarin climbed the stair and opened a door. Sherwood wondered if he was calling for his whip. Instead he heard him giving orders for Natalya to be brought down.

A few minutes later, Natalya appeared, looking pale. Zagarin told her and Sherwood, in simple terms that Sherwood found convincing, what he planned to do with Greg—mainly extract information from him. He thought Greg would be eager to cooperate.

"You don't suppose I mean to hold him as a hostage? What use would that be, when his own brother has been trying his best to destroy him? Nor do I suppose that Gregori Ivanovich would be anxious to defend his brother, after what his brother has done to him."

It had been Maxim's special agents who had taken Greg from the convoy and were hurrying him north. Zagarin hinted that he might be ready to help in the next attempt to rescue Greg—*after* the business of the American plot had been brought out into the open.

That was Zagarin's main topic, from which he never strayed for long: a plot by certain Russian officers to declare a vast region of Siberia an independent state, with a view to later joining the United States of America, either as a territory or as several states. To

Colonel Zagarin, the presence of Sherwood here in
Siberia, involved with the Lohmatskis and very likely a
secret agent of the American government, seemed to
support these suspicions.

Sherwood, now clinging to the bars with weak
human hands quite vulnerable to metal (these bars
would certainly keep him in, unless he Changed again)
saw no possibility of convincing Zagarin that he was not
an American agent, that he had never been sent to help
detach vast areas of Siberia from the Russian empire
and put them under the control of Washington.

Historically it was no secret that certain treacherous
groups of Russian officers had talked about such a
project from time to time, for almost a century, ever
since the Decembrists' revolt of young officers in 1825.
Natalya mentioned these facts now, and suddenly
Sherwood could begin to understand Zagarin's readiness to believe.

In response he could only continue to argue that he
had never heard of any such scheme. He insisted that
he was only a private citizen who had originally come
to Russia on a hunting trip.

"What were you planning to hunt?"

"Bears. *A* bear."

That answer evoked a roar of laughter. But Zagarin
was probably shrewd enough to see that there was
almost certainly some truth in it.

"At the beginning I never dreamed—nor did Greg—
that we were summoned to hunt the bear that goes by
the name of Maxim Lohmatski. At the beginning it
would have been impossible for me or Greg to imagine
any such thing."

"Have you no *obaraten* in America?"

"I never saw one there. How about letting me out of
this cage?"

"In good time, in good time. First let us talk about
your instructions from the American government."

Zagarin remained stubbornly convinced that his suspicions were correct, and was operating on the theory

that he could turn the American agent and use him for his own purposes.

At last he jingled his keys and silver rings at Sherwood. "I am afraid, old man, that I must lock you up again."

Feeling his human nose, Sherwood discovered without surprise that it was still pierced, as the bear's had been. His fingers told him that the rim of the puncture in his nose, like that in the bear's, was now healed.

He protested: "What's the point of doing that?"

"Come, you must be a bear again, for a little while only." Jingle jingle. "If an American spy is discovered here, you will certainly be taken away, out of my jurisdiction, and I suppose that neither your family in Ohio nor the lady here will ever see you again. You can stay hidden much more easily as a bear."

Sherwood thought that he had no real choice. He peeled off his clothes and once more became a bear.

Eva wondered what her master meant to do with this were-bear that he'd captured.

She mobilized such cleverness as she possessed to keep Zagarin from suspecting that she knew the marvelous secret of the bear. They were discussing the creature one evening in the comfortably furnished drawing room, while the colonel put the final touches on his uniform, making ready to go out on business.

"Dear Sasha, he's meant as a present for someone? Is that it?"

"Not for you."

"Of course not for me. I didn't think that . . . I'd set him free if he were mine."

"You'd loose him right here in the middle of the city, I suppose."

"I know! You mean to give him to the Minister, when he comes to visit? To Stolypin?"

Zagarin laughed. "That'd fix me up great! Offer a present of a bear, worth a thousand rubles or so, to a man who constantly rails against corruption—I don't know if he'd take a present or not, but certainly not anything as conspicuous as a bear."

After a pause he added thoughtfully: "If I make the Minister a present of anything, it may be of—Siberia."

"I don't understand, Sasha."

"Never mind. Don't worry your pretty head."

Eva was well satisfied to be considered mindless. "And what will the great Minister Stolypin do for you?"

"He has it in his power to do very much indeed." Colonel Zagarin, gazing at his mistress, shook his head. "Stolypin is a good man, but in many ways too innocent for his own good."

"Does an innocent man ever become a minister?"

"If I were you, I wouldn't worry about these things." Turning this way and that before a full-length mirror, the colonel made an adjustment of his sash. "I'm off, then. You needn't look for me for dinner."

Eva nodded, putting on an appropriate expression of resigned sadness at the last bit of news. Privately she was well pleased at the prospect of having more time to try to communicate with the Bear.

Zagarin waved to his mistress, joined Miushkin, who had been waiting at the door, and went out.

The bomb blast, sounding from just outside the building, followed less than a minute later. The explosion was so close and so powerful that Sherwood in his cellar could feel it in the timbers of the house around him, and his furry back was showered with light debris shaken down from his cell's roof.

TWENTY-EIGHT

Colonel Zagarin, along with his two closest advisers and Miushkin, had been blown to pieces immediately after the four men had boarded the colonel's carriage. Fanatical assassins, materializing out of snow and darkness, had succeeded in detonating a bomb right between the sled runners of the horse-drawn vehicle.

Within two hours, the Ministry in St. Petersburg, informed by telegraph of the disaster, had appointed an acting district chief. Vassily Fedorovich Volkov was a civilian with the rank of Councilor of State, the equivalent of a brigadier general in the army or police. Volkov, a small, pallid, mustached man, took over with a show of energy, and immediately concentrated his energies on the hunt for the surviving revolutionaries—one of them, a known rebel, had died in the blast, but at least two more had been seen running away.

The keys to Sherwood's silver collar and nose ring, along with many other keys, had been turned over to Volkov within hours of Zagarin's demise.

The bear in the basement was hardly the new chief's

primary concern. Volkov did not believe in *obaraten* and remained serenely unaware that he was now living under the same roof with an example. When he did come across the beast, in the course of inspecting his new headquarters on the day after Zagarin's death, he naturally proceeded on the assumption that Sherwood was simply a bear.

"Well, excellent material for a bearbaiting! We'll have some sport one of these evenings."

Eva had stayed on, and now, only twenty-four hours after the blast, she was clinging possessively to the arm of the new boss. Going into mourning had struck her as inappropriate; she was wearing as many jewels as ever.

Catching Sherwood's eye, she shook her head slightly, as if trying to assure him that the casually mentioned bearbaiting was not going to take place. But she looked so frightened that it defeated her intent of reassurance.

Continuing on the subject of the bear as she walked upstairs again with Volkov, Eva tried to hint at the truth about Sherwood. She began, as she thought, in a cautious, roundabout way, commenting on how quaint and delightful peasant superstitions could be. But at the mention of superstition, the new boss only looked at her with calculation, in the manner of one not at all sympathetic. Eva quickly changed the subject.

Meanwhile the new chief was treating Natalya with a certain wary respect. The Lohmatskis were a substantial family, and she seemed a figure of political importance, with one brother prominent in the Ministry and the other a political prisoner. Obviously, she was being housed under Zagarin's roof because of some intrigue. Maybe she was to be called as a witness in some investigation—it was quite possible that she herself did not know the true reason.

Neither did Volkov, but he meant to find it out. Not easy to do, when Zagarin's close advisers had been murdered with him. When the new chief questioned Natalya, quite diplomatically, over tea in the parlor, she did her best to convince him that she was here voluntarily—never mind the official records showing her arrest. She ought to be allowed to leave whenever she wished. And, of course, to take her bear with her when she departed.

"The animal is yours, then? My goodness! Where did you get it? Whatever do you do with it?"

"I'm not sure what I shall do. But it's mine, a gift of the colonel."

Volkov gazed thoughtfully at the attractive young woman he had inherited. "Well, we'll see. Anyway it's the beginning of winter. Surely you don't want to set out on a long journey with a bear?"

Natalya protested her uncertainty. The new chief, realizing his own ignorance, temporized. She remained, for the time being, housed as a guest.

Volkov was aware in a general way of the struggle for power that had been waged between his predecessor and the distant Maxim Ivanovich Lohmatski. He had learned also of Zagarin's suspicions regarding a plot to detach most of Siberia from the empire. But the colonel and his close advisers were dead, and the details of plots and suspicions were nowhere written down. Volkov had not the faintest idea of where the "American agent" might be found.

The assassination had not much slowed the whirl of the winter's social activity. On several occasions over the next few days the Councilor brought visitors and party guests downstairs to admire the bear.

The sight of such a powerful, healthy, and yet well-trained animal made some people reminisce about earlier days in Moscow or in the capital. In those cities, in accordance with a long tradition, bears were sometimes kept in the town houses of eccentric noblemen. The tradition went back two hundred years at least, to the time of Peter the Great.

Someone at a party, in Natalya's presence, began reading from a book published in 1722:

"It was the Master's habit to compel each of his guests to swallow a cup of brandy, seasoned with hot pepper. This draught was brought to them by an enormous bear, who carried the cup between his paws. For the amusement of the gathering, the bear pulled off hats and even wigs, and held by the clothing anyone who refused the peppered brandy."

Having heard that, everyone wanted to see the bear, and conducting the beast upstairs was easier than bringing all the guests down, a few at a time, through narrow, dingy passages. Natalya assured everyone that it would be perfectly safe; and everyone being at least somewhat drunk, everyone agreed.

In 1908, the bear who was also John Sherwood, on being brought upstairs to attend his first party in Irkutsk, observed to himself that the great majority of the guests needed no forcing to get them to drink anything alcoholic that was put in front of them.

In his first few days on the job, Councilor Volkov, having talked over the affairs of the District with such of Zagarin's associates as had survived the blast (though these were not the best informed), began to suspect that there might indeed be a vast, treacherous plot involving the detachment of Siberia from the empire. The business seemed to be connected somehow with the Lohmatski estate somewhere in the far north, land supposedly given the family by old Ivan the Terrible himself.

Zagarin's successor would have very much liked to get his hands on that original land grant. It seemed to him that the document might be instrumental in a Lohmatski effort to turn half a continent over to America.

Sherwood was relieved that the knowledgeable Zagarin was gone, and that his interrogation sessions had ended. Natalya, coming downstairs to look at the bear she claimed as her property, managed to whisper

scraps of information and a few words of encouragement. But he was somewhat worried by the fact that
Eva now seemed to be avoiding him.

The more Sherwood thought over the business of
the great Siberian plot, the crazier it seemed.

By early November, Sherwood, after having been confined for many weeks almost continuously in bear-
shape, began to fear that he could feel his human
intellect slipping away, his mind being lost to the inadequate support provided by whatever compound brain
now lived in his bear's skull. Several times he frightened himself with the noises he made on awakening
from dreadful dreams.

Maxim, whose tour of inspection had now brought him
to the end of the most northern telegraph line in
Siberia, received the news of Zagarin's death within a
few hours of the event. But the destruction of his rival
somehow failed to bring the sharp joy it would have
afforded him only a month ago.

By all reports, Volkov, the colonel's replacement,
was a relative nonentity. No competition. Still, Maxim
experienced no sense of triumph. He found himself
still going through the motions of his job, but as he
proceeded on his journey, everything about the Ministry, about the government, was beginning to seem—
relatively unimportant.

He was coming to understand that the real keys of
power and success were not to be found in offices and
corridors and titles. No, they were buried deeper in the
world than that.

His official tour still had a long way to go. But in fact
he was now beginning to feel that his real goal was
much closer. He thought he was now within a hundred
versts of Taimyr, the village where, if all went well, he
was going to encounter his brother.

Over and over in memory and imagination Maxim
relived that catastrophic, violent and crippling encounter with the American. He had felt his right

forepaw make glancing contact when he lunged up the broken stairs and struck at Sherwood. He knew that his claws must have wounded Sherwood and probably hurt him seriously. He had ordered the woods in the area of the abandoned estate searched for the American's body and had had a foreboding of unpleasant consequences when it was not found.

Since Sherwood had obviously survived his wounding, there was a chance—probably a very good chance—that the American too now enjoyed were-bear powers. Maxim's attempt to kill his enemy might only have strengthened him.

Eventually, accompanied by his dogsled driver and a couple of soldiers, he arrived at Taimyr. The scattering of small huts, surrounded by stunted trees and snowy waste, looked exactly like what it was: a remote, tiny village, buried and lost in emptiness, in which political exiles were interned as punishment.

The village before him, like the surrounding landscape, was enveloped in mist. And this was the place where he expected to find his brother.

Three men, all armed and two in uniform, accompanied Maxim as he advanced. He had chosen his sled driver and his two police guards carefully. They were all peasants, all ready to believe in the *obaraten*, even before the private demonstration he had given them when they were alone in Siberia, with only one more village lying between them and the emptiness of the north.

But naturally Maxim had returned himself to man-form before he approached the cluster of huts situated beside a small stream between the last straggling forest and the open tundra.

The political exiles in this small village were standing around outdoors (fortunately today's twilight of low wintry sun, passing for daylight, was practically windless) trying out their dialectics. Maxim recognized his brother at once, although, like everyone who went to prison, he had been changed. Gregori Lohmatski stood among the other exiles, but it was only the warmth of the fire that drew him, not the argument. Evidently prison had not awakened in him any interest in politics.

The Bolsheviks and Mensheviks, along with other flavors of revolutionary less easy to classify—one of the exiles was a short, vaguely Oriental-looking man called Koba—who had gathered around the wood fire peered at the world through their round, steel-rimmed eyeglasses, and stamped their feet in their felt boots, and shivered, and held out gloved hands toward the fire.

The samovar was steaming in one of the neighboring huts, whose door was shut. There everyone would spend at least one night, trying to sleep crowded together, with the roaches. After that the regular occupants of the sterilized hut would move back in, and another dwelling would take its turn at standing open and fireless for a day and a night to slay its vermin.

Indoors or outdoors, the politically active spent much of their time tirelessly arguing. It was as if they could not help it. With sublime confidence they told each other in detail what the members of the working class were going to be compelled by historical necessity to do, exactly how the revolution in the factories was going to take shape.

Gregori had been listening as one of his fellow exiles, an apolitical scientist, commented that forty degrees below zero was the same on both scales, Fahrenheit or Centigrade. It was the value where the two scales coincided.

Immediately the intellectuals had begun to argue over whether this was reasonable or not. Was such a coincidence to the advantage of the working classes? Several argued that the existence of two scales was in itself a cunning ploy of the oppressors, enabling them to manipulate people's perception of the temperature.

But soon the focus of debate was shifted. The main topic for the day, as it had been for the past several days and nights, was considered to be scientific too. It centered on a certain pamphlet published thirty or forty years earlier. A frayed and smuggled copy was one of the group's prized illegal texts.

The original was a small German pamphlet, written by Friedrich Engels in 1876. Someone in the group around Gregori pronounced the title with relish: *"The Role of Labor in the Ascent from Ape to Man."*

Gregori had never read the copied pamphlet or taken part in the debate. But he had now heard certain phrases and sentences so often quoted that he could have recited them from memory:

" 'The primary biological factor was the change to an upright posture . . .' "

" '. . . the strengthening of group instinct . . . among social animals . . .' "

" 'The change to a carnivorous diet promoting the development of the brain, also led to the use of fire and the domestication of animals.' "

A sudden silence fell. Gregori, who had been standing with his eyes closed, opened them to see his brother Maxim, accompanied by three attendants, trudging toward him through the snow. For just a moment Greg felt a fierce stab of joy at the thought that his brother had now also been arrested.

But soon it was obvious that that was not the case.

Maxim, well dressed and well fed as ever, crunched to a halt in the snow just before him. He inspected the scrawny prisoner and nodded. "I cannot say that you are looking well."

As the powerful visiting official, Maxim had no trouble getting his brother to take a walk alone with him. They went into a nearby scraggly patch of woods, one of the last stands of trees before the North took over utterly. When they seemed to be out of sight of all the others, Maxim stopped.

Greg was much thinner than when Maxim had last seen him. He was bearded now, gaunt and lice-ridden and disheveled, much of his body wrapped in layers of rags for warmth. Facing his brother in the seemingly interminable Arctic twilight, Greg asked: "Are you going to kill me now?"

"No. Nooo!" Maxim spread his hands—his wrists looked stiff, like a bear's forearms—in a kind of soothing protest. "What an idea!" He paused. Struck by a thought, he ungloved one hand and reached into one of his many pockets. "Would you like some chocolate?"

"Of course." Gregori had begun to salivate at the mere word. When his brother held out the candy, he seized it and stuffed it into his mouth.

Watching him critically, Maxim asked: "What do you think of them—back there?"

"The political ones in the village? Always arguing. They are idiots, for the most part. Have you any more food on you?"

"Not at the moment. I've heard a great many like them, believe me."

Words began to pour from Gregori. Obviously he was bursting with the need, almost as great as the craving for food and warmth, to talk to someone, even an enemy, who would understand. "Not one of those who were so loud, so certain, has ever been a worker. The only one who had ever labored in a factory was standing quietly in the rear, shaking his head, listening to the rest. He tells me that he understands only about half of what they say—only partly because they keep speaking French. The Russian words he hears from them make little sense to him. They seem, he says, to have no connection with the reality of the factory in which he had been arrested for trying to organize a strike." He paused. "Anyway, you sent me to prison; why shouldn't you murder me as well? Why have you come here, if not to finish me off?"

Maxim shook his head. "I could easily have finished you off, as you put it, from a distance. As to why I'm here, the answer is simple: I want you to come away with me."

Gregori's jaw, with its new beard, dropped. "Where?" he demanded suspiciously.

"I want your help in finding Padarok Sivera. I want to go there. It's in this region somewhere. You listened to Father's stories more than I did. You were always studying the old book."

Gregori blinked with surprise, then somehow seemed to find the idea not really so surprising after all. He thought it over for the space of several puffs of frozen breath. At last he said, in a voice that threatened to crack: "I think you are mad."

Maxim considered the suggestion calmly. "No, I don't think so. The estate where our grandfather lives—oh, yes, I have a strong suspicion that he still lives!—is perhaps no more than a hundred versts from where we stand. Certainly not much more than that. I think the truth lies there, in Padarok Sivera. I mean the whole truth about humanity. And when a man has faced that—and understood it—then he can rule the world."

"I still say you are mad. What is the truth about humanity?"

"I'll show you as much as I have already learned."

With that, Maxim Changed. Most of the garments he now wore were of loose fur, and he had become skillful in getting out of them even as the Change came upon him. His body grew fur quickly, and the very process seemed to generate heat, enabling him to avoid frostbite in the coldest weather.

In Maxim's bear-form, which he assumed only when outdoors and alone, he was still crippled. Having been wounded by silver in both of his left-side legs, which almost always prevented those portions of his body from Changing, he continued to have great difficulty in bear-form, getting around, or even standing up. But he was sure that he could still stand on his feet firmly enough, move fast enough, to take an unsuspecting human by surprise.

Greg watched the process. He showed no emotion, except that his right hand in its fur mitten came up to grip tightly the trunk of a young sapling that stood beside him.

Maxim Changed back, deftly sliding his two feet into his boots, slipping on furs taken from dead animals, before the cold could succeed in killing his human flesh. It seemed that even his human skin must now be tougher than it had been before he started Changing.

Once more possessed of a human voice, he demanded: "Well?"

Gregori showed little reaction to the monstrous transformation he had just witnessed. He said: "I have been a lifetime in prison—or is it only a month? I have already learned that men can change to animals."

"That should make it unnecessary to waste time in explanations."

"You had me arrested so you could get the property."

Maxim shrugged. He seemed to have become almost contemptuous of the idea of wealth. "I know what to do with an inheritance, and you do not. Anyway, Father's lands really ought to belong to me, since he made such a treacherous attempt to kill me—but perhaps you haven't reasoned that out yet. He was going to shoot me with a silver bullet and then announce a hunting accident."

"Father? Tried to kill you? Why?"

"Because of this. Because he knew—or suspected—what I had become."

"You killed our father! You damned monster!" And Gregori, releasing his pent-up rage, hurled himself on Maxim.

Taken by surprise, hampered by his clothing from immediately Changing once again, the younger brother went down before the rush.

At that moment both of Maxim's soldier-guards, who had been watching this political offender suspiciously from a little distance, now burst out of concealment among the trees, determined to protect their master. They dragged Gregori away from his brother, and one of them struck him with a rifle butt. But by now the Bear had sprung up, snarling, and knocked both the soldiers away. In self-defense, one of them dared to raise his Mosin-Nagant and fire.

Gregori sat in the snow, stunned by the heavy blow on the side of his head.

Other people, a modest horde of them, came running at the sound of a shot.

When a dozen people from the village arrived at a run, they found a half-human, bearlike monster sitting in the snow with two stunned men, raising a human head from where he had begun to chew, with human lips and teeth, upon the body of a third.

The natives fled back to their small houses, barred their doors, and prayed.

Out in the snow there remained almost a dozen unarmed politicals, with the two soldiers, who were now slowly recovering their wits. Confronting them was a creature that seemed neither animal nor man.

"Hear me!" said the man's head on the Bear's monstrous, partly human body. Blood stained Maxim's lips and mustache, smeared his chin. "Listen to me if you want to hear the truth!"

A spokesman (his round, steel-rimmed eyeglasses were fogged with the frost of his own breath, generated by running, and he thought he was looking at a man in a great fur coat) for a majority group of politicals, five or six men, two or three woman, stammered to the being who had killed the soldier, that "we want to hear it."

"Do you want to know the truth about the things you always argue about? Then gather your things in the village, and make ready to come north with me."

Now Maxim, his bear-jaws drooling a soldier's blood, having killed for the first time since being wounded himself, received his first inkling that human flesh and blood might be the medicine his bear-self needed to be restored to full power. He could feel his pallid, hairless, left hind leg and human arm stirring with new life and power.

Gregori, having been hit violently in the head, appeared to be seriously hurt, and Maxim did not want to wait for him to regain his senses. He began to make

arrangements to have his brother carried north, help-
lessly, in a sled.

While all the sleds available were being made ready,
Maxim confided to his groggy brother that it had
proved surprisingly easy for any Bear who could think,
or at least gave the impression of sapience, to acquire a
following of revolutionary intellectuals. Ordinary
people would not normally be foolish enough to submit
themselves to an animal as a leader, but once assailed
by charismatic beards and impassioned oratory, they
could be swept along.

Greg, still dazed, only looked at him and muttered
something.

Within a few hours, all the dogsleds and teams in
the village (there were only three) had started north,
not hurrying. Maxim rode for a time in man-form
because he thought perhaps he could think more
clearly that way.

Maxim informed the still-befuddled Gregori that,
before the new and perfect society could be constructed,
it was necessary to escape all vestiges of the old.

The exiles and the two soldiers, about a dozen
people in all, who had volunteered to follow the Bear,
found it hard traveling, but simply existing in the
roach-infested villages was scarcely less difficult.

The somewhat undersized man called Koba, fascinated but wary, had silently volunteered to come
along, trudging and trotting with the others after the
sleds.

TWENTY-NINE

Volkov, believing that he now had a firm grip on the job of District Chief, and eager to take advantage of those who wished to present the new chief with gifts, gave parties almost nightly. Many of the guests were businessmen, others police and army officers, in this city surrounded by mines and camps, its days and nights occupied by the great bureaucracy of policemen and prison officials.

Eva, as with his predecessor, enjoyed the role of hostess—Volkov's wife and children were a long way off in Moscow. Winter, when nights were long and roads were smooth, was the social season in Irkutsk. The nightly meals were feasts, including veal, suckling pig, caviar, and sturgeon, along with a hundred other delicacies.

Sherwood, now thoroughly recovered from the wounds suffered in his battle with the dogs, was brought out almost nightly in the form of a dancing bear. Natalya, doing everything to establish her claim to be his owner, had remarkable success in getting the beast to perform.

He would have been ready now to make a break for freedom—except that such a move was impossible until he had freed himself of silver.

Natalya sneaked downstairs, on various occasions by day or night, when she had the opportunity and thought she might find Sherwood alone. At these times she gave him the latest news in a few hurried words. "I can't find the keys; Volkov must be carrying them on him; I'll get them as soon as I can."

He wanted to urge her: *Get a saw instead!* But to speak with his nose and neck bound in a vise of silver was quite impossible. All he could do was lick her hand and try to growl encouragingly.

The fortified residence of the District Chief, like most of the other local mansions, boasted a grand piano. In every room, tall stoves of decorated porcelain radiated the heat of burning coal and wood.

Eva had intervals of being very angry with Volkov, a feeling she naturally did her best to conceal. She continued to be uneasy about Natalya, though she was relieved to see that the other woman had no intention of trying to challenge her for the position of Volkov's mistress.

In her days as Zagarin's mistress, she had when bored or dissatisfied amused herself with a couple of affairs. But one of her foolhardy partners in those earlier transgressions had simply disappeared from the face of the earth—this despite the fact that the colonel had been intensely occupied with other matters at the time—and her other partner had hastily distanced himself.

In trying to plan an escape, Sherwood's first thought was that conditions would probably be most favorable in the hour or so just before dawn, when most people in the compound were asleep. But the trouble was that even more guards were generally on duty then, and they seemed more alert. The best time might very well be earlier, up to an hour or two past midnight. Then, amid the usual drunken confusion of a party, with people coming and going in all directions (he could plainly hear them from his cell), whole gypsy troupes of bears and their attendants might leave the establishment with no one being the wiser.

A brief hiatus in the social season was created when the telegraph announced the long-expected visit from Minister Stolypin himself. In his coded message, Stolypin gave explicit orders that he was not to be formally entertained; this visit was for purposes of business discussions only.

Councilor Volkov, suddenly sober at all hours, and intensely concentrated on his duties, saw to it that the Minister's picture on his office wall was dusted, as was the larger portrait of the tsar and his family.

Stolypin himself arrived on schedule. He was in Volkov's office bright and early on the morning after his arrival. The exalted Minister of the Interior was, at forty-six a tall, pale, aristocratic figure. Two years ago, several members of his family had died in a terrorist bomb attack on his suburban villa. He had not made the time-consuming and difficult railway journey from Petersburg to Irkutsk to attend parties, and certainly not to waste time in discussion of marvelous bears.

When Natalya first saw him, he reminded her, despite the obvious differences due to sex, a good deal of Comrade Svoboda.

Gold smuggling was one subject Colonel Zagarin had been investigating, and the colonel's successor reported on it to the visiting Minister.

Certain Chinese residents of the district were engaged in preparing the body of one of their own for shipment south, across the border, for burial at home. Hidden in a shed or in a tent, they were getting the corpse ready by unobtrusively removing the brain, utilizing an ingenious suction device to siphon out organic matter, and then blowing gold dust up into the nostrils to refill the intracranial cavity. Stolypin on hearing this commented that the dead man would have a very heavy head indeed.

Volkov gave his opinion that the local police chief, routinely and relentlessly corrupt, was heavily involved in this smuggling. Possibly the colonel, too, had been involved, operating at a much higher level of rank and graft.

Minister Stolypin did not seem surprised. The powerful visitor, famous as an archconservative in many ways, was quite accustomed to corruption, though there was no evidence that he ever took part.

The talk moved on to the real object of the Minister's visit. Zagarin had apparently been unable to find proof of the American plot. But the Colonel's assassination could be interpreted as evidence that he had been hot on the trail of something.

The Minister was not convinced of the existence of an American scheme to seize control of Siberia—not sure enough, by a long way, to make an open diplomatic protest. But he half-believed the allegation, and could not afford to ignore the possibility; it seemed to him just the kind of thing that might tempt the adventurous Teddy Roosevelt.

The Minister, in conversation with Councilor Volkov, thought aloud about the possibility of trying to get Alaska back into the empire, even after that territory had been in American hands for forty years.

The question of the missing American naturally came up, while Stolypin and Volkov were in the midst of their discussions.

The new District Chief said: "Sir, I have the feeling that my predecessor knew where this Sherwood could be found, and was perhaps about to order him arrested."

"What about the woman who seems to have been traveling with him?"

Volkov was ready to produce her. Natalya Ivanovna, smiling graciously at her interrogators, claimed not to know where Sherwood was, and to be not particularly

concerned about him. She did not—could not—deny
that she and the American had entered Irkutsk
together, but the idea that he was an agent of the government in Washington was utterly ridiculous. And so
was the accusation that poor, well-meaning John had
murdered a policeman. No, some terrorist was certainly responsible for that.

Stolypin, regarding her sternly, insisted on the truth.

Natalya, who could be very much the lady when she
wished, demanded to know what grounds he had to
accuse her of telling anything else.

Privately she had decided, simply by looking at the
eminent visitor, that Stolypin did not believe in were-
bears. He was the type to stare with cold pity at anyone
who made such a suggestion. But Stolypin must also
know that many of the people did believe, and Natalya
thought he would not object to that—just as he did not
much object to parties and drunkenness, though he
was an abstemious man himself. Such beliefs, along
with the tenets of the Orthodox Church, and the divine
right of the tsar, were part of a much greater fabric, the
old inward truth of Holy Russia, whose fundamental
articles of faith had to be preserved at all costs.

The men looked at each other, both feeling unsure
of their ground and not knowing quite how to proceed.
Well, time would tell. Zagarin's purpose in keeping the
lady here would doubtless come to light sooner or
later.

Natalya smiled at them both. She felt secure, impenetrable. She hated men like these so much that she felt
she could conceal her feelings from them, where a
merely violent dislike would have somehow made itself
apparent.

Stolypin raised the point that Sherwood's relatives
back in Ohio represented themselves as deeply concerned, reluctant to believe either that he was dead, or
that he had shot and killed a policeman without great
provocation. Their letters from home piled up for him
at Padarok Lessa. By now the American legation had
been trying for months to find out what had happened

to him. Zagarin, like many other officials, had received inquiries.

Volkov mused that this attention could be taken as evidence that Sherwood was indeed a secret agent of the American government, of President Teddy Roosevelt in particular.

But Natalya, temporizing, her mind seeming to wander, managed to make herself look innocent but not too innocent. She succeeded in raising in Stolypin's mind grave doubts that she had anything to do with any plot. In the process she began making Volkov and his predecessor look like fools.

Around noon, a heavily guarded sled came to take the Minister secretly to the railroad station, where his private train awaited. He was in a hurry to move on, to pursue his investigations elsewhere.

Having had no word of Natalya for a day, Sherwood the Bear was overjoyed to see her come hurrying downstairs. Since Zagarin's passing, the bear no longer rated a special guard, and the two of them were quite alone.

She brought word of Stolypin's visit and reported that Volkov was in a bad mood. On top of everything else, the Councilor had just been informed by telegraph that his wife, having settled the family affairs in Moscow, would soon be on her way to join him with the children. In that case, Eva would soon have to find herself another situation.

Sherwood, after Natalya had hurried upstairs again, pondered the contrast between Comrade Svoboda back in Nizhni Novgorod, and the government officials here, in their attitudes toward certain things that some people lumped under the heading of superstition, although others believed implicitly.

Paradoxically, Sherwood in bear-form had more time to think than ever before. His physical activities were now quite limited in scope, and the way was clear for mental enterprise.

It occurred to Sherwood that one set of his enemies,

die-hard supporters of the old regime, like Zagarin, obviously knew the truth about his Changing, and were ready to accept it as part of the nature of the world. But his other set of foes, the atheists and modern thinkers on both sides of the power struggle, were at a disadvantage because they would not or could not believe. Now it occurred to Sherwood to wonder if they would try to fit the miracle under the heading of Evolution. *That* was something modern thinkers were supposed to believe in.

Volkov was in a mood to punish Natalya for her failure to cooperate, for making him look bad in front of his boss. He met her when she returned upstairs, and announced his intention to use the bear in an exhibition of bearbaiting. He had some idea of the version wherein the bear is chained and then set upon by savage dogs, as an entertainment.

A second possibility, one which many folk found very amusing, was the whipping of a blinded bear.

A third would be to pit the bear, once it was fully recovered from its previous wounds, against a large aggressive bull.

Natalya, her heart threatening to leap out of her throat, struggled to maintain her composure while she protested violently against any such destruction of her property.

And Eva, who happened to be eavesdropping, was aroused to a desperate urgency to free the bear.

Getting Natalya to herself a minute after the angry Volkov had dismissed her, the Councilor's mistress confessed that she too knew the animal to be a man.

That evening, with the Minister on his way back to the capital, and Volkov's wife not yet on the scene, the routine of drunken partying resumed, signaled to the bear in the cellar by laughter, dancing feet, and loud phonograph music.

Tonight no one had yet thought of summoning the bear to join the fun; the beast was becoming too familiar, commonplace. No one at the moment was paying much attention to him. Sherwood considered that there would probably be no more than the ordinary complement of guards on duty, and they would be concentrating on the possibility of terrorist attack from outside the house or compound.

In the end it was Natalya who came hurrying down to the cellar, suddenly dressed for winter travel and carrying a hacksaw filched from some workplace somewhere in the compound. Sherwood never asked her for the details.

Eva came with her, lending support, the two women obviously working together to save Sherwood's life. When Eva saw the bear again, she snarled at it in French: "I suppose you may be shot, John Sherwood, but that will be quicker than being torn to bits by hounds."

He quickly thrust his head close to the bars. The saw in a woman's inexpert hands wobbled over the collar's metal, but at last started to bite through, sprinkling the cell's floor with bright silver dust. Despite the discomfort, the bear held very still.

The collar went first, then the nose ring. In only a few minutes, though to Sherwood it seemed like many more, his silver bonds had fallen free.

THIRTY

Sawn free of his silver nose ring and collar, Sherwood had no trouble forcing his way right out through the iron grille covering the door. It was not the bars that gave way under the pressure, but the were-bear's flesh. But his body could not be harmed by the iron, and the seams that were opened in guts and bone and muscle closed again at once as soon as the barrier was past. The strong bars like dull knives sliced his body bloodlessly, almost without pain, and his body came smoothly together, healed without a trace of injury, as soon as it had passed completely outside the cell.

The sight set Eva trembling on the verge of panic, muttering about ghosts. Even Natalya, who had already witnessed greater miracles, was impressed.

At the moment of Sherwood's departure from his cell, the Karelian bear-hounds in their nearby kennel set up an absolute uproar.

Meanwhile Natalya was lamenting their lack of preparation for this moment. "We have no clothes for you, Sherwood, no sled, nothing . . ."

Eva, still determined to help, offered: "I have

brought you clothes!" And she held up the bundle she had carried down the stairs.

In a nervous voice, she explained that she had raided a closet and a trunk containing stuff which had belonged to Zagarin, and was being held for shipment when the colonel's next of kin had been determined. Especially handy, thought the bear eyeing these treasures, would be the late chief's spare winter coat and fur hat and boots—not, of course, the ones he'd been blown up in, which could hardly have been worth saving.

Mixed in with Zagarin's gear had been some of Sherwood's own clothes—most notably the vest, one of whose cartridge loops still held a silver bullet. Most of his own clothes had been ripped to shreds when he had Changed to a bear in his desperate effort to fight off the dogs.

But Sherwood was not waiting to debate the question; he was out of his cell and intended to stay out. As long as he remained in bear-shape he had all he needed, and he would worry later about the more elaborate requirements of humanity. Instead of hesitating or Changing he was heading straight for the back door that would afford him passage out of the house.

But he had scarcely started before he froze in his tracks, staring at an intermediate door in the passageway. He could hear—moments before the women heard them—the footsteps approaching on the other side.

The bear could recognize the purposeful footsteps, even above the background of the party's racket, before the door swung open, catching Eva behind it.

It was Volkov himself standing in the doorway, swaying as if he were somewhat drunk. The Councilor's eyes went wide at the sight of the bear before him. He had just time to draw his pistol before Sherwood's great paw brushed the man aside, slammed him into a wall with paralyzing force, though with no intent to kill.

Volkov bounced off the wall and went down as if shot. Eva, with a sharp little cry, took the fallen man's head in her lap, and began trying to soothe and comfort him.

Sherwood slammed the door shut again with his great paw, and in the same moment realized that he had to Change briefly, to talk to Natalya.

Eva, without ever really thinking about the matter, had somehow been nursing the assumption that the Bear when restored to humanity would become a handsome prince, as in certain ancient stories—beyond that point her thoughtless dreams had never carried her.

Now she was stricken by disappointment. Before her stood just another man, scarred and rather ugly, undistinguished in his nakedness, swearing and grumbling as he groped through the clothing she had brought.

His beard, like Maxim's earlier, had been growing, in potential, on his potential man-form face, his hair atop his potential head, even while that phase of his existence was suppressed. But full beards and wild hair were common here on the frontier, even among the soldiers.

The look on Eva's face reminded Sherwood that no one now alive in Irkutsk, except Natalya, had ever seen him in man-form. Walking on two legs, he ought to be able to get past any of these folks without being recognized. Volkov's dazed eyes, looking up from where his head lay cradled in Eva's lap, were now following Sherwood's movements with a complete lack of comprehension.

Somewhere a few yards away, the Karelian bearhounds were sustaining their frenzied racket.

Eva muttered dazedly, in Russian: "You? You were the bear?"

Over the last months, Sherwood's total immersion in a Russian world had greatly improved his familiarity with the language. He found himself now able to understand what Eva said. He nodded to her, but made no further effort to identify himself.

Then hastily he conferred in English with Natalya. There was no time to waste. A bear running for a long distance through the city streets, even at this late hour, could not fail to draw a crowd, provoke a relentless pursuit. And Natalya could not escape the town by running. A sled had to be obtained—of course with a party in progress, a dozen sleds were on hand, ready to go at short notice. Horses and drivers were waiting more or less together, in the large stable, out of the worst of the cold. But Natalya was known; she could not simply commandeer transportation without the Chief's authority.

Quickly they decided on a plan. Moments later the Bear, having padded through interior hallways to the back door of the house, burst out into the street, in the process knocking over and stunning a sentry. With a burst of speed the four-legged beast got round a corner and out of sight, before anyone else took notice.

Once he had fought his way clear, out into the open air, the Bear's sense of smell was almost completely nullified by heavy snow and wind. But so would be the noses of any pursuing hounds. Vision was also handicapped by heavy snow, but hearing retained its superiority over the corresponding human sense. Some instinctive sense of direction also seemed to come into play.

Beset by the most blinding snow as it went shuffling instinctively toward the north, the bear could only dream or imagine that a special smell came from that direction, the domain of seals and ice and ocean, half a continent away.

Two or three streets away from the fortified compound, Sherwood pounced out of shadows in a darkened street to commandeer a sled, loaded with well-to-do celebrants who were doubtless on their way from one party to another.

The ambush required precise timing, and delicate judgment regarding the wind, to keep the horses from scenting their attacker. A sleigh drawn by frightened horses would outrun a bear, unless the pursuer was able to overtake it in the first swift charge.

Sherwood knew he had in his ursine bones and muscles the ability to run twice as fast as any man. But he knew in his lungs and heart that the massive body of a bear could not sustain such speed for any distance, could never overtake frightened horses in a long chase.

The problem was complicated by the need to keep from injuring the horses. But by threatening to leap in at one side of the vehicle, Sherwood terrorized the driver and passengers into leaping out on the other. Then, as soon as he had two feet firmly aboard, he himself changed into man-form and seized the reins. He managed to stop the horses, then grabbed up a providential lap robe and wrapped himself in it before any important parts were seriously damaged by the cold. The impromptu driving lessons he had received from Natalya now proved very useful. In nightmares suffered during his long confinement in bear-form, he had been crushed by the certainty that his humanity was gone forever. But the routine human skills he had been most worried about came back with reassuring quickness.

Meanwhile Natalya, wearing Sherwood's vest, had picked up Volkov's pistol, and also the Mosin-Nagant dropped by the frightened sentry. Hastily she followed Sherwood out the back door. She leaped onto the sled as soon as the bear had stopped it and took over the task of driving.

Once Sherwood had regained his humanity and freedom, he felt a great repugnance to the idea of ever becoming a bear again—he knew he still had the capability, but he had sworn to himself that if he were ever allowed to regain his humanity, he would never make that Change again.

Eva, acting on impulse as she always did in important matters, had gone back, repenting, to her relationship with the new District Chief. She petted the stunned

Volkov, whose head still lay in her lap, trying to nurse him back to full awareness.

What she really needed was someone or something to take care of.

Eva Pavlovna had been extremely angry with the Colonel before he was killed, and of course at the same time afraid of him.

She was angry at Volkov too, but less afraid.

Eva had no wish to get away. She knew that Natalya and Sherwood were fleeing together, and vaguely she wished them well.

But she greatly missed the beautiful bear.

In the morning, when the snow had ceased to fall, and Volkov had more or less fully recovered his senses, he posted men at the railroad station, and on all the roads, with orders to look out for a woman matching the description of Natalya.

Also an abortive attempt was made to hunt the escaped bear with a pack of Karelian bear-hounds. But the pursuers could not agree on which way the bear might be expected to go; and in any case they never succeeded in picking up the trail of either the woman or the bear. It was as if the driving snow had blown them away completely.

THIRTY-ONE

❧

The first hours of their flight went smoothly.
Natalya during her enforced residence in Volkov's house, had kept her eyes and ears open,
and now knew the best route to take out of town at
night without being observed or challenged by police.

Sherwood rejoiced fiercely in the cold air blasting the
small exposed portion of his thin human skin. He took
joy from the violence of the wind that drove the snow,
because it meant that any trail their sled might leave
was going to be obliterated.

The pistol and rifle Natalya had picked up when
fleeing Volkov's headquarters rode in the sled. When
Sherwood had the chance, he examined them to see if
either might accept his remaining cartridge loaded
with a silver bullet. But unfortunately neither weapon
was of the proper caliber.

The couple made several stops near the edge of
town, gathering from shops that were still closed more
provisions, clothing, tools, necessities for their journey,
even a small tent. No ordinary shopkeeper's locks

could long withstand a bear's strength directed by a
human intelligence.

By the time Sherwood and Natalya had left Irkutsk
behind them, the sled was carrying a fairly large supply
of food, largely in the form of ice-blocks, frozen portions of soup and gruel and stew which, when thawed
would once more become suitable for human stomachs.
Each roughly cubical block, about eight inches on a
side, had the ends of a short length of rope frozen into
it, thus forming a convenient handle.

Natalya and Sherwood were frequently buffeted by
the frozen blocks of soup, milk, and other liquids,
which although customarily shipped and stored in this
form during the winter, battered the sled's passengers
and other cargo heavily as its runners slid up and down
the uneven ice.

On several of the streets and on many roads in and
near the city, the stony ice composing the road surface
had been carved into frozen waves and humps by
heavy sled traffic, and the ride was very uncomfortable—especially at high speed.

Summer was only an unreal memory now, and its
events seemed to have taken place in another life.
"What month is this?" Sherwood demanded when he
had Changed again to man-form, and was riding with
his companion in the sled.

"November."

Before morning the snow had ceased, the cold intensified. The wind had ripped away the clouds, and the
broad, untrodden snowfields glistened under the stars
and moon, displaying the beauty of a savage fairyland.
When dawn approached, finding them still near the
city, they encountered a fair amount of traffic on the
frozen road.

When the tardy winter daylight arrived at last,
Irkutsk lay well behind them. Around them and ahead,
the land was vastly transformed from the scenes Sherwood remembered, approaching Irkutsk at the end of
summer. Green had disappeared, leaving only shades

of gray and white, relieved by the stark black of the
trunks and limbs of trees. Sherwood felt he had
entered a different continent, a different world. During
the weeks of his confinement, the trees had gone
through their display of autumn foliage, when the
weather for a brief period had been still mild. Come
and gone were the signs of harvesttime: wheat, grapes,
other fruit, other grains.

"Do you think they'll throw Gregori in prison now?"
Natalya asked. "Or move him to a different village?"

"Because we're free? No. First, they don't know
about me; Eva won't say anything. And it'll never dawn
on them that Greg's sister, a mere woman, might be
going after him."

When she moved in revolutionary circles, Natalya
had heard of the village called Taimyr, which among
exiles and their friends had acquired a modest degree
of fame for its isolation, remarkable even for a Siberian
settlement. She thought she could eventually find her
way to the spot. "But it will take us months to get there.
Perhaps a year. We won't be traveling on railroads."

"I'm still game. Lead on."

"The geography is confused in my mind, and there
are few useful maps. Or none. But I wonder—"

"What?"

"If Maxim might have chosen Taimyr as the place to
put his brother away because it lies near Padarok
Sivera."

A choice of wide, clear highways lay before them—the
Russian winter highways leading into the north; the
winding surfaces of frozen rivers. The broad Angara
ran northeast through the city of Irkutsk, then curved
north to flow eventually into the giant Yenisei.

They rested for part of the morning in a shelter run by
a monastery, and pushed on shortly after midday.

The signs of industry, farming, population, fell away
with amazing swiftness. The Siberian forest was dense,

and for the most part intensely quiet. From the frozen riverbed, it presented two dark green walls, almost unbroken, seemingly impenetrable. The pines and firs often reached a height of a hundred feet or more.

Now and then wildlife, on wings or feet, started into view. There were flights of wildfowl, woodcocks, partridges, and grouse. Gray hares, startlingly large. Once Sherwood's eyes were quick enough to discern the fluffy tail of a fox.

The days passed, and the long nights. At each resting place, they built a fire. And Sherwood hunted, on four legs, saving ammunition.

The body of a were-bear, perhaps nine times the weight of the corresponding human form, required correspondingly greater amounts of food. For that reason, it was better for Sherwood to do as much of his eating as possible in man-form. On the other hand, the Bear consumed, and delighted in, varieties of food that Sherwood the man would not consider tasting unless forced by starvation.

Once one got a few versts away from any railroad, especially if one were also distant from the major rivers, the population density dropped off sharply. Settlements of any kind became smaller and scarcer, roads thinner and less common.

A month after their flight from Irkutsk, and a thousand miles farther north, the land was empty indeed. But as yet the village of Taimyr, the Arctic sea and the mystic, invisible domain of Padarok Sivera were nowhere near. Siberia still stretched on to the ever-receding horizon, and endlessly beyond—an ocean of land, that in Sherwood's soul, and in the nightmares his soul produced, began to take on the limitless quality of the sky itself.

As winter deepened, the sun's appearances became ever more brief and feeble. The light swung up a little distance above the horizon for a few hours each day, and then sank back.

Eventually the shortest day of the year was reached, and passed.

"Merry Chirstmas," Sherwood said one morning. He was really only guessing at the date.

"And the same to you."

They both had happy childhood memories of Christmas trees.

And a few days later he began with "Happy New Year—nineteen-oh-nine."

Adopting new identities as necessary, the American and Natalya began to pass openly through the increasingly infrequent villages and towns.

Eventually whole days of travel passed without sight of any humans, or even of any marks left by humanity. This world contained no road, no smoke from even an isolated fire.

The heavy snows Sherwood had been expecting failed to materialize. Natalya knew, from those who had been here, that comparatively little snow fell in northern Siberia—the cold there tended to be dry.

But incredibly intense. Only in Arctic North America had Sherwood ever experienced the like.

Here it was easy to get the impression that humanity was in danger of extinction, while every other kind of life still thrived. The treetop level was lower now, with great gaps between the individual trees, whose trunks were also growing thinner. More and more flatlands, certain to be swampy when the snow was gone. Here and there the snow had been dug and pushed away by grazing animals, revealing scanty bushes and moss.

They continued to work their way farther and farther north, groping for the river that came closest to the village called Taimyr. They were hoping to meet someone who could tell them where they were, alert for any further word they might be able to gather concerning Gregori's fate—but now there was almost never anyone to talk to.

The sheer immensity of Siberia had begun to sink into Sherwood's consciousness.

He remembered now a peasant proverb that he'd heard somewhere: *God is high up, and the tsar is far away.*

Eventually they reached a settlement whose people had heard of the village called Taimyr. No one here seemed to speak Russian, but when they heard the name, they pointed—farther north.

Coming at last to a village of respectable size, safely distant from any telegraph line, Sherwood and his companion traded in their big sled and its team of horses for a much smaller, lighter vehicle complete with furs and heavy robes and pulled by dogs—not bear-hounds, these, but huskies. The owner threw in some fishing tackle.

On most days, Sherwood moved for long hours in bear-form, while only Natalya rode the sled or loped along behind it. He had to travel at a distance, downwind, to keep the dogs steadily at their task.

For a time Sherwood considered pulling the sled himself. But a quick trial proved that the bear was not very good at such a task, except over very short distances. He tired too readily.

Natalya had hazy recollection of the names of certain rivers, forests, villages; Father had spoken of them once, or many times, when he had been drinking, and recalled his own trip to Padarok Sivera.

"But Greg was always more interested in Padarok Sivera than I was."

The couple were now working their way north along a broad river they were unable to identify with any certainty, a sheet of snow and ice that grew broader with the entrance of each tributary.

More than a month after Christmas, with the days beginning perceptibly to lengthen, they decided to leave it, and strike out along a tributary which seemed likely to bring them eventually close to Taimyr.

At least once a day they stopped and built a fire, here a necessity of human survival. Bears seemed to carry their own internal fires with them, and to Sherwood in that form the cold was not uncomfortable. If he meant to Change on the trail, he'd strip off his clothes under the cover of a large fur robe. Momentary exposure to these temperatures was enough to sting, to put in danger of freezing any of the body's outlying possessions such as toes or earlobes.

The tributary was yet another huge Russian river, of whose name they could not be certain—not the Yenisei, Natalya thought, for that stream's banks would be more thickly populated, even this far north. But of comparable breadth and volume.

Now they feared that their map, which Natalya had managed to steal in preparation for the escape, was beginning to play them false. They were on a huge, broad river, but were again uncertain of its name—or if it even had one.

On a comparatively sunny day, Sherwood in manform caught and pulled up a fish through a hole chopped in the ice. The live catch twisted once in air, twice—and then, before it hit the snow, was struck by frozen rigidity as if by a bullet, slain in midair by one snap from the fangs of cold.

Meanwhile days were also passing for Maxim on his own bold journey into the unknown north. A total, finally, of many days. But Padarok Sivera failed to appear, and the inside of Gregori's head had still not recovered from what the rifle butt had done to it. When Maxim ordered the sleds to stop, the injured man was kept warm, and as comfortable as possible, in a tent of reindeer skin.

Gregori had rarely spoken during the weeks since his brother had carried him away from the village of Taimyr, and what he did say was almost inconsequential. But Maxim listened carefully to every word, and continued to consult with the injured man on the progress of their journey.

With his helpless brother and an entourage of about a dozen followers, Maxim continued to work his way in the direction of the Pole, confident that he was getting near the mystic domain of Padarok Sivera. As they progressed, they encountered fewer and fewer natives.

Maxim had been making plans for a long time, beginning even before he left St. Petersburg, on how to challenge Grandfather's power at the estate if that turned out to be necessary. But first he wanted to be completely healed of the crippling that afflicted him whenever he assumed, or tried to assume, bear-form. Then it would be time to think of challenging the old man.

The true healing, Maxim's experience had now demonstrated to his own satisfaction, came with a diet of human flesh.

At one of their rest stops Maxim tried to talk to his brother, about the wonders they were going to discover, tried to tell the brain-injured man the following story. Halfway through the telling, Koba came to squat beside them in the snow, to listen without comment, his eyes gleaming.

More than a century ago (as the story went), one of the afflicted Lohmatski clan, putting his shape-changing condition to practical use—meanwhile glorying more and more in the power if afforded him—became a Siberian fur trapper of legendary prowess. Very few of his contemporaries understood the abilities behind his great success. He roamed the land in bear-form, gathering sables and lesser trophies with his own keen nose and ears, his deftly brutal paws. He sniffed out trails and dens where he, or some colleague restricted to working with two good hands, could set steel traps or deadfalls in exactly the most productive places.

The were-bear was also very good at robbing other people's trap lines. And in violently eliminating other trappers.

There also turned out to be a large profit in intimidating native tribes into providing a large harvest of furs.

Sooner or later, other trappers realized what was going on. But whoever tried to stop the thievery met a violent end, somewhere out on the trail.

Trapper Bear eventually went west to European Russia with a fortune, to die peacefully as a human, in his bed at home.

Gregori's recovery from the smashing blow to his head was still ominously delayed.

At almost every stop, Maxim petted and cajoled his brother, saying he depended on him for help in locating Padarok Sivera.

"Maybe Grandfather will find a way to help you, once we reach him. He's a very wise man, you know."

"Wise man," Gregori repeated softly, watching Maxim's lips. The man on the pallet gave the impression of someone whose thoughts were very far away.

Someone came to Maxim with a question about the timing of their next rest stop. It turned out that Koba had suggested asking him.

Maxim observed privately that Koba was never the one to take the lead, among the exiles and villagers, in communicating with the Bear. No, that one would bear watching. He generally stayed in the background, watching intelligently, letting someone else assume the initial risks, waiting to see how he might profit by whatever happened.

Maxim had never met Koba before encountering him in Taimyr. But somehow he felt that he had come to know the man during the days of their journey.

Continuing his progress toward Padarok Sivera, moving with his small party through a loneliness as intense as the cold, Maxim had encountered no other villages, not even a hunting party or the trail of one. He was disappointed. Followers were good to have, and the more fanatically devoted, the better.

At almost every halt he entreated his brother to give

him guidance. Sometimes he received what might have
been a meaningful answer.

Twice on this leg of his journey Maxim dined on one
of his supporters. This depleted his thin ranks further,
but he had now almost completely recovered his full
bear-form. He took these meals in isolation, and none
of the survivors ever asked him what had become of
the missing ones.

*If one is only completely sure of oneself, and completely
savage, then they will follow.*

Of course not all who listened to a Bear would
become his followers. Some were certain to turn into
dedicated enemies. But there could be a satisfaction in
acquiring enemies as well. To devote one's life to being
the enemy of some belief, or some person, was also a
form of discipleship.

Sherwood and Natalya, making their way toward the
Pole Star, still at an unknown distance from Padarok
Sivera, were given very little warning when a blizzard
hurled itself upon them. The dogs could no longer
move the sled, gave up trying, and disappeared into
the howling white inferno.

Sherwood turned to bear-form, Changed back long
enough to shout "Wait here!" above the wind, and then
reverted once more to furry bulk. The Bear's senses
probing through the blast had signaled the nearness of
several caribou.

Leaving Natalya huddled against the overturned
sled, he disappeared into the driving snow. In two minutes he was back, dragging a slain caribou. Another
minute sufficed for claws and teeth to disembowel the
kill, hollowing out the carcass sufficiently to allow a
tender, shivering human to crawl inside and thus avoid
death by freezing. The bear clung on outside, sharing
what warmth the carcass radiated, sheltered from wind
by the snowdrifts building up around the sled.

In the morning, with the storm abated, Sherwood
assured his partner: "An old trick I learned from the
Sioux."

The dogs had all disappeared, presumably frozen dead, and the sled was useless. Once again, as during their escape from the police at Nizhni Novgorod, Natalya rode astride a cooperative bear, carrying a bundle of essentials and clutching handfuls of fur as necessary to stay on. For the next few days, in deep snow, this mode of transportation was the only one possible.

Wandering hunters who saw the bear carrying someone on its back muttered prayers and incantations, believing the rider a powerful wizard indeed.

THIRTY-TWO

❦

A week after they survived the blizzard, Sherwood
and Natalya, her outer clothing still matted with
dried and frozen caribou blood, at last walked
within sight of the village of Taimyr.

Whenever Sherwood stopped to consider all the difficulties of their journey, he could only marvel at the
fact that he and Natalya had not become hopelessly
lost, wandering for a year or even longer before
finding their way to this remote spot.

But in fact the travelers, aided by some combination
of guidance systems possessed by woman, man, and
Bear, had needed only about six months to reach their
goal. At the time of their arrival, Sherwood estimated
that the month was May. At this latitude, about seventy
degrees north, the spring thaw had not yet begun in
earnest, but the bear walking on river ice could feel
new flow and pressure underneath, the transformation
impending upstream, in the south. The Arctic sun was
above the horizon for many hours each day, but
remained low in the sky. Fog created a kind of eerie
twilight.

Whenever Sherwood had Changed, during the last few days, his fur appeared and remained white, and he thought his size was slightly smaller. He could only conclude that a were-bear might assume the form of any of several different ursine species, consistent with the territory he happened to be in at the moment. A week earlier he had found himself appearing as a hybrid or crossbreed, reminding himself of the North American subspecies known as the barren-grounds grizzly.

At the moment of sighting Taimyr, the couple were virtually holding their breaths in hopes of finding Gregori. They tried to find encouragement in the fact that the settlement was unusually large for one this far north. It consisted almost entirely of log huts with sod roofs. A few dwellings boasted small windows of oiled paper.

In a hasty conference the couple decided it might be wiser for the Bear to scout ahead alone, then to appear as two human travelers with no obvious reason for their presence.

The inhabitants of Taimyr, when Sherwood approached them, were surprisingly not all that astonished to meet a second sapient bear.

The people who had seen Maxim as a Bear, but had declined to follow him, were universally reluctant to talk about the experience.

Those who remained in the village were mainly innocent victims of the system. None of them wanted to accompany Sherwood and Natalya on their journey north.

Once again, as on the occasion of Maxim's arrival a month earlier, the wretched unfortunates of Taimyr had put out the fires in one of their huts, and were leaving the door and windows of the dwelling standing open for a day and a night, in a desperate attempt to put an end to the ubiquitous cockroaches and other pests. Meanwhile the remaining exiles of the village, three or four men and a couple of women, were standing outdoors in the twilight, in a temperature well below zero on anybody's scale, and argued—what else?—political and social theories.

When Sherwood in bear-form appeared before this debating group, its members at first retreated warily. They talked among themselves of borrowing firearms from one of the natives. But soon, seeing that the animal appeared quite tame, they returned to the vicinity of the fire, and took the presence of the bear as an example that might serve to illustrate the subject of their argument. Still the bear did not appear menacing.

Some of the villagers, seeing how tame the beast appeared, discussed the advisability of throwing it some food; they were not starving, but suffering mainly from the grimness of their environment, and the sameness of their diet. Bread, fish, and dried meat. For a treat they occasionally thawed out a block of soup that had been frozen in the autumn. Also the creature looked so tame that it seemed harmless.

The scientist among the exiles, he who had tried to discuss the different temperature scales intelligently, took the opportunity to comment learnedly on the resemblances, and differences, between the human and the ursine species; that, for example, the male bear had a bone in his penis.

"But look at the scoundrel! I swear, he is listening to our debate." The man's voice changed. "I wonder if . . ."

Meanwhile the exiled factory worker, under the impression that Maxim Ivanovich had returned, at last could stand the suspense no longer. Coming round the fire, he advanced on the second bear, berating it in terms of loathing and defiance.

Sherwood, confronted by this eminently brave if not entirely reasonable man, retreated, and lurked in the background while Natalya advanced to do the talking.

As soon as Sherwood was sure that things were going

peacefully, he restored himself to man-form and joined Natalya and the others near the fire. Already he could read in his companion's eyes her bitter disappointment at learning that Gregori was no longer here.

"He was here, yes," said one. "But then—he was taken away."

"What do you mean? Taken away how?"

The worker told them what his fellow exiles soon confirmed; that Gregori had been hurt, and had been carried off by his brother, taken north on some kind of crazy-sounding search. "Like you, his brother was cursed—or is it blessed?—with the *obaraten* power."

Sherwood interrupted urgently. "Did any of them say where they were going?"

"The man who—who Changed—kept saying something, over and over. The Gift of the North. That was it, the Gift of the North."

Sherwood, determined to press on along the route where Gregori had been taken, had no wish to encourage any of its people to follow him. The thought that they might choose to worship him as he appeared in bear-form was totally repulsive. He would accept followers only if he thought their help essential. Natalya urged him to think about it, but in the end his attitude did not matter: there were no volunteers.

Over the next few weeks, the two travelers pressed on as best they could toward their unseen goal. Sherwood had begun to worry that they might not recognize the place when they found it. How had the borders of this estate been specified, in old Tsar Ivan's original land grant? As far as Natalya could remember, the old writings, authors quoting at second or third hand, said it had been defined in terms of the area drained by certain rivers. Nothing was more certain than that rivers meandering through flatlands would change their courses from time to time. Adding to the difficulty was the fact that no one, even in the early twentieth century, had mapped these streams with any certainty.

Remembering the Wright brothers and their Paris

demonstrations, Sherwood thought that in another hundred years, someone might be flying over this land in an aeroplane, mapping the rivers from the air.

Lost in his own journey, Maxim had understood from the start that his ultimate goal, the estate where, he was convinced, Grandfather Lohmatski still ruled, would be actually less difficult to reach in the dry, extreme cold of the dark Arctic winter, illuminated by moon and stars, and by the multicolored blaze of the aurora, than in the summer of low continuous sun. In winter the ground was hard as iron. Seldom did the soft snow on level ground drift high enough to seriously impede progress by sled or skis or snowshoes; but always there was the terrible cold, an almost-visible god that ruled the land.

As long as everything was frozen, one could make good progress even in human form, traveling behind dogs or reindeer on a sleigh over frozen streams, down one of the long rivers, then up some tributary, and by snowy road overland to a smaller stream; then down-stream on that watercourse. In summer the top foot or so of earth, down to the permafrost, dissolved into shallow ponds and quagmire, nurturing incredible swarms of biting insects. Such roads as existed were mere tracks.

Migratory reindeer herders traversed this landscape in great seasonal migrations, bringing with them no more than faint echoes of the outside world. And once in a while some determined agent of the tsarist government found his way this near the tip of the world—if this agent should disappear, it was only natural that he would be presumed lost in one of the many ways by which people here were wont to disappear. A replace-ment would be appointed in due time.

Since leaving Taimyr with about a dozen followers, Maxim in bear-shape had devoured half the cadre, preferring to consume his most fanatical revolutionary theorists. He found that he could easily down two undernourished intellectuals at a sitting if he was really hungry. Continually he doubted and questioned the loyalty of the remainder.

Plainly the survivors were all terrified. But with amazing stupidity they clung to the idea that without the Bear in this wilderness they would quickly be lost altogether. Besides that, Maxim was quick to let them know that anyone who tried to run away would be eaten ahead of his regular turn.

Every two or three days he killed a reindeer or a seal, in excess of his own needs, so his followers would have something to subsist on. His own diet toward the end consisted almost entirely of human flesh. The benefits were obvious: his silver-bullet wounds had now almost completely disappeared.

One day, which was otherwise much like other days, Maxim and what was left of his party, the number of survivors no more than half a dozen, at length reached the mysterious realm called Padarok Sivera.

From the moment of Maxim's arrival in the shadowy village of skin tents, he felt sure that he had come to the right place. One thing that assured him he had left the ordinary world behind was a huge, enigmatic, translucent structure that had been reared on the right bank of the frozen river. It was many times the size of any building that one might expect to find in a small village. And it looked like an enormous house, or the start of an enormous house, constructed entirely of ice.

Maxim ignored this strange construction for the moment. On foot and in man-form he advanced toward the huts, most of his remaining entourage shuffling at his back, while two stayed with the sleds and dogs. Several people, Ostyak or Tungus by the look of their heavy clothing, stared at their approach, then hesitantly advanced to meet them.

Communication with the inhabitants went better than he had feared it might. The first old man who approached and greeted the newcomers turned out to speak Russian, though with a most peculiar accent. He even gave a Russian name. It occurred to Maxim that some of the inhabitants of this place might very well be the descendants of the Russian sailors who must have come here with Grandfather, or of other explorers.

Speaking slowly and with pride, Maxim identified himself as the Lohmatski heir and then demanded: "Where is the old man? My grandfather?"

By now a small gathering of natives had surrounded him. They understood at once. They took him to the doorway of one of their dwellings made of reindeer skin, drew back the hanging flap, and showed him the frozen object mounted on tent poles just inside.

Maxim knew a thrill of triumph, of recognition. This was no ordinary bear's skeleton before him, nor was it that of any commonplace human being. From the distorted shape of Grandfather's corpse, he could see that the old man had still retained the ability to change into a Bear.

Grandfather's skeleton had been preserved in the transitional form in which he'd evidently died. It was a monstrous hybrid shape between ursine and human. Death had overtaken him in the middle of a spasmodic transformation.

Maxim wondered if matters would someday go that way for him as well. But then he shook himself, and resolutely thought of something else.

Shedding his clothing, he quickly showed them who and what he was.

The natives stood back in awe from him the newly arrived were-bear, as the great beast shouldered forward through Arctic sunshine and entered the shrine in the reindeer tent.

He did not really need the confirmation that came with the discovery of Grandfather's freeze-dried body, which the natives were keeping wrapped as a relic, so no dog or wolf or bear would chew on it. Speaking a kind of pidgin Russian, they told Maxim that the old man had died a month ago.

"It is well. It is all right. I am here now, and I am the true Bear."

This settlement where Grandfather had ruled, and where Maxim had now assumed the role of living god, was on the tundra, a treeless area of permafrost, and a great distance from any other settlement of any kind. The Arctic Circle lay hundreds of versts to the south. Only the camps of the tribes of reindeer herders, and of the Eskimo who dwelt in perpetual ice and snow, lay so far north.

Padarok Sivera in fact was so near the realm of eternal ice, the climate so inhospitable, that Maxim could easily believe no agriculture of any kind had ever succeeded. Yet it was evident that people had been surviving here for a long time as hunters and gatherers, eating fish and seals, roots, berries, and wild birds, along with other game.

One of Maxim's first acts on assuming absolute command of the estate was to forbid the hunting of any bear.

Another of his very early orders was that his brother be lifted from the sled and carried into one of the reindeer tents. The previous inhabitants had brusquely been evicted by the Bear. They went out quickly, without murmuring, and then in the snow outside prostrated themselves before their newly restored deity.

The wounded man, as he had been doing lately in such intervals of lucidity as he was granted, muttered vague protests and warnings to his brother.

Maxim listened carefully, then frowned and shook his head. "But you must not think me a cannibal, dear Gregori. These fools I am consuming can hardly be thought of as members of my own species—or of yours. We Lohmatskis and a few others, the natural leaders and rulers, are a race apart."

Even with the modest resources of the village now available, it was still a lot of trouble to care for an invalid, or a prisoner. Much easier simply to kill him. And eat him.

Maxim had to think seriously about how long he

could continue to rely upon his brother as a source of mystic inspiration.

Returning frequently to the shrine, Maxim lost himself in intense contemplation of the freeze-dried corpse of Grandfather. He gave orders that whale-oil lamps should be kept burning in front of it. For what seemed a long time, he forgot about his problems, his sister and his American rival—even his brother.

But the inattention was only temporary; Gregori's knowledge could still be useful. He was still being taken care of, at Maxim's orders.

The new master of the estate planned a prominent mausoleum for Grandfather. Or what was left of that relic after he'd gnawed it. Now he considered ordering the building of a superior shrine—make it an integral part of the new ice palace. Yes, that would be the way to go. Grandfather would be frozen like mammoth meat into a permanent block of ice.

At moments, casting his gaze across the stark extent of his new domain and almost dizzy with satisfaction, Maxim recalled with wonder and amusement his previous hopes and plans of promotion in the Ministry of the Interior. How superficial! What man would want to rely on offices and organizations to give him power when he could have sharp teeth and claws, and bulky muscles? And, as here, the freedom to exercise those advantages to the fullest without restraint!

Someday, someday, doubtless years from now, he would return in triumph to Petersburg and Moscow. Then all men would know and fear him as the Bear. But patience was essential; the conquest of the world could wait. First he had to perfect his grasp on the essentials of power and life.

As for Gregori—well, he had to be fed now, and tended like an infant. Maxim had to admit to himself that the man was slowly dying. Well, perhaps his usefulness was now about at an end anyway.

~

Gregori was no doubt dying. But there were times, in the darkness of the long nights, after Maxim had enjoyed one of the native women and then ordered her from his bed, when he realized that the old man was still alive and speaking to him from the security of his shrine.

Ordinarily, bears aged much more rapidly than humans. But did were-bears stick to an age corresponding to that of their human component?

Maxim had determined that he would obtain from Grandfather the secret, the means, to fully restoring his own health as a were-bear.

By now he at last had proved to his own satisfaction that a diet of human flesh was bringing about a full cure. But to feed on nothing but the intelligentsia—no, that couldn't be very healthy.

It occurred to the Bear that he ought to make sure that Grandfather's powers had all become his own, and to emphasize for his followers the transfer of power, by eating part of Grandfather. As he had eaten Father before him . . .

As Maxim meditated on this plan, he felt a sudden impulse to offer Koba the chance to take part in the same communion. But a moment later Maxim rejected the notion as frivolous.

THIRTY-THREE

From the moment when they first sighted the cluster of twenty or so skin tents, huddled at the mouth of a river with an inlet of the sea directly beyond, Natalya and Sherwood were sure they had discovered Padarok Sivera. Surely no more than one settlement of such size could maintain itself in this barren region. Beyond the inlet loomed a broader arm of the Arctic Ocean, dark, sullen, and immense; beyond that, the northern horizon was lost in endless grayness.

There were a few kayaks and other small boats of indeterminate design visible in the distance, resting on the snow near where the mouth of the river emerged at last into the darkness of open water.

Standing atop a low hummock of land, squinting into the low sun and wishing he had field glasses, Sherwood was able to make out in the distance the wreckage of a ship, showing broken masts and bowsprit. The hulk appeared to be bound in permanent ice, its crooked shape a shadow hanging black against ice and water. Natalya at his side spoke in a halting voice, recalling the family story; how Grandfather had come here by ship, more than forty years ago, bringing tools and supplies and determined to carve out his own domain, an estate whose master need not answer even to the tsar.

But something stranger than the ruined ship demanded Sherwood's attention. The nameless object loomed up, occupying a site on the east bank of the frozen river. It had the shape of an irregularly truncated pyramid about three stories high, and appeared to be made of glass. When Sherwood shifted his position by a few steps the low sun moved directly behind the structure, seeming to set it afire.

Dots that could only be humans clad in furs were slowly moving on and about the peculiar object, somehow grasping and dragging and lifting tiny crystal blocks. More moving dots were chopping and plowing slabs and chunks of ice out of the nearby river. A pair of reindeer were pulling one ice plow, a broad, harrow-like device, while sled dogs tugged less successfully at another.

The plows reminded Sherwood of a machine he had seen on his last visit to Ohio—the New Acme ice plow, forty tons an hour, from Sears, Roebuck. Meanwhile, on land, small dots that might be women and children appeared to be scraping at the snow. Probably they were digging under it to forage moss and other plants in competition with the reindeer.

But Sherwood's gaze kept drifting back to the glassy pyramid. To his companion he muttered: "What in the hell *is* that?"

Suddenly something about the building, the sun-fire shining through the ice, reminded Sherwood with a shock of something said to him, in a summer that seemed very long ago, by a holy fool standing on the bank of the Volga.

Natalya drew a deep breath. "I say we both just walk in. Any people living here are probably going to try to kill a polar bear on sight."

Sherwood nodded.

"And our first business is to discover the truth about Gregori if he's here, if he's still alive."

He nodded again. "That's why we're here. And if we run across Maxim . . ."

"We deal with him. Any way we have to." Natalya was still carrying the rifle she had taken in Irkutsk, and she checked the loading now. It was something she did frequently, a habit picked up from Sherwood on their long trek.

Maxim had been standing in man-form at ground level, near the base of his ice palace, which had been Grandfather's, and impatiently watching the work as it progressed. He was doubly impatient with anyone who interrupted him and threatened to delay the project.

Around him rose a babble of work-related talk, a pidgin mixture of several dialects. Tungus as well as Ostyaks formed the basic population of Padarok Sivera. Here had accumulated a number of outcasts, the disaffected, from several tribes. Among them were descendants of the crew of Grandfather's coastal sailing ship.

Evidently Grandfather, who had been the earlier incarnation of the Great Bear, had acted with cleverness and stubborn patience, using a variety of means to gather the necessary workers for the job. Remarks made by the natives had convinced Maxim that the old man had made a habit of capturing hunting and fishing parties from other, distant villages, and recruiting any wanderers who happened by. As a result, Maxim on his arrival at Padarok Sivera had found a population of almost a hundred people. He was able to dispatch hunting expeditions without depleting the ranks of workers too severely. The inhabitants survived on fish and the meat of seals and whales, their diets now and then augmented by a reindeer, and the scanty plant life in the vicinity.

For a short time everything had seemed to be going beautifully. But here, in the form of a child with an excited voice, came interruption to divert him yet again: the news of a pair of strangers approaching the village.

"Great Bear, they are a man and a woman, traveling on foot."

Maxim turned quickly, focusing on the distant dots. From his first look, he knew, with a mystic certainty, who they were: his sister and the American.

Well, let them come. Too bad that he had no silver bullets to finish Sherwood with. But he would find some other way.

Koba kept to himself his real opinion on many subjects, including the ice palace. He had been cunning, sub-servient to the Great Bear, and ruthless to everyone else. So far he had been able to get out of doing manual labor. He supervised work and enforced terror. When a worker laboring under a heavy ice cake slipped on the glassy steps and almost dropped his load, he cursed brutally at the man and menaced him with his rifle.

When a messenger arrived with a summons to attend the Great Bear, Koba responded quickly. The short man had quickly become one of the few privileged members of the settlement, one of those who, at the Bear's direction, carried a rifle. Other guards were armed with whalebone bows, and arrows tipped with bone or crystal, dipped in some lethal essence distilled from certain internal organs of the great white bear. Koba himself was intrigued by the idea of this poison and meant to learn more about it before he left this place (as he was secretly determined to do, when a good opportunity arose)—another bit of esoteric and valuable knowledge to carry with him back into the great wide world. He was seriously considering whether, when he had got safely out, it would be worth his while to report Maxim Lohmatski to the authorities in Petersburg.

Meanwhile, Maxim studied the two approaching fig-ures, and noted carefully that the smaller one was carrying their single rifle.

By now, almost a year after his wounding and con-version, the scars on Sherwood's human face and arm were still highly visible through slowly fading tracks of pink and tender and angry skin. The remnants of Natalya's crude stitches had long since been picked out of his skin. But it seemed likely that he would carry some remnant of the claw marks on his arm, and also those on his forehead, until his dying day.

"You have come to join me," were Maxim's first words, when the pair had trudged within easy speaking distance.

"We have come to find our brother," Natalya told him accusingly. Her face was weathered, as if she had lived in the open for a long time, and she looked older and tougher than Maxim had ever imagined she might.

He felt disappointed. "I was hoping you had come looking for the truth."

"What?"

"Gregori is in there." He nodded toward one of the larger tents, near the center of the village.

His sister turned her gaze toward the doorway of the tent, which was sealed by hanging skins. "Gregori has been hurt?"

"He's doing as well as can be expected."

Sherwood, who had been standing by in silence, suddenly put in, in broken Russian: "Why have you brought him here? What are you doing with these people? And what's that—thing, that they are building?"

Around them, the cutting and hauling of ice had faltered to a halt, and a small crowd of emaciated laborers had begun to gather, staring at the amazing phenomenon of new arrivals. Possibly to them it seemed even more amazing that the newcomers spoke to the Great Bear with such familiarity. Ordinarily such slacking on the job would have been enough to send the Bear into a rage. But at the moment Maxim had to concentrate on something he considered even more important.

Sherwood, on observing Koba, who had come up with rifle in hand to stand beside his master, had the feeling that he'd seen the man somewhere before. But the short man gave no sign of recognition.

In English Maxim said to Sherwood: "The answer to the question of what I am doing here is very simple. The real power, the real secret, is not in Petersburg, or Moscow. Or London or Berlin or Paris. Or Washington, for that matter. No, the secret which is really necessary lies out here."

Maxim smiled at his visitors, who were both gazing at him blankly. He added: "Grandfather has told me this. And many other things as well."

Natalya stirred. "Grandfather is still alive? Where is he?"

"Come, let me show you."

Maxim led them to the shrine the villagers had made inside a tent. There Grandfather's dried and frozen corpse, now little more than a skeleton, had been mounted upright, supported by a frame of poles. At first glance, the relic appeared to Sherwood as that of a large animal. When he looked at the thing more closely, he could see it as the body of a badly misshapen old man, with patches of long white human hair still clinging to the deformed skull. A small scroll that might have been parchment was gripped, like some kind of scepter of shamanic power, in one skeletal hand. The hands seemed to have nothing ursine about them—but then Sherwood remembered that bears' paws when stripped of skin and flesh looked notoriously like human hands.

Sherwood thought he was beginning to understand. Death had overtaken Grandfather when he was in the middle of a Change. He asked: "When did the old man die?"

"About a month before my arrival here—say two months ago."

Natalya put in sharply: "Before you got here? But you said he spoke to you."

"Indeed he did. And does."

Natalya thought she could feel the hair on the back of her neck trying to stand on end when she listened to her brother and observed the look, insanely certain and condescending, on Maxim's face.

The two newcomers exchanged glances; Maxim took note of this but said nothing. Soon enough his sister and the American would come to understand—and perhaps nothing would be lost if they did not.

Bear's skulls, along with a miscellany of other bones, including human skulls, decorated the interior of the tent that had become a shrine.

Maxim pulled from the old man's dead hand the plans, still intact, which the old man had drawn up for the building of his ice palace. Then he showed them to his visitors, who found it difficult to interpret the faded lines and figures.

Maxim was ready to interpret for them. Once he had begun on the subject of the ice palace, he needed no encouragement to keep going. He envisioned this monument to the Great Bear, as he called it, as an enormous structure. When finished it would comprise a thousand or more glittering translucent rooms, with towers of indeterminate height. At the top, the pinnacle of the pyramid, would be a small room, which only he, the Great Bear, could enter.

Another improvement on Grandfather's original plan would be the eventual subdivision of the lower levels of the palace into scores or even hundreds of cells, to serve as a commodious prison.

"Prison?" Sherwood couldn't decide whether the man before him was joking, or insane. "For whom?"

The Russian raised an eyebrow. "For the enemies of the Bear, of course."

"A prison of ice?" Natalya asked. "How could anyone survive?"

Maxim made an impatient motion, brushing such concerns aside. "The Eskimo survive in igloos. Anyway, what happens to individuals does not matter in the least. The number of incidental deaths will make no difference at all in the historical result."

Then he smiled suddenly at his visitors. "Being a Bear has taught me some very important truths."

Sherwood felt numb. "We want to see Gregori."

"In a moment." Maxim raised one finger, a lecturer making an important point. "For one thing, people in general—unlike bears—yearn to be told what to do. What they crave most of all is to be ordered to attack their enemies. And their enemies—whether they are Jews, or terrorists, or capitalist oppressors—are always less-than-human evildoers, whose destruction will make the world safe and enjoyable for all decent folk."

"Why do you—?" Natalya began. And then she let herself fall silent. It was as if she had given up.

Giving up was obviously the last thing on Maxim's mind. "Constant vigilance is essential," he assured the two before him. He was smiling, and there was no way they could tell if he was serious or spoke in mockery. "Evildoers who pretend to be loyal followers must be unmasked."

Maxim seemed to have run out of speeches for the moment. He told the newcomers that they were welcome to move into the tent where Gregori was staying. It was right next to his own.

"We must see Gregori," Natalya repeated as she started to turn away.

"You may do so. But one more thing, first." Standing now with folded arms, Maxim spoke graciously, as the tsar might do. "You may rest for the remainder of the day. Tomorrow, of course, you will have to join in the work on the great project. Work begins at sunup, which comes very early this time of year." He seemed to be perfectly serious.

In a neutral voice Sherwood asked: "You expect us to dig and carry ice?"

"Everyone must work, of course. There are no slackers here."

"We are going to see our brother," said Natalya again, and this time she turned away decisively.

Maxim went briefly to his own tent, where he had provided himself with such near-luxury as this remote half-migratory settlement could afford—of course he could enjoy such things only when in man-form. And these days he tended to a Bear almost continuously, unless he needed a human tongue to make his meaning clear to his followers. A Bear was not concerned with material luxury; when in that shape he required but little shelter from even the fiercest cold, and tended to be uncomfortable inside walls of any kind.

Except—perhaps—for walls of ice.

The thought carried him back irresistibly to thoughts of how the palace would look when it was completed. Grandfather had been a glorious genius to conceive such a project!

Natalya and Sherwood entered the tent which Maxim had indicated and found her brother there, lying wrapped in furs on a raised bed. A woman of the village, who was sitting beside him and trying to feed him from a bowl, looked up startled at the entry of two strangers. Gregori looked ill, almost comatose. His bearded face was tragically thin, and it was hard to tell whether he recognized either of his two visitors.

The native woman fussed about for a few moments, then left, as if frightened by the presence of newcomers.

Making themselves at ease as much as possible, sitting on the spare bed of old ship's planking, the invalid's sister and friend made every effort to talk to him.

Gregori muttered a few words from time to time, but all were incoherent.

Natalya took up a bowl of soup which the attendant had been trying to feed him, sniffed at it and tasted it, then tried to feed her brother, but with little success.

"We'll get you out of here, dearest brother!" she burst out impulsively, putting down the bowl and spoon and hugging him.

Neither Sherwood nor Greg said anything to that.

But Natalya thought that her brother responded by shaking his head ever so slightly, *No*.

Struck by an idea, she turned to ask Sherwood, "Who was that man with the rifle who stood beside Maxim? I have the feeling I've seen him somewhere before."

"I thought so, too, but I don't know where. Or if I ever heard his name."

From the natives they met in casual encounters among the tents, mostly children and the aged engaged in housekeeping chores, Sherwood and Natalya learned that Grandfather had started the ice-palace project early in the winter, months before he died. Long months of labor had been required to advance the construction to its present stage. Tons and tons of ice had been cut and put into place, with tools forged of iron wrested from the abandoned ship. The construction was basically crude, showing no trace of the traditional craftsmanship and artistry that went into such structures back in Europe—or that Sherwood had once seen in St. Paul, as a child in 1888. The building now under construction in Siberia was some thirty feet high, and growing higher, and covered as much as a quarter of an acre. He thought it must have been going up all through the long winter. It had thoughtfully been located on the low bank very near the river, to minimize the distance ice blocks had to be hauled.

Construction of the building had come to a halt, or almost, before the arrival of Grandfather's successor as Great Bear. But Maxim had speeded up the pace again, and quite a lot had already been done.

When the couple had withdrawn again into their tent, with only the dazed Gregori to overhear, Natalya repeated a certain old story to Sherwood in English:

"One winter in St. Petersburg, almost two hundred years ago, the Empress Anna gave orders for an ice palace to be built. It was planned and executed as a great amusement for the whole court. The entire structure was carved and built from ice. Furniture, dishes, kitchen utensils, all of the same material. Nothing was left out, except of course heating and the people to live in it.

"Then one of the favorites of the empress came up with a brilliant suggestion. A pair of clowns—court jesters as you say—were married with great ceremony, and the Empress gave her blessing on them before they were sent to spend their wedding night in their new house.

"Next morning, of course, they were found frozen to death. But none of the important people paid much attention to that."

Meanwhile the Bear had left his tent and was back on the job site, growling orders. Work had resumed on the pyramid of ice, and an intense level of effort was being maintained.

Gradually Sherwood, looking out at intervals from the doorway of the tent, realized that almost all waking hours of the population, not absolutely required by the tasks of basic survival, must be devoted to the ice palace.

A score or more of men and women had been put to work carving all the blocks and decorations, and scores of others were engaged in the assembly. Some used mere slings of reindeer hide, instead of the metal tools with which Sherwood was familiar, to haul and lift the heavy ice blocks. Water, hauled up in covered buckets to keep it from freezing solid on the way, served to weld the blocks together solidly.

The sounds of chopping, carving, scraping, plowing ice rang out clearly in the frozen air.

Teams of laborers were struggling at peril of their lives, to lift into place the huge slippery blocks required for the next highest level.

Looking at the villagers, seeing blue eyes and Russian features on their hungry faces, Natalya decided that some of Grandfather's crew had evidently survived that voyage of forty years ago, and had interbred with the native women.

Sherwood murmured to her: "We'd better take turns at trying to get some rest." Then he added: "Comrade Svoboda was crazy, in her way. But she was never as crazy as Maxim is now."

Natalya, half-asleep, murmured something in return.

"If being a bear has done that to him . . ." He left the sentence unfinished.

"No, you mustn't think that." Opening her eyes, she put a hand on Sherwood's arm. "You are a good man, whether or not you become a Bear. You're not going to . . . what was that noise?"

He had turned away from her, toward the doorway of the tent, and was listening intently. "I heard it too. Like—groaning, or . . ."

"Not a voice, though."

"No, not a voice." Sherwood stood up and went to the doorway and looked out toward the river. In the gray twilight he could see gouts of water splashing up, rising ten feet or more without any visible cause, through the most recently cut holes.

The figure of Maxim, walking in man-form, materialized out of the dusk. In a moment, both his visitors were wide awake.

Maxim said to them: "You asked what I am doing here with these people. Maybe I can explain it to you this way. The flag of my empire will display the perfect white of the polar bear."

"Why?" Sherwood asked, still hoping for some way to predict the lunatic's intentions.

"I'll tell you why. The polar bear presents us with our emblem, an example of the perfect body, the perfect spirit. Nothing, nothing at all is required by this animal, but air, and ice, and meat. Flesh to kill and tear and swallow." Smiling genially, he turned and went away.

~

When the sun had reached its lowest point on one of its
brief spring trips below the horizon, and Maxim
thought it the most likely time for his visitors to be
asleep—if they trusted him sufficiently to sleep, or were
simply too tired to stay awake—he summoned Koba,
then ordered his lieutenant to arm half a dozen men
and go and kill the newcomers in their tent.

"If there is a Bear in the tent, use no bullets on it but
only poisoned arrows. They will kill it." Maxim put
great authority into his voice, though he was not at all
sure whether the poison would be effective. Nor was he
even sure that he wanted it to be so. Then he added in
the same tone: "And my brother Gregori must be
spared, do you hear me? He shares the blood of the
Great Bear, and there is a special thing that I must do
with him."

Still fearful that the rifle in Sherwood's or Natalya's
hands might be loaded with silver bullets, Maxim
refrained from taking part in the foray himself. The
Great Bear would remain prudently in the background, at the far end of the village, until the business
had been taken care of.

Inside the tent, the couple were taking turns at
standing watch and sleeping.

Sherwood in bear-form, his senses intensified, happened to be on guard when the enemy approached.

Alerted in plenty of time by the faint crunch of feet in
snow, the smell of human fear, he wakened Natalya
where she sat dozing at her brother's side.

Then he charged out of the tent, skirmishing with
the human attackers, knocking down two of them,
driving off the others, who fled almost at the first sign
of resistance. Arrows, and a couple of bullets, fired in
panic at this Bear missed.

Natalya, following her man outdoors, held her fire
coolly, not wanting to waste a single shot on figures
running away in semidarkness.

Koba was not directly involved in the struggle. Like

his master, he had hung back, unwilling to risk his own skin if there were any reasonable alternative.

For a moment Sherwood thought the fight was over. Then, tasting the air with all his senses, he caught the scent of another bear, somewhere incautiously upwind.

He beckoned to Natalya, making a gesture with his paw, and charged out after it.

Natalya could not tell whether he had been signaling her to come with him, or stay where she was. But it made no difference. Taking a firm grip on her rifle, she came running after him.

A quarter of a mile from the village, their quarry, a great white bear, turned at bay.

The chemistry of the creature's scent was much clearer at this range. This bear was only a bear—in fact a female, followed by a half-grown cub.

"That's not Maxim."

Sherwood had Changed, just momentarily, to discuss tactics with his partner. Then both turned their backs on the snarling female bear and hurried back to the village. Over the distance, Natalya could move as fast on two legs as he on four.

THIRTY-FOUR

At this time of year and at this latitude, night meant no more than a few hours of extended twilight. Running through the dusk back to the village, instinctively concerned about Gregori and determined not to abandon him, the couple heard the great groaning sound again, accompanied this time by rumblings that seemed to come from underground.

Sherwood paused momentarily. "It's the ice."

"What?"

"I've heard that sound before, in America. The river ice is starting to break up. Somewhere south of here a big spring thaw's in progress. The ice cutting and the building are going to have to stop."

Koba, reporting to Maxim, informed him that the two interlopers, both gravely wounded by poisoned arrows, had gone staggering off into the dusk to die. The Great Bear accepted this report with some suspicion, and returned to the tent where Gregori still lay.

"How now, brother? Have you anything to say to me at last? No prophecy at all, no secrets to reveal? You were to be my guide!" In a rage he grabbed the recumbent form with both hands and shook it. "Have you made me bring you all this way for nothing, after all?"

Alerted by a stir, an urgent murmuring outside the tent, he let Gregori's all-but-inert body fall back upon the pallet. Still in man-form, Maxim turned and went to the doorway.

One of the surviving exiles, a taller man than Koba, stood there pasty-faced with fear, wearing eyeglasses with one lens missing. "Sir. Oh Great Bear. There are cracks in the ice!"

"What? In the river?"

"Sir. Oh no, sir." The man's eyes were filled with terror. "The very structure of the palace . . ."

Maxim snarled something and spun away, his gaze once more lighting on the still figure of his brother. The family. The blood of the Bear. Yes, Gregori would fulfill a mystic purpose after all.

Hastily the Great Bear Changed. Then Maxim seized his brother's clothing in his teeth and hurried from the tent, dragging the helpless man along.

Returning cautiously to the tent where they had left Gregori, Sherwood and Natalya discovered that he was gone. The fresh tracks of a huge bear were discernible in the trampled snow.

Moments later, Sherwood, also moving in bear-shape, left the tent and went loping toward the palace of ice, following the trail of the Great Bear that had once been Natalya's brother.

Rifle in hand, she came trudging steadily after him.

The trail led Sherwood toward the glassy pyramid, then became impossible to follow as it entered the intensely trampled area close to the structure. Looking warily for an entrance, Sherwood got his best look yet at the ice palace.

Somewhere inside the pyramid, above ground level, he could hear a growling. Maxim, in the shape and character of a dancing bear, was urgently calling his community together, conducting some kind of ceremony. The workers had set down their tools and were beating on their drums of reindeer skin with sticks of bone.

At close range it was easy to see that after six months or so of work, the building was still far from completion, even according to Maxim's description of Grandfather's relatively modest original design. Currently it was no higher than three stories, with a few impressively tall columns and one rudimentary balcony. The finished portion of the ground floor might have accommodated all hundred villagers, but there would have been little room left over.

Sherwood's rapid advance discouraged the guards Maxim had posted near the entrance, sent them scattering into the brightening twilight. The sky toward the east was red, the Arctic sun in its perpetual flirtation with the horizon was just about to rise.

Sherwood on entering the pyramid at ground level found himself in a room much bigger than any of the village tents, walled and ceilinged by ice, in curves and arches and columns. His appearance threw the handful of workers present into consternation and turmoil. Fur-clad bodies, screaming, hurled themselves out of the low openings between the heavy, glassy columns supporting the upper floors.

Outside, the risen sun was just touching the uppermost walls of ice with liquid fire.

At the far end of the ice hall from the entrance, there rose a well-designed but very slippery-looking stair, mounting in a not-ungraceful curve, with each broad tread sloping in toward the next highest riser. At sight of Sherwood, a pair of workers armed with ice tongs, tools doubtless painfully forged out of ship's iron, gave up their struggle with their frozen burden, and went scrambling wildly up, small bone spikes on their boot soles providing traction.

Sherwood crossed the long room and started up the icy stairs, as he moved hearing Natalya enter the palace behind him. He heard the metal barrel of her rifle scrape very gently on the sharply defined door frame of pure ice.

Having ascended the first curve of the broad stair, Sherwood paused to listen, look, and sniff at what might be above him. Up there brilliant sunlight cast down through clear ice a dazzling interplay of distorted images and shadows. Surely that great white shape moving slowly had to be Maxim.

The outline of the phantasmal image suggested that the bear was carrying a human figure—a helpless victim—in its jaws.

Gregori.

"Greg. Greg!" And Natalya, who beheld the image also, cried out more words in violent Russian, too fast for Sherwood to understand them.

Sherwood advanced, wary of traps and ambushes, thinking that Greg was a dead man anyway. Here and there the palace contained a few furnishings that were not of ice. On the second floor, real furs lay scattered here and there on ice ledges that might have served as Eskimo couches.

The upper floors seemed to have few windows, and certainly none were required to give light. Whenever the sun was above the horizon, the palace must glow with light. When only the moon and the aurora illuminated the atmosphere, their light augmented by that of a few interior lamps would be enough to create a strange and wonderful vision.

All the ceilings seemed to be arches or domes. Room after room had been constructed without the use of beams of any other material than the frozen water itself. Even a short, thick beam of ice could very well be flawed, and therefore precarious.

Sherwood had just resumed his passage up the stair, when there came a sharp sound, as of the structure cracking. Natalya standing at the foot of the stair cried out in alarm.

Looking out through one of the ground-floor

windows, she could see that the ice on the surface of
the river, in places two feet thick and more, was
breaking up. Great chunks, fragments weighing tons,
were being shoved brutally aside by an uncontainable
current, forced up on the banks in heaps. The earlier
eerie groaning had been replaced by slamming,
grinding sounds. The palace stood so near the bank
that now the rising water streamed furiously past its
foundations, assaulting them directly.

The bear that had been Maxim climbed from the
second floor of the palace to the third and highest. As if
forsaken by the power of speech, the beast seemed to
be urging on the work of construction with roars and
snarls. But even the Great Bear could no longer
enforce obedience by terror. Screaming workers ran
away, went sliding and leaping from the glassy roof.

The claws of Sherwood, stalking his enemy above,
dug effectively into ice as he climbed the icy stair. Once
he thought he felt the stairs, thick as they were, crack
under his weight. Natalya, with no bone spikes and no
claws on her boots, slipped and fell trying to keep up,
but fortunately was able to regain her footing.

Sherwood reached the second floor, but looking up
could see that Maxim was still above him. The image of
the Great White Bear, wavering as if the beast were
dancing, was still there, visible through the walls and
arching overheads of ice. Maxim was visible as a distorted phantom, dragging his brother with him among
the upper rooms of the ice palace.

Looking up, to where fresh sunlight burned against
the highest walls and pinnacles, Sherwood saw a single
drop of water, newly formed and diamond-sparkling,
trembling on the lip of a cleverly carved cornice, which
was now about to turn to melting ice. . . .

Up there, somewhere, another figure moved abruptly;
another mere human being, trying to escape. Koba
sought now to dart away from the Great Bear's teeth and
claws, but was knocked down with one swipe of a great

white paw. The injured man came crawling, sliding and whimpering, down the broad slick stairs past Sherwood, who ignored him.

Other sounds, grown hideously familiar to the Bear who was still Sherwood, came from up above. A chomping, slavering and chewing. And at the same time, hitting his sensitive nostrils with almost numbing intensity, the smell of human blood.

"Sherwood! Up there! He's eating Greg!"

Natalya tried to run upstairs past him, but slipped and fell again. She lay on her back, firing at the glassy image of the highest bear, working the bolt action of her repeating rifle. Under the barrage of bullets, heavy sprays of powdered and chipped ice flew from the arched ceiling.

The gunfire weakened the support of a structure already cracked in several places. In another moment, the high arch had collapsed under the Great Bear's weight. Tons of loosened, fractured ice and white fur, all laced with bright fresh blood, came down in a crystalline, crashing slide.

Sherwood, uttering a primal growl, leapt in to finish off his enemy.

Battered and bruised by falling ice, almost stunned, Natalya heard the bear-growling drowned out in a greater roar—the river ice was now totally shattered, swiftly breaking up under the impact of the spring thaw marching relentlessly poleward from the south. The flood, seemingly sprung from nowhere in mere minutes, was hurling huge floes and cakes against the foundations of the palace.

Water inside the building was rising, rushing, swirling around Natalya's legs. Still clinging to her rifle, she left the palace and struggled to reach safe ground.

Only one other followed her out. Sherwood, moving slowly though seemingly not much hurt, came out of the rushing water a minute after her, and like a wet dog stopped to shake his white fur dry. He did not Change to man-form until he was back inside the tent where he had left his clothes. There he reported to Natalya that both her brothers were dead.

With the flooded river still rising rapidly, huge ice floes were being hurled, dragged and shoved by the swift current, into the ruins of the palace. By the time the couple emerged from their tent to look around, not a trace of even the foundation still remained.

Minutes later, Natalya and Sherwood were standing with other survivors outdoors in front of a roaring fire, which prodigally consumed reserves of wood earlier salvaged from the wrecked ship. Already the couple were making plans as to how they were going to get away.

One scheme involved taking one of the village kayaks or other boats, and moving by sail or paddle, or as the current took them, east or west along Siberia's north coast, which was sometimes navigable for great distances in the summer. Somewhere there would be another river, another village. There ought to be good hunting, in either direction.

The other possibility would be to wait through the brief weeks of Arctic summer, and depart from Padarok Sivera by land when winter came again.

At the moment there was no need to decide. In any case, they would be together.

The hours of the long day were moving on, the sun, constrained to low altitude, marching steadily around in what would be almost a complete circle of the horizon.

Natalya and Sherwood, feeling thoroughly warmed and dried, soon moved away from the village fire and began a search. She decided that Gregori's bones, or as much as could be found of them, ought to be gathered and burned.

When Sherwood came upon the relic of Grandfather's preserved body, which someone had already cast out of its tent shrine, he seized the fabric of distorted bones and hurled it into the river, then watched while it was swept out to sea.

He snarled at any villagers who tried to genuflect to him, or to address him as the Great Bear.

"That beast is dead. I saw his throat torn out." He did not say by what agency that feat had been accomplished. "I saw his corpse washed out to sea." And Sherwood was determined not to change again, where any of the people of this settlement could see him.

The scores of people who through the winter had been forced to devote their lives to the ice palace were now in a precarious condition regarding their own survival. Several, besides Maxim and Gregori, had died, and others were missing. But at least the survivors could now concentrate on working for themselves.

An hour later, three people, searching desultorily for more survivors, were prowling along the near bank of the still-rising stream, among a litter of enormous cakes of ice. In the long-slanting rays of the sun, some patches of muddy earth appeared nearly as lifeless as the crumbling, melting ice itself. But here and there small plants, looking as determined as the rocks they sprang from, still clung to life.

Everyone in the village could begin to feel sure of it now. The Great Bear was dead and gone.

Thus Natalya and Sherwood, moving along the riverbank with their companion, came upon the body of a man, muddy, wet, half-frozen and half-stunned, but inwardly still as full of life as the small plants under the snow. He was a tough young man, and not to be so easily disposed of.

"Koba? Are you all right?" The bearded exile, wearing glasses with one lens missing, bent over the recumbent form. Then he lifted his head briefly to remark: "I know this man by a different name. He's one of us, I'll testify to that—a real revolutionary, a comrade from Georgia."

Now that the Bear was slain, the old purposes, old ways of thought and speech, had already started to come back.

The one who had been called Koba moved and sat up. He still looked dazed, leaning awkwardly on his left arm. He was holding his right arm, which had been bleeding, stiffly in front of him.

The searcher who had said he knew the man bent over and inspected his wound with moderate concern. Then he announced with satisfaction: "That arm's hurt. It looks as if the bear took out some meat—but I've seen worse. You're lucky, Comrade Stalin."

On the evening of th the very presence o Kiev, Pyotr Stolypin third Minister of the Interior since the turn of the century. No the gunman, Dimitry Bogrov, was i terrorists or of the police, or had acce both organizations.

Five days later, the youthful Georgian and revolutionary called Koba by his asso name Iosif Vissarionovich Dzhugashvili, aka Stalin, is known to have arrived by train in the following one of his suspiciously frequent, seemin effortless escapes from detention in custody of tsarist government.

On this visit in late 1911 Stalin remained in Pete burg for only a few days before being rearrested ag and sent back into exile, this time in the small village o Vologda. Which on the map appears to be at no enormous distance—as distances are best measured in that world—from Padarok Lessa.

He snarled at any villagers who tried to genuflect to him, or to address him as the Great Bear.

"That beast is dead. I saw his throat torn out." He did not say by what agency that feat had been accomplished. "I saw his corpse washed out to sea." And Sherwood was determined not to change again, where any of the people of this settlement could see him.

The scores of people who through the winter had been forced to devote their lives to the ice palace were now in a precarious condition regarding their own survival. Several, besides Maxim and Gregori, had died, and others were missing. But at least the survivors could now concentrate on working for themselves.

An hour later, three people, searching desultorily for more survivors, were prowling along the near bank of the still-rising stream, among a litter of enormous cakes of ice. In the long-slanting rays of the sun, some patches of muddy earth appeared nearly as lifeless as the crumbling, melting ice itself. But here and there small plants, looking as determined as the rocks they sprang from, still clung to life.

Everyone in the village could begin to feel sure of it now. The Great Bear was dead and gone.

Thus Natalya and Sherwood, moving along the riverbank with their companion, came upon the body of a man, muddy, wet, half-frozen and half-stunned, but inwardly still as full of life as the small plants under the snow. He was a tough young man, and not to be so easily disposed of.

"Koba? Are you all right?" The bearded exile, wearing glasses with one lens missing, bent over the recumbent form. Then he lifted his head briefly to remark: "I know this man by a different name. He's one of us, I'll testify to that—a real revolutionary, a comrade from Georgia."

Now that the Bear was slain, the old purposes, old ways of thought and speech, had already started to come back.

The one who had been called Koba moved and sat up. He still looked dazed, leaning awkwardly on his left arm. He was holding his right arm, which had been bleeding, stiffly in front of him.

The searcher who had said he knew the man bent over and inspected his wound with moderate concern. Then he announced with satisfaction: "That arm's hurt. It looks as if the bear took out some meat—but I've seen worse. You're lucky, Comrade Stalin."

AFTERWORD

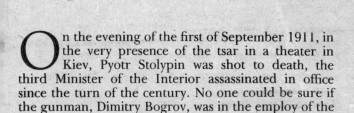

On the evening of the first of September 1911, in the very presence of the tsar in a theater in Kiev, Pyotr Stolypin was shot to death, the third Minister of the Interior assassinated in office since the turn of the century. No one could be sure if the gunman, Dimitry Bogrov, was in the employ of the terrorists or of the police, or had accepted money from both organizations.

Five days later, the youthful Georgian bank robber and revolutionary called Koba by his associates, full name Iosif Vissarionovich Dzhugashvili, aka Comrade Stalin, is known to have arrived by train in the capital, following one of his suspiciously frequent, seemingly effortless escapes from detention in custody of the tsarist government.

On this visit in late 1911 Stalin remained in Petersburg for only a few days before being rearrested again and sent back into exile, this time in the small village of Vologda. Which on the map appears to be at no enormous distance—as distances are best measured in that world—from Padarok Lessa.

TOR
BOOKS The Best in Fantasy

LORD OF CHAOS • Robert Jordan

Book Six of *The Wheel of Time*. "For those who like to keep themselves in a fantasy world, it's hard to beat the complex, detailed world created here....A great read."—*Locus*

STONE OF TEARS • Terry Goodkind

The sequel to the epic fantasy bestseller *Wizard's First Rule*.

SPEAR OF HEAVEN • Judith Tarr

"The kind of accomplished fantasy—featuring sound characterization, superior world-building, and more than competent prose—that has won Tarr a large audience."—*Booklist*

MEMORY AND DREAM • Charles de Lint

A major novel of art, magic, and transformation, by the modern master of urban fantasy.

NEVERNEVER • Will Shetterly

The sequel to *Elsewhere*. "With a single book, Will Shetterly has redrawn the boundaries of young adult fantasy. This is a remarkable work."—Bruce Coville

TALES FROM THE GREAT TURTLE • Edited by Piers Anthony and Richard Gilliam

"A tribute to the wealth of pre-Columbian history and lore."—*Library Journal*